BRYANT & MAY
Oranges and Lemons

www.penguin.co.uk

BRYANT & MAY
Oranges and Lemons

CHRISTOPHER FOWLER

doubleday

TRANSWORLD PUBLISHERS
61–63 Uxbridge Road, London W5 5SA
www.penguin.co.uk

Transworld is part of the Penguin Random House group of companies
whose addresses can be found at global.penguinrandomhouse.com

Penguin
Random House
UK

First published in Great Britain in 2020 by Doubleday
an imprint of Transworld Publishers

A CIP catalogue record for this book is available from the British Library.

ISBN 9780857525703

Typeset in 11/13pt Sabon by Jouve (UK), Milton Keynes
Printed and bound in Great Britain by Clays Ltd, Elcograf S.p.A.

Penguin Random House is committed to a sustainable
future for our business, our readers and our planet. This book
is made from Forest Stewardship Council® certified paper.

1 3 5 7 9 10 8 6 4 2

For Peter Chapman

And Sophie Christopher
6/9/90 – 3/6/19

PART ONE
The Bells of St Clement's

Clement Danes stands all forlorn and destitute;
Bells that rang out yestermorn today lie mute.
I hear children in my mind all singing there;
But oranges are hard to find and lemons rare.

Harold Adshead

I

OLD WHITE MALES

'Everything I tell you is a lie.'

The old man had a face like a cheap cushion. It had retained every crease, wrinkle and furrow imprinted upon it by the tumultuous cavalcade of London's history. It might have staved off the worst effects had it been treated to regular use of moisturizer from about 1955 onwards. Instead it was 'lived in' and 'full of character', appealing phrases used to describe old men's faces for which there was no similar vocabulary about women.

'I'm afraid that's a bit on the nose for the first line of a memoir,' said Simon Sartorius. 'It might put readers off.' He tried to rebalance himself on his galvanized stool but the café's tiled floor was uneven. He should never have let Arthur Bryant pick the venue for their meeting. The café was tiny, loud, overcrowded and steamier than a Turkish bath.

'I think my readers should know what they're getting into,' said Bryant, tucking a paper napkin into his shirt collar as he attempted to read the 8-point Futura type on the menu, which was printed on a brown paper bag. 'You're always complaining that I misremember the past so I thought I'd be honest. Every act of recollection alters a narrative. Stories are strange fruit that ripen and mutate.'

'Yours are meant to be based on fact.' Bryant's long-suffering editor waved at the waiter, but it might have been faster and easier to contact life on other planets. 'You're an officer of the law presenting his police unit's true cases to the general reading public. It's not *Lord of the Rings*.'

'A fair point,' said Bryant, 'but in this case it's appropriate to question everything you read.' He dug what appeared to be a sherbet lemon from his top pocket and managed to hit the waiter on the back of the head. 'We'd like your second-cheapest bottle of red,' he called.

'You still haven't told me anything about the investigation,' Simon reminded him.

'Oh, it has all the ingredients you're looking for minus the sex, OBVS,' said Bryant cheerfully. 'I've given Cynthia, my ghostwriter, all the case notes.'

'That's another thing,' said Simon. 'I understand that the lady in question recently spent some time in prison for counterfeiting.'

'That was a political act, FFS.' Bryant had lately discovered online abbreviations and was trying them out in everyday conversation, even though he had no idea what they stood for. 'Cynthia is an extremely skilled forger. I used her dud fivers for weeks before noticing that Churchill had a moustache. She's a numismatist and IMHO a fine prose stylist, but apart from that she is first, most passionately and above all a terrible kleptomaniac.'

The waiter slid between them and unscrewed the top from a bottle of red, sloshing it into the editor's glass with ill grace and poor aim.

'Are you sure she's right for the job?' Simon asked. 'You haven't had much luck with your biographers.' As Bryant's first biographer had been murdered, he realized that this was something of an understatement. 'Can she be relied upon?'

'She isn't likely to wander off,' Bryant reassured him. 'She's currently under house arrest. She stays cheerful. She has attractively customized her ankle bracelet.'

Simon tried to steer the conversation back to the book. 'Tell me about the case you want to cover.'

'Sometimes I look back and wonder if I didn't dream it.'

'Let's hope your readers don't.'

'The writer H. H. Munro said that the young have aspirations that never come to pass and the old have reminiscences of what never happened,' Bryant replied unhelpfully.

Simon winced, not at the *aperçu* but upon examination of the wine label. 'Château' was spelled wrong. 'How did you find this place?' he asked.

'The ABC Café poisonings,' said Bryant. 'I wouldn't have the mackerel.'

That was the problem with Mr Bryant, his long-suffering editor decided. One never knew if he was joking. Looking across the plastic counter at this twinkle-eyed trickster, ancient yet somehow forever stuck in those teenaged years that could make any parent commit murder, he weighed up the risks of publishing something that might prove to be a farrago of nonsense. Volumes One and Two had no pending lawsuits and were modestly in profit. *So long as it's entertaining*, he decided. 'When do you think we'd be able to take delivery?'

Bryant's innocent blue eyes swam up at him. 'Do I get more dosh if Cynthia bangs it out in a fortnight?'

Simon began to doubt the wisdom of recommissioning the series of memoirs that the *Sunday Times* had called 'the very definition of unreliability', but London's oldest detective was already raising his glass in a toast.

*

Introduction to the forthcoming book The Nick of Time: Memorable Cases of the Peculiar Crimes Unit, Vol. 3, *as told to Cynthia Birdhanger, Random House, Hardback, £18.99*

My name is Arthur Bryant, and I'm one of two senior detectives at a specialist London crime unit. Perhaps you've read my earlier memoirs. Working in homicide really takes it out of you. If you thought I was an old man in those days, you should see me now. My face looks like an apple someone left on a warm windowsill for a year. A list of my ailments would run to the size of a telephone directory, assuming there's anyone left alive who remembers what directories were. Strongmen tore them in half on television.

I admit I haven't taken care of myself. I'm in better condition than Naples, but that's about it. I'm still alive though, still working with my partner John May at the PCU in King's Cross, London, determined to soldier on even if I occasionally lose my keys, mentally speaking.

The investigation I'm about to describe occurred in strange days. It felt like the time of the Phoney War, that drifting period between Neville Chamberlain's announcement and the start of the Second World War when everyone was anxious but nothing much happened, except of course it wasn't wartime. It was somewhere around 2020, I forget exactly when, but a period of such global uncertainty that we couldn't discuss our fears without rancour.

Abnormal was fast becoming the new normal, and it was an abnormally warm spring. I was forced to shed one of my vests in March. Normally they see me through to 21 June, a time when Londoners ask themselves how it can possibly be Midsummer's Day when they're still wearing cardigans.

Strange days . . . did I say that already? Ranted politics in hoppy pubs, high-street shops posting closure notices, acrimony and ineptitude, a skittering spirit in the air. Where once there would have been torchlit riots to set the heads of the guilty upon the poles of London Bridge, instead there was only muddle, mess and moaning.

Nor were the law enforcement units exempt. After a decade of fighting budget cuts, the PCU had hit the buffers and could go no further. At our lowest point we were embroiled in our strangest case.

In order to present this account unambiguously, I must explain what the killer did, the how and why of it all, but that will not be enough. I still feel I failed and that justice was not served. I ask myself: what was it *really* about?

The majority of crimes are senseless. The few which are premeditated end up on our desks, but this nearly became another unsolved London mystery. Some of you may think that my career as a police officer sounds far-fetched, but what you consider shocking I regard as routine. We are daily steeped in the banality of violent death.

OK, Cynthia, over to you. You can work at my desk as soon as your anklet comes off but don't 'liberate' anything. I've counted my pens.

Cynthia's my ghostwriter. She's a lovely woman but a bit of a career tea leaf, and tends to go on the nick when she's got the itch for it. She's just returned from another little holiday at Her Majesty's pleasure after covering a CCTV camera in tin foil and whipping an Asprey's tiara into her bottomless handbag. I'm giving her my notes on the case so she can check them against the facts and tell me I got everything wrong, then write it up in a form that has 'reader appeal', whatever that means. I tell her all facts are adjustable. It wouldn't kill her to make me a bit younger. The trouble is, when you leave it to a biographer to fill in the blanks they get carried away. Cynthia's prose has a purple tendency and you can't always tell if what you're reading is real or a Jeffrey Archer, but apart from that she seems up to the job.

I'll be reading over your shoulder, Cynthia, so go easy on the adjectives, and if you leave the office after me remember there's nothing valuable here unless you can find a buyer for my 'I'm Backing Britain' tea mugs.

PECULIAR CRIMES UNIT
A specialized London police division with a remit to prevent or cause to cease any acts of public affright or violent disorder committed in the municipal or communal areas of the city.

The Old Warehouse
231 Caledonian Road
London N1 9RB

STAFF ROSTER MONDAY 11 MARCH

Raymond Land, Unit Chief
Arthur Bryant, Detective Chief Inspector
John May, Detective Chief Inspector
Janice Longbright, Detective Inspector
Dan Banbury, Crime Scene/Forensic
Meera Mangeshkar, Detective Sergeant
Colin Bimsley, Detective Sergeant
Sidney Hargreaves, Intern
Giles Kershaw, Forensic Pathologist (off-site)

PRIVATE & CONFIDENTIAL MEMO
FROM: RAYMOND LAND
TO: ALL PCU STAFF

Right, you lot, pay attention.

This will be my last email to you all. I know you've always relied on these bulletins to keep you up to date with law enforcement guidelines, so if you still need a bedtime story I could tell you about the latest promise to put more PCs on the streets by plucking them from the Magic Police Tree, i.e. shifting inexperienced officers from one dire crisis to another and giving us back some of the money the last PM snatched away. Whichever Old Etonian is in charge of our country these days would rather blame the current knife crime tsunami on sunspots than admit they've been draining our budget coffers. 'Austerity measures' means we're twenty thousand front-line officers down with no support and no back-room staff. Thank God we're cops and not doctors. I don't want to know how they're stitching patients up with parcel string and rubber bands in the corridors of the NHS. So let's skip all that and address the big issue of the day.

What did I *specifically* ask you not to do?

Don't get us closed down, I said.

It wasn't asking much. I just wanted you to keep a low profile, look busy and not turn us into social lepers. What happened? We've gone from a local embarrassment to a national disgrace. We have the smell of death about us, and this time it's not just coming from Mr Bryant. I keep looking to see if we've got a cross painted on the unit's front door. I know what you're going to say: We've been closed down before. This time it's for good. We've made it to number one on the government's blacklist of 'Organizations of Potential Detriment'.

9

Our commendation for catching the Lonely Hour Killer came with the kind of bill that's usually only seen by our commissioner after one of his dinners at the Dorchester. I'll happily itemize the cost for you. So far it's for the partial demolition of a Tudorbethan mansion in Hampstead, the destruction of an extremely rare Daimler motor vehicle, damage to various high-street shops, lamp-posts and statuary, several pending law suits from frightened pensioners who suffered gusset accidents after being forced to jump into hedges to escape your pursuit vehicle and of course, the *pièce de résistance*, costs arising from a multiple pile-up near St Paul's Cathedral, including an assault on a vicar and the wholesale looting of a doughnut van. So if anyone has some loose cash knocking about, feel free to put it in the reparations kitty.

The London murder rate is still a fraction of New York's but it isn't helped by gunfire taking place inside our own building. At least the perpetrator was apprehended and charged with attempted murder.

You probably want an update on John May's condition. I have his University College Hospital Patient Report:

'The patient was admitted with a gunshot wound to the upper right side of the chest wall, and suffered haemothorax and respiratory compromise, but it was not necessary to intubate as the small calibre of the round prevented significant bronchial injury.

'There were initially signs of neurological deficit (patient complained of loss of sensation in right arm), but these soon subsided. There is likely to be long-term cardiac and oesophageal damage. Formal echocardiography and bronchoscopy will be performed after patient has reached a significant level of stabilization.'

Short version: he's going to live.

Unfortunately he's facing a number of charges arising from the investigation. Sadly naivety is no alibi and I've been told that his prosecution is going to be aggressively pursued. Although he's expected to make a full recovery from his injury, he says he has no intention of returning to the unit. As for his partner, if anyone knows where he is

Here Raymond Land stopped typing. There was no easy way of explaining that his best detectives would never again work with each other. Arthur Bryant and John May were finished. Their unbroken record of successful murder prosecutions was undermined by their inability to follow even the simplest rules. The PCU was like a flatulent elderly relative in a roomful of silent millennials, a source of profound embarrassment to the newly streamlined Home Office, and John May's stupid error of judgement had given them the perfect reason to sell off the unit. Arthur Bryant was a stubborn, annoying old man who had refused to forgive his partner. Well, someone else could sort out the mess. After years of ridicule and dismissal he felt disinclined to get involved. His index fingers hovered over the keyboard.

For the rest of us life goes on, unfortunately. The removal vans are arriving this morning, so this is the last email I'll ever have to send. We can no longer fool ourselves into thinking we're needed in this increasingly unpleasant city. The government's position is clear: let society find its own level and to hell with anyone who doesn't come up to scratch. Dan Banbury tells me that a police constable can be replaced with a matchbox-sized surveillance camera. I'd like to see a drone sort out a domestic involving some paralytic pikey waving a knock-off *Game of Thrones* machete at his missus because she stood in front of the football.

'Can he say "pikey" in a memo?' asked Colin Bimsley as he read the email.

'According to the dictionary it means "any person of low background",' said his colleague Meera Mangeshkar, checking her phone. 'Probably an abbreviation from "turnpike-keeper". Oh God, I'm looking up words even though old Bryant's not around.'

Of course we can't be allowed to remain open. Our mission is to prevent, not cure, and remove the long-term causes of public disorder. But prevention is an unaffordable luxury now, so they're closing us down to save a few bob, and making London a bit more unbearable in the process.

You probably want to know if you still have jobs. I'm told that all staff will be notified about their employment options in due course. I understand that most of you are going to be reallocated to other specialist divisions, although I'm afraid they may not all be centrally located.

'Not centrally located?' cried Colin. 'Is he having a Turkish? I'll do anything for my job so long as it's in Zone One. I'm not going up the arse-end of the tube map every day. Epping? That's in the woods, isn't it? Morden, well that's from *Lord of the Rings* and Theydon Bois sounds suspiciously French. Not on my watch.'

'It won't be your watch much longer,' said Meera. 'What if the only job you're offered isn't in London at all?'

'What do you mean, *not in London*?' Colin replied, genuinely mystified.

So that's it. The unit is now officially shut.

Your contracts don't expire until the end of the month but you're free to go off and enjoy yourselves. Summer's just around the corner. The King's Cross drug-dealers have already started wearing shorts. The two Daves are staying on, having been hired to refurbish this dump, which is now set to become a 'plant-based tapas bar', whatever that is. It seems we wasted years training as law enforcement specialists when we should have been learning how to put sprouts on sticks.

It seems I am the only one who'll be left without a new position, which suits me perfectly as I plan to retire and go as far off the grid as possible, in this case a bungalow with faulty wiring on the Isle of Wight. I no longer want to live in a metropolis that thinks it's acceptable to charge fifteen quid for a cup of artisanal coffee that's been passed through the digestive system of a tapir.

Adding insult to injury, I have received a letter of complaint that our most senior detectives used inappropriate language during the last investigation and are guilty of being, I quote, 'old white males in a woke world'. I don't know about 'woke' but Mr Bryant certainly needs to be woken in our meetings. I imagine being old and white is somewhat beyond his control unless he's planning to reincarnate.

You may have noticed there's an unfamiliar name attached to the recipients at the top of the page. Sidney Hargreaves is a girl. She's happy to be called either Sid or Sidney because her name is, I quote, 'non-gender specific in an identity-biased profession'. It's not for me to pass comment on gender, I got lost somewhere between Danny La Rue and RuPaul. She was due to start this week as an intern. Her scores from Henley College were exceptional but came with a warning that she is 'unusual', so she was assigned to a unit where she could be rehabilitated by like-minded people, which suggests that they see the PCU as a mental facility-cum-toy hospital.

As you can see, it's not all good news this week. Wherever you're relocated to, I'm given to understand that you'll be reverting to your former job titles, as your upgrades were never fully ratified before the wheels fell off our

investigation. Feel free to take it up with your union repre-
sentative, i.e. me.

On to practical matters. The evidence room will need
clearing out today, and I think we should do it before anyone
else sees what we're up to. I don't want our so-called superiors finding out about Mr Bryant's little witchcraft museum.
As for the staff fridge, I know it's the only temperature-
controlled device we own but leaving a human nose in the
salad crisper is going to attract the wrong sort of attention.
Dan tells me it's being stored until it can be examined for
teeth-marks, so for now it's in a sandwich box in the kitchen. Don't do what I nearly did.

I think we might also consider shredding certain internal
files, as some of our recent investigations read like a fanta-
sia on policing themes. If they get out we'll be a laughing
stock.

Make sure last month's log entries are legible and put
your stuff into boxes. Don't think about nicking anything.
The black market Chinese brandy in the evidence room did
not diminish 'due to evaporation' as someone with Colin's
handwriting scrawled on the label.

To be honest, I never imagined we would end up like
this. I thought we'd probably get blown up or quarantined
again, not quietly closed down and moved on because of a
compromised operation. It's undignified. Three decades in
the force, I finally get some grudging acclaim and you have
to go and stuff it up. I don't wish to apportion blame, but
it's entirely your fault.

Good luck in the future, what's left of it.

Land felt like dropping his head to the desk. *Take a deep
breath*, he told himself. He was free at last. Free to go and
sit in his bungalow in Ventnor, watching grey clouds decant
themselves on to an even greyer sea. He should have been

over the moon yet he did not feel, in Churchill's phrase, the exhilaration of a man shot at without result. Quite the reverse. It felt as if he had taken John May's bullet himself.

The future suddenly looked ghastly. He had nothing more to put in his memo, no protestations about the capricious plumbing, no suggestions for the unit's monthly film night, no complaints about Colin eating durian fruit at his desk or Meera wearing her pyjamas on late shifts or Bryant causing the video entry system to pick up old *Carry On* films or Janice leaving the cat's litter tray in the operations room, because there would be no more films or working nights and anyway the cat was dead.

I'm not sure I want to live on the Isle of Wight after all, he thought. *This may be a ridiculous anachronistic dead-end job in a government department that should have been closed down decades ago, but it's* my *dead-end job and I'm rather proud of it.*

Then fight for it, said a small voice inside him. *Some poor mug has to get us out of this mess.*

It's just not going to be me.

Pushing back his drooping comb-over, he hit *send.*

2

COOKING THE BOOKS

MAKING A MURDERER

I've always known there was something wrong with me.

The knowledge was stuck beneath my skin like a thorn, right from the time of my earliest memories. On my first day of school at Albion Mixed Infants in Deptford, South London, I was shaking with fear, trying not to wet my shorts. The teacher, Miss Piper, introduced me to the class and asked who would like to share their bench and poster paints. Not one hand went up. They had seen the way I walked, with my elbows raised and a rolling gait like a sailor on a storm-swept deck, or a dressed-up chimpanzee performing for an old-time circus, and started whispering behind their hands.

Finally Miss Piper made the best of it and set me up on my own with a jigsaw of a pet-shop window that only had about fifteen pieces, and I thought to myself: Is she a moron? We were supposed to be playing for three-quarters of an hour and the jigsaw took me ten seconds to finish, so what was I supposed to do then?

But the teacher was talking to the children who didn't make her feel uncomfortable, so I surreptitiously stole another child's poster paints, turned the completed jigsaw over and painted a fairly decent landscape on the other side.

I got sent to the head teacher's office for damaging school property.

I won't bore you with my difficult formative years. It's enough to know that I was shunned in the playground, avoided during team selection, bullied in class and usually ended up hiding in the library, where I would read murder mysteries and books about magic until it was time to go home. At the age of eleven I was fitted with a black rubber brace that would straighten my leg over time, but I hated wearing it because it chafed away at my skin, leaving crescent-shaped callouses, so I often left it off.

I was never a comfortable child. My clothes never fitted properly; my hair was cut at home; I didn't have nice stuff.

My mother couldn't collect me from school because going-home time fell in the middle of her shift at the super-market, so I walked home alone. I was usually ambushed somewhere along the way, and quickly learned to keep my money in separate pockets so that I wouldn't lose all of it.

I was supposed to exercise for at least half an hour every day, and was nearly always alone. If anyone had asked what I remembered most about being young I would have said walking by myself in the rain. I preferred the empty back-streets of rough neighbourhoods where none of the other kids in my class would dare to follow me.

My mother was harassed and panicked and worn thread-bare by work. No matter how many hours she put in she was always broke because she surrendered her wages to whichever bullying thug had currently latched on to her. She cried a lot. One day she explained why I was different. She told me about the Event.

I wished she hadn't.

After that I was pretty much uncontrollable. I was thrown out of schools for being disruptive (I learned too fast and grew impatient, then became bored and angry). I began wearing my brace over my clothes so that people could see I was proud of being different. I exaggerated my rolling walk and made myself stand out until I provoked fights. I learned to punch first. I did not get good grades, and then I stopped going to school altogether. It had never been easy because we never stayed in one place very long. I was smart, but self-taught, and applied to colleges. But my thinking was undisciplined. I could not conform.

My mother's death brought my childhood to an abrupt end. An aunt arranged the funeral, then conveniently disappeared. I was left not knowing what would happen to me.

It turned out my mother owed money to everyone. I found a shoebox full of unpaid bills under her bed. Her few relatives had long ago disowned her. One night men from a debt collection agency tried to break in, so I left for good. Broke and friendless, I was forced to squat in an empty mildew-smelling council flat off the Old Kent Road.

Begging for small change in the piss-reeking underpass of the Elephant & Castle Shopping Centre is lower than most of you will ever go. I became obsessed with the idea of taking back control of my life, but try getting anywhere without spare cash or special abilities. I needed to find someone with money. I knew how to make friends in theory: you help someone, joke with them, make them trust you – but I had never been able to put it into practice. That was when I discovered I had a gift of cracking life's problems by turning

each of them into a puzzle that needed to be solved. By looking at them differently.

I am the child of many fathers and part of me died before
I was born, so it seemed only fair that six should die to bring
about my rebirth. I had no lover, no friend, no brother to
stay by my side and keep my resolve, but I had learned
from an early age to think for myself and trust no one.

I worked on my plan and made strategic alliances with
people who would unwittingly help me to fulfil it. I stole
his watch and her laptop and their savings, and arranged it
so that no one was ever looking in my direction when it
happened. I studied everything I needed to know and a lot
I didn't. It was a long journey filled with dangers that took
me from the derelict church all the way to the burning
bookshop.

I should have known that books would be the cause of
all the trouble.

Bookshops suit the austere grey terraces of Bloomsbury. At
dusk they glow invitingly with yellow light and warmth. The
bookshop in Bury Place was called Typeface, a small double-
fronted brick house with windows framed in grey-painted
wood, its interior finished in the kind of muted natural colours favoured by fashionable independent shops. Its left-hand
display was reserved for bright bestsellers about family secrets
uncovered in Mediterranean climes, while the right side was
kept back for academic publications, debuting authors, greet-
ing cards and rubber stamps. It made very little profit, even
in bookish Bloomsbury. On a wet Monday night it was deserted outside and should have been dark inside, but George
Bernard Shaw was on fire.

The splash of blue flame flickered up and spread quickly
along the tops of the bookcases from Plays (*Pygmalion*, first
edition, £4,500) to Bolshevism (*The Legacy of Lenin*, 3 vols,

slightly foxed) to Avant-Garde Poetry (*Why We Scream*, damaged frontispiece, £6 ono). Then it spilled in a fiery waterfall on to the General Fiction shelves. As it fanned and flooded out across the freshly varnished floorboards, the flyers on the cork noticeboards scorched and lifted free of their drawing pins, spiralling upwards in the blackening calyx of hot air. There was a pop of glass and a soft whoosh of drawn heat.

The sprinklers failed to open because some idiot had painted over them, and the ground floor became an inferno. When the windows blasted out into the street the fire's grip on the little shop tightened. Before the emergency services could reach the scene all was lost. It didn't help that one of the finest fire stations in the area was now a fashionable brasserie.

Senior Fire Officer Blaize Carter had been off-shift, and arrived just as the flames were being brought under control. The first floor of the narrow building was still dense with oily smoke. The ground-floor ceiling had carbonized and was starting to sag. Carter and her team drew back as someone pointed up at the roof. A stack of orange clay chimneypots, appearing to defy gravity, was leaning gracefully and falling slowly inwards, taking most of the roof tiles and attic beams with it.

The fall of wood and brick slammed down to the first floor, releasing the bookshop's heavy ceiling. The plaster put out the last of the flames but filled the building with dust, increasing the danger of reignition. The ground floor was given more water. What the flames hadn't damaged, the hoses obliterated.

'There was nobody in there,' one of the lads came over to tell her, Sandy someone, a nice kid based at Shaftesbury Avenue. Carter remembered him because nobody was called Sandy any more and he looked about fifteen. 'We've checked the buildings on either side; they're both empty.'

Carter wedged a yellow glove under her arm and matched

the building against the diagram on her phone. The department knew every building in its ward and could theoretically summon up their fire-safety plans, except that the app rarely loaded properly. 'Built in 1702. All wood beams and lath and plaster ceilings. Incredible.'

'Sorry?' The lad looked at her, missing something.

She glanced over at him. 'Incredible that it survived three centuries of candlelight, gas mantles and dodgy electrics, only to burn down in an era of cold-light LEDs and electronic sprinkler systems. It's a listed building. The paperwork will be a nightmare. Queen Anne was on the throne when this place was built. I hope none of her chairs were still in there.'

'Think it was an insurance job?' Sandy looked back at the billowing black smoke.

'Books? I doubt it. Dry paper is always a disaster. Ever hear of Paternoster Row?'

'No.'

'No reason why you should, I suppose. It was a three-hundred-year-old street of stationers and bookshops just behind St Paul's. It went up with a roar they heard streets away. Burning paper everywhere. Wiped clean by a stray bomb during the Blitz. The firefighters couldn't get near it. This isn't clean. I can smell linseed oil.' She sniffed the acrid atmosphere. 'Something else too. Citrus. Aftershave?' She crinkled her nose. 'Nope, it's gone.'

As water flooded back out of the ground floor she broke protocol by setting aside her breath-pack and climbing through the shop's smashed window in her yellow headgear and gloves. The breathing apparatus was essential for deep exploration – it gave a whistle when it was running out of air – but this little place only went back a few dozen yards. Once, far inside a warehouse, an acetylene tank had exploded in a storage room and melted one side of her helmet. It had taken two months for her hair to grow back. The bookshop's scorching air stank of blistered varnish, but underneath it was another unmistakeable smell, much stronger now.

Oranges.

The fall of rubble from the roof had bowed the exposed ceiling beams of the ground floor. She stepped forward, tapping her steel-capped boot on the boards as she went, making sure they were solid enough to take her weight. The fire had not reached the basement, so it had presumably started here on the ground floor and flared upwards via the wooden staircases.

She glanced back. They were supposed to have two crews, one to extinguish, the other to search, but staffing problems had left them short. Lately, too many of her friends had quit.

There was an ominous yawn of stretching timber from above. The first floor now had the weight of the second plus the roof on it, so it was time to get out. As she crunched back over broken glass and soaked paper she saw the line of primary ignition clearly etched on the floor, running like a meandering black river from the bookcases at the back of the shop to the front. Oil had been poured straight from a can, its flow mimicking the walk of the carrier. Arson wasn't uncommon, but in a place like this it didn't make sense.

'We haven't been able to get hold of the landlord yet,' said Sandy. 'Someone at the Met's asking for a report.'

'I'll deal with them,' she told him. 'Keep trying the owners.'

Her phone pinged. 'Thought you should know John May is going in for surgery tomorrow morning.' It was from the Operations Director of the Peculiar Crimes Unit, Janice Longbright.

Blaize eased off her gloves and walked back to the fire truck thinking about the message. Even though she had broken up with John she felt bad for him. He had no family who would come visiting, only his co-workers, and his partner had apparently disappeared without telling anyone where he was going.

She walked beyond the fire truck to breathe some fresh air and clear her lungs. That was when she spotted the trainers. Blue and white Adidas, sticking out of the archway that led to the narrow courtyard behind Galen Place, with its terrace of elegant Edwardian apartments. As she approached, she saw that the trainers were attached to a man in his early thirties. He was sprawled on his back in the centre of the arched alley, neatly dressed in a navy sweater and jeans, but soot-blackened and barely conscious. When Carter leaned over to check his breath she was hit with a sour blast of whisky. His sweater reeked of oil.

'Come on,' she coaxed, 'get up, you can't stay here.' She pushed a hand under his back as he tried to lift himself.

'What – Where we going?' he asked, slurring his words. He had startling green eyes.

'I'll decide in a minute, after you tell me where you got that.' She pointed to the uncapped can of linseed oil that lay beside him.

'You understand why you've been arrested, don't you?'

Sergeant George Flowers took a bite out of his apple and set the core aside, balancing it on its end. When no answer was forthcoming he tapped the suspect to stop him from falling asleep again and sliding off his chair. 'You did a *Fahrenheit 451* on your gaff.'

Flowers read a lot of classic science fiction on night duty. Holborn Police Station was deadly quiet this evening and the sergeant had been halfway through an Arthur C. Clarke when they brought in the suspect, reeking of flammables, booze and burned paper.

'I didn't do it. I wouldn't set fire to my own shop,' said his detainee, coughing so hard into his blackened fist that the sergeant's apple core fell over.

Flowers gave himself a scratch and looked about for a biro.

'Don't jump the gun, mate. Let's do it properly and get a witness statement. Do you need a doctor? I'd go without one if you can, 'cause it's a minimum four-hour wait for a non-emergency.'

'I already told the fire officers I don't.' He had an Eastern European accent – Baltic perhaps. 'How long do I have to stay here?'

'Until we've got your statement, your lawyer's been and you've sobered up,' said Flowers. 'You should be able to get some kip after that.'

'You mean I'll be able to go home? My wife—'

'—is on her way here. You won't be going home tonight. What part of "arrested on suspicion of arson" is confusing you? What's your name, mate?'

'Cristian Albu.'

'Spell that for me, pal.'

'I'm the owner of the Typeface bookshop and I didn't—'

'Ah-ah-ah.' Flowers wagged an index finger at him. 'No point in telling me what you've done before I know who you are. Are you Russian?'

'Romanian. I've lived here for eight years. My wife is English.'

'So what does this shop of yours sell then?'

Albu was mystified by the question. 'It's a bookshop. It sells *books*.'

'Yeah? What else?'

'Nothing else. Books. I know who did this—'

'Ah-ah-ah.' Flowers warned him with another finger-wag. 'What did I tell you? Let's take this one step at a time. Spell your name.'

Elise Albu cast one last look around the basement flat, then checked her bag. Toothbrush, soap, pyjamas – nobody had told her what he would need, so she packed as if she was taking him things in hospital. Cristian had once been arrested on a demonstration but had not been kept in overnight. She was married to the tidiest man in the world, and therefore couldn't find anything. Having met the other members of his family, she had decided that personal neatness must be a Romanian national trait.

She set off with her bag from Dalston Junction and sat with her husband in Holborn Police Station while he made his statement. He looked smudged and frayed, all done in. He had been appointed a lawyer who ignored him throughout the process, answering briefly and under sufferance before leaving at the first opportunity. Cristian seemed confused about the order of events, but she gleaned this much . . .

He had closed the shop at 7.00 p.m. and stayed for an hour finishing the accounts. As he was leaving, a customer had tapped at the door and asked him about a book. For reasons that Cristian was unable or unwilling to explain at the moment, he had gone for a drink with this customer to the Museum Tavern. The next thing he remembered was being woken up by a female fire officer and shown the remains of the burned-out shop. He had drunk a single pint of lager and had no idea why he smelled of whisky. Similarly, he had not been aware of the oil can before the fire officer had pointed it out to him. He recognized it; it belonged to him. He was devastated about the destruction of the shop, which was, as he explained to the patient but clearly bored Sergeant Flowers, his life's work.

'What have I done?' he asked his wife as she wiped his sweat-slick forehead. He had the face of a desperate child. She hated having to talk here on a bench in front of the sergeant, pinned under the shadowless light. 'You know what that shop meant to me, Elise. I've failed you.'

'You mustn't think like that.' She rubbed his hands, trying to calm him. 'Please, Cristian.'

'It wasn't me. It couldn't have been me, you know that.'

'Tell me more about the man who called at the shop.'

'I've met him before. We've had a few dealings.'

'What was his name? What did he look like?'

He held her arm. 'I don't want to get him involved. He's very private. I told him I respect that.'

She had seen this before in her husband, an anxiety to please that weakened him in the eyes of others. 'But did you argue? Did you do something to make him angry?'

'No, we just had a little business. He pays well and in cash.'

'It was off the accounts?' She tried to think. 'What were you selling him?'

He ran a hand through his hair and studied the floor, clearly embarrassed. 'There were things he wanted which are hard to find. I have to finance my imprint, you know that.'

She glanced back at the sergeant but Flowers was paying them no attention. 'Cristian, you must help me find him. I don't trust the lawyer. We can't rely on anyone else. We have to do this ourselves.'

Albu stayed silent for so long that he began to frighten her. 'It's all gone.'

She held his face and forced him to look into her eyes. 'Tell me everything and I'll get you out of here. I won't judge you. I just want to get to the truth. Who was he?'

He could not bring himself to answer.

'Have I met him? What does he look like?'

'It's nothing to do with him, Elise, it couldn't be. I got hold of a couple of books he wanted, very rare.' Shame was clearly silencing him.

'Cristian, where did you get them?'

'Some libraries – they have reference books that haven't been taken out in years. Nobody wants them. They don't even know what they have.'

'You mean they were stolen to order.'

'This time he wanted a book from the shop. We reached an agreement on the price and he said we should have a drink to celebrate.'

'You never drink with clients. Why did you go?'

'I wanted to. I had something of his. It's a pleasure to discuss books. I can't remember what happened after we had the first drink.'

'There must be something else. Please. What does he look like?'

'I don't know – ordinary, smartly dressed. He has trouble walking, a problem with one leg, I think. He was wearing a wedding ring.' He gripped her sleeve. 'They think it was me, Elise. They'll find out about the money we owe.'

'Even if they did, what does it matter now? They can't call in a loan on a shop that's gone.'

She didn't like the look in his eyes, as if he had surrendered his last hope. 'Elise, take me home. I don't feel safe.'

'I'll find this man. There are ways.' She smoothed down her husband's sooty hair and gave him a goodnight kiss. The dirt on his face made his eyes seem even greener.

As he was gently led downstairs, she waited knowing that he would glance at her one more time before turning the corner. He did so every morning as he left for work. When he looked back this time, the sight of him tore out her heart.

Sergeant Flowers was on duty at Holborn Police Station until 7.00 a.m. He didn't need to take the night shifts but during the week his wife worked in different surveillance centres around the country and could only get back to their home at the weekends, so he took the hours others didn't want.

The night was uneventful, but at least it allowed Sergeant Flowers to finish his novel and start a Brian Aldiss. A little before seven he made fresh coffee for the incoming sergeant and took down a mug to the prisoner.

Cristian Albu looked terrible. He asked to use the toilet and Flowers accompanied him, waiting outside. As there was only one holding cell, the bathroom was in general use by station staff. The main door had no lock, but the window situated above the sinks was bolted shut.

Flowers figured it was safe to leave Albu in there for a few minutes while he collected his bag from his locker. When he returned, he found that the prisoner had still not emerged, so he checked inside.

He discovered Albu on his knees, hanging from the wash-basin. He had choked himself to death by looping the elasticated belt from his jeans around his neck and tying the other end to the sink's cold tap. Albu had allowed his body weight to pull the makeshift noose tight and cut off his air supply.

Sergeant Flowers was mortified.

Holborn nick had not had a death in custody for years. If anybody saw that he had failed to take away the prisoner's belongings he would be done for negligence. He had meant to do it but his mind had been elsewhere.

He looked down at Albu's trainers and remembered that he had removed the laces, but the belt was the same colour as the jeans and had simply escaped his attention. It had been an honest mistake on his part, but unfortunately Sergeant Flowers had a bit of a history when it came to unfortunate mistakes. He could not afford to let this go on his record.

The Romanian was still hanging there, his face grey, a disgusting puddle of drool on the floor. The cleaner wasn't due in until tomorrow, but at least his shift was ending so it would be someone else's problem.

His shift.

The day sergeant would be arriving in a few minutes. Flowers took a shot of the scene on his phone, then carefully removed the belt from Albu's neck and lowered him to the ground. Stuffing it into his pocket, he ran back up to his desk and searched for the Swiss Army knife he always kept in the drawer.

He returned to the cell and cut into the bed's tough blue plastic cover with the knife, tearing off a long strip. He knotted it into a makeshift noose, fitting it around the prisoner's neck in exactly the same manner as the belt had been tied, then returned Albu to the position in which he had found him. He arranged his mouth above the pool of spittle and made sure that his head hung in the exact same pose.

By the time he had finished, Sergeant Flowers was positive that no one would ever know the difference. There were cameras in the station entrance and the cell. He would have to figure out a way to deal with those. He deleted the shot on his phone and headed upstairs to his duty desk, where he added the belt to the laces he had taken.

Then he sat down with his book to await the arrival of his replacement.

3

FALLEN ANGEL

'Arthur, is that you?'

The change in light told John May that the door to his private room had opened. He tried to twist his head, but his chest felt as if it had a burning rock inside it. He could make out a dumpy figure in a cheap grey leisure jacket and an open-necked shirt.

'No, I'm afraid it's me.' Raymond Land gingerly seated himself in the visitor's chair beside May's bed and set down a bag of obligatory grapes.

May usually had a light tan but now he was the colour of an Elastoplast, the veins in his hands prominent and sore from his saline drip.

'I see they got you a room.' Land patted his knees, looking about. 'The old lady must have died.' He raised a thumb. 'Result.'

May closed his eyes.

'It's nice and clean. I like University College Hospital. People reckon it's a good place to come when your time's up.' He pantomimed remembering something amusing. 'Oh! The revolver she fired at you? We're having it made into a cigarette lighter.'

'I don't smoke.'

'Well, it's the thought. The nurse says I can only have five minutes.' Land pushed back a wayward strand of his combover. 'We sent you a card.' He plucked a condolence card from the bedside table, the front of which read 'Sorry For Your Tragic Loss' above a painting of dying lilies in an urn. Inside was a handwritten note, which he read aloud.

'Hey, John,

Congratulations on being the second person in our unit ever to get shot in his own office. We came to see you but you were out cold and it was boring just sitting around doing nothing so we went home. We ate your cake. Sorry. The main thing is that you're not dead. They've assured us you're going to make an almost full recovery, so you won't be a burden on state services. Not yet, says Meera.

Also sorry for the card but the Get Well Soon ones didn't seem appropriate as we didn't know if you were going to pull through.

We had to forge Mr Bryant's signature because he has gone missing. We couldn't get you a private room. They've promised you can have one if the pensioner in 14A carks it. She's not looking good, so try to hold on.

We'll be back when you're awake. We hope you're a bit more vivacious next time.

Love,
Janice, Meera, Colin, Raymond, Dan, Giles, Mr Bryant

'They're taking you down shortly,' said Land. 'You'd better not have the grapes yet, patients can choke to death under anaesthetic.'

May said nothing. Land hummed a little, breathed out noisily, looked around. 'Don't they smell funny, hospitals? I'm surprised you're having another operation. The nurse said the removal of the bullet wasn't as clean as they'd hoped. There's some kind of perforation – I didn't get the full gist.'

'They need to drain the fluid from my right lung.' May attempted to pull himself upright but had to stop. 'They're cleaning out the tissue debris to reduce scarring.'

'How long is the healing process? Has anyone given you a timeline?' Land grimaced in an attempt at sympathy.

'Up to six weeks at home. I'll be able to do some work from there.'

Land hastily skipped over the remark. 'We thought we'd lost you, you know. It's a good job the other bullet missed. It ruined the skirting board. It was quite a shock, finding you lying there on the floor of your office. You had a nasty crack on the head.'

'Apparently I have a thick skull. What's happening at the unit?'

'The Home Office sent in a team to seal all documents and pack everything away. We tried to get rid of as much as we could before they arrived. Janice was shredding like mad. It was like Watergate. The atmosphere is awful.' Land did his duck face. 'They've already started clearing the building. They reckon it will only take them a couple of days. The computers were removed yesterday. Dan went bananas. They nicked all his cables.'

May stopped trying to sit up and fell back. 'Have the staff been told where they're going?'

'That's just it. Nobody knows.' In the next room something electronic began pinging ominously and two nurses pelted past. 'I suspect there are no placements available in any of the London specialist units. Most of them are being closed down and centralized. We'll try for voluntary redundancies first.'

'And my prosecution?'

'Are you sure you want to hear this before going into surgery?'

May regarded him with a steady eye. 'How much worse can it be?'

Land pulled an envelope from his pocket and skimmed through its contents. 'It says here they're going to pin a whole raft of misdemeanours on us using your case as an example to others. As far as I'm concerned you've committed no offence. You've seen a lot of changes in your life; it's not always easy to adapt to new rules.'

'Stop being so polite, Raymond.' May lifted his eyes in exasperation. 'It was my own bloody fault, mixing my personal life with business. God knows it happens often enough in the Met.'

Land tried a puckish smile. 'Well, I'm sure they'll wait until you're fully recovered before starting proceedings against you.' As reliable assurances went, it was on a par with Neville Chamberlain returning from Munich.

'Did you come bearing any good news, by chance?' May asked with some testiness. 'Where is Arthur? He hasn't been to see me.'

Land fidgeted about awkwardly on his orange plastic chair. 'Nobody's seen him. Even his landlady doesn't know where he is. He's disappeared before. You know what he's like.'

'I thought he might have changed his mind about how he felt.'

'I wish I had better news, John.' Land pocketed the offending letter.

'You need to find him. He's out there somewhere and may be in trouble. You know he's not good by himself.'

A nurse appeared at the door and pointedly waited.

'I'll make some more calls.' Land fiddled with the buttons of his jacket in a prelude to departure. 'It's raining out. I suppose I should—'

'They'll let you know how my operation goes.' May sank further back on his pillow, dismissing his boss. Land had never been the most inspirational of men and now seemed physically diminished, a faded photograph found tucked in an unread paperback, unplaceable and out of time.

'We're going to take you down now,' said the nurse as an orderly crashed a gurney into the door frame.

'I don't need that,' May snapped. 'I can still walk.'

'We don't want you raising your blood pressure, do we?'

'Who's "we"? Don't use a plural when you mean a singular.'

'You sound just like your partner,' said Land unhelpfully.

'We have to make allowances for him, don't we?' said the nurse, attempting to collude with Land.

'You may have to, I don't,' Land replied, confusing things further.

'Please, somebody knock me out,' May begged.

The nurse and the orderly took over. A feeling of hopelessness sank into him. Everything was out of his hands now. In the course of their careers the detectives had been admired and hated in equal measure, but never before had they been ignored.

As John May was taken down into surgery, further along Euston Road the barbarians were storming the gates of Rome. Specifically, the Home Office agents in the employ of their police liaison CEO, Leslie Faraday, had entered the PCU's headquarters on Caledonian Road and were ransacking it room by room.

'Oi, give us that back,' warned Dave Two, one of the builders who had taken up permanent residence at the unit, 'that's DS Bimsley's exercise bike.'

'Sorry, squire, evidence,' replied the burly lad who was dragging Colin's gym equipment into the street.

'I don't see how an exercise bike is pertinent to the investigation,' said Dave Two.

'It's a good job you're just a handyman then, isn't it?' The lad vengefully threw the red steel frame into the back of their van. 'We're stripping out the operations room next.'

The two Daves had been working at the PCU for so long that they felt like part of the family, bringing in baklava and Turkish red velvet cake on Fridays, offering suggestions on policing the capital and attending the monthly film night.

Dave One patted Dave Two's back consolingly. 'Let's take up a couple of floorboards in the hallway. That'll slow them down a bit.'

'And the light switch outside the operations room could give someone a nasty shock,' Dave Two surmised, unsheathing his electric screwdriver and heading back into the unit.

'It must be here somewhere. We have to find it.'

Janice Longbright stood astride the mess with her knuckles on her hips. 'I have no idea where to start looking. How close are they getting?'

Meera Mangeshkar peered around the door jamb. 'One of them is going into the operations room with a trolley and a stack of boxes. They won't reach this office for a while yet.'

There was a crackle and a yell and the lights momentarily dimmed. When Meera looked again she saw one of the Home Office agents sitting on the floor with sports-car hair.

Longbright was standing in the office used by the unit's most senior detectives. Today she had abandoned her 'Forgotten British Stars of the 1950s' look for a more practical outfit of jeans and a red sweater, although she had knitted the top herself from a pattern created by the late singer Alma

Cogan. Before her was a habitat without its inhabitants, part man-cave, part bat-cave.

One side of the room was John May's, bare, pristine and Bluetooth-empowered, its clean glass desk sporting a silver laptop, a notepad and a squared-off Montblanc pen.

Beyond this arctic border lay Arthur Bryant's territory. It was the difference between the room at the end of *2001: A Space Odyssey* and the junkyard in *Steptoe and Son*. Janice was convinced that the air changed as she crossed the other half. Even the Bluetooth connection disappeared. May's side smelled faintly of electricity and aftershave. Bryant's smelled of old dog, rolling tobacco, dope, gravy, horsehair cinema seats, Jeyes cleaning fluid, sherbet lemons, Vicks vapour rub, aniseed balls, hops, tea and, for some reason, burning coal.

In the middle of his desk was a galvanized bucket filled with receipts that had not been emptied in four years. There were hummocks of paperwork that would never find their way to the Cloud, brown cardboard folders tied with green string and balanced like rock formations, a mountain range of books not organized under any currently recognized system because the alphabetized shelves were all full, a boneless armchair and a filthy roll-top desk covered with what appeared to be unpopular exhibits from a provincial museum, including a ceramic statue of a goat being torn to shreds by hounds, a tea mug commemorating Daniel Defoe's description of the hanging of Jack Sheppard and a satirical etching of an eighteenth-century French water closet.

'Give me a clue,' begged Meera. 'What does it look like?'

'If it was anyone else I'd say an address book, but he calls it his Dead Diary. Knowing Arthur it could take the form of an Enigma machine. He's very precious about anyone touching it because it holds all his private contacts. He told me it never leaves the room.' Longbright rolled up her sleeves and prepared to shift the dusty volumes from the desk.

'There must be an easier way of finding him.'

'I know Arthur. He's far more likely to have confided in one of his contacts.'

'How about this?' Meera held up a black leather book with an embossed head of Lucifer on the cover. A single page stuck out from it, encouraging withdrawal.

'What does that say?'

'I think it's poetry.'

She was about to cast it aside but Longbright stopped her. 'Let me have a look.

'Grip my coat and hold on tight!
Here we reach a central height,
Where the mountain brings to view
Fires of **Mammon** *shining through.*

'The word Mammon is in bold type.' She turned it over and read out the note on the back: ' "It's from Faust's flight with Mephistopheles if you must know – you won't find the key to begin with – AB." '

A brass lock kept the book's pages safely sealed. 'We could try smashing it off,' Meera suggested.

'If it really is his Dead Diary he'll already have thought of that,' she told Mangeshkar. 'He's set the finder a puzzle.'

'Why does he have to turn everything into some kind of obscure board game?'

'Because he knows that we'll be able to find the information but nobody at the Met will. It's the way his mind works. He doesn't know how to encrypt passwords on his laptop so he hides things on bits of paper. He's always done it. You have to remember that the unit started out as one of Churchill's secret ministries, full of boffins hiding passwords and encrypting everything.'

Out in the hall, the Home Office agents were calling to

each other, coming nearer. Once they entered the room it would automatically become off limits to staff. 'Think. Where would he have hidden the key?'

'Maybe he has it on him.'

Longbright turned around on herself. 'No, we're meant to find it.' From next door came a crash of dropped furniture. 'I have to phone a friend.'

Raymond Kirkpatrick was one of the country's leading experts in semantics and cryptography, even if he did look like a nineteenth-century naval commander crossed with a yeti. He was currently in the medieval map restoration department of the British Library listening to a Mongolian death-metal band on his headphones, which was his favourite thing to do after verbally duffing up the students who dared to cross his path looking for places to charge their laptops.

'Janice, you gorgeous beast, where have you been keeping yourself?' he boomed into his phone, clearing his study area and plonking himself down on a protesting desk.

'Rather short of time,' she said. 'You don't know where Arthur is, do you?'

'His every movement is entirely mysterious to me. Mr Bryant's thoughts fall into a special category that includes my wife's erogenous zones and the city of Perth. I'm fairly sure they exist but I can't be arsed to go there. Why?'

'We need to find him urgently and our best bet is to go through his address book, which of course is locked. The key must be in his room but everything's about to be confiscated. We thought you might know this.' She explained the Goethe quote.

Kirkpatrick sucked the end of his beard, thinking. 'That's the Philip Wayne translation, if memory serves. I won't ask a more obvious question, *exempli gratia*, why his office is being emptied out. If you're looking for something that appears in

Faust you're royally shagged, because Faust is stuffed to the gunnels with arcane symbolism: Walpurgis Night, jars containing images of Cabirian deities and all that stuff about Helen of Troy. Mammon is the personification of wealth. Faust and the Devil look upon the lights of the rich—'

'The rich.' He heard Longbright turn aside. 'Meera, what's the most valuable object in this office?'

'There's nothing here I'd want.'

'What about that hideous thing? It's not telling the right time. Mr Kirkpatrick, there's a baroque carriage clock on Arthur's mantelpiece. Any clue there?'

'Ah, I know the one. The definition of *Mammon* is "wealth regarded as an evil influence or the false object of worship and devotion". I reckon it would cover a naff fake gold clock.'

'Hang on. It's got a cable hanging off it. Meera, is there a switch?'

'I'm sorry to interrupt your little treasure hunt,' Kirkpatrick shouted, 'but I've got a 1560 map of London to get under glass before one of these spotty twerps spills his mungbean latte on it.'

'I think we could be on to something,' said Longbright. 'I'll call you back.'

'I'd rather you didn't. I'll have to bill you for my time. May I go now?' Kirkpatrick cranked his death metal back up and rang off.

The door to Bryant's office opened and one of the Home Office agents pinned it back. The face above the tie was young, doughy and quite punchable. 'What are you two doing?'

'You wouldn't believe us if we told you,' said Meera.

'Don't touch anything, either of you,' he warned. 'We're boxing it all up so you have to leave right now.'

'Give us two minutes.' Meera turned on the carriage clock's light. A soft yellow glow shone from its face. A plaque beneath the glass read: 'To Mr Arthur Bryant & Mr John May in gratitude from the Rector of St Bride's Church'. Meera opened the glass and ran her fingers behind the minute hand. 'There's something here.'

Longbright waited. The agents waited. Meera withdrew a miniscule key, holding it high between thumb and forefinger. She tried the lock on the address book, but it was too small to fit. 'There must be another one,' she said. 'What is this, Alice in bleeding Wonderland?'

'That's it, we need you two outside this minute,' said the foreman of the removal team.

Dave Two appeared alongside them in the doorway. In terms of chest measurement and moustache luxuriance he outranked the foreman. 'Mate, show some manners and give them a moment, all right?' he suggested in a tone of friendly threat.

'This entire building is now under Home Office jurisdiction,' the foreman warned him, taking half a step back just to be on the safe side.

'Wait, is there a copy of Faust on his shelves?' Longbright squeezed past the men, who were now starting to remove books. *Thank God for Arthur's alphabetizing fetish*, she thought, locating a battered paperback. She turned it over and shook it out. The only things that fell from the pages were other pages.

'If you don't put that down and leave the premises immediately, we'll have to remove you,' said the foreman, lifting a rather club-footed ceramic angel from the mantelpiece.

Longbright ignored him and studied the note her boss had left behind. ' "You won't find the key *to begin with*",' she repeated. 'That sounds clumsy. Did he mean we'd get it eventually?' She turned to the front of the book and read the opening lines. ' "Philosophy have I digested, / The whole of Law and Medicine . . ." '

'No,' said Meera, 'he means you won't find it at the beginning.'

Longbright turned to the very end. 'Now what?' She glanced back up at the clock. 'It's stopped at seven minutes to five. Seven, five. The final chorus is eight lines long.' Her finger ran down the page. 'The last sentence starts on the penultimate line and has five words. "Eternal Womanhood / Leads us above." The infinite feminine.' She looked at the home-made statue of the angel in the removal man's hands and nodded to Meera, who grabbed it from him and dropped it on the floor.

Inside the smashed meringue of china she found the key. 'Why couldn't he have just said it's in the sodding angel?' she asked.

'Right you two, bugger off before you cause any more damage.' The foreman ushered them out and started to tape the door shut.

'Watch it, mate,' warned Dave Two in the crowded corridor outside, 'they're ladies, even the short one, so treat them with some respect or you'll get my claw hammer across the bridge of your nose.'

'You heard him,' said Longbright. Armed with the key and Bryant's address book, she and Meera beat a retreat, leaving behind the shattered seraph.

4

EXISTENTIAL

The operation on John May's lung proved successful, and the detective was returned to his bare bright flat in Shad Thames for a period of enforced recuperation. Over the next three weeks he organized the place to within an inch of its life, including the micro-calibration of his home entertainment system and the cataloguing of his music, and learned how to navigate the byzantine structure of his streaming services. It was easy to empty the small plastic drain in his chest and change the dressing, but being forced to remain still for long periods had brought on a bout of cabin fever.

During this time he received an unexpected visit from Fire Officer Blaize Carter, whose feelings he had hurt most deeply during their last investigation. Ashamed, he apologized and she ostensibly forgave him, but he sensed that she watched him now with a jaundiced eye. She made it clear that what they'd once had could never be repeated.

Of his partner there was not one single word.

The building on Caledonian Road had been stripped out

and the staff dispersed to their homes to await notification of their transfers. The city continued its diurnal ebb and flow without noticing that its most venerable specialist crime unit had ceased to exist. London's beautiful curse is its ability to completely forgive and completely forget.

At the close of March, four members of the PCU staff decided to commemorate the end of an era by going for a drink. The Racketeer on King's Cross Road was named after the nineteenth-century term for pickpockets who used fire-crackers to distract their targets. It was fake, of course, a Dickensian makeover of an actively unpleasant 1970s boozer, but somehow appropriate in its newly minted incarnation. Carrying their drinks down to the candlelit, crimson-curtained basement, the team settled in old armchairs and tried to come up with a plan of action.

'We could firebomb the joint,' said Meera Mangeshkar, taking a pint of bitter from Bimsley's proffered tray.

'Bit extreme, Meera,' said Colin.

'It wouldn't be the first time the unit burned down. We could fill it full of rats. Health and safety would have to clear the place.'

'How about something that doesn't involve blowing up buildings or poisoning everyone?' Colin suggested.

Janice Longbright took her gin martini from the tray. 'Meera, I think you have to accept that the unit has gone. Has anyone received a Home Office communication yet?'

'Not a dicky bird.' Dan Banbury lifted his Guinness.

'I went to see John last night,' Longbright told them. 'He's up and about now but . . .'

The others waited.

'Well, it's hard to say exactly. He's not himself. He's depressed.'

'No shit,' said Dan. 'He's going to trial and Mr Bryant hasn't bothered to get in touch with him.'

'You don't suppose Bryant's old memory-loss problem has come back?' Colin asked the group.

'I don't think so. I checked all the hospitals, hostels and homeless shelters. I even called a number of high-end hotels where he knew the concierges well enough to blag a room. He hasn't been seen anywhere. Here.' Longbright opened her handbag and removed half a house brick from it along with her mother-of-pearl compact and a startling number of post-war lipsticks. She held up Bryant's Dead Diary. 'These are some of the people I've tried so far: Fraternity DuCaine, Maggie Armitage, Coatsleeve Charlie, Audrey Beardsley, Edwardian George, Raymond Kirkpatrick, the Friends of the British Library and those crazy tramps he befriended. Meera and I are working our way through every contact but it's tricky. A few are dead and some seem to be completely fictitious, plus he's alphabetized them thematically rather than by their last names. We started with academics, anarchists and astrologers, and now we're up to creationists and conspiracy theorists. I'm even trying the ones in prisons and mental health institutions. And all the addresses are in code, of course. Luckily I have his symbol key. He used an Atbash cypher.'

'What's that?' asked Colin, picking something out of his beer. His bulky, well-proportioned frame overwhelmed the puny stool he was perched upon.

'It's just the alphabet backwards. It's designed to slow down users, not stop them.'

'Look, I know he's brilliant and everything,' said Dan, 'but he's a royal pain in the arse.'

'It's a very British habit,' said Janice. 'The BBC used to help espionage units by sending coded messages to private individuals via the radio.'

'Bryant's landlady must know where he is. He tells her everything, doesn't he?'

'Either she genuinely doesn't have a clue or she's covering for him. I couldn't get anything out of her.'

'Have you talked to Raymond? Maybe he's heard something.'

Janice shook her head. 'He's at his cottage on the Isle of Wight. He hasn't spoken to anyone.'

'So that's it.' Colin examined his pint philosophically. 'After all we've been through, we're just going to leave it like that and go our own ways, are we? Who's going to hire us now? Mr Bryant saw talents in all of us, but individually we're just not special enough. I mean, look at us. Dan's a geek, I have diminished spatial awareness, Janice thinks it's 1960, Meera's got anger management issues—'

'Say that again and I'll split your lip,' said Meera.

'But together – that was what made it work. We've got to remain a team.'

'I don't know, Colin.' Meera looked doubtful. 'At this rate we're going to end up as another of old Bryant's weird old societies, like druids or evangelists.'

'Yeah, you be a team,' said Dan. 'I can get a job tomorrow outside of the police service. I'll put in for something closer to home. I've already been offered a job in Sevenoaks mending digital readouts on refrigeration units.'

'That sounds pulse-racing,' said Meera.

'I want to spend more time with the kids.'

'I thought you only had a boy?'

'I've a little girl too.'

'You didn't say.'

'You never asked.'

'No, because it's boring.' Meera said this as if it was obvious. 'It's like when people drag their partners along to company parties; nobody wants to talk to them – we'd rather hang out with our co-workers. You won't be doing that with fridge-parts people.'

'Look here, I spent my days and nights in that building with hardly any free weekends and no life of my own,' said Dan vehemently. 'I'm amazed my wife didn't leave me like Raymond's did. Now I can have a proper work–life balance.'

Janice wondered where her gin had gone. The glass was empty and she appeared to have eaten her slice of lemon. 'I don't want a work–life balance. My parents were both coppers, it's in my blood and there's nothing I can do about it. I don't want to get married and I don't trust anyone except you lot, so what else is there?'

Colin was crestfallen. 'I just fancied a beer with my mates. I wasn't expecting a basement full of existential grief.'

'I'm getting sick listening to you lot,' said Meera. 'You're all talking as if you're washed up. I'm the youngest here. I was just getting started. I admit I hated the unit at first because nobody explained how anything got done and even when they did it didn't make any bloody sense. And I got stuck with dustbin duty. I'm not built for inactivity. It feels weird not having any cases on.'

'But we have got a case,' said Longbright, handing them the pages she had scanned from the Dead Diary. 'Your mission is to find Arthur Bryant.'

5

DOWN THE STRAND

Script extract from Arthur Bryant's 'Peculiar London' walking tour guide. (Meet at Embankment tube, duration 1 hr, sausage rolls provided, tips gratefully accepted.)

In London, nothing is ever where it's supposed to be.

To turn right you may first need to turn left (on roundabouts), to go north you must sometimes head east (on the Underground), to travel between stations it might be quicker to walk (Leicester Square to Covent Garden) and to cross a road you must wait for the green man except when his appearance has nothing to do with the passage of pedestrians or traffic, which is most of the time.

It comes as no surprise, then, that just as Islington's Upper Street is in fact its lower street, the Strand, one of London's grandest streets, is not a strand at all. A strand is the edge of a river but the river in question here is the Thames, which follows a path only in the sense that you can eventually follow one end of a hurled rope to the other. The river meanders, but the Strand, its edge, does not.

This is because the Strand is not a bridle path but one of the straightest thoroughfares in the capital, paved as the royal road to London, connecting the City's Square Mile to Westminster Abbey via the little village of Charing. It now finds itself lying inland, high and dry because of the Victoria Embankment. The ornate cross of Charing Cross inconveniently stuck outside the station is one of twelve monuments erected in the thirteenth century to the memory of Eleanor of Castile. They mark the resting places of her funeral procession. There are three others still knocking around.

What else can I tell you? There's a deep and ancient holy well just outside the law courts. It was used by the Saxons who lived in Aldwych because they were too scared to live in the haunted Roman ruins of the City.

Once the Strand was the home of dukes and earls. The governors of the Empire headed here to purchase their solar topees. Dickens enjoyed the Roman bath on Strand Lane, the *Strand* magazine introduced the world to Sherlock Holmes and Strand cigarettes told smokers 'You're never alone with a Strand'.

The Wig and Pen Club, the only Strand building to survive the Great Fire of London, has now been closed down, trapping the headless ghost of Oliver Cromwell inside it. The gaiety theatres and music halls, the brothels, taverns and supper clubs have nearly all vanished in the twenty-first century, unable to compete with office rents.

One end of the Strand is guarded by a dragon-like beast: the silver Temple Bar gryphon. Theoretically the Queen is not allowed to go east of it without receiving a formal invitation from the Lord Mayor.

The Strand was ahead of its time. It had the first gas lamps, the first public electric lighting, the first plate-glass windows along its length. But it was also a steadfast barrier between rich and poor. While the royal family owned the land from the south side to the river, its northern half was threaded with dark alleyways and ginnels where mountebanks, stage-door Romeos and good-time girls loitered to smoke and flirt. A few of them are still there.

The Strand is full of surprises. The playwright Ben Jonson used to drink in the Palsgrave Head Tavern, which was turned into London's most elegant bank, Lloyds, covered in mosaics of beehives, fish and owls. The story goes that the dining room of Lloyds was air-conditioned by two ladies riding a tandem in the basement to power a pair of bellows. It sounds ridiculous, but when the building was renovated workmen found the bicycle and its attached airpipe. So a bank was once a pub, and a tea shop was once a coffee house: Twinings, the world's oldest tea shop, took over Tom's Coffee House in 1706. If you head down the tea-caddy-lined hall you'll find a wooden box with the gold-painted initials 'T.I.P.' on it, standing for 'To Improve Promptness'. If you wanted your beverage a bit faster you'd drop a few pence in, from which we get the word 'tip'.

Just a hint there.

We shall be stopping at a nearby hostelry for oesophageal easement, so for those non-drinkers among you: bad luck, the tour is now over.

Nineteen-year-old Koharu Takahashi had been in London for less than twenty-four hours and was struggling to cope with the chaos of the city.

There seemed to be no standard codes of behaviour. People

wandered out into busy roads, changed their minds halfway and came back on to the pavement. It was cool and wet but they stood about as if it was a hot day, and were strangely dressed even though they weren't *kogals* or *men-gals* or part of any urban tribe she had ever seen in Tokyo.

After breakfast she had walked from her hotel in Trafalgar Square along the Strand, looking up at the ornate buildings, but there was hardly anyone around. It was a Sunday morning in a Christian country so she had expected a few stores to be shut, but there was nothing open at all.

Her parents had forced her on the trip because they were fearful that she was developing *hikikomori* from spending too much time shut up at home with her laptop. They had heard about the phenomenon on TV and had paid for the two-week vacation to London, although they had sent her older brother along as a chaperone.

This morning he was sleeping in, so she had ventured out into this alien world alone. The streets were grey and quiet, glossy and rained-on even though it was not raining, or at least not quite. A fine wet mist hung in the air, a kind of semi-rain that reminded her of home.

If she tipped back her clear plastic umbrella she could see an ornate white church with a tiered spire. She could hardly have missed the building, for it was stuck right in the middle of the road so that traffic diverted around it on either side.

The surrounding terraces were low and grubby and *old*. There was a building connected with colonnades, with ships on the top of it, and another old off-white block with fake Greek columns like some kind of temple, and a crimson-tiled Underground station called 'Strand' that appeared to be closed, and some ugly offices and lots of tall trees that made an avenue of interlocking branches, and there were no helpful signs, just one that said, randomly, 'Elephant & Castle', and no shops open anywhere.

It was all highly confusing.

That was when she looked up at the building with the col onnades and saw the man coming out of the entrance, a fellow with a neat grey beard, dressed in a black suit with a carnation in his lapel and a white silk shirt, like a figure from a steampunk manga. He disappeared from view. She walked about for a few minutes, trying to match the street scene with the map on her phone. She was worried that if she wandered off into any of the narrow lanes she might not find her way back out. Perhaps she should head back to the hotel.

The smartly dressed gentleman was back. He was about to cross the road but suddenly a pulse of buses and cars streamed past him. He stepped from the kerb between two parked vehicles, a tall-sided delivery van and a council bin lorry, but never emerged from the other side.

When Ms Takahashi looked again she saw that something very strange had happened. The spot through which the smart gentleman had passed was filled with wooden crates that had fallen from the back of the van. The van was pale blue and said 'Kent Farmhands Organic Fruits' on the side above a painting of oranges and lemons. There was no sign of the man at all. Further along, a smartly dressed middle-aged lady had stopped and was also staring at the van in amazement.

She could not help feeling that, even for London, whatever had just happened was not a normal occurrence.

Ms Takahashi was one of two witnesses. The other was Mrs Margot Brandy, who did not want to be at the Inns of Court on a Sunday morning but had no choice; one of the lawyers she looked after had managed to mislay his notes and as a court officer she had agreed to check the offices for him.

The clouds above were the colour of boiled fish. The wea- ther was in a very British state, in that it was trying hard to rain. Margot's little flat was on Gray's Inn Road, just a few minutes' walk away, but it meant that she could always be called upon at the weekend. She had passed the red and silver dragon that marked the boundary of the City of London and was now on the Strand, hoping to find a shop open that would sell her some Superkings. Running out of fags on a Sunday morning around here was as fatal as smoking them.

She at least had the consolation of knowing that there were others working today. On her right were the mean-windowed offices of various government quangos, many of which employed weekend staff to perform admin chores. Margot had a full house in court this week, including a major fraud case going to trial, too many ill-prepared defendants and too few police witnesses. Unless her lawyers could get more coppers into the box their cases would collapse, but that was the legal system for you, forever on the edge of disaster yet somehow scraping through to fight another day.

Margot was dying for a gasper and a doughnut. And a coffee, ideally as strong and bitter as her ex-husband. There was nothing open, not even the funny little kiosk run by the old Korean lady whom she suspected of sleeping behind her stacks of cartons. She caught sight of something moving just past her eyeline. The back of a fruit van had opened, and there was someone trying to get across the road.

Margot recognized him mainly because of his goatee. She'd seen him often enough on the news, the former firebrand lawyer who had shone a light on police corruption and entered Parliament to eventually become the nation's upholder of procedural civility, Michael Claremont. She could hear his familiar voice rage as he called order in parliament. The sighting forced her to rummage through her bag for her distance glasses. She watched dumbfounded as a tall stack of crates from the back of the van toppled forward and engulfed Claremont at the exact moment he chose to cross the road.

The crates were wooden and filled with fruit, and some

must have split on impact because in a moment Claremont was buried beneath them. She ran over to help, pulling at the boxes and stabbing splinters into her palms.

Claremont was at the bottom. She assumed he would be bruised and shocked, possibly cut, but when he was uncovered she saw that a stave from one of the crates as sharp as any dagger had punctured his ample stomach. A single scarlet flower had blossomed through his silk shirt. Six inches of rough wood protruded from it but it was impossible to tell whether it went deep or was a surface wound. Then he coughed and blood welled around the stave's entry point, pouring off his belly in a thick stream. That was when she knew he was in serious trouble.

The Speaker of the House of Commons lay on his back, surrounded by sun-brightened oranges and lemons from the smashed crates, the straw that had settled over his midriff soaked with blood. Fruit lolloped across the tarmac as cars slowed to avoid them. A Japanese girl was staring at the scene, frozen to the spot.

My God, Margot thought as she rose unsteadily to her feet, *there are going to be questions asked in the House about this.*

6

A SPYING JOB

'I won't do it.'

Leslie Faraday believed in structure. His emails required responses, his tea needed biscuits and his working day had to proceed in an orderly fashion, which was why, whenever he committed some appalling political gaffe and was forced to hide from the press for a few days, the thing he hated most was the way it disturbed his calendar. He needed order. At university he had been nicknamed 'the Olympic Flame' – because he never went out.

He was particularly unhappy about being called in early on a Monday morning and having to be here before his PA Deirdre had had time to put the kettle on, but his protests were starting to sound like petulance.

Timothy Floris had come over from the Independent Police Complaints Division on the other side of the building, and was too sharply dressed, too healthy and too young to be working in a Home Office back room. He knew it and Faraday knew it, with the result that Faraday cut him out of the loop whenever he could.

Floris decided to try again. 'I know you've had a long, fractious relationship with the Peculiar Crimes Unit, but the Home Secretary believes that it's time to reconsider your position.'

Fractious didn't begin to cover it. There were still a number of senior officials at the Home Office who would have been happy to dismantle the unit with their bare hands, especially since Bryant had once led three of their wives out of Claridge's restaurant in handcuffs.

'After all the grief they've given me?' Faraday stared at Floris in frank disbelief. 'Just when we finally get rid of them once and for all? Do you know how much they were costing us?'

'I have the budgets here,' said Floris, tapping his tablet mainly for effect. 'The unit was cheaper to run than almost any other.'

'But why them?' Faraday almost pleaded.

'Perhaps I can explain,' said Floris with infinite patience. 'The Speaker of the House of Commons is required to be politically impartial. Speakers must ensure that the rules of parliamentary law are adhered to. When a new one is elected she or he must resign from their party and remain separate from all political issues, even in retirement. Claremont is a highly respected Speaker. If he dies he could trigger a fight for succession that has tremendous political ramifications.'

'How so?' Faraday asked, trying to sound interested.

'Whoever steps into his shoes will have to be as independent as he was. Unless they're not.'

'Meaning . . .'

'Meaning the members cannot be trusted to choose an unbiased parliamentarian.'

'I'm a civil servant, Mr Floris. When my paymasters change I barely look up from my desk. The Serious Crime Command can handle the investigation. I will not have those lunatics at the PCU running around destroying everything again, particularly when the matter is so sensitive.'

This was a bit rich coming from someone who, on a stag weekend in Brussels, had been photographed pretending to post a letter in a burqa-wearing woman. Nobody knew it was Floris who had anonymously dropped it on Twitter.

Faraday looked across at Floris and felt threatened. This pipsqueak with threaded eyebrows and manicured nails belonged to an ambitious new generation that was entirely alien to him. Floris was the type who favoured protein boxes and palm-held technology, who talked about 'drilling down' and 'leaning forward', and was out of place in a department that had only just abandoned secretaries and wire-mesh in-trays. Faraday, who had been known to scoff pork pies at his desk, hated him. But Floris wasn't a *real* civil servant, he reminded himself, just someone whose parents both worked in the murky cross-hatched section between the Single Intelligence Account and the Home Office, which probably explained why their son had sprung up through the ranks with such celerity. There were even rumours that he was related to the Home Secretary, although no one was quite sure of the lineage.

There was a chill wind blowing through the corridors of power these days. The millennials were after his job, waltzing around their open-plan creative spaces with almond milk lattes. One by one they were being foisted on him, and were probably checking to see if he was trustworthy. He would have to keep his eye on these Midwich Cuckoos and make sure his job stayed secure.

Floris tapped at the screen of his ridiculous little tablet. 'Mr Faraday, you need to look at this from a different POV.'

'A different what?'

'A different point of view. The SCC can't take it on, but the PCU can.'

Faraday gave an adenoidal snort and surreptitiously wiped

his nose. 'You're forgetting that I disbanded it. Its senior detectives aren't available any more and the rest of the staff have been placed on gardening leave.'

'There's another way to conduct the investigation that could benefit everyone.' The screen was turned around so that Faraday could have read it if only the type size hadn't been so small. 'I think you should call in the head of the unit.'

Raymond Land had been looking forward to retirement on the Isle of Wight, partly because of the time difference (it was always 1965 there) and he would be able to go to the shops in his carpet slippers. But it hadn't quite worked out like that.

He rocked back on his heels and set down his trowel. It was a late Monday afternoon at the start of April and the perfect time for spring flowers, but nothing had bloomed in his garden. He had started out simply with daffodils and bluebells but they hadn't come up. He couldn't understand it. Schoolchildren managed to grow daffs, for God's sake, and you couldn't stop bluebells from sprouting like unwanted hairs. There were supposed to be some hyacinths in there too, but all he had managed to grow so far were a few ugly green potato stems covered in some kind of weevil.

Rising, he stretched his back and looked down to where the Ventnor pier had stood for over a century before collapsing into the sea. It was the first sunny day in nearly a month. The ground was spongy and welled beneath his wellingtons. The air smelled of rotting seaweed and cow dung. Something was trilling in the distance: not a springtime bird, just the phone he had left in the kitchen. Making his way through the nettles and bindweed, past the mossy, partially collapsed garden fence that shielded his paranoid neighbours, he reached the back door just as the trilling stopped.

57

How had he ever thought his retirement would be idyllic? The house was falling down, the locals were Neanderthals and the nearest pub was half a mile away. In one month he had read two-thirds of a novel, half completed an Airfix model of HMS *Ark Royal* (he had abandoned it after gluing one of the radar masts to his eyelid) and watched half a TV whodunnit before his satellite dish was blown off the roof during a storm. The most exciting thing to happen so far was a duck climbing in through his toilet window.

Seagulls wheeled about the bungalow screeching like knives on plates. Sometimes the odour of cow methane forced him to close his kitchen windows. When he looked at the missed-call number and saw that it was not someone trying to sell him double glazing but the Home Office, his pulse returned to a faint blip.

He rang the number back and was put through to Leslie Faraday. *This could go either way*, he thought. *Faraday's probably furious after our last encounter, and he has a vested interest in getting us out of the building.*

Faraday's tone caught him by surprise. 'Land, is that you? I've got Deirdre on my extension. I have something to tell you that can go no further.'

'I'm retired, Leslie,' Land answered. 'Who on earth am I going to tell? The woman in the local charity shop?'

'The Speaker of the House of Commons was just seriously injured in a freak accident.'

'I fail to see what this has to do with me.'

'The SCC can't handle it because it's not a criminal case.'

'I don't understand what you're saying.'

'The matter is far from straightforward. There are – elements.'

'Elements,' Land repeated.

'I can't get into it on the phone. You need to come in right now. Alone.'

*

Having travelled up to London the previous evening, Raymond Land put on an unironed shirt and left his Travelodge, heading to the Home Office's Marsham Street headquarters.

In the chilly marble reception chamber he was given an ID lanyard, passed through a turnstile and was greeted by a black-suited young woman with flawless skin and tied-back blonde hair.

'Mr Land? Follow me, please.' She stopped before the lift and ushered him in with the sympathy of a student offering a tube seat to a pensioner.

Land was delivered to a glass-walled office on the third floor and greeted by the portly liaison officer. Faraday, he had always felt, was a fat cork on the ocean of law enforcement. His initiatives sank without trace around him but he always resurfaced, bobbing along with the political tide until he could insert himself into another career fissure and bung everything up again.

Faraday introduced him to Fatima Hamadani, a young Muslim woman from Manchester who, Land later discovered, had suddenly found herself transferred to the police liaison department a week after Faraday's unfortunate stag photo surfaced online. She sat as still as a rock, her hands folded neatly together over a notepad, and looked incredibly fed up.

'We're just waiting for two more,' Faraday explained. 'From your old unit.'

For a brief, mad moment Land entertained the thought that it might be Arthur Bryant and John May, until he remembered that even if they could be at the unit they couldn't because it had gone.

Instead, he looked up through the glass wall and saw Janice Longbright and Meera Mangeshkar being shown into the room. Janice looked magnificent, as if she'd caught up on a lifetime's missed sleep. Freed from the restraints of active duty she had returned to her glamorous post-war stylings, complete with a coppery coiffure and a polka-dot blouse with a pinched waist and a turned-up collar. Meera, on the other hand, looked impatient, annoyed and suspicious.

'Goodness, a lot of ladies,' said Faraday, the female-to-male ratio clearly unsettling him. 'Make yourselves comfortable. Deirdre has left tea and biscuits in the corner, and the loos are just outside to the right. The first door says "gender free" but it's actually the men's. Fatima, perhaps you could lead us off?'

Hamadani did not need to consult her notes. She had already realized that her legendary efficiency would mainly be required to cover her new boss's failings. 'We have a preliminary report on Mr Claremont's condition. His wife is with him. I understand her request for privacy but she's being quite obstructive.'

'What's the prognosis?' asked Longbright.

'His skull is badly grazed and a sliver of wood has pierced his stomach lining. It missed his vital organs but two years ago he had a heart valve replacement and his doctor is concerned that the trauma has put it under strain. I believe the wife wants to move him to a private clinic in Scotland.'

'And where did this accident take place?'

'Outside Marconi House in the Strand.'

'That building has been redeveloped, hasn't it? Why was he there?'

'It's residential now,' Hamadani explained. 'Mr Claremont has a town flat there. It happened at nine o'clock on Sunday morning.'

Faraday stopped dunking his custard cream for a moment. One half fell into his tea. He raised a hand. 'I think we're getting a little ahead of ourselves here, ladies. Mrs Longbright—'

'DI Longbright is fine,' said Janice, nettled. 'I am not married.'

Land raised his right hand tentatively. 'May I ask a question? Why are we here?'

'Well.' Faraday carefully set aside his broken biscuit. 'I thought you might be wondering that. I'm sorry we haven't been able to reallocate your boys and girls.'

'But you're planning to,' said Land, alarmed.

'Unfortunately it hasn't been possible.'

'But you closed the unit down. You must have made some bloody provision.' Incarceration on the Isle of Wight had blunted Land's manners.

'It's become a little more complicated.' Faraday took up a fresh biscuit and baptized it. 'As you know, we decided to terminate the unit because a number of controversial actions contravened procedural guidelines.'

'The PCU achieved its success rate by *not* following your guidelines,' snapped Land.

Faraday was not to be goaded. 'I have been convinced that it would be in the government's best interests to allow the PCU to operate as an independent investigative body just in this matter.'

A slow smile crept across Land's face as he looked from one civil servant to the next. 'You want to open us again as some sort of pop-up? Perhaps we could sell pulled-pork bao buns and designer handbags at the same time. What are you up to?'

'It's a jurisdictional problem. The SCC can only examine the cause of Mr Claremont's injury and its circumstances. We need to know more than that.'

'How did it happen?' asked Longbright.

'He was trying to cross the Strand between parked vehicles,' Hamadani told her. 'A van shed its load just as he passed, burying him under a stack of crates, some of which smashed and injured him. We want to understand what was going through Mr Claremont's mind at the time.'

'A lump of wood, by the sound of it,' said Land.

Faraday took over; he couldn't have Hamadani doing all

the talking. 'We need to know if Claremont has been acting out of character lately, and if so who he's been talking to.'

'Isn't that something the Minister of Security should be handling?'

'Ordinarily, yes, but she feels that there are certain . . .'

'Elements,' Land completed, catching Longbright's look of puzzlement. 'You want to know if he was bonkers.'

Faraday carefully chose his words. 'There have been concerns about his behaviour in Whitehall for some time now.'

'Of course there have, Leslie. Claremont acts according to his conscience, which must terrify you lot. He's the enemy of rich lobbyists pushing vested interests. You know – your mates.'

'If Mr Claremont isn't in full possession of his faculties it's important to know whether he shared any privileged information,' said Faraday primly.

'Oh, so it's a spying job?'

'It's not quite as dramatic as that, but—'

'I think what Mr Faraday means', Hamadani cut in, 'is that it's an unorthodox investigation and something for which you would be ideally placed. You would be allowed to take it over on the condition that you could reassemble your staff.'

'I see,' said Land, knowing that one detective was recuperating and the other one had vanished.

'You'd have to start immediately,' added Faraday. 'Time is of the essence. According to the SCC, your unit is better equipped to deal with this because of your unique approach to such matters.'

'And what *is* our approach?' asked Longbright, who was fascinated to know how their methods were perceived.

'From the side.' Faraday waved his hand as if suggesting Tote odds or an approaching shark. 'Unexpectedly. You would have to be fully functional within the next twenty-four hours.'

'I don't see how that's possible,' said Land. 'We have no premises, you've taken away all our equipment and we're missing—' Meera kicked him under the table.

'Well, we'd have to come to some sort of arrangement, obviously,' Faraday conceded.

'You mean you'd allow the unit to remain open?'

'Just for the duration of the investigation.'

'Mr Claremont had just undergone a full psychological evaluation,' said Fatima Hamadani. 'He was granted the highest level of clearance, which allowed him full security access.'

'Why are you questioning your own evaluations?' asked Land.

'Because this accident seems improbable and is therefore highly suspicious.'

Land shrugged. 'A lot of accidents are improbable. My grandmother was bitten by a horse and died after falling off the stretcher.'

'When will it be possible to interview Mr Claremont?' asked Longbright.

'We're hoping to be able to speak to him within the next forty-eight hours,' Hamadani replied.

'What was a van doing unloading at nine o'clock on a Sunday morning? Have you questioned the driver?'

Hamadani passed her a single sheet. 'Unfortunately the driver went missing moments after the accident. Presumably he had his own reasons for not wishing to be interviewed by the police. He may have been in violation of his employment terms or knew he would be liable for failing to secure his cargo.'

Longbright read the page through. Mohammed Alkesh had been hired to deliver forty crates of fruit to the church opposite Claremont's flat. Had he stuck around, he would have been taken to Holborn Police Station to make a formal statement. A young constable had tried to keep the scene under control until the ambulance arrived. Descriptions of Alkesh were tentative and unedifying; he was young and wore a black sweatshirt with a brown leather baseball cap. Nobody at Kent Farmhands Organic Fruits seemed to have met him, but that was not unusual.

Faraday closed his blank notebook with finality. He liked the kind of meetings that shifted responsibility to others. 'The Home Secretary needs to be one hundred per cent sure that Claremont was of sound mind. If you find anything that suggests otherwise we'll advise an immediate overhaul of the vetting process. Both the Home Office and the Foreign Office will have to withdraw clearances across Europe and resubmit everyone for testing. We need answers by the end of the week.'

'How can you prove someone sane by then?' asked Longbright. 'It's not possible.'

'Perhaps not,' Faraday agreed, looking at Land because he was senior and a man, 'but we need you to try. I'll have you liaise with, er . . .' He waved his hand vaguely in the direction of Hamadani, who was scribbling furious notes on her pad and suddenly looked up like a rabbit sensing it was about to be shot. 'She'll supervise the operation.'

'Perhaps we could have someone impartial this time,' Land suggested.

'I think you'll find Fatima very fair-minded,' replied Faraday.

Hamadani quickly raised her hand in protest. 'I don't think that would be appropriate.'

'Why not? If you're based at the unit you'll be able to keep the Home Secretary directly informed.'

'I have no experience of working in the field, Mr Faraday.' It was clear that the thought of operating from a run-down King's Cross building surrounded by unemployable officers and drunken academics horrified her.

'No,' said Faraday, remembering he had been forced to accept Fatima to improve his image and the department's diversity quota, 'it has to be you.'

'Of course we would welcome an independent Home Office observer,' said Land, seizing the moment. 'Unfortunately, it won't be possible to rehire our staff or rebuild the unit in time.'

'I may be able to help there,' said Longbright, ignoring her boss's tensed look. 'I think I can get the team back together.'

Faraday rose and packed away his still pristine notebook. 'That's excellent news. I'm sure I can sort out something our end, money-wise. I'll leave it to you to make all the arrangements.' He was on solid ground once more, mentally moving the office chairs back into place to protect his fiefdom.

'What on earth were you thinking?' cried Land as they headed back to the tube. 'You can put the team back together? This isn't *The Blues Brothers*. John is laid up at home with his chest bandaged, Bryant is off-planet somewhere and the unit doesn't even have any furniture. The building's in a worse state than it was when we first moved in. It's entirely out of the question.'

'What would you have had me say?' asked Longbright. 'Sorry you want to entrust us with an incredibly high-profile case but there's nothing we can do?'

'Raymond has a point,' said Meera. 'We were put on the spot back there. Fatima didn't seem keen on being seconded to us. We'd have to get her on side.'

'That is *literally* the one thing she can't do,' Land replied. 'She wouldn't be much of an independent observer if the first thing she did was choose a side. And I'm *Mr Land* to you. And – what's the other thing?'

'You don't know where Arthur is,' Longbright reminded him.

'Exactly.' They were standing on Whitehall, the drab grey Westminster street that had become a metonym for the British civil service. 'I hate this bloody road,' Land complained. 'The centre of government and it doesn't even have a sodding paper shop. It's about to start chucking it down, I've got no overcoat and there are never any taxis.'

'This could be a very important case for us,' said Janice, unfurling a vast black umbrella and holding it over her boss. She and Meera were used to being outside in the rain.

'What, a politician buried under an avalanche of groceries? Most humiliating case, more like.'

'But what if it's not? Wouldn't you rather retire in a blaze of glory?'

'No I wouldn't,' said Land stubbornly, 'because that isn't what will happen. I'll retire in a blaze of destruction and public humiliation.'

'Then think about John. If we pull this off they'll have to drop their case against him. Faraday is more concerned about preserving the Home Office's image than pursuing a vendetta against an officer.'

Land stopped in the middle of the wet pavement. 'You honestly think they'd drop the prosecution?'

'If we insisted on it.'

He shook the dream from his head and carried on. 'Forget it. It's out of the question. We have no way of finding Bryant.'

'You don't know where he is,' said Longbright, sending Meera a private smile. 'But we do.'

7

GOLDEN BUDDHA

He heard the spinning of the golden prayer wheels and the low rumble of the mantras: *om mani padme hum*, the repetitive droning eventually blurring into a single infinite note. He smelled the dry sweetness of the incense mixed with the scent of Febreze emanating from the monks' freshly laundered robes. Crimson ribbons hung from the ceiling of the temple; flags and swathes of saffron silk wafted gently in the warm air.

Arthur Bryant stretched his legs and spread his fingers, breathing deeply. He tried to imagine himself floating in a pastel-blue aura of pure calm.

'Mr Bryant, are you eating?' asked the Master, leaning over him.

'It's only an aniseed ball, your graciousness,' Bryant replied, displaying it between his gleaming dentures.

'The noise is distracting the others. I've told you before.'

'Last time wasn't my fault. We'd had sprouts.'

'Your aniseed balls are all around the hall. Several of the monks have slipped over.'

'Yes, there's a hole in my pocket.' He pulled the pocket from his trousers to show the Master.

'That's another thing. Your manner of dress. You're wearing a suit under your robe.'

'I couldn't get a meditation spot near the fan heater. And I can't do the legs-crossed thing. That's why I brought my rubber ring.' He clambered to his feet. The ring deflated flatulently as he folded it.

'Nevertheless, this is your . . . let me see . . .' The Master checked his little gold notebook. 'Ah yes, your seventeenth infraction in four days.'

'How many am I allowed?'

'I don't know, nobody's ever incurred this many before.' Worry lines furrowed the Master's brow. He carefully smoothed out his crimson robe. 'How long do you intend to stay?'

Bryant counted on his fingers. 'Let's see, I did three days at the Shri Swaminarayan Temple, then the Brick Lane mosque, a synagogue in Golders Green – amazing bagels – a refugee camp in Earl's Court, the Silent Order of the Monks of St Benedict – they asked me to leave because I didn't know how to turn my phone off – the Quakers on Euston Road and an ashram in Highgate. Oh, and half a morning at Our Lady of Perpetual Misery in Clerkenwell. They chucked me out for cleaning my pipe with one of St Sebastian's arrows. It wasn't my fault it had fallen off his statue. So I think I'm just about done with the enlightenment thing.'

'Well, I can't say all of us will be heartbroken to see you go, Mr Bryant, but I hope we've been able to guide you towards spiritual illumination.'

Bryant gave the old fellow a friendly pat on his saffron arm. 'I think you have, your magnificence, although it's been rough on the knees. And I've been able to give something back. I took your novices through some of our more interesting murder cases.'

'As violence is expressly forbidden here I'd rather you hadn't stirred them up.' The Master tried to recompose his sagged features into an optimistic smile. 'You came in very late last night.'

'The chanting left me parched so I slipped out for a quencher.'

'You came back singing.'

'Nothing too rude, I hope.'

'Unfortunately yes. Something about a gentleman from Devizes. So if you'll just let me have your finger-cymbals back I'll bid you good-day.'

'Oh, I thought they were a gift. You've a touch of Felix Aylmer about you, have people said that before?' Bryant shook his hand vigorously. 'It's been a pleasure, your delightfulness. I'm sorry to miss the end-of-term knees-up.'

The Master paused and thought for a moment. 'Tell me, Mr Bryant, what did you come here seeking?'

'What everyone seeks,' Bryant replied. 'An explanation. You see, I am an incomplete person.'

The Master looked down. 'Oh, I'm sorry.'

'I mean psychologically. I view the world as an outsider. I have no patience or empathy with the common man. I am like the Tin Man, missing a heart, and it has grievously affected my work. Happily, over the years my great friend Mr John May covered for me. And in his hour of need I failed him.'

The Master looked sympathetic. 'Then I hope your time with us helped to return you to the path of understanding.'

'Not really, no.'

'Oh.'

'But it allowed me to consider what I might do to make

amends. I thought I'd buy him something nice as a peace offering. A new whistle.'

'I didn't know the police still used them.'

'A suit.'

'I like to think that we can rise above the material, Mr Bryant.'

'Don't worry, it'll be quality schmatta. He's a bit of a clothes horse. I want him to know how important it is that he lives.'

'It's important for us all to live.'

'Yes, but with all due respect you haven't had a bullet up the jacksie.' He poked at the Master's saffron robe.

The Master's face furrowed further. 'I've been watching you, Mr Bryant. I think you've been at war all your life with those whom you perceive are trying to undermine you.'

'Not the French?'

'You have been contemplating your future here, but you cannot resolve it because you are trying to achieve the impossible, when your goal should be to discover what lies in your heart.'

Bryant pointed a finger at him. 'Right, got you, no idea what you're talking about but it's been lovely. I want you to know that I've had a great time, and I adored the food. Don't listen to what the others say – nobody ever gets fed up with pad thai.' He gave the Master a nudge. 'After I've gone take a look in the collection box. I know people can be mingebags when the plate comes around so I've tried to make up for the inconvenience of you having me. Tell the lads to have a few ales on me.'

The Master had a feeling that he and this peculiar old man were fighting the same fight, just from different points of view.

Even so, he was glad to see him go.

As Bryant collected his stuff and strolled out, he stopped before a statue of the smiling golden Buddha and set an offering of pear drops before it, then returned to the street with a small leather suitcase, his homburg, his four-loop scarf and his mackintosh. The Golden Buddha temple was situated in a former chapel in suburban Wimbledon. Looking back at it with affection, he set off through teeming rain for the station.

Bryant had hoped that spending a few weeks exploring his spirituality would restore his equilibrium, and besides, he could not bear the thought of watching the unit dismantled before his eyes. As no one had come knocking at the temple door, he assumed that his landlady had kept his secret well.

As he walked, he switched on his phone and was bombarded with dozens of missed calls and messages. Raymond Land had rung eighteen times, which seemed rather excessive.

When he turned the corner he was shocked to find Land standing in the middle of the pavement, right in front of him. He looked back at his phone in puzzlement. 'Raymondo. How did you do that? Is it an app?'

'Bryant, there you are.' Land was holding a sodden *Daily Mirror* over his head and dripping ears.

'That's me, what do you want?'

'What do you mean what do I want?' He bellowed so loudly that Bryant had to turn his hearing aid down. 'You really are the most irresponsible – where the bloody hell have you been?'

Bryant blinked bluely. 'There's no need to shout. I went out. Is that all right with you?'

'Out? Out is nipping to the shops for a paper, not vanishing into limbo.'

'This isn't limbo, it's Wimbledon,' Bryant said. 'They've got a Fired Earth store and a Farrow & Ball, it's dead posh. I've been looking for the real me.'

'So have we, for nearly a bloody month. Why didn't you tell anyone where you were going?'

'I needed some time to think. My partner made the kind of mistake any normal human being could make in the line of duty, and I should have forgiven him. Instead I behaved abominably.'

'You always do. John is recovering at home, no thanks to you.'

'Alma sent me a message. I'm glad he's on the mend. How did you find me?'

'I didn't. Janice did. One of your loopy academic pals set her off on a ludicrously complicated treasure hunt involving a schedule of your whereabouts hidden in an apothecaries' hall.'

'So she got the Dead Diary open. Smart lass.'

'Have you seen the news?'

'No, I've been in a temple. We weren't even allowed to get racing tips.'

'The Speaker of the House of Commons got buried under half a ton of fruit. You need to come and take a look.'

'It may have escaped your notice, *vieux haricot*, but the unit no longer exists.'

'The Home Secretary himself has intervened,' said Land. 'I've been called to a meeting with someone who's sorting out our accommodation. If he tries to get away with offering us a Portakabin he can stick it up his arse. Just get yourself over to Marconi House on the Strand, and read this on the way.' He gave Bryant a thick envelope of notes.

'Aren't you going to say it's good to have me back?' Bryant suggested.

'I don't know if it is yet.'

'Well, I'm glad to see you.' Bryant looped his arm through Land's. 'Would you care to share a hansom back with me?'

Land looked horrified. 'A handsome what?'

'You've never really been on my wavelength, have you?' said Bryant.

'I've never been on your planet,' said Land, releasing himself.

'I suppose not. All I can offer you is my essoinment,* my dear obganiatory† mataelogian.‡ I shall bid you *au revoir.*'

'I'd rather you just said goodbye,' muttered Land as his bungalow on the Isle of Wight started to look appealing once more.

---

* Excuse for absence.
† Boringly repetitive.
‡ One who speaks pointlessly.

8

A LIVING PARADOX

'Mr B., my word, you do look well,' said Dan Banbury, the PCU's crime scene manager, delightedly shaking the detective's hand, even though he then had to wipe his fingers with a tissue as Bryant was eating a jam doughnut.

Arthur Bryant stood before him in a squashed homburg and a cobra-like red and green scarf, an oversized tweed coat and baggy grey trousers. One hand was leaning on a snake-head walking stick and the other was wrapped around a fat doughball oozing raspberry glue.

'I'd given you up for dead,' Banbury admitted, leading him inside Marconi House. 'I've been monitoring the Thames Police chatter in case you turned up at low tide.'

'How very kind. I am very much alive, thank you. It looks like we're back in business, thanks to this Claremont fellow. I'm not sure how we're going to work without a unit, though. What have you got?'

'Apparently Claremont's being moved from Chelsea and Westminster to a small private hospital in Scotland.'

'He can't do that. We'll need to interview him.'

'His wife won't let anyone near him, and she has a doctor to back her up. Come upstairs – you need to see something.'

Claremont's apartment was a dark library with a bed. Every wall was lined with leather-bound legal volumes and documents. Mahogany, copper, brass and gold created a welcoming womb. There were low orange lamps and a gigantic green leather sofa smothered in periodicals, court circulars and parliamentary papers. Best in winter, Bryant imagined.

'Apparently he was some bigwig in government,' said Banbury, carefully ushering the detective through a pinned-out route to the sitting room.

'Some bigwig?' echoed Bryant. 'He's the guardian of the nation's democratic process. He monitors the debates and maintains order. He represents the Commons to the monarch and the Lords. There's only ever been a hundred and fifty of them in the whole of British history. They get their names inscribed in gold leaf in the House of Commons Library.'

'He must be under a bit of pressure then.'

'Which is why the Home Office thinks he's having a breakdown and is shooting his mouth off to anyone who'll listen. They want to know who's behind the attack on his life. The Home Office is pursuing its own agenda.'

'Where did you get that from?' Banbury asked.

'It's why we're being resuscitated, Dan.' Bryant rolled his eyes. 'Obvs. What did the porter have to say?'

'Just that Claremont's a friendly chap, always stops by for a chat.'

'How's his family doing?'

'The wife never leaves his side.'

'And her reaction?'

'No idea. I'm on the side of the dead, Mr B., not the living. That's your job. This is what I wanted you to see.'

On the sofa sat Banbury's fingerprinting equipment. Next

to it, a cardboard box had been opened. Bryant pulled its wrapping free and examined it.

'Don't do that!' cried Banbury, angry with himself for having failed to issue the standard warning.

'Sorry, I've got jam on it.'

Bryant unstuck the wrapper from his fingers and looked into the box. It contained six oranges and six lemons. 'No return address or courier details.' He went to the window and looked out. 'Very suggestive.'

'The porter says it wasn't delivered.'

Bryant headed to the kitchen and turned about on himself like a dog taking in new surroundings. 'Brand new, unused, no juicer. What was he supposed to do with the fruit? Either somebody thinks he needs vitamin C or it's a warning he failed to appreciate. Anyone else been in or out?'

'The porter wasn't here on Sunday morning – it's his day off.'

Bryant picked up a bronze figurine of Hermes and turned it over. 'See if anyone was in the building when this happened, would you? I hear there are a couple of witnesses.' He headed back to the kitchen for a poke about in the cupboards.

'They're being brought up here, seeing as we don't have an office,' said Banbury, checking his watch. 'Don't touch anything in the—'

Bryant upturned a silver salt cellar to see who'd made it. 'I understand the PCU building is going to house a new dining concept, Casa Beansprout or something.'

'You're getting salt everywhere— What's wrong?' Banbury asked as Bryant started emptying out the contents of a shelf.

'Has Claremont got health problems?'

'Why?'

'His cupboards are full of painkillers. That's the best part about being old; you get to do a ton of drugs. I know most of these. I'll have a word with his doctor. How old is Claremont?'

'Not as old as you.'

'*Nobody* is as old as me.'

'Mid-fifties, I think. Have you spoken to your partner yet?' Banbury's tone was deceptively casual.

Bryant tipped a tablet into his palm and touched his tongue to it. 'No, but I heard he's out of danger.'

'Go and see him.' Dan took the pill pot out of Bryant's hand. 'You're going to need him on the case.'

Bryant ignored him. 'There was a bin lorry at the kerb – anyone in it?'

'The driver was asleep in the cabin when it happened.'

'Did you check the pavement and gutter?'

'I didn't find anything out of the ordinary. Junk food wrappers, a few empty bottles and an abandoned skateboard.'

Bryant checked the other cupboards. 'Was Claremont just incredibly unlucky, Dan? Head in the clouds, stepped out without looking? Or does the Home Office really think there's a conspiracy? He talks to the wrong person and says something so revealing that they try to kill him in a staged accident?'

'Accidents are easier to establish than conspiracies,' Banbury told him.

Bryant stood on the front step of the Marconi building and drew out his pipe. He looked on to the street and tried to see where Claremont's body had fallen, but the pavement had been cleaned and reopened. It was city policy to reduce the impact of any public drama as quickly as possible, but he wondered if some detail had been swept away in the process. Why had it occurred on a Sunday morning in daylight and in public? Why had the driver run? Why were there oranges in Claremont's flat?

Bryant looked up at the windows and puffed at his Spitfire. He called Banbury. 'Can you make sure that Westminster sends you their forensic report on the van?'

'There may not be one. They only took it away because it violated parking regulations.'

'Then put in a formal request to go over it.'

'I'll try. We're only on this to ascertain the Speaker's mental health, remember?'

I'll have to do something about that, thought Bryant, drawing deeply on his aromatic leaves.

Seated on a bench in Claremont's kitchen, Koharu Takahashi looked small and frightened. This was not how she had imagined she would be spending her holiday in London. And now, to be confronted by this tramp-like old man with luminous outsized false teeth and a hearing aid was enough to make her feel like crying.

'He is very strange,' she whispered in a microscopic voice.

'Strange in what way?' Bryant asked. 'Please be more exact.'

'Like *wafuku* but for westerners,' she said, watching his uncomprehending eyes. 'Um, formal – suit.'

'Did you see him close up? Was this him?' He showed her the photo on his phone.

Koharu looked around for help but none came. She wasn't sure how to answer. 'Beard,' she said finally. 'And this.' She tapped her lapel. 'Chrysanthemum.'

'Ah, carnation.'

'Flower, no flower.'

Bryant tried again. 'Did you see him step out between the parked vehicles?' He mimed the action.

'He goes under the fruit.'

'What did you do?'

'A lady comes to help. I go away.'

'I know it was a couple of days ago but is there anything else you can tell us about the accident?'

'Is dangerous to cross the road in London.'

'Thank you, Ms Takahashi. Utterly useless, we have your details, you're free to go. This thing that happened, it's not normal. London is safer than you think, and welcomes you. Enjoy the rest of your holiday.' Bryant smiled briskly and dismissed her.

Margot Brandy had helped the PCU many times in the past. She gave Bryant a peck on the cheek and slipped off her faux-leopard coat. 'I'm glad you're all right, lovey. I've been hearing all sorts of stories about you.'

Margot's voice always came as a shock to him, even now. She sounded like an East End bricklayer, solid, rough, fundamentally warm-hearted. Her voice was the secret weapon in her arsenal because it caused some of the plummier lawyers to underestimate her, to their lasting regret. 'How's your hand?' he asked.

She turned over her bandaged palm. 'It's fine, darling. I think there are still some splinters in there but I'm not going to sit around in A&E all day. I shouldn't have waded in like that. I might have known it would be organic fruit.'

'Why?'

'Fancy, expensive, delivered in cheap wooden crates full of straw – more "authentic-looking", I suppose.'

'A bit of a coincidence, you passing,' Bryant said.

'Hardly, love – I'm only over the road.' She lit a Superking from a match and fanned it out. 'I'm smoking inside, don't judge me. I know him, of course. A charming dinner companion, always wears a buttonhole. I don't usually warm to podgy men. The wife's nice too, a bit prickly, ambassador for a European charity, saves churches in the Netherlands.'

'When was the last time you saw him?'

'About six months ago, at an Inns of Court dinner to honour a retiring judge.'

'What's your professional impression of him?'

'He's honest. Impassioned. An accomplished public speaker.'

'Level-headed?'

'Implacable. It comes with the job.'

'Did you see Ms Takahashi?'

'Yes, she was standing further away than me.'

'Tell me about the van and the bin lorry. Why did Claremont choose to cross there?'

'The gap was right outside his door. And Sunday morning, I assume he was heading for the church.'

Bryant chastised himself. 'I'm such a heathen. That would never have crossed my mind.'

'The driver of the bin lorry was asleep with his boots up on the dashboard. They don't start until ten on a Sunday in Covent Garden.' Her left hand cradled her right elbow as she smoked. 'I didn't see the door of the fruit van come open but I heard the crash as the crates came down.'

'Did you see anyone else with him?'

'He was alone. I ran over and dug through a great lethal pile of wood and nails. Most of the fruit had scattered. I couldn't move him and I couldn't see the driver around. I was amazed that the crates could do so much damage, but we've often had cases of negligence involving unstable loads. The driver is usually thrown to the wolves for failing to tether his load correctly.'

Bryant shook his head. 'Unfortunately he did a legger the moment the officer's back was turned. His whereabouts are unknown.'

Margot blew smoke through a gap in the kitchen window. 'What do you think happened?'

'According to the CCTV footage Claremont came out of the entrance twice. Pity we have no facial recognition cameras there.' Bryant opened the fridge and had a poke about inside. 'This pâté will never keep. Would it be wrong to take it? There's a space in front of Marconi House exclusively reserved for diplomatic vehicles. I guess he was going to tell the driver to move his van. The cab of the vehicle is out of shot, but it looks like they talked briefly, then he headed back inside. Five minutes later he reappeared. Presumably the driver said it was a Sunday and he was entitled to unload—'

'Was he? Allowed to unload there on a Sunday?'

'Yes, but not in the diplomatic space. Then the back of the van opened and the crates came down.'

Margot pinched out her cigarette. 'So maybe the driver lost his temper and gave them a push.'

'And there's my problem,' said Bryant. 'The crates fell and one piece impaled Claremont. People can injure themselves on anything. But oranges and lemons? Well, it's the bells of St Clement's, isn't it? Just along from the flat. The church of St Clement Danes, the oranges and lemons church, although I'm not sure why we call it that. And Claremont. Clement. Was the assonance deliberate? I wonder if the church sent him the box of fruit that was found in the flat.'

'Darling, you can't use me to bounce your ideas off,' said Margot gently. 'You need your partner. You know what your problem is.'

'Oh, I hate it when friends say that.'

'You're a living paradox,' said Margot. 'You venerate the law above all else, yet you break all the rules that govern it.'

'Because the law has to be flexible. I understand how it works. But I don't understand people.'

'Then you have to learn. It's time you listened to John on that subject.'

'If anyone else gives me advice—' Bryant began.

Margot rose and slipped into her coat. 'Dan says you've got

the unit back just for this case. I'd make the most of it if I were you. If you want to understand what really happened, you have to get inside someone's head.'

'I have no idea how to do that,' he said.

'You don't but John does. Take the pâté; it'll only go to waste.' She blew him a kiss and left.

9

WELCOME BACK

The first illuminated hoarding on Piccadilly Circus was the Perrier sign, which went up in 1908. Over a century later it had been replaced by a vast curved LED screen showing a hyper-realistic hamburger seventeen metres high. Very few of the one hundred million people who passed through the circus every year realized that behind the signage was an old office building. One of the suites backing on to the suppurating hamburger was the office of Dr Arnold Gillespie, FRCP. As its windows were permanently boarded up the doctor relied on artificial light that had the effect of giving him eyestrain, depression and insomnia.

Today he was also bruised about the face and wearing a supposedly flesh-coloured eye-patch, so he was not in the mood to deal with any difficult patients. Unfortunately a knock at the door revealed Arthur Bryant, who had turned up unannounced.

'You were supposed to come in a fortnight ago.' Dr Gillespie irritably waved Bryant to a seat.

'I forgot about it.'

'It was for a memory test.'

'There you are. You should have reminded me.' He seated himself with a grunt. 'What have you done to your eye?'

'I got hit in the face by my wife's reconnaissance drone. She was taking photos of next door's crazy paving.' Dr Gillespie patted his paperwork. 'I'm very busy – what do you want?'

'I understand the Right Honourable Michael Claremont is a patient of yours.'

'So that's what this is about? I've already had a call from the Home Office. I can't tell you anything unless it's a criminal case. Patient confidentiality – you know that.'

Bryant dismissed the notion. 'Are you treating him for depression?'

'He's been under some stress. He feels his parliamentary impartiality is being tested.'

'Has he said by whom?'

Dr Gillespie gingerly touched his eye-patch. 'I'm his physician, not his priest.'

'Do you think he has any serious mental health problems? Thoughts of suicide?'

'I doubt it, although we don't fully understand what triggers them because there are too many variable factors. For decades doctors believed that overwork killed people. We used to ask patients if they were under stress in their jobs, and no one ever said no.'

'I'll need a full list of his medication. One other thing: does he have a vitamin C deficiency?'

'Everybody does, in the sense that some vitamins aren't stored in the body. It's worse in the city. You just have to eat an orange.'

'Why is he taking so much medication?'

The doctor sighed wearily. 'Because he wants to, Mr Bryant. Ultimately we're largely responsible for our own health and like most people today he's a hypochondriac, so I mainly prescribe placebos.'

Bryant regarded him with a sharp eye. 'It's a piece of cake being a GP, isn't it? A few referrals here, a few happy pills there. I could do it.'

'You could try.' Dr Gillespie gingerly adjusted his eye-patch. 'I've got a sick dog at home. If you care to come round I'll set him on you.'

Bryant punched a groove in his hat and jammed it back on his tonsure. 'I shall trouble you no longer. By the way, I left a stool sample on your reception desk.'

'I didn't ask you for one.'

'Think of it as a souvenir.'

As the rowdy cosmos of Piccadilly Circus closed about him once more, Bryant stood outside Brasserie Zedel on the newly pedestrianized and sanitized edge of Soho, and recalled walking these streets with his partner and Janice Longbright. They'd seen and heard it all under these arches: the catcalls from the prostitutes; the dark laughter of the rent boys; the shady deals and racy nights. Now there was a giant McDonald's.

He told the taxi driver to take him to Shad Thames.

While Bryant headed for a reckoning with his partner, Raymond Land was on his way to the Home Office Liaison Department in Marsham Street. He had been summoned back for a meeting, but as he approached the building he found the entire road filled with members of staff, coatless and in shirt sleeves. At the lobby doors security guards were ushering everyone outside.

Land stood with the others, wondering what to do. Approaching him was some kind of feminized male model with a trimmed beard, Tom Ford glasses, a tight suit and a severe haircut. He shook Land's hand warmly.

'Mr Land, I'm awfully sorry about this. The security alarm just went off again. It keeps happening but no one has been able to fix it – Whitehall in a nutshell. We should be allowed back inside in a few minutes. Timothy Floris. Call me Tim.'

So this was the publicity-friendly operative Land had recently heard about, appointed as an 'advisory interlocutor', one of the Home Office's new job titles introduced to add a fresh element of gibberish to their Kafkaesque world.

'It isn't really my field,' Floris admitted in a voice that was rather too high and thin to command respect. 'One of my tasks is to damage-limit the department's relationship with the media, mainly by keeping everyone away from microphones and Twitter.'

'That must be a full-time job,' Land sympathized. Faraday rarely spotted his own foot without trying to insert it into his mouth.

'Mr Faraday and I came to an agreement. We've got your old building in King's Cross back for the duration of the investigation. Obviously you have no equipment so we'll bring in the essential tech kit if you can rustle up some furniture. I'm calling in every favour I can to get you kitted out and fully operative again.'

Land made a noise of agreeable consent but was waiting for the catch. There was always a catch with the Home Office.

'Mr Faraday is not keen on handling the details himself . . .' Floris began awkwardly.

I bet he's not, thought Land. *We've run out of ways to humiliate him.*

'He's asked me to act as an independent observer, which means I'll be seconded at the unit.' He winced in apology. 'Obviously I won't interfere in any way. You should think of me as a . . .'

'A spy,' said Land drily.

'A resource,' said Floris with an ingratiating smile. His teeth were bleached.

It was a reasonable price to pay for a chance to clear their name, Land decided. 'We'd better get started,' he said.

John May's flat looked as if it was between tenants. Arthur Bryant walked into a bare-boarded hall with white walls. Beyond it was an empty white room overlooking the grey high tide of the Thames. The room had a special feature: even weak sunlight reflected from the waves and shone ripples of light across the ceiling, creating a calm underwater atmosphere.

Bryant went to the open window and looked out. He drew a deep breath and smelled the musk of Thames silt, sharpened through oxygen blooming from the embankment trees. A narrow balcony overlooked the river, upon which an iridescent patch of oil was moving sluggishly downstream like a vast undulating brooch. There was light everywhere even on this purblind day, the sky pushing its way in and filling his vision with furious clouds.

He turned and studied the room. There were no mantelpieces, no shelves, no flat surfaces for the arrangement of books. May's flat was an idealized department store layout, a theatre set for some obscure futurist entertainment. Why would such a naturally warm-hearted man choose to live this way?

'I'm in here,' called May.

Bryant stepped back, overwhelmed by the panorama, and followed the voice.

His partner lay propped up in bed so that he faced the picture windows. His chest was bandaged and he was wrapped in a grey blanket that matched his leonine silver hair. Elegance came naturally to him even in adversity, so that he appeared to have been art-directed into place in this sparse, ascetic home. His enforced inactivity had added a little weight to his bones.

87

'Arthur.' He fought down a smile, determined not to look grateful.

'You shouldn't leave your front door open, I could be anyone. Are you well? When we asked you to take a bullet for the team we didn't mean literally.'

'Very funny. This is coming out in a couple of days.' He showed Bryant the drain in his chest.

Bryant inwardly recoiled. The plastic tube made him realize just how closely his partner had brushed against death. He stood awkwardly before the picture window that framed the Thames like a Canaletto, not knowing what to say or what to do with his hands, so he took out his Spitfire pipe and fiddled with the stem. 'Don't worry,' he managed, 'I won't light it.'

'If you have to. The window opens.'

'Best not. Your lungs, FFS.'

May looked at him. 'You have no idea what that means, do you?'

'How are your lungs?'

May smoothed the counterpane. 'At about sixty per cent of their capacity. It hurts if I breathe too deeply. I'll probably never run anywhere again.'

'Running at your age is undignified anyway.'

'I'd just like the option.'

'We'd all like the option, John.' Bryant stuck the pipe in his mouth unlit. 'By the time they reach sixty most people have around six health problems. Then it's just a matter of gently coasting downhill to senility and death.'

'I'm so glad you came by to cheer me up,' said May. 'You must come again.'

'I would have visited you earlier but I was under a vow of silence.' He picked up a packet of medication and examined the contents, clattering his pipe. 'You know I'm not very good at this.'

'I know.'

'How long before you can go out?'

'A couple of weeks. The staples are out but I have to wait for the stitches to dissolve. The doctor says I have a good chance of completely—'

Bryant was unable to contain himself a moment longer. 'I was in the wrong, all right? I admit it. I was furious because you jeopardized the investigation. I didn't take human error into account.'

There was a moment of silence. 'You never could. I know you're still angry with me.'

'Well, of course I am.'

'I don't understand.'

'Of course you don't.'

'Can you stop saying that? I made a mistake and now they're going to throw the book at me. Happy?' May winced as he tried to sit up.

'Of course I'm not.' Bryant found his face heating up. 'All my life I had to fight for everything and you had it all and nearly chucked it all down the drain. The handsome one, the charming one, the likeable one, women chasing after you, men looking at you in admiration and respect. Me, the short fat ugly one with the obsessive ideas and the boring conversation. I was grateful for every advancement, no matter how small. It was so easy for you, you probably never even noticed. You're blind.'

'Is that all?' asked May. 'Have you finished?'

'Yes,' said Bryant.

'Well, I hope you feel better for getting it off your chest. You think I'm blind? Take a look at yourself. You're the reason why the unit still exists.' He air-poked Bryant in the chest. 'It's *you*. You're the main attraction. They come for you, not me. I'm the straight man, the line-feeder. But you know what? I'd be perfectly happy with that if we could only keep the unit.'

Bryant felt the last shred of his annoyance evaporate. 'I need your help,' he said. 'You like people. Civilians bore me to tears with their talk of marriages and babies and *feelings* but it's something I need to learn. I've tried every major school of spiritual teaching and they've done nothing except leave me with a craving for pad thai.'

'I don't see what I can do,' May answered.

'Teach me about people, John. I'll try not to look bored but I'm not promising anything.'

'Arthur, it gladdens my heart to hear you say that, but we no longer have the unit.'

'Ah. Yes. There's been a development.' He looked around. 'I presume you have a television hidden in here somewhere?'

'No, I have a tablet.'

'Of course you do. You've seen what happened to the Speaker of the House? He didn't have an accident, he was attacked. Someone tried to kill him and slipped up.'

'How do you know that?'

'My dear fellow, all the signs are there. It's as plain as the drain in your chest. The Home Office is giving us back the unit because they think Claremont divulged parliamentary secrets while he was in an unstable state and we're going to do a bit of spying for them, but instead we will be investigating the attack.'

'On whose say-so?'

'Mine, obviously. Of course we'll be defying orders and have no money or resources and you're laid up but it's this or me wandering around the park trying to remember where I live again.'

May's head hurt. 'Let me get this straight. You still want us to work together?'

Bryant nodded so vigorously it looked as though his teeth were about to fall out. 'Of course. Are you in?'

'I was never out.'

Bryant grinned. 'I'd give you a hug but I don't do the touchy-feely thing, and – ribs.'

May looked down at himself. 'As you can see I'm somewhat incapacitated at the moment, but I can work from here. You could start by feeding me anything you've got so far.'

'Stout fellow!' He made to slap May on the shoulder but managed to stop himself. 'We'll get started at once.'

'Your first lesson in caring more about people,' said May. 'Try to sound concerned about my health.'

'OK.' Bryant thought hard for a moment. 'Is someone looking after you?'

'Blaize brought me some things. I should be able to—'

'Fine, whatever, I'll have Janice send you the witness transcripts and make sure you're copied in on everything, although we'll only have mobiles and bits of paper so I don't know how it's going to work, but if we pull this off without upsetting anyone or destroying anything we could at least show them we're still employable.'

'—get around a little in a day or so,' May finished lamely.

Bryant clapped his hands with relish. 'The preliminary files have already been uploaded to the cloud-thing so you can access them, yes? I haven't a clue how to do it. I asked Dan to explain but he said if he did so again he would have to be restrained from strangling me, so it's best to let him handle the technical bits and bobs. We've a lot to do.' He paused for a moment in the doorway, trying to recall something. 'Oh yes. Sorry. Caring. You're looking as well as can be expected for someone who managed to get himself shot. Right: get on with your work; there's no time to lose.'

'Not good enough, Arthur.' May's tone stopped him. 'Ask me how I really am.'

Bryant waved away the thought. 'We're police officers, we don't do that sort of thing.'

'*Ask* me.'

He tried to clutch words from the air. There was a faint squeak first, like someone stamping on a stoat. 'How – are – you – in – yourself?'

'Funny you should ask because when I was shot and felt myself falling, do you know what I thought? Arthur will be fine because he lives for his work, but I don't. I'm leaving behind nothing. I have no legacy. My wife and children have gone; there's very little left. There are barely even any photographs. Who *was* I? Nobody should die with that thought in their mind.'

'It's just as well you didn't then.'

'What I'm trying to say, Arthur, is—'

'I understand, John, I really do,' said Bryant impatiently. 'When we get really old I'll help you up the stairs and you can tell me what day it is but right now the important thing is to keep working and the seconds are ticking by.' As he wasn't wearing a watch he looked pointedly at his bare wrist. 'It's time to turn the ignition key. Start all the clocks. We have a lot to do before the world comes to an end so we'd better get a move on. Are you with me?'

'Well, I suppose I might be able to help.'

'Thank God for that. Now let's go out there and upset a few carthorses.'

'Apple carts.'

'If you prefer. Just don't worry about the cow going blind.'

'Horse.'

'Whatever.'

And with that he was gone. May prepared for the pain of sitting up and found, much to his surprise, that it was suddenly easier to move about. He flexed his wrist, then his arm, and found them more pliant. Perhaps seeing Arthur had done him some good after all.

There was something in a brown paper bag sitting on the

window ledge. He carefully raised himself from the bed and went towards it.

The bag of glued-together sherbet lemons had a biro-scrawled note stuck to them: 'I hope you are feeling better we all missed you esp me stop lazing about feeling sorry for yourself we have work to do.'

10

NEW BLOOD

Like most London addresses, the Peculiar Crimes Unit had had many previous lives. In 1786, number 231 Caledonian Road had been a notorious brothel. In 1873 it was a shabby coffee house visited by Rimbaud and Verlaine. In 1900 it had been a dubious hotel owned by Catherine 'Skittles' Walters, the last Victorian courtesan. Between these raffish incarnations it had also found time to serve as stables, a working man's pub called the Hoop and Grapes, a boarding house where Aleister Crowley had held spiritualist meetings and a cocktail bar. Housed in an awkward corner on what might best be termed a pedestrian black spot, it had, during the tenure of the Peculiar Crimes Unit, been set on fire, quarantined and declared unfit for habitation.

Now it was opening again.

A truck had delivered furniture from a derelict Met building in Gravesend but most of it was too wide to go up the stairs, so Colin Bimsley and the two Daves sawed three inches off the legs of all the tables, and now they were too low to fit chairs beneath them. Dave Two had also accidentally sawn through a desk leg, so they set that one aside for Raymond

Land. The main staircase smelled of fresh-cut wood and was stacked with pine beams and plasterboard. From above came the constant noise of sawing and hammering.

The Daves' first job was to put hardboard over the gaping holes in the floorboards and lay tripwires of electrical cables across doorways. Half of the ceiling in the operations room was missing. Worst of all was Land's old office. Someone had put a sledgehammer through a partition, breaking a pipe. Rusty water was meandering down the wall into a hole that led who-knew-where. Somewhere a junction box fizzed and sparked as water dripped on to it.

'I never thought this dump could look worse,' said Meera, climbing out from under a table with several electrical cables in her fist. 'This is Dan's job. Why isn't he helping?'

'Because he's at a crime scene,' said Longbright reasonably. 'Do you know how to connect them?'

'I'll try all the permutations. I'm bound to find the right one eventually.' There was an ominous creaking from above like a heavy truck crossing a plank bridge. Clouds of sawdust sifted down on them.

'It sounds like they've taken too many support beams out,' said Janice, looking for somewhere to set down an armful of folders.

'Has anybody seen my office?' Raymond Land asked from the door.

Colin was busy unrolling an oddment of crimson carpet over several uneven floorboards. 'Why, has it moved?'

'I mean have you *seen* it? When I left it had no door. Now it's got a water feature. I know King's Cross used to be a spa but this is ridiculous. I thought they were supposed to be rebuilding the place, not tearing more down.'

'At least you've got a desk,' said Colin.

'I've got *most* of a desk.' Suddenly a buzz saw started up. 'How are we supposed to work with all this racket?'

'We need a toilet door. I've put a blanket up for now.' Janice wiped sawdust from her forehead. 'Colin, did you steal that carpet from an Indian restaurant?'

'I got it from my gran, actually,' said Meera, bristling.

'Also there's a woman downstairs who wants to make a formal complaint to someone in charge.'

'I'll deal with her,' said Land. 'Has anyone seen the electric kettle?'

'She wants to see someone *in charge*.'

Colin pointed to a box of tea mugs on the window ledge. 'I'll do it but she can't just tip up without an appointment.'

'Apparently she has one. It was originally booked for the week we were disbanded. She's been kicked around the system for the best part of a month.'

'OK, I'm on my way.' Colin stamped the carpet flat and was about to set off when he stopped and his mouth fell open. 'Mr Bryant.'

Arthur Bryant stood in the doorway of the operations room with a carpet-bag in one hand, looking like a disreputable relative of Mary Poppins. Some plaster dust dropped from the ceiling and spattered his homburg but he failed to notice.

'It's looking good.' He beamed. 'Nice to be back. I hope everybody's well. John sends his regards. Close your mouth, Mr Bimsley, we are not a codfish.'

'You've been to see him?' Colin was still incredulous.

'Of course. He's in fighting form and can't wait to get started.'

'But I thought you weren't on speaking terms any more,' Colin began.

'We're far above such childish behaviour. John wants – hang on.' He unscrambled a shred of paper and held it at the end of his nose. 'Open access codes for the Bakerloo secure cloud documents, whatever that means – I may have written it down wrong. Colin, can you take care of that? Janice, *lumière de ma vie*.'

Her eyes softened. 'Arthur.'

He held out a wrinkled hand. 'I wasn't being difficult, you know.'

'About what?'

'The address book. I couldn't leave it lying around with so many people coming in.'

'One of your contacts sent us to the Apothecaries' Hall in Black Friars Lane. There was a painting over the fireplace of Elizabeth the First watching the Spanish Armada. But we knew she didn't. Watch it, I mean. I know how your mind works; you always look for anomalies. We found your schedule stuck behind its frame.'

'Alma knew where I was too,' said Bryant, 'but she was under strict orders not to tell anyone unless I allowed her to do so.'

'Why does everything have to be so bloody complicated with you?' cried Land. 'Why can't you just do things in a simple, straightforward manner like everyone else? Look at this place, utter chaos, and that's how you like it, isn't it? You function better when you're in a madhouse.'

'What was the other key for, the tiny one hidden in the clock?' Meera asked.

'It unlocks my family photo album,' said Bryant. 'I'm sparing you from the sight of me as a pie-faced ten-year-old in a sailor suit.' He turned to Land. 'It's delightful to see you, Raymondo, you're a brick, in the sense that you're dense and blocking progress, so you can potter back to your water feature and let us take over now.' He dumped the electric kettle and its cord in Land's arms. 'When they put you on gardening leave you didn't actually have to do any gardening.'

'How do you know I did?' Land asked.

'I got one of the lads in your local nick to keep an eye on your house. Your herbaceous borders are a let-down. I spoke to Margot Brandy and Ms Takahashi and have drawn some clear conclusions from their witness statements. Can we get a whiteboard up by the far wall?'

'We thought of that,' said the extravagantly moustachioed Dave One, who had painted a sheet of hardboard with white gloss and leaned it against the wall. 'Only it's not dry yet.'

Bryant dug into his carpet-bag to produce his folder of statements and a pencil box. He drew directly on to the wall with a purple child's crayon, setting out a rough plan of Claremont's flat, the street beyond and the site of St Clement Danes church.

'I'll keep this brief. Both witnesses saw Claremont for a couple of seconds before he stepped between the two high vehicles. Miss Takahashi didn't see what happened next – she was at the wrong angle. Margot Brandy had to find her glasses. The box of fruit upstairs seems like the equivalent of Robert Louis Stevenson's black spot, a warning that Claremont acted upon, rushing out into the street. But perhaps it has nothing to do with it; sometimes a black cat is just a black cat. Of course there's a simpler way to account for it; when Claremont went downstairs to remonstrate with the van driver he was given it as a placatory gift, which he took upstairs. That makes the whole thing look more like an accident, which makes me more suspicious.'

'While you were off looking for nirvana did you read a lot of murder mysteries?' asked Land. 'Because that is the most ridiculous thing I've ever heard. Death by fruit? It's impossible. You might just as well invite your victim to Hyde Park in a thunderstorm and wait for lightning to strike him.'

'Exactly,' said Bryant. 'If you think it's impossible then there's a chance that it really happened this way. Raymondo, go and shoe the goose while we find Mr Claremont's attacker.'

He might have explained that 'shoeing the goose' was a sixteenth-century English expression meaning to undertake absurd or futile work, but Land wasn't listening. 'You cannot just decide that a misfortune is suddenly a murder attempt,' he said almost pleadingly. 'You have no proof.'

'Truth first, proof later.' Bryant tapped the side of his head. 'We'll turn the impossible into a possible.'

Without the rationalizing influence of his partner in the office, Bryant was free to untether his more fantastical theories. Land stormed out of the operations room. He should have foreseen that this would happen. Unfortunately he did not foresee the approaching hole in the corridor floorboards and nearly broke his ankle.

Land found he was being watched by a clearly bemused Tim Floris. As he tried to free himself from splinters of plank he tore open the left leg of his trousers. 'There are bound to be a few teething problems,' he said, trying to make light of it. 'Things have been much worse than this before.'

'Well.' Floris cast about for something positive to say. He had dressed down into a very expensive pair of jeans and an immaculate black sweater. 'Mr Faraday doesn't have to know everything.'

Land felt like falling to his knees and thanking the government interloper, but he was also ashamed of having to beg favours from someone who looked like a character from a Netflix science fiction series.

'Am I in the wrong place?'

Both Floris and Land turned around. A girl stood before them in a bright orange jacket, purple leggings and black ankle boots. Her auburn hair was tied back, her eyes strikingly alert. There was an air of expectancy about her, as if she was waiting for someone just out of sight to fetch her a chair. Land wondered if she was real or if he was imagining an Instagram story being played out by teenaged fashion influencers. Fashionable people did not belong in a police unit.

Even so, he was tempted to check his comb-over. 'Miss Hargreaves?'

'Technically. I'm Sidney. Are you Raymond?'

'I'm Mr Land, yes.' Land felt his hand rising to his hair. Floris seemed to have glitched and frozen.

'I believe we're going to be working together?'

'Well, you'll be working for me.'

'It's just a figure of speech.' The girl put her chin forward and looked about. 'I suppose I'd better get started. Will somebody show me where to go?' She removed her jacket and studied Land expectantly.

'Let me get – um – you'd better – step this way.'

'That's probably not a good idea.' She pointed down at his torn trouser leg. 'Why don't I lead?'

He remembered now. The college had warned him that she was a handful. Well, he would quickly put his foot down – carefully – and let her know who was boss.

'So you came from Hendon,' he said, trying to squeeze beside her as they passed through the minefield of floorboards.

'Henley.'

'I think you'll find the college is in Hendon.'

'I live in Henley.'

'So you commute?'

'It's not really important how I get here, is it?'

'I'll take you to Mr Bryant,' said Land.

He found Bryant in the operations room balanced on a chair with a Dualit four-slice toaster held out in front of him. On the floor was an enormous green watermelon. 'Stand back,' he warned. 'I don't want to hurt you.'

'What on earth are you doing?' cried Land.

'This weighs only slightly less than a small crate of oranges.'

He dropped the toaster and smashed the watermelon. Clambering down, he examined the mess on the floor.

'Overripe. I shan't be using the Moroccan corner shop again.' He looked up at the girl and held out his melon-sticky hand. 'Did it get you? Sorry, I really need a skull. Hello, you're very' – he looked her up and down – 'bright. Is that made of plastic?' He pointed to the orange PVC jacket over her arm.

'I think so.'

'May I?' He took it from her, gripped the hem and tried as hard as he could to tear it in half. She watched him without comment.

'Just as I thought. Sorry, testing a theory. Thanks.' He returned it to her, somewhat stretched.

'Miss Hargreaves is young enough not to understand any of your references,' Land pointed out, 'so perhaps you could refrain from quoting old episodes of *Round the Horne* at her.'

'Sidney, why do I feel as if I know you?' Bryant asked, examining her closely.

She picked pieces of melon from her leggings. 'Was his skull fractured?'

Bryant continued to study her with interest. 'No.'

'A glancing blow.'

'Exactly,' said Bryant. 'The skin was broken but the wood splinter didn't penetrate. A tear but nothing more.'

'So that part of it was chance.'

'You know what he's talking about?' Land asked her.

'I believe so.' She looked at Bryant, who was sucking his fingers. 'The intended fatal injury was to Mr Claremont's stomach. The blow to the skull was secondary and unplanned.'

'How did you know about this?' asked Land. 'It's not public knowledge.'

'I'm not a member of the public.' She looked about. 'We should talk. May I have a seat?'

Great, thought Land, storming out, *it's not enough that we have a robotic over-moisturized Home Office spy on the premises, we now have an over-entitled androgynous post-millennial waif-child to deal with.*

Nevertheless, he returned with a nice chair for her.

11

TWO WOMEN

On the ground floor of the PCU, in two makeshift front rooms, two women told very different stories.

The first was the Speaker's wife, Fenella Claremont. Dressed in natural colours that augmented her calm demeanour, she sat cradling a PCU mug of builders' tea as no one had been able to find the visitors' cups. Fenella liked to get on with things and find workable solutions, although nothing could rescue the beverage.

'Michael is not the kind of man to ever put himself at risk,' she told Janice Longbright. 'He is in a position of enormous responsibility. He's respected for his fair-mindedness. Last week we had dinner at Number Ten. One only gets invited there for a purpose, and the food is desperate. On Friday night we had dinner with the Sheriffs of London and Michael was in fine spirits. I had an Age UK fundraiser in Winchester on Saturday so he remained up in town.'

'I wasn't aware that London had sheriffs,' said Longbright.

'There are two elected annually. All London mayors must have previously served as a sheriff. I have a friend at the

Home Office who is currently a candidate. He always keeps an eye on Michael when I'm away.'

'Why would he need someone to keep an eye on him?'

'He likes a brandy or two at the end of an evening and the press are always looking for public figures with their guard down. You're regarding this as an unfortunate accident, yes?'

'That's the official line,' Longbright conceded.

'But is that what you believe or not?'

'We have to consider every possibility.'

For a moment her composure slipped. 'I do so tire of the official line. Do you honestly imagine that this is how my husband's adversaries would strike at him? Don't you think they'd rather damage his career by leaking a memo and discrediting his opinions in the House? If they wanted to physically hurt him, why not pay someone to rough him up instead of shifting the contents of a greengrocer's van on top of him?'

'Has he said or done anything that would make someone want to hurt him? Does he make enemies?'

'All Speakers do – how could they not? Enemies are to be expected. What cannot be allowed are allies. There's something you must understand. The House of Commons is like a clubhouse for amateur model-makers: cliquey, protective and childish. My husband is keen to restore faith in Parliament, but he is not a visionary. That is not what's required of him. The enemies he makes are not filled with the kind of passionate hatred that inspires assassins. They are people who dislike poor grammar.' She tried to sip her scalding tea, gave up and set it down. 'Parliament is a terrible building, falling to bits, damp, sunless, mice everywhere. There's a strong likelihood it will go the way of Notre-Dame. I can't imagine anybody wanting to spend a minute longer in there than is absolutely necessary. Even Michael's enemies have called with commiserations, presumably because it's such an odd thing to have happened. My husband isn't ill or mad and doesn't have a death wish. I wish I could tell you more.'

'Were there any enemies who didn't call?'

'Of course. Several people on both sides of the House were unhappy with his election. They thought he would try to exert a bias. My husband is a parliamentarian, not a politician. He keeps order with utter impartiality, but of course MPs some-times cross the floor and he finds himself with conflicting loyalties. Today's foe is tomorrow's friend, so it's hard to say at any one time who his enemies are.'

'Who else has keys to the flat?'

'Just the two of us, the cleaning staff and the porter. Our son lives with his family in Mexico City. He's a musician. We are not close. It's the most extraordinary thing. On my way here people stopped me in the street to offer their sympathies. I suppose Michael is a familiar face because of the televised parliamentary debates, but they must know me too.'

'You're public figures and therefore subject to public own-ership,' said Longbright. 'I'll need a list of names from you.'

'I used to think, *This is England, things like this don't hap-pen here*, but of course they do, don't they? Litvinenko, Salisbury and so on? I can give you the names of people with whom he's crossed swords at work, and a couple of muck-raking journalists who spoke to our son.'

'But if you had to suspect any one person above all others . . . ?'

Fenella Claremont could tell that this rather extraordinary-looking police officer with her 1950s hairstyle and heavy make-up was not going to give up until she surrendered a solitary choice. She thought for a moment. 'One above all others? That would have to be Peter English.'

'Who is he?'

'An extremely wealthy businessman with the kind of extravagant hobbies that keep him too busy to answer any of his critics. My husband's somewhat exaggerated sense of fair play offended him.'

'In what way?'

'Michael spoke at a dinner about tycoons with political aspirations and conflicting business interests. English manages to be both crass and over-sensitive. He takes offence and never forgets criticism. You won't get anywhere near him.'

'We will if he becomes a suspect in the investigation.'

Fenella shook her head in doubt. 'Not even then. He'll take great pleasure in proving to you that he is above the law.'

Longbright checked her notes. 'I have to ask: Could there be someone in your husband's life that you don't know about?'

'I believe he's true to me because truth is in his nature.' Fenella gave a rueful half-smile. 'He has certainly never given me cause to believe he has a mistress.'

'Can I ask why you're moving him to a private clinic?'

'I want him out of the public eye. His condition isn't critical. It's a place where the nurses know how to deal with invasion of privacy. If it *was* an attempt on his life, I don't see how it could have been engineered.'

'That doesn't mean we can rule it out.'

Fenella sat forward. 'You have no leads, do you?'

'We're interviewing the building's residents, searching facial recognition data, gathering forensic evidence.'

'But you have nothing so far.'

Longbright did not answer. Fenella Claremont picked up her bag and rose. 'Thank you for your honesty, at least.'

'Wish your husband well for me.'

'Thank you.' Mrs Claremont lightly shook her hand. 'Please try not to tell the Home Office every little thing you hear about my husband.'

*

On the other side of the ground floor Arthur Bryant was meeting with Elise Albu. The bookshop owner's wife had made such a strong impression on him that he felt it was the least he could do.

Elise was dressed in a similar fashion to Fenella Claremont except that her clothes were from Primark, not Fenwick's, and she was as slender as a heron. She looked as if she had barely slept in a month, and her answers arrived slowly after struggling thought. She sat with her hands pressed hard on her knees, anxiety drawing down her pallid features.

'So all this was reported and no one came back to you,' said Bryant, checking his notes. A scribble at the bottom of the page read: 'Remember to be nice to people.'

'I need some answers, Mr Bryant.' An electric saw started above them. She looked up in concern. 'What is this place?'

'It's a police unit,' he replied, looking for a single thing that would back him up.

'And you're a police officer?'

Her incredulity annoyed him. He felt his niceness ebbing. 'Yes I am. We have copies of your husband's death certificate, the fire officer's report and the police report. What is it that you don't understand?'

'The certificate says "Death by suicide". That's a verdict they give to people who fall off mountains taking selfies. How could his death have been accidental? It's ridiculous. I tried to talk to someone about it but got nowhere.'

The case had been handled by the City of London Coroner's Office. It was a bit late to start looking into it again. Bryant wondered what he could say or do.

'My husband was from Timişoara in western Romania,' Elise said.

He was about to ask why he needed to know this, but bit his tongue. *Nice*, he reminded himself. 'Tell me about him. Something important to you.'

'Cristian wanted to be a writer, but somehow he never settled to it. He inherited his father's bookshop in Cluj-Napoca. The shop's rent had been raised and it had fallen on hard times, but he made it profitable again. It became the centre of his life and the community. Everyone knew the shop and stopped by there. They didn't always buy something but that didn't matter.'

Bryant wondered how long this would take. He was hungry and his bunions were playing up, although these facts were not related.

'I met him in the park because a beetle got tangled in my hair. As he was helping me get it out, I saw the underside of his left arm. There was a curious tattoo: an elderly man's hands, sewing together two pieces of cloth that perfectly matched. It was very beautiful, like a painting, and ran from his elbow to his wrist.'

She continued before he could stop her.

'As he pulled the beetle free I asked him what the tattoo meant. He explained that his grandfather had been the town tailor, and under Nicolae Ceauşescu's monstrous regime officers would call by every year and tally up the family's belongings. If the officers felt they had two pigs too many, they would cite the *Communist Manifesto* and cut the allowance in half, taking away whatever they wanted for themselves. Cristian's grandfather explained that he shared the animals with his community, but the officers never listened. They were all corrupt, and took belongings from everyone.'

Bryant opened his mouth to interject but was too late.

'So the grandfather offered to make each of the officers a suit if they would leave the animals alone, even though it meant working through the nights.'

This was what came of being nice to people, Bryant thought. Given half a chance, everyone he interviewed would start opening up their hearts. The idea was appalling. He forced his attention back.

'The grandfather promised that when Cristian married he would make his grandson the best suit in the whole of Romania. But Cristian still hadn't met the right person and soon the old man's hands shook too badly to make a suit, so Cristian had the tattoo made to honour his grandfather, and to show that some things don't have to be finished to be appreciated and loved. I fell for him instantly and we married soon after, but by that time the old man had died, so the wedding suit was never made. But it was there, imprinted on my husband's skin.'

Bryant found that his eyes were itchy. 'How extraordinary,' he said, patting her hand. 'But I don't see how—'

'When he came to London he continued to follow his dream, and was able to raise enough money to open a small bookshop with a controlled rent. The shop was very precious to him. He worked late almost every night. So you see, it's unthinkable that he would burn down his own shop.'

Bryant consulted his notes. 'Your husband was found unconscious in an alleyway, soaked in whisky and with an emptied can of oil still in his hand.'

Elise was vehement. 'He only ever touched beer. He had seen the damage that drinking *ţuică* had done to the men in his family. It's a strong spirit made from plums; they all drink it.'

'Then what do you imagine happened?'

'He committed suicide because the idea of not being able to support me without the shop was deeply shameful to him. That was how he thought. But there's something else. A customer called that evening to purchase a book. He took my husband for a drink. I asked Cristian why he agreed to go, but he had no real answer for me. I think it was a set-up.'

'But why?'

'I was hoping you could find out.'

'Mrs Albu, there was an official verdict of misadventure delivered, although I assume the arson case is still open. It wouldn't be an official investigation but I could make some inquiries. What's happened to the shop?'

'We forfeited the lease. Obviously the insurance won't pay out. There's nothing left for me here.' She dug out a pitiful scrap of tissue and wiped her nose.

'What will you do?'

'I'll go to Romania.' She caught a look in his eyes. 'I can see you don't understand. I'm English but I owe Cristian everything. So I'll go there and start a new life, and run a bookshop just as he did. That way I can repay the debt I owe him and balance things out. I just want someone to tell me what really happened.'

Bryant checked his notes. 'Unfortunately the trail will have gone cold by now, but I'll do some asking around for you. Did anyone look for this mysterious customer?'

'No. I was given a number to call in case there were any further developments, but I was told he wasn't a factor in the investigation.'

Typical, thought Bryant, his sense of indignation rising. 'Did the bookshop stock anything that would upset someone who was unbalanced? Radical political manifestos, perhaps?' He thought of Bookmarx, the Marxist bookshop just a short walk away in Gower Street, which had been attacked on numerous occasions.

'No, not at all. It specialized in art, design, European literature. Cristian was setting up his own imprint. He self-published some short stories but to be honest they weren't very good. He was passionate about discovering other writers, though.'

'Did he have any financial difficulties?'

'There aren't many independent booksellers who don't. I need to sort out the accounts but they're in a mess. I can't find anything.'

'When do you plan to leave?'

'After my husband's funeral,' Elise replied. 'I applied to take his body back to his family home, but it was too complicated and expensive to do so. I don't want to wait any longer. I'll travel with his ashes instead.'

Bryant rose and held out his hand, looked at it, wiped it and held it out again. A piece of smoking metal fell through the ceiling and bounced across the floor. Elise eyed it in alarm.

'Perhaps this isn't something your unit can help me with,' she said uncertainly.

'It most certainly is.' Bryant's sense of pride made him grip her hand too tightly. 'I am going to find out what happened between the time your husband left his shop and the time he was found dead. There is one thing you can do for me: go through anything he has written down – notes, addresses, books, diaries, stock orders. Let me know if you find anything out of the ordinary.'

As he watched her leave, stepping around stacks of timber, cables and torn linoleum, he wondered if he could be as good as his word. For a moment the strangest feeling crept over him that he might be able to make a difference, and that it might finally happen because he had understood a fellow human being. Elise Albu's story had touched him, but that was the problem.

Emotion got in the way of work. He couldn't take another story like that, so it would probably be in everyone's best interests if he went back to only pretending he cared. It was safer for him, and for everyone else.

12

MAY *IN ABSENTIA*

John May's bed was not suited to long-term confinement. It was a sofa bed, and had a steel strut running down the middle that he could feel through his thin mattress. He lay watching the reflections of the crane lights dancing across the tidal pull.

The Thames was no longer obscured by wharves and ships but nor were there many signs of life. A wall of office blocks and empty apartments rose beyond the black waters like so many mirrored bathroom cabinets. London's most spectacular views had been stolen away by people who never saw them.

His tablet lay on the bed unused. There were twenty dinners in the freezer so he had no need to think about cooking. The laptop dinged with incoming mail but he ignored most of it, only opening the file that Janice had sent him on Michael Claremont.

It was clear the Speaker had few friends outside of his parliamentary circle. Perhaps it was difficult making social arrangements when you knew that at any given moment you might be summoned to a high-level meeting.

May read on through the pages. Claremont was a man of the people who liked a beer in a Somerset pub, but he owned an Elizabethan manor and was in dispute with his neighbours. His wife's charity had once been accused of misappropriating funds, but that turned out to be a smear which had originated in Canada. Clearly there were no white knights, but Claremont and his wife came up cleaner, fairer and more balanced than most.

Neither of the witnesses had been able to observe the full passage of the victim from door to road. Once Claremont entered the gap between the two vehicles he was briefly lost from sight. May considered the attack as a whole. It was feasible but it didn't ring true.

Dead end followed dead end. There was only so much he could do online. Pushing the laptop aside, he swung his legs off the bed and sat up. The medication had dulled the pain in his chest but was slowing his thought processes. He poured himself a brandy and knocked it back. He imagined the hot bullet tearing a path through his musculature, leaving behind a shaft of cauterized tissue that would always feel like an arrow left in its wound. 'Lucky to be alive,' the doctor had said, but lucky was not being shot at all.

The doorbell rang. Walking to the door was easier now but raising his right arm to the latch made him cry out.

The woman who appeared before him was bent over, tying a knot in a black plastic bin bag. 'I wonder if I could borrow your basement key? The managing agent was supposed to send one through but it hasn't arrived.' She straightened up and saw his bandages. 'I hope I didn't disturb you. I was beginning to think this flat was empty. I haven't seen any lights on.'

'I've been mostly asleep.' He pointed at his chest. 'This is keeping me home at the moment. John May.' He shook her right hand with his left.

'Jenny Handler. I put in weird hours too. Work.'

'Whom do you work for?'

'A games company in Shoreditch. Our motto: "Nobody sleeps".'

'Please come in.' He led her to the bleach-scoured kitchen.

'Have you just moved in?' She glanced around the bare surfaces.

'I've been here six years. In the building, anyway. I changed flats.' It felt as if he should apologize for lacking the outward indications of a personality. 'I'm not in very much.'

'Oh, is this your pied-à-terre?'

'No, it's where I live. I have a spare key here somewhere.' He winced pulling open a drawer.

She moved to help him open it, watching his movements as if analysing them. 'Do you mind me asking how you did that?'

He wondered whether to tell the truth, but recent experience had made him wary. 'I had an operation on a torn ligament,' he said. 'Working on games must be fun.'

'Everyone thinks that. It probably is if you're a member of the design team. I'm a QA tester.' She didn't bother to wait for his quizzical glance. 'I look for fixes and improvements in gameplay. It means rerunning sections hundreds of times. You have to be very patient and detail-oriented. Sometimes I close my eyes and all I can see is a space trooper trying to climb over a wall. Leg up, leg down, over and over. I remember playing *Tomb Raider* as a kid and wondering why half of Lara Croft was stuck in a rock. I didn't know I'd end up stopping it from happening. How about you?'

'I'm in law—' He was about to say 'enforcement' but swerved to 'legal'. '—a legal unit. How long have you been here?'

'Just moved in. I was way out in the sticks before.'

'It must have been a shock moving here.'

'Whenever I see the subway at Old Street tube it makes me glad to be working in a nice clean virtual world. That's something designers don't factor in, just how scuzzy real cities can be. They always call Shoreditch edgy, never dirty.' When she reached into her back pocket he flinched. She drew out her door keys. *Muscle memory*, he thought.

He kept things brisk and distant. 'You've probably noticed there's nothing much open around here. I keep a list of places where you can buy essentials. I can send it to you if you like.' He knew he sounded as skittish as Norman Bates describing the motel facilities.

'I'm sure I can find everything I need.' She went to the window, in no hurry. 'You have a great view. I'm jealous. I'm at the back of the building. My bedroom is right over the electric motor that raises the garage door. My little boy hasn't been here yet – he's with his father at the moment – but I know he's going to love it.'

As they chatted May lowered his guard a little. The stress of the shooting had affected him more than he'd realized. Neighbourly conversations rarely involved him. Most of the other tenants worked in the City and were in too much of a rush to pass the time of day.

Listening to Jenny talk about her son produced a fleeting moment of jealousy. Occasionally he glimpsed a life he might have had.

'I should probably let you rest.' She looked at him, trying to understand more. 'You don't need me chattering away.'

He gave no answer. After she left he went back to work, looking for clues to Michael Claremont's state of mind, but drew a blank. He had never worked well alone, and, after struggling through the Speaker's notes on the month's parliamentary meetings, he drifted off into uneasy dreams.

'I need John on this,' said Bryant. 'I can't think clearly without him. Do we really have to have new people working with us? I don't like change.'

Longbright dragged Bryant across the busy Strand. 'Floris doesn't like it any more than we do. We can't pretend he's not there.'

'The Home Office clearly wants us to issue a statement refuting Claremont's credibility.' Bryant sought out her hand as they crossed, as a child would with a parent. 'We can deal with Floris but this other one, the girl with the attitude, we can't put an intern on a murder case.'

'No,' Longbright agreed. 'She can handle some of the paperwork I shouldn't be doing at my age.'

'I suppose some new blood will do us old 'uns good.' Bryant removed an orange from the voluminous pocket of his overcoat and bit into it, spraying juice everywhere.

Longbright was not thrilled at being lumped in with the seniors. 'You didn't take that from Claremont's flat?'

Bryant peered at her over the orange, his dentures buried in its skin.

'Are you sure they're all right to eat?'

He dragged a chunk of peel from beneath his dental plate. 'Let's see what the church has to say.'

St Clement Danes might have been marooned in the middle of the Strand but its magnolia trees were blossoming with fat pink petals that shielded the passing traffic and gave the churchyard an air of becalmed grace, like a ship stuck on a sandbank. Bryant climbed the flagstone steps and wandered inside for a nose around. The interior smelled of candle wax, damp and . . . yes, a definite tang of citrus fruit.

' " 'Oranges and lemons,' say the bells of St Clement's",' he murmured, running a hand along the back of a pew. 'Ah, here's someone who can help us.'

As the Reverend Sarah Boscastle came forward to meet them, Longbright realized that the meeting had been prearranged. That was a rare thing for Arthur, who usually preferred to capitalize on the element of surprise by simply barging in. He only made appointments with people he respected.

'I hope I haven't kept you.' She beamed at them both. 'I was catching up with my music director. We had a piano recital last night.'

Longbright introduced herself. The Reverend Boscastle shook their hands warmly. Bryant's hand appeared to make hers sticky; the Reverend surreptitiously wiped her fingers on her surplice.

'We did know him,' she said. 'Mr Claremont and his wife came to the Christmas service last year, and have attended recitals in the past. Such an odd thing to have happened. He was always in such high spirits.'

'Well, his spirit was almost a lot higher,' Bryant pointed out.

'Is he going to be all right?'

'As far as we know, but you can put in a word for him.' He pointed at the ceiling.

'Was the van delivering to you?' Longbright asked.

'I'm afraid so.'

'What do you do with all the fruit?'

'It's placed around the church for the day of celebration, and is given away at the end of the service, and again after the recital. The leftovers go to the schoolchildren of St Clement Danes.'

'I'm surprised there are any schoolchildren left in the West End,' said Bryant. 'Why do you celebrate?'

'Well, we're the oranges and lemons church, Mr Bryant. Our bells ring out the nursery rhyme. The Reverend Pennington-Bickford instigated the service exactly one hundred years ago, so this year's celebration was a special one.'

'Did you also send a box of fruit to Mr Claremont?'

'I don't think so. I can check.'

'Would you please.' He looked up at the vaulted ceiling.

'I've always liked this church. One can be an atheist and still appreciate the architecturally divine. What's its history?'

Oh, don't ask her that, thought Longbright.

'Before the Great Fire there were a hundred such churches packed into this single square mile,' said Reverend Boscastle. 'This little corner of Holborn was once Danish, hence the name. Several royal Danes were buried here. The ones who married Englishwomen had places of worship on this site consecrated at the end of the tenth century. The church burned down in the Great Fire but Christopher Wren rebuilt it. Samuel Johnson worshipped here with Boswell, and one of our rectors invented the game of rugby.'

'So why is it known as the RAF church?' Bryant tapped his boot on the squadron badges set in the church floor.

'The Blitz bombs shattered the coffins in the crypt and all ten bells in the tower came down. The air force paid for it to be rebuilt after the war.' Reverend Boscastle stepped back to reveal more emblems. 'All the squadrons are represented. We have their names inscribed in our book of remembrance.'

Longbright was getting fidgety. Bryant had never been able to keep his interviewees on topic for long, especially when it came to the history of his city. It seemed to clarify his thoughts, as if by veering off course he could consult forgotten figures from the past and obtain their help. Even so, she felt the pressure of time upon them even if he didn't.

'Well, Reverend, they're charming stories even if they're not all true.' Bryant dug in his pocket and produced a paper bag of boiled sweets.

'What do you mean?'

'You're not the oranges and lemons church, are you?' He popped a sherbet lemon into his mouth and offered them around. 'There are other St Clements. One in Eastcheap holds a better claim because freighters docked there with crates of oranges. And nearby St Clement's Inn charged toll fees for allowing fruit through to Clare Market.'

'I suspect what happened was that one of our rectors claimed the right to it, true or not,' Reverend Boscastle admitted. 'The Victorians embellished every old London tradition. We can't trust the past, Mr Bryant.'

'Perhaps a little more than the present,' Bryant countered.

Longbright needed to steer the conversation back on track. 'How did you book the delivery?'

'We always use the same company. They're very reliable.'

'And the same driver?'

'I doubt that, seeing as we only need them once a year.'

'Did anyone meet him?'

'No, because we heard he left after the accident. Someone else came and unloaded the van.' The Reverend checked the time and began to bring the meeting to a close, manoeuvring them back up the aisle. 'Please send my best wishes to Mr Claremont's wife.'

'What did you think of that?' asked Bryant as they left through the blossoming churchyard.

'I think the bells of St Clement's aren't saying much,' replied Longbright, checking her phone. 'Dan got a match on the driver; Mohammed Alkesh. Looks like he used his real name. Why would he have done that if he was planning to attack Claremont?'

As they walked back to the tube station, Longbright called the delivery company. While she waited for her questions to be answered Bryant hopped about, now contrarily impatient. 'Well, what's happening?' he snapped.

She put a hand over the phone. 'They're not going to admit liability. They're consulting lawyers. To prove negligence it'll be necessary to show that the crates were incorrectly tethered and that the normal safety procedure for unlocking the doors wasn't followed.'

'I don't care about their culpability case, I want to trace the driver.'

Tired of waiting for further snippets of information, Bryant decided to conduct his own online search. He had seen enough people staring at their phones in the street to know it was possible to do this while walking, but at his age he didn't trust himself to google anything without vanishing under a bus.

There were more than 7,200 matches for *Mohammed Alkesh*. 'The stupid thing is broken,' he complained. 'Why doesn't it match his name to his facial features and give me an address?'

While she was on hold Longbright looked over his shoulder. 'That's not how it works,' she told him gently. 'Don't worry, I've got someone on it.'

'Did you get anything out of Mrs Claremont?'

'She said that if her husband had one real enemy it was a man named Peter English, but she thinks none of us will be able to get near him.'

'Oh she does, does she?' Bryant continued to stab his phone until it emitted a sound like a baby trapped in a drainpipe. 'That's it, I've broken my phone now. John's good at dealing with people who think they're above the law. Let's put him on it.'

Longbright took the phone from him and rebooted it. 'Good idea,' she said. 'We need to get him working again. He's not good alone.' *And you're not good without him*, she thought.

13

ONE BIG TRICK

Four weeks had passed since his surgery. John May had reduced his painkillers and begun light exercises to strengthen the muscles in his chest, but he missed the stimulus of having other people around. As the sun sank behind a palisade of fiery glass he read back over his notes on Michael Claremont. Parliament housed rat-kings of ambitious power-seekers – where did he start looking for someone who would be prepared to kill for revenge or advancement?

On Bryant's instruction he ran a background check on Peter English. The tycoon's Wikipedia page felt as if it had been written by committee, so May applied for an MI5 file and received it within minutes.

There were few details on English's early life. He had attended art college before taking over his family's newspaper, where he gained a reputation for editorial meddling. After several bankruptcies he started investing in data retrieval. The MI5 file suggested he had skirted the international laws surrounding the sale of arms.

May followed a number of websites used by journalists

whose articles had been spiked due to legal infringements. Here he hit pay dirt: English sat on the boards of acronymic organizations with buried agendas and twilight lobbyists fighting progressive policies. His detractors hardly knew where to start, but English was litigious and vengeful. His public objection to Claremont read like the eruption of a long-fermenting hatred, and was reason enough to interview him.

By now May had begun to realize that arranging a meeting would not be easy. He came up against a brick wall of polite deflection. First he called English's official numbers, but was told that English preferred not to have direct contact with the general public. When May explained that he was calling on official police business, the responses became colder. Enquiries could be directed via the Metropolitan Commissioner only. A personal assistant suggested submitting a formal request for an email interview which would then be subject to legal vetting. He was being set on a course designed to wear him down, but it had the opposite effect.

Still, there was a problem; since the preliminary inquiry on Claremont had been held *in camera*, interviewing English could not be made mandatory. May called every number suggested to him, then many that weren't. In desperation he rang the new editor of the online magazine *Hard News*, Paula 'The Mauler' Lambert.

'Good luck with that one,' she said, shouting over the noise of a bar. 'Peter English works through a handful of official communication lines. His lawyers got him security protection under the Terrorism Act.'

'Why would he have that?'

'Someone posted bombs to his data company. One of them detonated, injuring a post-room assistant. It's never been established where they came from. One of our journalists suggested he sent them to himself to get the protection. She was sued. I had to bail her out. Hang on.' She broke off to shout at someone. 'John? Don't underestimate who you're dealing with. He has a forensic knowledge of the law.'

'So he's smart,' said May. 'What's he like as a person?'

'Streetwise, manipulative. We once described him as a "Machiavellian jokester" and he sued us. We won the case but it was a Pyrrhic victory because he continued to sue over every article in which he was mentioned for months after.'

'And he won them?'

'No, he lost them all. But by keeping us tied up in litigation he drained our coffers and very nearly bankrupted us. He enjoys rough sports.'

'His falling out with Michael Claremont – how did that end?'

'Oh, you're on that, are you?' He could hear her thinking through the possibilities. 'English told Claremont to mind his own business and made an unspecified threat that Claremont took seriously – then it all went quiet.'

'And now Claremont has been badly injured,' said May.

'Well, now you have our problem.' A cheer went up in the background. 'Sorry, somebody's birthday. Listen, the average household wealth for Britain's richest decile is now three hundred and fifteen times that of the poorest, which means access across the divide has declined. The walls have gone up. It's almost impossible to hold anyone at the top accountable these days. Trust me, you will never speak to Peter English in person, only through a battery of lawyers who will blue-pencil, edit and rewrite every word that's exchanged between you.'

'You're telling me he's above the law.'

'No, John,' said Lambert. 'I'm telling you he's *making* the law.'

Arthur Bryant was trying a different way into the case. While the rest of the PCU were interviewing Claremont's colleagues and trying to trace the van driver, he went to speak to a magician.

Everyone in entertainment called Dudley Salterton a trouper, which was a polite way of saying he should have retired thirty-five years ago.

Salterton was sitting on the steps of the London Palladium with a Starbucks coffee cup. A woman dropped twenty pence into it as she passed.

'Oi,' he shouted, 'I'm not homeless, I'm an international cabaret artiste.' He pulled a withered roll-up from his lips and coughed hard, spitting a green globule into the cup before remembering the money and fishing it out.

'You all right, Dudley?' asked Bryant, arriving beside him. 'You got a piece of cigarette paper stuck on your lip.'

'Piss off, Arthur, I'm on in a minute.'

'Yes, I thought you might be. I wanted to catch you first.'

Bryant looked up at a lurid poster for the Old-Time Music Hall Variety Show. 'I didn't know they still did evenings like this.'

'They don't. It's a seat-warmer, keeps the theatre from going dark between musicals. I bloody hate 'em. We get bewildered pensioners wandering on to the stage looking for the lavs, no offence to you.'

Dudley was ancient and sepia with nicotine, but vanity required him to take sunbeds, wear an orange wig and dye his eyebrows chestnut. Since his wife had died his features had grown baggy with alcohol and he had stopped shaving properly. He was still living in one of the last truly disreputable bed and breakfast joints off the Euston Road. He smelled of sweat, rolling tobacco and Old Spice aftershave, and performed the same banter-laced magic tricks he had made popular in the 1970s. Not that the audience cared; they came to catch up with each other, to wave and eat and chat. They came because the seats were cheap and they wanted to live in a distantly remembered past populated by familiar faces, when you could make mother-in-law jokes without getting into trouble.

'I'm doing a guest spot in the second act because their magician, Lo Fun, got pissed and took his finger off in rehearsals,' said Dudley. 'His wife used his magical chopper on her carrots and forgot to change the setting back. I told them I don't mind stepping in but I'm not doing it Chinese, I'll play it straight, thank you. We're modern now, it's nineteen – twenty – something, there's Chinese in the audience, they'll take offence. I do "The Birdie Song" while producing doves from unlikely places and let Barnacle Bill tell a couple of off-colour jokes, then I'm off over the Argyll Arms for a pint.'

Barnacle Bill was Dudley's ventriloquist's dummy. With its rolling eyes, lascivious wink and odour of rotting rubber, it haunted the sleep of many an impressionable child. Lately, Dudley had started looking more like his dummy than ever. Both had been at their peak of popularity after the war and were soon to be shut up in boxes.

'I thought you'd retired Barnacle Bill,' said Bryant, sitting down alongside him.

'That were just me messing about,' Dudley explained, finishing his fag to the last strand of tobacco. 'I told the children he'd died of woodworm just to get rid of them. I thought they'd never stop crying. He had a lingering death in Blackpool, I'll bloody tell you that. We did the panto season there. It were bloody awful. Our Widow Twankey went to prison for molestation. How he got a job asking children to pull his bloomers down I'll never know.' He pointed towards the box office. 'You're welcome to a comp. There's nobody in except a party of special needs from Dagenham. They're not getting many of the jokes but they're good laughers.'

'Is there an orchestra?'

'Piano, drums and a bassoon. Not exactly the Philharmonic. The producer's added one of them burlesque acts, a lovely big lass from Huddersfield. She's got a bust on her that fair makes your ears wiggle. She takes a bath in a champagne glass but it's not going to hold her weight for much longer. There was an ominous crack last night when she started waving her swizzle stick about.' He flicked his fag end away. 'The writing's on the wall for us lot. This audience is the last generation that'll put up with such rubbish. I suppose you're after advice again.'

'I am, as it happens,' said Bryant. He was still getting over the fact that Dudley was alive, sober and working. 'You remember that act you used to do with Lavinia?'

'You mean the Ali Baba cabinet of swords? We had to give that up after I nicked her. I thought she was going to bleed out before the band finished.'

'This was different,' said Bryant. 'She was in a swimming costume and you filled a shower cubicle with coloured water, and when you drained it she'd gone. She came out from the flies and took a bow in a mermaid tail.'

'She did until the zip went.'

'How did you make her disappear?'

'Oh, that were easy. The water's inside a double layer in the Perspex, like them old pens you used to get where a girl took her clothes off when you turned them upside down. But the cubicle kept springing leaks. She always gave me grief about soaking her fags. I told her to lay off the roll-ups. A magician's assistant shouldn't have a smoker's cough.'

Bryant looked disillusioned. 'It's a bit of a let-down when you know how it's done.'

'And even when you don't.' Dudley pulled something from under his wig, examined it and tossed it into the gutter. 'That's why magicians never give away their secrets. They're bloody boring.'

'It's just that I'm faced with a criminal problem and thought of you.' He explained the circumstances of the attack on Claremont.

Salterton rubbed his stubble, thinking. 'It all sounds pretty straightforward to me,' he said finally. 'You didn't happen to find a rope lying around?'

'No.'

'Or something that could move quickly, like a platform on wheels?'

'There was a skateboard found nearby.'

'Was there a vehicle with a high wheelbase behind the van?'

'Yes, a council bin lorry.'

'That would have acted as a good shield. As I understand it, between the pavement and the road this fella was pretty much out of sight. That's why we put blinds around magicians onstage; the audience sees before and after, and their imaginations fill in the bit they miss. Our eyes aren't much good by modern technical standards. We see less than the average phone camera, but our brains compensate. What you've got is classic stage magic transferred to the street. The fella who got injured – easily recognized, was he?'

'Very. Distinctive clothes and a goatee.'

'And the witnesses, quite far away?'

Bryant nodded.

'Then I reckon it was a substitution,' Salterton said. 'Very easy to stage. The victim came out of his place a few minutes earlier, yes?'

'To talk to the van driver.'

Enthusiasm descended upon Dudley. His eyes seemed suddenly clearer. 'Except that's not what happened, see. When he came down the first time he was pulled into the van and taken care of. The fellow inside put on his clothes or was already dressed like him, down to the goatee. He left the body in the van and used the victim's keys to go back into the building.'

'We have a view of his back on CCTV doing just that,' said Bryant.

'A few minutes later he came back out, got himself seen and passed behind the van, pulling the rig down.'

'What do you mean, the rig?'

'Give over, Arthur, you weren't born yesterday. He pre-loaded his props! A stack of crates with a gap at the bottom, into which he'd dropped the body, rigged to fall down when he touched them.'

'But—'

'Try not to interrupt, you. Where was I? So, the van driver emerges dressed as your political fellow and walks behind the truck. The bin-lorry driver is high above him and doesn't see what's happening, nor do the pedestrians. He touches the rigged crates, drops to the floor and slides under the lorry just as the whole lot comes down, so that when all the debris is removed the original victim is on the ground below the crates and the lookalike has slipped away.'

'Would you need an accomplice for something like that?'

Dudley resettled his wig. 'I don't see why, although it would have to be rehearsed and timed with precision, but that's any magic trick for you. Anyway, it didn't go according to plan because he failed to kill him.'

'It just seems risky,' Bryant pointed out.

'Any riskier than poisoning someone with radioactive tea, like that Russian fella? And what about that MI6 bloke locked in a holdall in his bathtub with the key underneath him? I used to be an escapologist and even I couldn't have managed that. You say he was a government high-up, so it stands to reason he'd get special treatment.'

'Dudley, you've been a great help,' said Bryant, 'but I'm going to have trouble selling your theory to anyone.'

'That's your job, Arthur,' said Salterton. 'If I can convince 'em that dragging a half-suffocated pigeon out of a top hat is the height of sophistication, you can make them believe a politician was stabbed in a van.' He let out a sigh that contained the weight of the world. 'Life is one big bloody trick played on the unsuspecting.'

14

INVISIBLE

'A total salad.' Meera Mangeshkar tried her other eye at the crack in the door. Beyond it, Tim Floris was talking to Raymond Land at the entrance to his office.

'He can't help how he looks,' Colin whispered.

'It's not his looks, it's his attitude. Privileged plonker.'

'Apparently he and the Home Secretary are cousins,' Colin tried to see through the door crack. 'You haven't spoken to him yet. He might be very nice. I like the new intern.'

She threw him a look of deep suspicion. 'Oh really? I wasn't aware you'd spoken to her.'

'I haven't.'

'So you're just rating her on looks.'

'Only to start with. I'll probably qualify that opinion once we've become more familiar with each other.'

'I'm looking forward to you impressing her with the way you eat sausages. Did you rate me on looks before we first talked?'

'No, I didn't think you were my type.'

'What part? Indian? Female? Breathing?'

'Height. If you must know, I thought you were a bit short.'

'When I first saw you I thought you had arms like a monkey but do go on, this is fascinating.'

'You weren't like the others. You played hard to get.'

'I wasn't playing. I didn't fancy you.'

Colin was affronted. 'Why not?'

'I thought you'd be my intellectual inferior.'

He stared at her. 'How did you decide that?'

'I watched you trying to get a Pringles tube off your fist without letting go of any crisps.'

'But you liked the look of me.'

'I thought you were like a mongrel dog with abnormally big arms.' She grinned and scratched his cropped head. 'Good dog. I'm going off to rate the intern.'

The operations room had not been restored to a level that warranted the recapitalization of its door lettering. Just enough of its Tetris-like floorboards were missing to keep it from looking respectable, or safe. A random assortment of borrowed, stolen and rescued furnishings included a pink dressing table, a child's chair in the shape of a boat, a horsehair ottoman and the kind of folding seats that were set out for flute concerts. They had been arranged around the room so that staff members could help themselves. The old allocated spaces could still be discerned from the positioning of the floor sockets and chair-leg scuffs, creating the image of a phantom workforce that had died but refused to leave.

Unbothered, Colin Bimsley squatted on a pile of rubbish with his laptop on his knees. The others had salvaged enough household items from grandparents to make the room resemble an amateur production of *The Mousetrap*.

Timothy Floris was clearly amazed to find himself surrounded by working-class people. He wandered about looking like a foreign ambassador visiting a leper colony. But he was young, Longbright decided, and as yet unformed. It would do him good to get his hands dirty and knock some of the edges off his perpetually stunned demeanour.

'Why don't you grab a folding chair and take that desk?' she suggested.

Floris eyed it with trepidation. 'It's very low.'

'We nicked half a dozen of them from the primary school around the corner. They'll have to do for now.'

'I'm meant to be observing,' he said, 'but there isn't anything to observe.'

Longbright set down another charity shop table with reduced legs. 'I'm afraid it's often like this. Mr Bryant tends to pursue his own leads. He rarely remembers to tell us what he's doing.'

'I don't understand how it works.'

Longbright puffed out her cheeks, trying to decide how best to explain the unit's methodology without sounding certifiable. She was concerned that anything she said would make its way back to Faraday, or worse, go right to the top.

'Our senior detectives decide the course of the investigation and brief me on everyone's respective roles. Mr Bryant has a separate set of contacts, mostly field authorities who can provide specialist information. Mr Land oversees operations and approves the collated reports in terms of effectiveness and expenditure.'

When put that way it sounded almost plausible, she decided, omitting to mention that the reports usually appeared to have been assembled by stroppy art students and the field authorities were certifiable.

Floris nodded thoughtfully. Just as Longbright thought she had got away with it Raymond Land came in. She knew at once that he had already forgotten there was a spy in the room.

'Right, you shower, let's see if we can give old Faraday a knicker sandwich by burying this as soon as poss.' He rubbed his hands with static-building energy. 'We've got testimonials from two colleagues saying that Claremont is medicated up to his hairline and has been "in a state of anxiety" for several months. You've got all the bits, they just need tarting up before I bang them off to Fatso.'

Floris watched Land from behind his miniscule desk. The recipient of his congealed stare looked as if he had been caught standing before a broken window with a brick in his hand.

'What I mean is,' Land said with a cough, 'we now have significant intelligence that should reassure the Home Office, so if you could carefully review your data and submit it before midday tomorrow I'll set about closing the investigation.'

With Raymond on our side we don't need enemies, thought Longbright. She became aware of something blocking the doorway.

When Arthur Bryant crossed a floor, one could never be entirely sure that he would end up at his chosen destination. He liked to time his entrances, and this one was only impeded by his need to check that there was a floor beneath his boots. His clothes looked as if they were attempting to consume him. He was buried to his ears inside his red and green scarf and had a bag slung over his shoulder like an itinerant.

'You can't close the investigation. I have evidence that the attack on Claremont was carefully planned.' He set down the black bin bag and tore it open, revealing a skateboard. 'This was found stuck under the back wheel of the council bin lorry. We have been deceived.'

Making his way to the whiteboard, he drew the positions of the van, the lorry, the Marconi building and the church, then pointed them out with the broken end of a Harry Potter wand (Banbury's son had foolishly left it on his chair).

'The first time Claremont went down to the van he was pulled inside and stabbed.' He prodded the diagram with half a wand. 'The attacker took his place and went back inside Marconi House. Being a lookalike merely involved wearing a similar jacket and a goatee. If you dress as a sailor and walk along a pavement, the uniform is the only thing anyone remembers. He knew that when he re-emerged he would only be seen for a moment. All he had to do was trigger the van doors and scoot under the bin lorry as Claremont's body fell out with the crates. He emerged from the rear, walking away as the crowd gathered, all of them facing in the other direction.'

'That's ridiculous,' cried Land. 'What made you even think of it?'

Bryant tapped his buttonhole. 'He was wearing a carnation in his lapel. Both witnesses commented on it. But Koharu Takahashi said, "Flower, no flower." She meant there wasn't one on him afterwards, because his attacker had lost it in the jacket swap.'

'Why make it look like an accident at all?' asked Janice. 'Why not attack him on the street?'

'I haven't the faintest idea,' Bryant admitted.

'What about the inside of the van? Wouldn't there be blood everywhere?'

'We don't know because Westminster won't release the vehicle to us.'

'Is there a problem?' asked Floris.

'Their officers say the interior was clean, but they've refused to cooperate with us in the past, so perhaps you can have a word with your cousin.'

'Tissues,' said Sidney, perched demurely on a wooden children's stool shaped like a duck. 'Knocking Claremont out creates the anterior skull wound. Then he's stabbed in the stomach through a wad of tissues. The stake is left in place to keep the wound staunched, the tissues are taken away. There are probably traces of paper on the stake.'

Everyone stared at her.

'What?' she asked. There was something impassive in her gaze. She might have been considering a chess board.

'You haven't even spoken to anyone at the site,' said Bryant.

'You can gather evidence without interpersonal skills,' Sidney countered.

'Let me explain something to you, Miss Hargreaves. Beat coppers are nurses. They have "interpersonal skills". Detectives are doctors. They search for the truth, as unpalatable as it often turns out to be. In 1963 Detective Chief Superintendent Jack Slipper tracked down the Great Train Robbers—'

'Before I was born,' Hargreaves pointed out.

'So was Queen Marie of Romania but it doesn't mean you shouldn't know who she was.'

'I *don't* know who she was.'

Bryant begged the ceiling for strength. 'While we rewrite history to include only the people we can be sure were around after the momentous advent of your birth, Miss Hargreaves, consider Slipper of the Yard. His imprimatur was stamped on every case he handled. The great detectives think differently because they develop a singular outlook. Share your ideas with everyone and you end up in a committee that achieves nothing.'

'Perhaps we'll agree to disagree on that,' Hargreaves observed.

'No, let's just disagree,' said Bryant.

'You're very old,' she said suddenly, as if she had just noticed.

Bryant's nose hairs bristled. 'This conversation is ageing me.'

'I meant in a good way.'

'When you get up four times a night to pee you'll realize there is no good way.'

Sidney was about to reply but Longbright touched her lightly on the shoulder.

Bryant studied the girl with interest. 'Are you on the spectrum?'

There was a small horrified pause, although not from Sidney. 'I prefer to think of it as somewhere over the rainbow,' she said.

'Interesting.' He tried to steal a glance at her forearms to see if there were any scar-obscuring tattoos. Her skin was clear. She was of slight and slender build, but commanded an audience. He noticed that she sat on the edge of her seat as if ready to sprint off at any moment.

Banbury drew their attention with a counterfeit cough. 'Thanks to the wonders of modern tech, it looks like we may be about to get an address for Mohammed Alkesh.'

'Shouldn't you be prioritizing the investigation into Claremont's mental health?' Floris asked. Nobody answered.

Land looked for somewhere to sit, and sank on to a pink boudoir chair that accompanied the dressing table. 'Where's the forensic proof for all this?'

'Oh, *evidence*.' Bryant batted the idea aside. 'This isn't about Claremont revealing state secrets.'

'Hang on, hang on.' Banbury held an index finger to the side of his head.

'He's wearing an earpiece,' Janice explained to Sidney.

'We have an address for the driver, a flat in South London. He's not answering. Someone has to go around there.'

'Let me go with Colin,' Meera suggested. 'I'll take the Kawasaki; it'll be faster at this time of the evening. We know what to do.'

The Royal Woolwich Dockyards had been opened by Henry VIII, and for centuries after the area remained resolutely military. Even though the Royal Arsenal's football team had decamped to North London, the town, centred on a rambling market, was rough-hewn and rowdy, beset by squaddies looking for a laugh and a beer. Woolwich had once been distinguished by the great brick wall of the dockyard that loomed over the town, but that barrier had fallen to the wrecking ball, opening up the wide riverside, and with gentrification had come a kind of windswept bareness. Now salvaged chunks of military hardware formed a decorative motif, war fetishized as commercial opportunity. From here to the sea, the southern side of the Thames was ugly and bad-tempered.

Mohammed Alkesh lived in a prefabricated 1970s block of flats in serious need of repair. Colin had trouble finding a porter who would let them in. The young Bangladeshi sat behind an acid-etched sheet of wired glass and still looked apprehensive even after he had seen their ID.

They showed him screengrabs of Alkesh. 'He was here last night,' said the boy, 'except that's not his name around here.'

'Do you know what it is?'

'Something like Dex or Jax? I heard him on the balcony on his phone. I can take you up.'

He led them along a corridor that smelled of dope and stale burgers, and unlocked a scuffed door with his master keys.

Meera went first. 'Did you ever talk to him?'

'Not much. He's an illegal.'

'How do you know that?'

'You just know. All their stuff fits into one bag.'

'Did he have a vehicle, a pale-blue van?'

'No, man, he has nothing. Sometimes another guy lends him a car, a bashed-up Fiat. It's parked outside.'

'How does he seem to you?'

'Kind of invisible. Skinny, with a busy haircut – I don't know what. I see guys like him everywhere. He has *nothing*. No stuff, no family.'

'No furniture,' said Colin, looking around the bare whitewalled flat that smelled of bleach and damp carpet.

'I never seen inside,' said the boy. 'Where does he sleep?'

Meera found a single mattress stored upright in a cupboard. 'How long has he been here?'

'A few weeks. It's a sublet. I don't know who owns it. Not my business. Illegals. Close the door as you go.'

'You don't want to wait for us?' asked Meera.

'You see anything worth stealing in here?' The boy gave a shrug and trudged back to his booth.

'So, nothing for Dan,' said Meera as they came out of the living room. The slamming-back of the bedroom door caught them by surprise. Someone small with ragged black hair went hurtling past them.

In the corridor Meera saw the fire-escape door swinging and ran for the stairs. Colin stayed close behind but stretched out his fingertips to touch the walls, unable to judge the width of the gloomy staircase.

The boy unlocked the silver Fiat as he was sprinting towards it and launched himself inside. Colin was running towards the vehicle when it pulled away in a blast of blue smoke. Meera was already starting her motorcycle.

'Could he make himself look more guilty?' she called as Colin climbed on to the Kawasaki behind her.

'You can take him, Meera, just don't smash up half of London this time.' Colin pushed himself back into the pillion seat as they took off in pursuit.

The Fiat led them into a shabby high street filled with the kind of shops once associated with rustbelt America: burger joint, nail bar, tattoo parlour, chicken shop, every fifth property empty. There was nothing of this part of old South London left.

'Do you want local back-up?' Colin called.

'No time.' Meera cut in hard behind the Fiat, watching the traffic up ahead. She would be able to overtake him before they reached the red lights.

'Get ready to drag him out,' she called. 'Are you wearing a stab vest?'

'No, they make my nipples itch. I'll stay out of his reach.'

As Meera braked and pulled in behind the Fiat Colin got ready to run for the car, but the lights changed and they were off again.

Grimy Edwardian terraces gave way to unadorned council blocks separated from each other like prisoners ordered to stand apart. The threadbare bushes and trees dividing Bevan House from Chamberlain House turned to indiscriminate brambles that overran fences and substations.

The Fiat flashed through patches of light and shade, pulling ahead every time Meera accelerated.

'Where the hell are we?' Colin asked, looking around.

'I can't get ahead of him,' Meera shouted back.

'You have to do something. If he's going to make a move it'll be now.'

'Hang on to me. This could be more tricky than—'

15

GENERATIONALLY CHALLENGED

'The car in front suddenly drops down on to a slip road and vanishes,' said Colin, talking through a bite of fried-egg sandwich. 'Meera swings the bike as sharp as she can but he's gone. They find the Fiat torched on some wasteland near Dartford at two o'clock this morning.'

'It still doesn't explain how you got that,' said Niven, pointing to the plaster stuck across the bridge of Colin's nose.

At 8.00 a.m. the Ladykillers Café was already crowded with staff from the railway stations and publishing houses of King's Cross. What Niven, the proprietor, lacked in stature he made up for in volume, but for once Colin realized it might not be a good idea to confide in him fully. Mr Bryant was notorious for his indiscretion, but even he would think twice about sharing details of the investigation with the owner of a packed café.

'This?' He touched the plaster gingerly. 'Meera cut across an emergency access lane but there was a concrete traffic calmer on it. She braked so suddenly my mobile hit me in the face.'

'While you were holding it.' Niven screwed the lid back on a jar of peach-gin marmalade. 'What's the point of pretending you can protect us when you can't even protect yourself?'

'Give me a cheese and chutney on white for Mr Bryant before I arrest you for being irritating,' Colin said. 'I have to get a move on.'

Colin pushed the remains of the sandwich into his mouth and tapped his card on the reader as he left. At least the unit's main entrance now had a front door, even if it was only chipboard and the lock didn't work. He and Meera had argued after losing the Fiat and she had gone home to her own flat, more angry with herself than with him.

'Here you go, Mr B., quartz cheddar and pickle, don't pay me in old money again.' Colin threw Bryant the greaseproof paper packet.

'I wasn't going to pay you at all,' said Bryant as the sandwich bounced past him. He had not looked up from the document he was reading. Although his old office had been returned to its former glory, he'd found himself unable to settle without his partner, and had temporarily set up in the operations room.

'It's no use, I can't work like this.' Bryant sneezed and blew sawdust everywhere. 'Why is John lying around at home doing nothing? Why can't he heal faster?' He twisted around in his chair to face Floris. The young official looked as if he had spent the night in an airtight container. 'I can feel your gaze dropping upon me as the gentle rain from heaven, Mr Floris.'

'I'm sorry?'

'*The Merchant of Venice.* You're staring.'

Floris ran a finger through the air. 'I'm interested in your dynamic.'

'My dynamic what?'

'The way you operate together. You seem to have very little

in common beyond the fact that none of you are married or have active social lives. Mr Land accepted the Home Office's terms without negotiation. He must have known you would all agree to return here.'

'Are you suggesting we have nowhere else to go? There are plenty of other things we could be doing. Are you serious about filing reports on us?'

'I already sent the first one.' Floris tapped at his tablet. 'I copied you in out of politeness.'

'I read it, that's why I'm asking. We had someone in here who used jargon once before. That didn't end well. I don't know what *interface* means when you use it as a verb but it sounds rude.'

Floris smiled blandly. 'Mr Bryant, people of my generation prefer to share and communicate.'

'Well, people of *my* generation – the ones who still know where they are – prefer to get on with their work.'

'I appreciate the difficulty,' said Floris. 'I'm not too thrilled about being here either.' He checked himself. 'Perhaps that's unfair. Perhaps our divergent methodologies can be bridged.'

'Perhaps you should say *perhaps* less often.'

Floris had adorned his desk with a framed photograph of Faraday's liaison team at a formal dinner that ostentatiously included Floris and the Home Secretary himself. Bryant wondered what kind of man would choose photos of office colleagues over family and friends. Perhaps nobody loved him. Good.

The detective was unwrapping his sandwich just as the door opened and Sidney Hargreaves came in, pulling up a chair and turning it backwards to sit astride it.

'Ah, Miss Hargreaves, how may I offend you today?'

'It's the millennials who take offence.' Sidney took the document he was reading from his hands and cast her eye over it. 'I'm Generation Z.'

'So apart from a short attention span and no working knowledge of *Are You Being Served?*, what can you bring to the table?' Bryant asked, snatching back the document.

'I want to be a detective.' She returned his gaze with a placid frankness.

'So do a great many others.' Bryant blew his nose violently.

'But I want to be you.'

He observed her over the top of his handkerchief. 'I really don't think you do. Not with my bowels.'

'You were my case study at college,' said Sidney. 'I covered every PCU investigation I could find on file. The ones that weren't still sealed *pro bono publico*, anyway. You frighten them.'

'I'm sorry, whom do I frighten?'

'Your superiors in the Special Operations Directorate. I talked to them. They're scared that your methods are too unique.'

'A tautology, young lady.'

'They could mutate and cause chaos. Law is control. Perhaps we should discuss this another time.'

Bryant realized he had at last met someone who was completely unknowable. She stared and stared with her china-blue eyes like a rare artefact revealed in torchlight and he had no idea who or what she was.

'We're all still here, you know,' said Longbright, sticking her head around the door and passing him her phone. 'Dan wants to speak to you.'

'Are you checking on the vehicles?' Bryant bellowed.

'You don't have to shout,' said Banbury. 'Your mystery driver parked his Fiat on some wasteland behind a kebab shop. Nice neighbourhood, the kind of place where you can torch a vehicle and nobody notices. There was nothing left of it. I'm with the fruit van now, in Westminster. I have something interesting for you.'

Bryant listened and waited. 'Well, what is it?'

'I'd better bring it in and show you in front of our observer. Otherwise Mr Floris will think we're hiding information.'

'Good plan. Get back here.'

As he rang off, John May rang in. 'Arthur, I've hit a wall with Peter English. All enquiries have to go through a senior security officer with prior approval of the Home Office. English has a reputation for destroying anyone who tries to humiliate him.'

'Humiliation isn't against the law, John. Sounds like he's used to getting his own way.'

'One of his companies created a program that aggregates algorithms to detect false news. The program proved inaccurate and the investors lost fortunes, so they're pretty disgruntled. It may be a way in to him.'

'You really think he's involved in this?'

'It's hard to know, working like this. I need to get out there.'

There was a creak of wood. Bryant could tell his partner was supine. 'How are you feeling? Are you getting any exercise?'

'I'm controlling the pain. I can't help much with just a phone and a laptop. I'm useless. How's the new blood?'

'They're very nice, if you don't mind interactifacing with generationally challenged pod people so young their mothers are still lactating. You need to get back here and help me deal with them; I have absolutely no idea what they're on about.'

'We are *still* in the room with you,' said Sidney.

May rang off and went to answer the door. His new neighbour Jenny had brought him a spaghetti Bolognese. 'I come bearing convenience products,' she said cheerfully, inviting herself inside. 'It says "artisanal" on the lid so maybe they've put some bits of grass in it. Are you working?'

'Just notes,' he said, closing the lid of the laptop. Recent experience had taught him to be wary of sharing any information, no matter how innocent.

'So' – she tapped the packets – 'spag bol, soup, juice, some kind of pie-thing and some veggie bits. That should keep you going.'

'It's very kind of you but I have food in the freezer.'

'I dare say you do, but you can also accept a friendly helping hand.'

'I'm not very good at that.' He sat back on the edge of his bed. 'Let me give you the money—'

'I'll take a coffee. Incredibly, I do know how to use a Nespresso machine.' She headed for the tiny kitchen. 'Do you cook?'

'I haven't for a while.'

'How long?'

'Maybe six, seven years.'

'So, the whole time you've been here.'

He hobbled behind her, feeling ancient. 'How would you know that?'

'You told me, remember? Plus I talked to the caretaker. He has the dirt on everyone. I treat cookery like a sport: push up the temperature, get into a sweat, wear yourself out – the perfect end to a day spent hunched over a screen. How long are you going to be away from your job?'

'I don't know yet. I'm seeing the doctor again next week.'

She turned on the coffee machine and wandered into the living room. 'You've got no books.'

'I download them.'

'Lots of lovely tech, though. I have the same headphones. I have a headphone fetish. Seven pairs and counting.'

She prowled around the flat peering closely at everything. He was glad he had put away the more unusual prototypes Dan Banbury had made for him.

'Watching for details,' he said.

'I'm sorry?'

'Your video games – they must make you notice small things.'

She apologized. 'It comes with the job. I know it looks like I'm being nosy. Where's your – legal practice, did you say? Is your office far from here?'

'Not far.'

'How long have you been with them?'

'A while now.'

She narrowed her eyes at him. 'You don't give out much information, do you?'

'I'm a bit out of practice, conversationally.'

'Throw me out when you've had enough.' She poured coffee like a barista. 'I talk too much. It's because I can't talk at work.' She tapped her ear. 'I wear the headphones all day long. I'm deprived of normal conversation. Not that I work with many normal people. They tend to conform to stereotype. Good at powering up to fight next-level bosses, not so hot on banter.' She laughed. 'You don't seem to have a TV.'

He knew that from an outsider's viewpoint the flat must appear devoid of creature comforts. 'I have a tablet,' he said. 'I don't amuse myself. I'm usually thinking about work.'

'But you must have friends outside of work.'

God, she wanted to know a lot. Was this how all normal people were? During investigations he interviewed them with unfailing kindness and consideration, but they really only existed to answer his questions. People were never comfortable with police officers. The innocent worked so hard to make themselves appear guilty.

'Your work makes you sound very mysterious.'

'I'm not that interesting,' he said. 'Tell me about you.'

She ran out a second coffee and tasted it. 'I moved south after Sheffield University. I have a son named Caden, a great kid, almost a teenager. You're not married, obviously. Any children?'

Her questions flagged themselves up like warnings and he found himself unable to answer her. He had spent too many years as a perpetual bachelor, refusing responsibility, determined not to act his now-considerable age, but the shooting had shifted everything. Things had to change. He felt much as Tom Jones must have done when he decided to stop dyeing his hair.

'You're miles away,' she said cheerfully.

'My wife is dead,' he blurted out. 'She had a breakdown and never recovered.'

Jenny was momentarily nonplussed. 'I'm sorry. I didn't mean—'

'I'm not very good company. My chest is rather sore.'

'You won't be feeling social if you're on these.' She picked up a packet of tablets and read the label. 'They're very strong. I'm intruding on your privacy. Call me if you need anything. I don't mind when.'

She drained her coffee and waved fingers at him, heading out.

He sank back into his sofa feeling relief that she had gone. He was suspicious of her for being so kind and curious about his life.

No more than three or four people had ever set foot inside his flat. After a lifetime in the force the young, gregarious John May had turned into a taciturn senior, institutionalized by work, uncomfortable with outsiders, discomfited when left alone. He no longer believed in the seven ages of man but in two states only: looking forward and looking back. Somehow the most important part, the time that fell between them, eluded him entirely.

16

FAKING IT

It was the first time in an age that Arthur Bryant had been by himself to see Giles Kershaw. The holly-framed cottage at the back of St Pancras Old Church cemetery housed the pathologist's office and looked like a Victorian stage set. In its backstage area was sunk the brutal grey concrete bunker where the science of death was navigated.

Bryant realized he would have to face Rosa Lysandrou alone. Usually when he made fun of Giles's dour housekeeper he had John to back him up.

She opened the door to him before he'd had a chance to knock.

'Blimey,' said Bryant, 'do you have ESP?'

'No, we have Sky,' said Rosa, peering around him. 'Where is the one I like?'

'Still shot, I'm afraid. He wanted me to thank you for the chocolates. I passed the hard-centred ones on to him. You'll have to make do with me today. Did anyone ever tell you how lovely you look in the morning light?'

'No,' she said suspiciously.

'They never will. But we must desist in this foolish dream. Our love can never be. I'm from leafy Whitechapel and you're from the wrong end of Mykonos. My father was a lowly tram conductor and yours was the head of the SS. Can Giles come out to play?'

'Do you have an appointment?'

'No, but I have a little badge that allows me to see him whenever I want.' He flashed his bus pass at her. 'I'll wait in your Chapel of Rest.'

'You will not. I've just polished it.'

'There's not much point in having a Chapel of Rest if you can't rest in it. Announce me, you espresso bar Jezebel.'

'Ah, there you are,' said Giles, coming to find him. 'Don't lurk out there annoying Rosa, come and see your corpse.'

'I've got wintergreen, sherbet lemons or rhubarb and custard,' said Bryant, rattling a bag of boiled sweets at Kershaw as they headed for the autopsy room. 'They're all horrible but it's better than smelling of your chemicals.'

Giles led the way. 'You're still finding plenty of cases "likely to cause public affright", I see.'

'That's our remit, old sausage. People default to a state of trust. It's the way we're programmed. As I see it, the unit is responsible for maintaining that trust. Which one is he in?' He pointed to the cadaver-storage drawers.

'You know, it always annoys me when you see morgues in films,' said Giles, 'all those half-naked bodies lying about. I've never met a pathologist who keeps a corpse out when there are visitors. Mind you, you're nobody's idea of a detective.'

'Then what am I?'

'A disrupter.'

Bryant popped in a sherbet lemon. 'Is that a good thing, do you think?'

'It's not a bad thing. I suppose you heard I didn't get a look-in with Michael Claremont.'

'Well, he's not technically dead.'

'I know, but I thought I might give you a hand by talking to a survivor. I'm a pretty good judge of character.'

'I don't see how you can be, when the only people you usually see are staring up at the ceiling.'

'Anyway, I hear he's been whisked off to the countryside. I guess the NHS wasn't good enough for him.'

'You went to a school for poshos, didn't you? I thought you had family connections to the Home Office?'

'*Had* being the operative word,' said Giles. 'She left me. Why?'

'I'm trying to find a way of interviewing someone who's too rich to return my calls.'

'Be careful not to confuse posh with rich, dear chap. The former are poor and the latter are vulgar.' Giles knew whereof he spoke, hailing from an ancient estate that was flogged off to pay taxes. 'How's John doing?'

'He's as well as can be expected,' said Bryant, reaching the crunching stage of his sherbet lemon. 'The case has given him something to aim for but at the moment he's in durance vile at his flat on the river.'

'Let's hope he's back soon. You need him to keep yourself anchored.'

'We are not a ship. Why did she leave you?'

Giles looked surprised. 'My wife?' He thought for a moment. 'We disagreed on the correct ingredients for a *salade Niçoise* and I had an affair. Let's see what we've got here.' He pulled open a drawer and unzipped its sanitized bag.

'Cristian Albu, late proprietor of Typeface Books, Bloomsbury,' Bryant murmured. He was always amazed by the human body in repose. 'How much did you find out?'

'Janice scanned your decoded notes for me but I still couldn't read them. Your handwriting is atrocious. This chap's been kicking around the system for far too long. He'd been mislabelled and put in storage at University College Hospital. What went wrong?'

'We did, I'm afraid. The case came in just after the unit was shut down. I need to make it up to his widow.' He sniffed inside the bag, then backed off.

'The most obvious thing is the distinctive smell, even after all this time,' said Giles. 'A mix of burning wood and varnish plus linseed oil.'

'It was used on his wood floors and stored in a can under the stairs.'

'So Janice told me. I thought I'd find splashes on his hands and trainers. Instead I found it under his arms. And no ashes on him, not an ember. There's alcohol in his system but not enough to put him out, so I looked for the presence of narcotics. I wasn't sure I'd still find anything but there are mineral traces from a neural blocker. They're factory-made synthetics, unfortunately very easy to get hold of these days.'

Giles moved around to the head of the drawer. It pleased Bryant to see him using the retractable steel pointer their previous pathologist had bequeathed to his successor. Continuity gave him an irrational sense of pleasure.

'There's a small contusion on the back of his head, specks of gravel on the heels of his trainers, as if he was dragged a short distance and dropped. No oil on his hands, yet the cap was off the empty can. Nothing unusual in his clothes: small change, a paperback, his wallet, a phone. He should have had everything taken off him. He'd made one call home.'

'So a scenario presents itself,' said Bryant. 'He takes a drink with this stranger to celebrate a sale, he's drugged and is half-walked, half-dragged across the courtyard into a corner of the alley. The stranger takes his keys, sets fire to the shop and leaves the can beside him.'

'A relatively easy frame-up in an empty backstreet,' Giles concurred.

'The next part is weirder. Albu is arrested and put in Holborn station's overnight holding cell. There's nothing in there you could hang yourself on, so he tears the plastic cover off the bed in a strip and asks to use the bathroom. Once inside, he ties it into a makeshift noose, attaching one end to the cold tap, the other around his neck. He then drops towards the floor, choking himself to death. And that's where my problem begins.'

'I'm glad you have a problem, Mr B.,' said Giles, 'because so do I. Let's see if they match.'

'OK, mine is the bed cover.'

'Oh.' Giles was surprised. 'Tell me yours first.'

'It's impossible to tear. It's thick, strong plastic and designed not to be ripped. Oddly enough I was testing my theories on deaths in custody and tried tearing a jacket made of roughly the same substance. I couldn't do it. Mind you, I can't get the lid off a jar of gherkins. You could tear it if you could find something to puncture it with first, but Albu had nothing sharp on him.'

'His teeth?'

'Not consistent with the marks on the bed. According to Dan the cover had been punctured before being torn, probably with a penknife – an item Albu did not possess. Tell me your problem.'

Giles traced his pointer across Albu's throat. 'See these livid crimp marks? There's blood trapped under the skin. You get them from elasticated material as the threads stretch and then contract, like the marks your socks leave when you take them off. There's no give in the plastic strip we found around his neck, so it couldn't leave a mark like this, and it doesn't quite match up. Sergeant Flowers says he took Albu's laces and belt away from him, and later found him hanging from the plastic strip. But his belt was elasticated and matches the earlier throat markings.'

'So it was swapped for the torn bed covering after he had already died.'

'Which is where I hand the problem back to you,' said Giles, looking around for a box of swabs. 'I've got something on your arsonist, too. If he lifted this fellow up to move him I assumed he'd lift him under the arms, so I smelled his armpits.'

'Nice.'

'All part of the service. I wondered if he'd left any transfers on the body but I didn't find any fibres, so sometimes it pays to use your nose. Smell this.' He ran a swab on Albu's armpit and waved it under Bryant's nostrils. 'It's a transferred scent. He doesn't just smell of smoke.'

'No,' Bryant agreed. 'He smells of oranges.'

PART TWO
The Bells of St Martin's

The English are bears in all places, except in their own houses; and only those who make their acquaintance in their dens know how amiable, kind and mannerly they really are.

Max Schlesinger

17

OVERTURE

Script extract from Arthur Bryant's 'Peculiar London' walking tour guide. (Duration 45 mins, meet beside statue of Dame Edith Cavell.)

In the year 334, Jesus appeared to St Martin in a dream. Martin wasn't a saint then, just another gormless Roman soldier, but he was canonized and buried at the edge of Covent Garden, where Henry VIII created the parish of 'Saynt Martyns-yn-the-Ffelds' in 1536.

His graveyard later came to hold the victims of the Great Plague, because Henry didn't want them coming anywhere near the Palace of Whitehall with their filthy germs. The original cockney thief and jailbreaker Jack Sheppard was hanged at twenty-two and buried there. William Hogarth too, and Nell Gwyn, at thirty-seven. She had probably been born in Coal Yard Alley off Drury Lane, went on stage as a man, became Restoration comedy's superstar and Charles II's mistress, although everyone still thinks of her flogging oranges in

Covent Garden because they never let you forget your roots.

St Martin's got grander. The church owns the adjacent alleyway so it has its own inscribed lamp-posts. Everyone hated the new design, yet it became copied all over the world, especially in America. It's the parish church of both the royal family and the Prime Minister.

But it's an oddly unlovable building, elegant within, severe without, rectangular and faced with a portico whose pediment is supported by giant Corinthian columns. It almost defies you to step inside, although the crypt is welcoming and you can have lunch on top of the gravestones in there. Don't worry, we'll be stopping there for a cuppa and a sausage roll with meatless option as I have a bit of a deal going on with the cook.

St Martin's commands the upper right-hand corner of Trafalgar Square. Forget finding it in fields; you're hard-pushed to find any trees. Surprisingly, it's always been a community church. It has a history of sheltering the homeless and in both wars soldiers were billeted in the crypt. And check out the arched central East Window, which looks like there's some kind of space-time warp going on. It makes a nice change from shepherds, halos and fat little children tangled in sheets.

'What do you mean, I can't come in?'

Raymond Land looked from one Dave to the other, trying to remember which was which. They stood on either side of the door in the chipboard wall that had been constructed around the Peculiar Crimes Unit. From the grim look on their faces they might have been set to guard a keep, armed with monkey wrenches instead of pikes.

'The front-door lock isn't working properly,' explained

Dave One. 'Mr Bryant has set up a password system to secure the premises.'

'Oh, this is ridiculous. Let me in, you know who I am.' Land looked around the door to the staircase, wondering if he should just push past them.

'He said you'd say that,' said Dave Two.

'How would I know what the password is? He hasn't bloody told me.'

'You could try guessing. We can give you a hint. It's something Mr Bryant stored in the evidence room.'

Land's eyebrows nearly met his comb-over. 'Dear God, that could be anything. Bomb-making equipment. A goat's head. The Dagenham Cannibal's Cuisinart. Crippen's corpse. Madame Blavatsky.'

'Fair enough,' said Dave One. 'In you come.' He took Land's right hand and smacked it with a rubber stamp. Land looked down and read:

ADMIT ONE
Santa's Grotto
Gamages Department Store
Valid until end of 1956

He ushered the unit chief inside. Land felt his way along the darkened plywood corridor and emerged by a blue plastic Portaloo with a sign on it reading: 'Raymond Land's Office – Please Knock'.

Furious, he blundered back and shoved the snickering builders out of the way. 'I know you think this sort of thing is amusing but police work is no laughing matter. I will not work in a toilet. A very important political figure has been buried under a pile of fruit.'

'Cheers, Mr Land,' Dave One called after him. 'Top bantz, you're a total ledge.'

'Ah, Raymondo, *mi idiota favorito*,' cried Bryant as Land stormed past his office. 'I'd like my desk lamp back.'

'I'll give you a broken back if you do that again,' seethed Land.

Bryant paused to take his Spitfire out of his mouth. 'I don't know what you're talking about.'

'Your little jest with the two Daves.'

'I only asked them to keep an eye on the door.'

'You've infected them with your appalling sense of humour. You've already turned a simple accident into a ludicrously complex murder mystery. I want results, not guesswork. If you're so sure Claremont was deliberately attacked find me some proof fast. And stop smoking that thing indoors, it stinks.'

Bryant took the tobacco pouch from his top pocket and read it. ' "Fort William Old Naval Bengali Hemp". Yes, it's a bit pungent, isn't it? Says here it's made with cardamom and marigold seeds but it smells like burning mice. I'd love to help out but this morning I'm dealing with the bookseller who killed himself.'

'What bookseller? I don't remember anything about that.'

'The case came in while you were fretting over your daffodils in Ventnor. Last month a bookseller burned down his shop, except he was framed and killed himself and nobody did anything about it.'

'Why are you getting involved when we still need you on Claremont?' Land demanded.

'Because I can't do anything on that until – what ho, Dan.'

Land felt sure that his detective had been about to reveal something important, but it was too late; Dan Banbury was bounding up the staircase as fast as anyone could, considering there were several steps missing.

'How did you get in?' asked Land, annoyed.

'I've been at the Westminster vehicle pound.' Dan swung his case on to a table and opened it. 'Looks like Mr B. was right. I found this under the van's front seat. Incredible. They hadn't even tagged and bagged it.' He lifted out a clear pouch containing an unprepossessing grey rag.

'I have no idea what I'm looking at,' said Land, mystified.

'It's a stick-on goatee made exclusively by a theatrical costumiers in Shaftesbury Avenue. Unfortunately they say they haven't sold any in months, which suggests it was nicked from the store.' He took a piece of wood from his bag and showed it to Bryant. 'This is similar to the one that speared Claremont. I experimented with several bits and they all broke into sharp pieces. If Claremont was attacked in the van, the driver had to have inflicted the blow before going upstairs. Here, push down on this.'

He held out the spear of wood. Bryant gripped it and pushed, but had to let go.

'There's no way you can do it without piercing your hands, is there? Imagine someone trying to fight you off at the same time.' Banbury took the wood back and closed up his bag. 'I think your new girl has some good ideas. Claremont's air passages were blocked with tissues and he was stabbed in the stomach while he was groggy. You were brought on board to find an information leak and got attempted murder instead.'

Bryant shook out his hands. 'I'm getting a tingling feeling in my fingertips.'

'Perhaps you're having a stroke,' Land suggested.

'Something wicked this way comes. I'm going to need my books. I'm missing certain key volumes. I can live without my *British Nautical Almanac* and my *Practical Guide to Keeping Geese* but I must have my *Encyclopaedia of English Folk Song*.'

Land looked around. 'Does anyone know what he's on about?'

'What I'm on about?' Bryant dragged noisily on his pipe. 'I fear the attack on Michael Claremont was just the start. The overture to the main event.'

18

ON THE STEPS

Chakira Rahman was late, and the BBC did not like to be kept waiting.

Broadcasting House was still a healthy walk away so she needed a city-bike or a taxi, but she was not dressed for the former and there were none of the latter available. It was occluded and inclement. The spring rain looked soiled, as if it had already been recycled through several city drains.

Rahman was recording an interview about the construction of the new Museum of London, but her nanny had chosen today to have her dog put down, so she had bundled her phone-focused girls into the car and run them to school herself, calling her assistant to collect the vehicle so that she could keep to her schedule and get to her next appointment before eleven.

It was always like this, running from briefings to construction sites, arguing with the architect, the client and the banks while making sure that her two girls were fed, watered and educated, but there was even more pressure on her than usual. She was in a position of privilege that had taken a long time to earn. When others fought hard she fought harder, but right now if she didn't get to the studio, turn on her formidable charm and explain why part of the museum project was running late, the press would be attacking her before noon and her directors soon after that.

She was lost in thought as she cut off the corner of Duncannon Street and St Martin's Lane, diagonally climbing the three-sided steps to St Martin-in-the-Fields. As much of her day involved sitting in windowless rooms, she tended to use London's street furniture like gym equipment, getting in her steps and turning stairs into thigh-and-glute exercises.

On the other side of the road a group of tourists had gathered for a new exhibition of Martin Parr photographs at the National Portrait Gallery, their colourful umbrellas hoisted against the famous English weather they'd heard about and now wished never to see again.

Chakira was thinking about her upcoming conference call with the German Minister of Housing, and wondering if her researcher had provided her with enough material about their project, when she became aware of the man limping towards her.

He suddenly moved his hand and her first thought was that he would ask her for money, but a moment later there was a pain in her chest. It felt as if she was experiencing a heart attack.

She heard the sound of coins dropping nearby. Her mind raced: a protestor, a terrorist, just a black shape, fleeting and gone.

Her balance went. She slipped and fell head-first down the wet steps. Somebody cried out. She fought to regain her equilibrium but the staircase was wide and sloped away at two different angles. It was impossible for her to break her fall. As she landed she felt something snap in her wrist. She slid to a stop on the corner of the staircase with the coins cast on the steps above her, extending from her heels like a row of copper raindrops.

The man had already gone. A woman ran over to help. Chakira wanted to say *don't move me*, but now there was an iciness spreading from the base of her skull, and her tilted view of Trafalgar Square sparkled and dissipated as bells began to ring.

'I'm afraid she's dead,' said the vicar of St Martin's, the Reverend Stephen Mallory, who was the first to understand what had happened. He called an ambulance and they called the police, who arrived and spoke to the Serious Crime Command, who summoned the Peculiar Crimes Unit, the entire process taking eight minutes, during which time Chakira Rahman lay on the steps with an overcoat covering her face. The drama coincided with a party of tourists being led out of the church, so Mallory was forced to divert them, and by doing so drew even more attention to the fallen woman.

Dan Banbury collected Bryant in his car, but by the time they arrived the body had been moved inside the church and shielded from public view by the Emergency Medical Team.

'The steps aren't very steep,' Bryant observed. 'Even I could get up and down them without slipping over. They're disorienting, though.' He stepped back under the eaves. The rain was sheeting down now.

'We had a bloke fall down these last month,' said the EMT leader. 'American. Aneurism. He was in sniper's alley.'

Bryant looked about. 'And where is that?'

'Not where, when. Forty-eight to fifty-two. Males who don't change their lifestyles in that age bracket have a tendency to drop dead. Went down like a toboggan, straight under a lorry.'

'You think she'd have survived being stabbed if she hadn't fallen as well?'

'Probably not,' said the EMT leader. 'The blade went in deep and was removed.'

Bryant wrinkled his nose. 'Are you chewing?'

'Fruit gum.'

'Can I have one? Dan, nobody's taped off the spot where she fell.' He waved at his crime scene manager, who was balanced on the rain-slick steps. 'Do something about it.'

'Sure you don't want to go and trample all over it with your big boots first, drop a few sweet wrappers, tread some mud in?' Banbury asked. 'It's what you usually do.'

'Just secure the site, would you? The Met officers can handle a weapon search, they're good at that.'

'Surely there's no need to bring—' Banbury began before he caught the trapped-wind look on Bryant's features. 'I'll tell them.'

'I don't suppose anyone saw where her attacker went.' Bryant sighed and looked about. 'Do we even have a description?'

Behind him was a ragged queue of tourists in rain macs. 'They'll start drifting away in a minute if you don't take their statements. Dan, run them into the narthex and make sure there are at least two officers with notepads.'

'Where's the narthex?'

'The porch bit at the front, you heathen. They can't phone anyone about this until we've put out a statement. If anyone's filmed it, take their device away. Chakira Rahman is an MBE so news of her death will get out there quickly enough, but we have to be in control of the information.'

Bryant stuck his hands in his pockets and looked out at the scene. The fat, inelegant plumes of the Trafalgar Square fountains were spattering over their basins in the wind. Rain had driven everyone from the square. Crimson exhibition banners clanged and slapped at their poles. A taxi was stuck across a junction. Tourists in clear plastic rain-hats advertising some kind of musical – ironically, *Singing in the Rain* – were politely waiting to get around the congested corner of the church steps. A Japanese couple in full wedding regalia, the bride in a frothy white frock that made her look like a shepherdess, were being photographed on the steps of a church where a woman had just been stabbed to death.

It's happened to another high-profile figure in public, Bryant thought. *Sheer devilry. I know where we're going with this, I just don't know how to tell anyone without being ridiculed.* John could have helped him explain, if only he could be here. The pistol might have been aimed at his partner but the blast had damaged him as well. Bryant took death more seriously than people realized.

Two constables guarded a roped-off corner beneath the organ where the body had been placed. Now that the coach party had left the church, the nave was almost empty. St Martin's was busiest during its evening concerts. Then the chandeliers would be lit so that the gold tracery of the white interior could glow and sparkle above the heads of the congregation. Today the seething grey morning had turned the wooden pews to charcoal, filling the space with deep shadows.

The ambulance team wanted to take the body away. An initial examination noted injuries caused by the fall, a broken wrist and a cheekbone contusion, and the cause of death, a single stab wound penetrating deeply and directly into the heart. It was Bryant's worst nightmare, someone struck down in a public place. He had seen the aftermaths of street bombs, innocents attacked by fanatics. It was as if the city, birthed in ancient paganism, periodically demanded sacrifices of its people.

For now he had to think about the practical. Banbury had checked Chakira Rahman's online profile and lifted her contact details, including her husband's office numbers. Her face was familiar to many in the capital. One of the most levelling characteristics of London was that the majority of its inhabitants, rich or poor, walked, biked or used public transport to cross the city. It was important to ensure that they never became afraid of doing so. He looked over at the waiting group of witnesses, corralled behind the rear pews.

'She's well known, isn't she?' said the vicar softly, staring in wonder at the covered shape being removed from the floor. 'She raises money for humanitarian aid. I've watched her being interviewed on television.'

'What did you see?' asked Bryant.

'I heard someone cry out and immediately came outside. I couldn't see her at first. She had fallen face down.'

'Was there anyone else near her?'

'Not that I noticed. My concentration was on Mrs Rahman. And there was the blood of course. I didn't want anyone coming into the church to see it but it had spread across the steps. We overlook the heart of the city. To have such a thing happen here is unthinkable. People have had accidents before but no one has *died*.'

'The medics said there was a fatality just last month.'

'Yes, but he went under a truck. That's not us.'

'Are there cameras covering the steps?' asked Bryant.

'Not from the church. It's a very old building. You can't just drill into the brickwork.'

'Perhaps we'll be lucky with the ones in Duncannon Street. We'll make sure he doesn't get away.' It felt like something he should say rather than something he believed right now. 'There'll be some disruption here for a while. We'll try to be gone as soon as possible.'

'I think I should say a prayer for him,' said Reverend Mallory.

For once, Bryant did not indulge his penchant for vicar-baiting. Instead, he turned his attention to the removal of the body, staying with the EMT while they made it safe for transporting down the steps. As he headed outside, an argument started.

He glanced back at the witnesses. 'What's the problem?'

'We've got half a dozen phone recordings of the attack,' said Banbury, 'maybe more, and they're kicking up hell. No one wants to hand over their phone. Two of them are arguing over copyright.'

'Who's the scariest Met officer on site right now?'

'Sergeant Maxfield.'

'Louise? Perfect. Let's put her in charge of the witnesses. We must be able to get an ID of her attacker.'

Bryant located the no-nonsense sergeant and had a word with her. Within moments she completely silenced the mob. Met officers cultivated that ability; they could put a full stop to arguments with as much efficiency and more warmth than British Airways counter staff. It was a skill no one at the PCU had ever managed to develop.

Banbury found him again. 'This is going to do your head in, Mr B. They were scattered at the spot where Mrs Rahman fell. One of the witnesses says she saw a man throw them down but she didn't see what they were.' He handed Bryant a plastic evidence pouch.

Bryant unsealed it and squinted inside. 'You have got to be joking.'

'Don't take them out of their—' Banbury began but it was too late. Bryant had already tipped them into the palm of his hand.

'Five farthings?' he said incredulously. 'Tell me this isn't what I think it is. Did anybody else see you pick them up?'

'I don't think so, no.'

'It has to be kept out of the press. Can you imagine the field day they'd have?' He handed back the pouch. 'Do whatever you feel is necessary to suppress it.'

Banbury caught his eye.

'What?' snapped Bryant, nettled.

'I've seen that look on your face before. You think it's all connected now, because of the churches.'

'I'm keeping an open mind,' Bryant lied. 'That's what John would do.'

He called Longbright. 'Janice, everything has changed. I need you to be with Giles Kershaw when he receives this body. And get Raymond to put a news blackout on the death until you and Giles have spoken.'

He heard her sigh of impatience. 'I was due to go to Holborn Police Station to discuss the Cristian Albu suicide,' she told him. 'You told me it was important.'

'This is going to override everything else for now.'

'OK, but it's your case.'

'Don't talk to anyone about Rahman's death.' He put his hand over the phone while a police siren passed. 'We have to keep the news from spreading until we're ready to release official information.'

'I don't understand,' she said. 'What haven't you told me?'

'I have to be absolutely sure first.' He tried to keep his voice low. 'We could soon have lynch mobs roaming the streets looking for a killer.'

'Why would that happen?'

'Because we'll have given them a map showing them exactly where to look for him.'

'I'm not sure I follow,' Longbright said.

'Oranges and lemons,' Bryant replied, and rang off.

19

ORANGES & LEMONS

Bryant was wrong; it took no time at all for the news to flare and spread across London. The rolling captions on Sky News were changed from 'tragic accident' to 'attack at church' and finally to 'police looking for assailant'. News teams began to congregate on the steps of St Martin-in-the-Fields, but by this time Bryant and Banbury had spirited the body away to St Pancras.

Seven witness statements went directly back to the PCU. Five called it an accident, pointing out that Chakira Rahman appeared to lose her footing on the steps and fall awkwardly on the corner where the two inclines met. The other two agreed that someone appeared to brush against her first. One suggested it was this collision that caused her to lose balance. The collider had been in a rush, and was wearing black sweatpants, white trainers and a grey hoodie with the top up, a common sight on a rainy day. That person had suggested he moved with a limp.

As soon as John May saw the first statements he understood the implications. Opening his laptop, he logged into the PCU's private site. In the chaos of cross-chatter that ensued he noticed Leslie Faraday contacting Raymond Land to ask him what was going on. Land appeared to have ignored the liaison officer's questions and instead of going on the offensive had shut down all communication with the Home Office. He had never been able to handle conflict.

May shifted restlessly on his sofa. He'd had enough of being on the outside looking in. Pulling a sports vest over his bandaged shoulder, he found a loose sweater that would allow him some movement, packed painkillers in his jacket and called a cab, telling himself that there would be plenty of time to rest after the case was closed. If he warned anyone that he was coming they would find a way to stop him, so he decided to head directly to the St Pancras morgue.

'*Oranges and lemons,*' *say the bells of St Clement's*, he thought. '*You owe me five farthings,*' *say the bells of St Martin's*. The idea was absurd, but it wouldn't take long for hacks to start putting the pieces together.

Where May saw something as mundane as an angry kid targeting strangers, he knew that his partner would be hunting for something more exotic, an elaborate plot to bring down the government, say, or a sociopath with a degree in Victorian campanology.

As it turned out, Mr Bryant was not entirely wrong in his assumptions.

They say the old are more fearless than the young because nothing surprises them, but there was something Arthur Bryant still feared, and it was facing him now. The sign on the wall said 'Sunny Days Nursery School'. From within came the sound of a hundred starlings being torn to pieces by cats.

He was in Bayswater, among the white stucco terraces and kebab shops, a schizophrenic neighbourhood that wanted to be Kensington but felt more like Paddington. The neighbourhood's

scruffy soul had been scooped out along with most of its renovated apartments' non-load-bearing walls, yet it was still not
quite reputable.

A scream split the air, rising so high that it vanished into a
range only dogs could register. Bryant turned down his hearing aid and pressed the door buzzer.

Ruth James was wearing yellow dungarees and quite a lot
of paint. She had a number of coloured pencils in her knotted
red hair. 'Come in, Arthur, how lovely to see you. This must
be important. I know how you loathe small children.'

'If they get too unbearable I'll make them cry by taking my
teeth out,' said Bryant, reluctantly pecking her indigo-smeared
cheek. 'How do you stand the screaming?'

'Earplugs.' She showed him the orange foam bullets in her
hand. 'Free expression brings out the worst in them. Their
parents think they've given birth to baby geniuses. The truth
is that most are uninteresting, a few have the electricity of
curiosity in their eyes and the rest have the intelligence of
molluscs. But in order to justify the cost of dumping them
here everyone goes home with a gold star, a shiny badge or an
important-looking certificate. They're all right most of the
time but occasionally I wish I could buy them guns.'

Ruth led the way through the rainbow-striped play area,
stepping over a dozing romper-suited boy so smothered in red
paint that he looked like an axe murderer's victim. Ruth lec-
tured in childhood studies, specializing in Victorian poetry,
but these days she made more money running the day nursery.
She summoned one of her helpers to monitor the room, then
led Bryant to her office. When she shut the door all outside
sound ceased.

'Isn't it blissful? Double glazing.' She poured two mugs of
tea from an enormous brown pot. 'I can't imagine why you're
here. There's not much call for my area of expertise these
days.'

'I'd have thought we could learn a lot from old English songs,' said Bryant.

'Many of them are deemed inappropriate for tinies now. I'm all for protecting them but I've seen a mother take an apple away from her little girl and give her a protein bar instead because she's never heard of the old saying.' She checked the wall clock. 'I have ten minutes to spare before they sense it's getting close to break time and go berserk.'

Bryant examined the spines on the bookshelf behind Ruth's head. 'Some of those look quite rare.'

'Folk songs.'

'Read me one.'

Ruth opened a volume at its marker. 'Try this:

'There was a man of Newington,
And he was wond'rous wise,
He jumped into a quickset hedge,
And scratched out both his eyes:
But when he saw his eyes were out,
With all his might and main,
He jumped into another hedge,
And scratched them in again.

'And there's a nice illustration of a screaming man with blood pouring from his eye sockets. It's a paradox poem, a subset of songs that present inexplicable situations with logical-sounding solutions.'

Even Bryant was shocked. 'Can you read that to a child?'

'Not any more, but it's how children think. We're the squeamish ones because we've seen grisly accidents and it's made us wary. They haven't.' She sipped her tea and visibly relaxed. 'The other day I read the older children a heavily bowdlerized version of *The Hunchback of Notre-Dame*, and at the part where the Hunchback sits by the dead Esmeralda

I asked them what would happen next. You know what one little girl said? "His tears will fall into her eyes and bring her back to life." Nonsensical to grown-ups but entirely sensible to children, who are naturally pagan. In Victor Hugo's tale the Hunchback betrays Esmeralda and starves to death beside her corpse.' She sighed. 'Maybe Disney's version is better. You wouldn't believe some of the songs that lot outside make up. They're particularly fond of adding verses to something called "Burn Nanny's Knickers". That's what we do, isn't it? Create. Stories exist in thousands of micro-variations. Look how childlike the creation myths are.' She jabbed him in the arm. 'You didn't come here to listen to me.'

Bryant attempted to raise his eyebrows innocently in a way that would indicate that he often travelled about London visiting old friends for no particular reason, but he failed to convince. 'It's strictly confidential,' he began, still eyeing the books. 'I know I always say that but this time it really is.'

'Who am I going to tell? This lot?' She opened the door a crack and the screaming rushed back in. 'Look at little Sheema over there; she's eating the paints. Not the brightest brush in the pot, I'm afraid. Hang on.' She called through the gap. 'Archie, don't do that, it gives the others ideas.' Resealing the door, she turned her attention back to Bryant. 'Do go on.'

' "Oranges & Lemons". I need a bit of background on the rhyme. I tried looking on the internet but kept taking a photograph of some woman's knees. She threatened to call the police. I was on the Piccadilly Line.'

'Well, there are all sorts of complicated theories. The longest version of "Oranges & Lemons" that I've come across has seventeen verses, but we know it best in a truncated form of just six verses and a coda. It's a side-choosing game. Two children form an arch for the others to pass beneath. One team is Oranges, the other is Lemons.' She flipped open a moth-eaten encyclopaedia. 'They sing:

' *"Oranges and lemons," say the bells of St Clement's.*
"You owe me five farthings," say the bells of St Martin's.
"When will you pay me?" say the bells of Old Bailey.
"When I grow rich," say the bells of Shoreditch.
"When will that be?" say the bells of Stepney.
"I do not know," says the great bell at Bow.

'Then the procession beneath the arch of hands speeds up as they say:

'*Here comes a candle to light you to bed.*
Here comes a chopper to chop off your head!
Chip chop, chip chop, the last man is dead.

'Each person chopped has to choose a side and get behind their choice, and once the last one is chosen they have a tug-of-war. It's very sing-song, which is why churches use it in peals of bells. And if you want to know more about bell-ringing, try *The Nine Tailors* by Dorothy L. Sayers.'

'I'm more interested in the song's hidden meanings,' said Bryant. 'Assuming it has any.'

Ruth pulled one of the pencils from her hair. 'I can give you a couple of books but I want them back in one piece, not like last time. Pages glued together with cod roe.' She searched the shelves. 'We suspect that almost every nursery rhyme has a basis in some forgotten event. "Rain, Rain, Go Away" is connected to the defeat of the Spanish Armada in a series of thunderstorms; "Georgie Porgie, Pudding and Pie" is a reference to King James I's lover, the Duke of Buckingham; "Old Mother Hubbard" is intended to be Cardinal Wolsey, although he's also supposed to be "Little Boy Blue"; and "Lucy Locket" was a barmaid at the Cock public house in Fleet Street who chose not to supplement her salary with prostitution. A lot of traditional rhymes were said to be satires on Henry VIII's wives.'

'So they're all true?' asked Bryant.

'Now you're asking the impossible,' said Ruth. 'We have no idea what was true and what was fabricated. Clearly some were retroactively fitted to historical events, but others definitely circulated outwards from courtiers to townsfolk, and probably vice versa. "Oranges & Lemons" – here we are.' She ran her finger down the page. 'The earliest printed version appeared in 1744, but that had references to sticks and apples and maids in white aprons, and doesn't have the "chopper" part. We think the end lines were added by children because church bells always marked public executions at Tyburn, and there were families living nearby. The churches featured in the song were most likely just inside or against the old city walls.'

'That would rule out St Martin-in-the-Fields,' said Bryant.

'Yes, it's more likely to be St Martin Orgar, just off East-cheap, because moneylenders used to live and work there. That church burned down in 1666. Most people assume it's St Martin-in-the-Fields.'

A child's penetrating shriek shattered the calm of the office. Ruth set aside her mug and peered out. 'That's Olivia. A quite extraordinary sound, isn't it? Fairly raises the follicles. She's caused our old caretaker to suffer a trouser accident on more than one occasion. Where was I?' She passed him another volume from her collection. 'People used to make up lyrics for sequences played by church bells. They're simple and memorable. My esteemed colleagues will write you monographs on the secret origins of rhymes until the cows come home. You've probably heard stories that "Ring-a-Ring o' Roses" was not actually about the Great Plague because the language isn't Middle English, but that rebuttal was based on a later version. In fact, the abbreviated "o'" and the use of "posies" suggest that it truly is a plague poem. As for "Oranges & Lemons", I suspect that the song's phrasing was created from the need to find assonance with church names, although "St Clement's" and "lemons" is a bit of a stretch. Stop me when you've heard enough.'

'You'll know when I'm bored,' said Bryant.

'Some believe the song is connected with "London Bridge Is Falling Down", because it was acted out with the same execution ritual, in which case it may have pertained either to the fate of some of Henry VIII's wives, or to a prisoner's final journey from Newgate Prison to Tyburn Tree. The curates of St Clement Danes stole the story as a nice bit of local colour for their church, holding special services with carillons of bells. It's still a macabre song though, reminiscent of funeral torches and public executions. The odd thing to me is that it never really changed, just got shorter. Even when it was first published there was only one line different: "Ring ye bells at Fleetditch". Most songs in use by the populace continue to evolve. One thinks of football-match chants, rhyming slang and the like.'

'Is there any significance in the farthings of St Martin?' Bryant wondered.

Ruth thought for a moment. 'Well, a farthing was originally "four things". A silver penny was pretty soft and could be scored with a cross to make two half-pennies or four quarters, which is why there were four farthings in a penny right up until 1969, when it was removed from circulation.'

Bryant's blue eyes brightened. 'Is there another interpretation in the context of the church, something to do with crucifixes?'

'That's five rather than four – the five wounds of Christ are the "five things" by which sinners are redeemed. But there is a religious reading that suggests the sacrifice of Our Lord must be repaid before the greatest bell of all heralds the end of time. The execution at the rhyme's end can be read to suggest that the church is founded upon the blood of martyrs.

One only has to think of John the Baptist or Sir Thomas More. Human heads must roll before salvation of the spirit.'

'Could the song contain a modern message of some kind?'

'I don't see why not. Minstrels used to spread messages of dissent from town to town by hiding secret meanings in their ballads, like medieval viral protests, just as religious runes were smuggled in the patterns of fabric. You could argue that the colours of oranges and lemons are the colours of paganism, alchemy and the transmutation of metals. You could also read it broadly as a warning.'

'Saying what?'

'The bells are metaphorically announcing a series of executions. Debts have to be paid, sacrifices must be made, a new order arises – you can fill it with anything you like. One could associate it with anarchy.'

'Why so?'

'Anarchy was a harmonic principle of life beyond government, but its modern incarnation revels in atavistic decline.'

'An unpicking of the social order.' He watched the children intent on their play through the window. 'I'm told you once campaigned against a businessman named Peter English. My partner has been trying to see him. Not an easy chap to track down.'

'Yes, I've been keeping an eye on his meteoric rise. Back in my more rebellious days I used to drop leaflets in his neighbourhood until one night our office mysteriously burned down. We always suspected him. Under all those grand statements about transforming society he's just a thug.' Another terrific shriek brought Ruth to her feet. 'That's my cue to get back in there before they start forming tribes.'

'I could never be a historian,' said Bryant with sudden passion.

'What do you mean?'

'Never getting to the bottom of things, never reaching a

definitive answer. History keeps fluctuating. We track down evidence and convict; we close the story. Yours stays open for ever.'

'That's the joy of it, always adding pieces to the puzzle,' Ruth said with a smile. 'Time's up, give me a hug, and don't leave it so long next time.'

He hugged her awkwardly. He wasn't used to it; people usually tried to get away from him. When he let go and stepped back, Ruth's hand went to her mouth and she laughed. 'You wanted some background colour. I've smothered you in pink paint.'

20

OBSERVERS

Rosa Lysandrou was so excited to see John May standing before her in his beautiful blue suit and pressed white shirt that she brought him a cup of lapsang souchong with two Bourbon biscuits in the saucer. Even though she spent most of her time in the Chapel of Rest with the cadavers and was therefore a bad judge of what constituted a healthy complexion, she still thought he looked remarkably well.

'It hurts when I lift my right arm,' said May.

'Because your body's telling you not to lift it,' Giles suggested, heading to a cadaver drawer. 'Listen to a doctor.'

'You're only a dead people's doctor. I'm not ending up on your slab.'

'Just as well, there's a waiting list. What's the word on this one?'

'Nobody has a bad word to say about Chakira Rahman.' May studied the construction manager's rested features. 'She was making real progress in a man's world. She set up training schemes for women in engineering and design, even opened a private members' club for them.'

'Well, now she's joined the ultimate private club,' said Giles. 'Everyone gets in eventually, you just can't do it while you're alive.'

'You did though,' said Rosa, making May jump. 'You came back to us. Did you see the light?'

'No, I saw the floor. I'm sorry, Rosa. If I recall anything about the afterlife I'll let you know.' He waited until she'd left the room. 'Can you make her stop creeping up on people? She's like an electric car. Give me your initial thoughts.'

Giles studied his instrument drawer. 'This lady has only just arrived, John. I don't know how you got here so fast.'

'I heard about it at home. Thought it might be a good idea to get a head start. I need anything you've got.'

Giles fixed his plastic hair cover. 'She was stabbed with a thin blade. The heart is a dense muscle that's not easy to penetrate, and it clenches, so it's hard to get some knives out. He didn't want to leave any evidence. Actually his aim wasn't as good as he'd probably hoped it was, because he only clipped the muscle. I'm wondering if there's another factor involved. She fell down seven or eight steps.'

'The rain had made them slippery,' May said. 'It's one of the most polluted spots in the West End so I imagine particles of engine oil settle on the stone. And the staircase is on three sides without guard rails.'

'So, injuries from a fall.' Giles leaned in close and checked the limbs. 'Broken right scaphoid, the most common bone you'd break when putting out your hand. Abrasions on the knees and the right cheek, swelling on the left side of the skull. She landed on a downward slope, which is bad for bleeding out.'

He ran his thumb down Rahman's spine, counting the vertebrae. 'I haven't found her medical records yet but I'm betting she had a spinal injury in the past. It took away the flexibility she needed to break the fall.'

'Why do you say that?' asked May.

'The C3 and C4 vertebrae are fused.'

'She's left behind an ex-husband and two daughters. They'd know.'

'Do you want to stay for the next part?'

'I've seen it before,' said May, taking a seat against the wall while Kershaw opened up the spine.

'You wouldn't expect a whole lot of flexibility there, but that's not the problem.' Giles delicately exposed the vertebrae. 'The hard landing didn't damage the fused pair. It impacted upon the one above, C2.'

May studied the strip lights and tried not to think of what Giles was doing, although he heard an occasional sound like someone cutting a rare steak.

'Yup, we have a bone shard. If it shattered and severed the spinal cord, she would have undergone neurogenic shock, so you could expect circulatory collapse and autonomic dysreflexia.'

May was forced to look. 'What's that?'

'A sudden burst of high blood pressure which brings on an aneurism. Obviously I'll have to open up the brain for that.'

He watched as the pathologist gently closed the spinal skin flap and moved on. He turned Rahman from her side on to her back, then flexed her wrists and ankles. He shook his head, muttered, shoved his hairnet back, muttered again, then gripped her shoulders. 'John, are you able to give me a push here?'

May did as he was ordered. Together they lifted the upper torso, then let it sink back. 'Interesting,' Kershaw said, putting his hands by his sides once more. 'Her muscle response is wrong.'

'What does that mean?'

'There's no rigor yet so it might be toxicity of some kind. Could be evidence of Botox, because the neck muscles are too soft. Of course everything's a poison, it's just about the dosage. The only other thing . . .' He studied Rahman's lips, then opened her mouth and swabbed it, placing the sample in a dish. 'Let's get that checked out.'

'Come on, Giles, you've got an idea.'

'I don't want to jump the gun but at a guess I'd say there was something nasty on the blade of the knife. I hope that's not the case because we're not sterile to the level of neurotoxins.'

'Why would he add a poison? Isn't it enough that he stabbed her?'

'Two possible reasons spring to mind. Either he wanted to be sure, because knife damage is unpredictable, or it was present on the blade without him knowing. People are scared of using poisons on their enemies. Remember the Aum Shinrikyo cult and the sarin gas attack on the Tokyo subway? Passengers saw liquid leaking from packages. You can't just spread a toxin around without taking major safety precautions. I think it's more likely that there were germs on the knife from whatever he sharpened it with, because it was extremely sharp. Anything invasive can cause sepsis. Maybe she would have lived if the knife had been clean.'

May turned away from the body. It felt as if the line separating life from death was becoming ever more transparent. He might have been looking at himself lying on the steel table.

By the time he had walked halfway back to the PCU his shoulder had started hurting, so he crunched two painkillers. The building on Caledonian Road was now surrounded by timber sheets and workbenches. He just managed to stop Dave One from slapping him on the back as he reached the entrance, then made his way up to the first floor.

Very quickly, the staff gathered and followed him like children after an ice-cream van. The last to arrive was Bryant, but only because he had become over-involved with his coat sleeves. May was taken into the remnants of the operations room. Everyone shook his hand and gingerly hugged him.

'I don't understand it,' Bryant complained, struggling to get his pudgy hand out of his sleeve, 'nobody here ever hugs me.'

'That's because you carry sharps in your coat,' Meera pointed out, 'and you put fishing hooks in your hat and you don't even fish.'

'And you're covered in pink paint,' Colin added.

'And as for you, you're signed off.' Land jabbed a finger at May. 'You're not supposed to be here.'

'Too much rest is unhealthy,' May replied. 'I want to help. I can't say I love what you've done to the place.' He eyed the cables dangling like tagliatelle from the ominous hole in the ceiling.

'You can't be involved, not while your case is under review.' Land face-shrugged in the direction of Timothy Floris, who was standing at a respectful distance, looking as if he was waiting for a wasp to move away. May only had to glance at him to see the problem. Class was rearing its ugly head in the office. Land's father had been a shopkeeper. The unit chief became uncomfortable around the sleekly confident upper-middles. They had business degrees and he had a swimming certificate (bronze).

May stepped forward with his hand out. 'Mr Floris, it's a pleasure.'

'He's our Home Office observer,' warned Bryant, ridding himself of his meddlesome coat. 'He *observes*.'

May pumped Floris's hand. 'So you're working for Leslie Faraday.'

'Technically he works for us,' Floris politely corrected. 'Our department acts under the command of the Home Secretary. I'm here to make sure that protocol is followed.'

'You've come to the wrong unit, then,' said May. 'We're rubbish at rules. We tend to burn things down.'

'I told him that,' said Bryant.

Sidney Hargreaves presented herself to May. 'Hello. I'm working with Mr Land.'

'She's working *for* me,' said Land. 'An intern.'

'You want to be a detective?' The girl standing before May wore mismatched clothes in artful composition. He had never seen her before, yet she was entirely familiar to him. It was as if the unit had always been awaiting her arrival. He tried not to stare.

'I'm more than that. A bee, perhaps,' she said.

He could not tell from her deadpan face whether she was joking. 'A bee?'

'There are up to a hundred thousand bees in a hive, with thousands of females making honey, hundreds of male drones doing nothing until we evict them and let them die, and just one queen.'

Meera gave an involuntary bark of laughter.

'Your apiary-based ambitions are duly noted, Miss Hargreaves,' said Bryant.

Land called back their attention. 'Can I remind everyone on my payroll that we are now dealing with a murder case, and that you lot need to start getting some bloody results? Is anybody listening to me?'

He looked around to find that the others had dispersed.

'It's good to have you here again,' said Bryant, leading his partner back to their office.

Land followed behind them. 'It was me who made all this happen, you know. Me who got the unit back, even if it's only for a week or so—'

Bryant shut the door in his face.

21

CANDLE, CHOPPER

'It's not exactly like your old chair but it's the nearest I could find,' said Bryant, ushering May to his seat. 'I'm not sure how poor old Raymond's going to take it when we break the bad news to him.'

'You mean the oranges and lemons part? I can already hear him.' May gingerly lowered himself into his chair.

'It's a disaster.'

May thought he was talking about the case until he saw Bryant pointing to his bookshelves. 'Faraday's gorillas completely wrecked my alphabetical order. It's obvious that *Jellyfish of the Cornish Coast* should come before *Dutch Chamberpots of the 18th Century*, thematically speaking. And where's my *Encyclopaedia of Victorian Drainage* gone? What? You're giving me a funny look. Is your bullet hole hurting?'

'You're right, it's good to be back,' said May.

'I was starting to think you'd never get here. I can't prove it but I'm sure all three cases are related.'

May was surprised. 'Three?'

'Cristian Albu, arson, suicide and the smell of oranges.

Michael Claremont, publicly stabbed outside a church connected with the same fruit. Chakira Rahman, knifed on the steps at the song's next site and pelted with farthings just to make sure that we get the point.'

It seemed to May that as his partner became more enthused the years fell away from him until he seemed suspended in time, held aloft by his passionate curiosity.

Bryant rapped at the scribbles on his desk. 'The killings are planned, timed and rehearsed. This is beyond mere premeditation, it's a battle plan!'

'Presumably Rahman was followed from home,' said May.

'Yes, but her killer had to act somewhere near the church in order to fit the rhyme. It means he had access to her schedule, John. The same holds true for Claremont; the attacker knew that he was going to be alone at his flat on Sunday morning.'

'But if Rahman was heading to Broadcasting House she could have gone up the other side of Trafalgar Square, then up Regent Street,' May pointed out. 'It's probably faster.'

'But nobody does, do they?' Bryant pointed out. 'It means crossing Piccadilly Circus. Most of us would go past St Martin-in-the-Fields and cut behind Leicester Square.'

May thought for a moment, drawing swirls on his notepad. 'Could Claremont and Rahman have known each other?'

'Janice thinks it's possible they met at a government function. Colin and Meera are looking for connections. I've been trying to see the broader picture. I keep coming back to the song.'

'Of course you do.'

Bryant got to his feet and dug out his Spitfire. 'The best known version of the "Oranges & Lemons" song has six calls to action. That leaves four more victims to be attacked in public places. It's no longer about deciding whether Michael Claremont is a security risk. This is something bigger.'

'You think that's true?' asked May. 'Or is it how you'd like the case to be?'

'You're suggesting I want the unit to make a name for itself again? I do, but not this way. Claremont and Rahman both seem to have been forces for good in an increasingly ghastly world. Who would wish them dead?'

'Someone who found them in the way, I suppose. While we're coming up with crackpot theories, here's mine. Many of the country's oldest churches are falling down, ignored and virtually empty. Both attacks have drawn attention to them. What if he's a religious extremist and is trying to say something about places of worship?'

'I like your thinking,' said Bryant. 'Churches are physical expressions of faith, built to lift sinners above the corrupt mire of the capital. Why were so many constructed in London? Because in medieval times the church had total control over knowledge. The counsel of God was deemed far more important than the evidence before your eyes. What if these victims are sacrifices? The churches involved are ancient and built over temples of pagan worship.'

The door opened. Sidney wandered in and stood before them. 'Just to say I haven't been given any structure?'

Bryant studied her as if examining a particularly trying piece of modern art. 'What?'

She looked from one to the other. 'Support structure? Like who can help me if I need support?'

'First,' said Bryant, holding up a finger, 'knock before you come into this room, then think about the consequences of your action and don't come in. B, don't turn statements into questions. And third, along with Santa Claus, the ozone layer and Raymond Land's love life, unit support does not exist. In your parlance: it is not a thing. Do you understand? Nod if yes.'

Sidney rubbed at her nose. 'That doesn't make me very comfortable.'

'I'm not here to make you comfortable. I'm here to make you vaguely afraid.'

'Also your connectivity is problematic. I like your office.'

'You're not having it.'

Bryant's sarcasm bounced off her. 'I'm very pleased to be working with you.'

'We're in a meeting. What do you want?'

'I should sit in. I want to see how you do it.'

'We are not a magic act,' Bryant snapped, losing his patience.

'Perhaps not,' Sidney replied, 'but I don't see how I can help until I fully understand.'

'Nobody expects you to help, you're on tea and envelopes.'

She stared at him with a hardening of the features that could have snapped pencils.

'And stop doing that.'

'What?'

'That accusing look. It makes you look deranged.'

'You can't say that to me.'

'Young lady, everyone here lives with their own form of madness. Out there you may be treated differently but in this unit you are not special. Furthermore, I can say whatever I like because I have long since stopped caring what anyone thinks. I hope one day you discover the delightful sensation of not giving a monkey's truss.'

She stared at him for just the right amount of time before continuing. 'A moment before I came in I overheard you saying that the "Oranges & Lemons" song has six calls to action. It has eight. The candle to light you to bed, the chopper to chop off your head. Just because they don't mention churches is no reason to discount them. Know what they suggest to me?'

'Please do tell us, Miss Hargreaves.'

She looked from one to the other. 'That the killer is going

to commit suicide after his task is completed. And he'll do it at night.'

'Why do you say that?'

'He wouldn't need a candle to light him to bed if it was day.' She closed the door quietly behind her.

'She's a piece of work, isn't she?' said Bryant. 'Are all young people like that?'

'Only to you,' said May.

'She's making me feel old,' said Meera. She was standing beneath a fritzing light in the first-floor corridor with Long-bright. They were waiting for the coffee machine to strain out an espresso, something it had been reluctant to do since Dave One had reinstalled it.

'It's good that she has ambitions,' said Longbright.

'I don't want it to turn into one of those situations where women can't support each other because they're too busy competing.'

'No, that would be wrong,' Longbright agreed.

'And she's obviously smart even if she's . . . you know,' Meera conceded.

'You always feel threatened when someone new comes into the unit,' said Longbright. 'There's no reason why we can't all be friends.'

'Even so,' said Meera.

Longbright turned to look at her. 'Then what's your problem?'

'She's got the old man wrapped around her little finger.'

Longbright smiled to herself. The door opened between them, and Sidney came out of the detectives' office.

'How did it go in there?' asked Longbright.

'I like them.' Sidney looked from one to the other, her face blank.

'You mean they liked you,' said Meera, folding her arms.

'I very much doubt that. I thought I'd walked into a World War Two film.' She stepped between them and studied the coffee machine. 'You expect everything to be in black and white.'

'Are you after a permanent position?' asked Meera.

'That depends. Mr Bryant gave me his case notes.' She looked down at the manila folder in her hand. 'Well, he's given me tree shavings, which is weird. Apparently he doesn't read screens?'

'But I gave him those notes,' Meera said.

'Yes, and now he's given them to me. Don't feel bad.'

Longbright tried to formulate a reply and failed.

'Shakespeare,' said Sidney. 'You either go after the lead role or you end up in the background playing Randombantz and Palpatine.'

'Rosencrantz and Guildenstern,' said Longbright.

'Probably.' Sidney smiled at Meera. 'I don't know anything about Shakespeare.'

'Well, I must remember to tune in again next week to *Let's Talk Bollocks*,' said Meera. 'We see through your little act, Little Miss Idiot-Savant who aced her exams and now thinks she can breeze into any job she pleases by waving her special mental health credentials.'

'You've got me all wrong.' She slapped the coffee machine and it sputtered into life, pouring a perfect espresso. 'I failed my finals. That's why I'm here.'

She headed off with her coffee and her tree shavings.

'We can't stake out every neighbourhood mentioned in the rhyme,' said Bryant, ransacking another bookshelf. His treasured volumes amounted to little more than a hodge-podge of bookshop clearances and charity-shop rejects, yet he treated them as if they belonged in the Great Library at Alexandria. He cast a baleful glare at his Special Reference Section. 'This office has to be put back exactly how it was, with the books all in perfect order, then I can start thinking clearly. Where's my goat's head lampshade? And my plant?'

'It was marijuana, Arthur.'

'It was *medicinal*. According to Raymond, that fellow Floris is holding the unit's purse strings. He may be a perfumed twerp with a ludicrously complicated beard but if we exploit him ruthlessly he can grease a few wheels for us. What I need most now is your marvellous common sense. I'm unmoored without it. What do we do?'

May had never felt that he truly pulled his weight on the team – Arthur had once called him his capstan because 'we can tie everything to you and none of it will float away' – but today he could see how much his partner needed help.

'First let's give the Home Office what it wants,' he suggested. 'The file on Claremont's mental health. There's enough material in it to keep them busy for a while.'

There was a knock at the door. Bryant opened it to find Meera standing with his plant in one hand and what appeared to be a furry dishcloth in the other. 'Raymond wants you at a meeting in the operations room right now,' she said, setting down the plant and turning to go.

'Wait, what have you got there?' asked Bryant. 'Is there a cat inside that?'

'He's a rescue moggy.'

'It smells horrible.'

'He got into the kitchen bin,' said Meera. 'I left some pilchards in there. I thought he would cheer Raymond up, seeing as Crippen died.'

'Does it have a name?'

'Strangeways.'

She set the cat down on the floor. It promptly fell over.

Strangeways was black and white and looked as if he'd been in a wind tunnel, and had quite a few clumps of fur missing and one eye partially shut. When Meera scuffed his half-chewed ear he started making a rasping noise like a baby with croup.

'What's wrong with it?' Bryant asked. 'It's got that squinty look on its face you only normally see on dead things, like it's just returned from the grave. I don't want another cat, especially one that looks like a zombie.'

Meera turned to May. 'It's nice to see you back, sir.'

'You've never called me sir,' Bryant complained.

'You might want to work out why that is,' said Meera.

Bryant turned to his partner. 'It's her, that girl Sidney. She's upsetting everyone, spreading her post-millennial malaise through the unit.'

'It might not be such a bad thing,' said May, rising.

Strangeways sneezed. Bryant decided to steer well clear of him. 'And why would you name that thing after a prison?' he asked.

'He's a *he*, not an *it*. Our last one was named after a murderer and changed sex,' Meera pointed out. 'Raymond says right now or you're all fired again.'

22

RADICAL ALF

'What is this?' cried Raymond Land, banging on the whiteboard with his pointing stick.

'It's your wand,' said Colin.

'This, *this*.' He slammed his hand over the words to 'Oranges & Lemons' that Janice Longbright had written out on Bryant's instructions. 'One attempted murder and one very public death, and you're linking them together with a nursery rhyme? I cannot have our Home Office spy reporting this back to Faraday.' He hastily checked to make sure that Tim Floris was not within hearing distance.

Colin shifted around on his seat. Out of the corner of his eye he saw something that looked like a hairy version of the facehugger from *Alien* scamper past. 'Did I just see some kind of animal?'

'We've got a new cat,' said Meera.

'What's wrong with it? It was moving like its legs are on backwards.'

'If I can have your attention, Mr Bimsley,' called Land, tapping his stick on the board. 'I do not want this theory handied about. We are here to extrapolate rational explanations from irrational events, not make up new irrational ones.'

Bryant and May seated themselves on chrome 1970s Indian restaurant chairs. 'I take it you don't think the deaths are in any way related to the rhyme,' said Bryant. He removed some items from the voluminous pocket of his cardigan and set them down on the table before him.

'No, and it's not your job to link them without evidence,' Land reminded him. 'You don't even have proof that the victims were linked, so don't start adding fairy-tale elements.' He saw what Bryant had set down. 'What's all this?'

'The evidence,' said Bryant, holding up an orange and a lemon. 'Claremont was surrounded by them when he was attacked. It was a complicated little trick that made everyone think it was an accident.'

He picked up the coins. 'Five farthings, thrown on to the steps of St Martin's beside Chakira Rahman's body in order to deliberately create a link. She died from a lethal toxin on the blade that was used to stab her. If he keeps to this pattern he has to kill four more times.'

'But for the love of God *why*?' Land was desperately trying to understand. 'What could he possibly hope to achieve?'

'That's rather the question, isn't it, old sock? The rhyme's rather vague.'

'You think this is all a game, don't you?' Land scrubbed the lyrics from the whiteboard. 'A storybook puzzle designed just for you to solve.'

'You don't understand, Raymondo, it's not about the puzzle.'

'You just said it was.'

'The victims aren't connected to the churches. They weren't christened or married in them, although the Claremonts occasionally attended services at St Clement's. The rhyme is simply being used to draw the public's attention. The attacker understands how publicity works.'

'And how does it work?' asked Land.

'By fixing on a colourful detail. When our Prime Minister says something spectacularly stupid it distracts us from the real issue. Most people in the country won't have heard of Claremont, but they'll remember the oranges and lemons. It's misdirection. The attacks serve a murkier purpose.'

'The trouble with you is—'

'Don't say it.'

'—you hate the idea of murder lacking a motive. Most are driven by hatred and anger and *nothing else*.'

'That doesn't make them motiveless,' Bryant said heatedly. 'Killers strike because they feel inadequate and powerless. I agree most are inarticulate with rage. This one is articulate.'

'Why not go with the nursery rhyme theory for now?' asked May in an effort to placate the pair.

'Because whenever your partner goes looking for crazy he always finds it,' hissed Land.

'It won't harm the investigation if we keep it in this room.'

Land looked around for something to grip and throttle. 'And how do you propose to do that when we have a government observer sitting in with us half the time?'

'He's easily taken care of,' said Bryant cheerfully, putting his coat on. 'Feed him the report on Claremont's mental health.'

'I know you're going to do something that will make me look bad again.'

'You had a shooting on the premises and lost the unit: how could we possibly make you look any worse?'

'But you can't just go wandering off,' Land cried, exasperated.

'I have a meeting to attend,' said Bryant. 'I'm off to practise my ollies with Radical Alf.'

He slipped out of the door before Land could begin to frame an answer.

It was a short walk to the Thameslink train from the unit. Crossing the grey expanse of York Way to reach it was like changing into a freshly laundered shirt. A gleaming new metropolis had arisen from the ashes of the old King's Cross slums, as if a city block from Dubai's business quarter had been airlifted into one of North London's poorest neighbourhoods. It had created a new social stratum: Google class, filled with small-portion restaurants, cushion shops and portly security guards watching for signs of disrespect.

Bryant reached the Thames by train in no time. As he marched along the South Bank with the skateboard under his arm, he wondered why people were giving him strange looks.

The Undercroft, a shadowy graffiti-spattered concrete space beneath the riverside buildings, had been co-opted by skaters for over forty years. The clatter and snap of boards echoed through the brutally geometric chamber day and night. The skaters were indifferent to the fact that they had become a tourist attraction.

Radical Alf was far too old to still be boarding, but if anyone told him so he always replied, 'Look at Tony Hawk.' He wore a voluminous Hawaiian shirt covered in tigers but was as thin as a sapling, with hair like a spaniel in a sports car. He pumped Bryant's arm energetically but his eye had already strayed to the board. He was twitching to get his hands on it.

'That's an old customized Sk8Mafia – what have they done to the wheels? Where did you get this?'

'I found it in the Strand,' said Bryant. 'What can you tell me about it?'

'It's brand-new but it's been given some kind of overhaul. May I?' Radical Alf dropped it on to the ground, set off and executed a 180-degree turn. He kicked it up and returned holding it before him in reverence. 'Fast and silent. I'm not sure what the wheels are made of but I've never seen anything like them. I didn't know there was a skate shop in the Strand.'

'There isn't. It was under a bin lorry. You can keep it. I can't introduce it as evidence. I just want to know where you'd get one.'

'You are a total dude.' Radical Alf pulled a yellow plastic tube from his top pocket and took a drag on it. He offered it to Bryant. 'It's a phytochemical vape. This one's called Gorilla Glue, very mellow.'

'Not while I'm on duty but I'll stick one behind my ear for later.' Bryant slipped the cannabis oil tube into his jacket as Radical Alf called to another skater.

'Hey, Trainwreck, have you seen one of these before?'

Trainwreck was limping badly and had lost enough skin on the left side of his skull for there to be little chance of growing his hair back. He examined the board like an antiques dealer doubting the provenance of a Fragonard.

'See, here's your problem.' Trainwreck ran the remaining nub of his forefinger along the board's deck. 'The ply is standard and available anywhere but the trucks and risers are custom. Chopping a board this way makes no sense. The grip tape would wear out first.'

'I don't think the maker cared about long-term usage,' Bryant said. 'This was put together for a single purpose.'

'Home-crafted, man. Sorry we couldn't help more.'

Radical Alf gave Bryant an odiferously skunky hug and bounced away.

As the detective made his way back to Blackfriars Station he saw the entire performance in his mind's eye. When Claremont's attacker went behind the van and triggered the crates, the skateboard was already in position beneath the bin lorry's cabin. With a little practice, dropping on to the board and pushing back to the truck's far end could have been accomplished in a single fluid motion.

The second performance was even simpler. A brush-past on the steps of St Martin's; a dab of toxin on a blade. In many ways a perfect crime, yet it could easily have gone wrong. He had assumed that the hardest part was getting hold of a poisonous chemical, but Dan had disabused him of the notion. 'You just have to look in your garden shed or under your kitchen sink,' he'd explained. Which made him fearful about what might happen next.

This is insanity, Bryant told himself. *Who in their right mind would kill like this?* But of course he had answered his own question.

23

MAKING A MURDERER

Fireman. Policeman. Magician. The things I wanted to be when I was a child.

Most of all, I wanted to commit murder. I wanted to think of myself as a hero.

When my mother told me about the Event everything fell into place, and I finally understood. She cried, how could she not, at the memory. I felt disgusted, then ashamed, and later when she couldn't stop crying I overcame my revulsion and comforted her.

She said it was because of the London streets, and that I would never understand how it was. The way the streets were laid out.

South London was different then, every neighbourhood had its character but the trouble began at the points where they butted up against each other. Every town has a bad spot, sometimes just a street or a pavement corner. In Greenwich the western part of the town was rich, the home of architects and playwrights, filled with museums and galleries. The eastern part was working class, decent but scruffy, lined with charity shops and takeaways. The two halves met at the top of the street where I was born.

At the end of this street, set back from the intersection, was an elaborate Victorian railing that had once belonged to the church. There was only about ten yards of it left but it had remained standing for well over a century, a gateway between the two worlds. That was where they gathered.

That's how she knew them.

Beyond the remains of the church were the fancy houses, the ones that had once had boot-scrapers and servants' entrances. They still had high hedges and ponds in walled gardens, while ours had a bicycle-filled back yard. The boys hung over the railing watching her pass, their long arms dangling. They never called out; they were too well educated for that.

My mother went to the local comprehensive school. One of the boys was privately educated in a grand Georgian house close to the *Cutty Sark*. The others went to different schools in the nicer part of the borough. There were all sorts of stories about them. They had a private clubhouse no one had ever seen. One of them had been sent home from school for defacing a portrait of Jesus in the chapel. They had secret rituals and initiation ceremonies and rules – lots of rules about who you could be seen talking to, who you could befriend, who you had to treat as a sworn enemy. One of them was a girl, an honorary member, nobody knew why. Nobody knew where the stories came from, or if any of them were true.

One day as my mother was passing the railing one of them spoke to her, gently and respectfully. He said as they saw each other so often they should be friends. He was the tallest and the most handsome, and as none of them had ever teased her or said anything nasty she smiled back, but went on her way. She was eleven, they were twelve and thirteen. The next time she passed, she stopped.

She never stayed for more than a few minutes, but as she got to know her new friend better he introduced the others. They were shy and uncomfortable around her, largely mute. The girl hung back, avoiding her gaze. On airless summer evenings they lay listlessly draped over the stumps of masonry beyond the railings, boneless with boredom. She suspected they saw her as a distracting interloper.

Finally she was invited through the railings to the other side.

The handsome one showed her the street's private gardens. He took her to the places where they congregated, showed her the comics they collected, the magic tricks they performed, the arcane games they played. Their most secret and sacred spot remained St George's Church. It had been bombed out during the war, but unlike wealthier churches it had not been funded and repaired. Locals said the vicar had been killed in a raid, and no one was ever appointed to take it over. Instead it had continued to crumble apart, the land untouchable because it was still owned by the Church. Rocket and mint sprouted between the bricks. The apse had erupted with broken tiles and rubble. There were a few crusts of stained glass in the windows. The rest had been destroyed with hurled bricks. Only the stretch of railing remained at the edge, like the lace hem of a rotted coat.

My mother lived with her grandmother in those days – her parents had long before fought and split up. The grandmother said she remembered the church when it had still been complete. There had been a nativity scene in the largest window, picked out in red, blue and gold. She had been christened there, back in a time when most people still had family in the streets where they were born. Continuity made people comfortable. All that has gone now.

My mother never told her grandmother that she was friendly with boys from the other world. She knew the old lady wouldn't approve. When the handsome boy invited her over she proved herself by joining in their games, silly sing-songs, tugs-of-war, catch games, hiding games. She was never one of the gang – she sounded too different – but they accepted her on their own terms, and I suppose that was all she had ever wanted. The other girl never spoke to her, hardly spoke to anyone.

As time passed she saw less of the boys. Under the instruction of their parents they put away childish things and spent more time studying. My mother had no such supervision and spent her days alone, helping her grandmother with the housework – she lived above a grocery shop – but sometimes she saw the handsome one out with his parents. The first time it happened he pretended he didn't know her, although she wondered if he simply didn't recognize her because her body was changing and she now wore her hair differently.

But he did notice her.

If he hadn't done so, I would not have set out on a path to burn this city to the ground.

PART THREE
The Bells of Old Bailey

The past is round us, those old spires
That glimmer o'er our head;
Not from the present are their fires,
Their light is from the dead.

Letitia Elizabeth Landon

24

LIFESAVER

Elise Albu sat on a stool restitching the torn seat of her husband's favourite armchair, and tried to think of him without crying.

She could not yet begin to grieve. She had promised herself that no tear would be shed until after his funeral, but the ceremony had been postponed pending the endlessly delayed police investigation. She would do what all the women in her family did: busy herself with something that could temporarily take away the pain.

The armchair had been his grandmother's, packed up and shipped from Romania. It had caramel-coloured upholstery and deep soft cushions, and was wing-backed so that Elise could rest her head in its corners and close her eyes, and smell his aftershave, his skin, his hair. Perhaps if she kept her eyes closed for long enough and waited for just the right moment to open them again the world would be reset back before that terrible night, and she would hear the click of the kettle in the kitchen and know he was making himself a cup of tea, and would come in carrying a mug for her, because he always made her one without needing to ask.

When she opened her eyes the flat was still empty and silent. Nothing had changed, but now it felt inhabited by one, not two. She could hear the traffic in Dalston High Street, and the tick of the old tin alarm clock in the bedroom they had set aside for a baby. She found a tissue in her sleeve and blew her nose. The nursery could be painted white and turned into an office.

The strange old man from the semi-derelict building in King's Cross had asked her to go through all of her husband's letters, notes and bills. Now they covered the kitchen table. Cristian would have hated the mess she'd made. Booksellers liked order. What she had found was too painful to think about: requests for loans and payment extensions, endless finance restructuring documents, politely desperate begging letters to relatives. He had never let her see the lengths to which he had gone to secure their future.

In the last month she had called Sergeant George Flowers at Holborn Police Station so many times that he stopped answering. Now he was on sick leave and the case seemed to have been taken up by Mr Bryant, but despite his promises the detective had not been in touch again.

She picked up her phone and looked for his contact details. She wanted to call him, just to know that there was someone genuinely trying to help, but he was a confused old man who should clearly never have been passed the case, and she did not know what to say to him. How could the police help her if they were prepared to hand her over to a pensioner after a month of doing nothing?

She returned to the task of sorting through her husband's correspondence. Cristian kept an empty Nike box in a kitchen cupboard that he used as his 'pending' file. She fetched it now and emptied it out on to the floor.

Here were the rest of the unpaid bills along with details of the loan they had taken out, several final demands and threats of private debt-collection agencies. Repairs to the shop roof that Cristian had paid for had not been reimbursed by the landlord, and private dental work for Elise that the NHS had been too stretched to handle had amounted to a small fortune.

She opened his laptop and checked his email account. In it was a file she had not noticed before marked *Titles Cash Only*. His record of under-the-counter sales.

She scrolled down through the volumes.

Richard Quittenden, Giant-Land, *author's own edition with hand-coloured plates.*

Oscar Wilde, Salomé, *first edition, one of fifty copies, printed on Van Gelder stock.*

Arthur Conan Doyle, The Maracot Deep, *four science fiction stories 1929. V. rare.*

There were dozens of titles, many more than she had expected. The sales had begun in August of last year and ran until just before Cristian's death. She tried to think of any sign that this shadow-trade had been going on behind her back but nothing came to mind. They had gone to work, eaten together and seen friends like any other couple. Their love life had lost its early urgency and there had been some money worries but otherwise their day-to-day affairs had run on the same solid rails as always, or so she'd thought.

With the exception of this one undeleted file he had covered his tracks very carefully. She could find email addresses for his buyers but what could she write that would elicit anything but furious responses and threats from lawyers?

As she tried to find a solution something broke inside her and she finally cried, the way a man cries, with head lowered in silent shame, swiping at her eyes so that no one would see her wet face. She had thought that his death was the worst thing that could ever happen, but this made it even more unbearable.

She found Arthur Bryant's number and deleted it. She would never be able to understand her husband now, so what was the point of asking anyone to investigate his death?

'I'm afraid he's asleep,' said Mrs Flowers, blocking her view. 'You should have called instead of just turning up like this. He's on official sick leave.' She had opened the front door by about a foot, the standard width preferred by those who were suspicious of unsolicited callers.

Janice Longbright was used to the response. Members of the public were easier to deal with than Met officers and their families, who treated her and the rest of the PCU staff like interlopers. 'I'll wait until he's awake,' said Janice, checking her watch and showing that she was prepared to settle in on the doorstep.

'He'll sleep right round the clock now.' Mrs Flowers opened the door wider and folded her arms across her chest, her husband's gatekeeper. 'It would be best to come back another day.'

'Mrs Flowers, I apologize for not calling first but if I leave without seeing him, George's career in the force is going to end tonight. Could you fetch him for me, please.'

That did the trick. Longbright waited patiently in the lounge, hearing muffled, urgent whispers behind the wall. She looked around the room. When you stepped into someone else's living space you always made assumptions; it was an observational skill that came with the job. Everything here had been chosen by a woman. Sergeant Flowers had no interest in his home because he chose to spend more time at work.

Six minutes later, George Flowers appeared, buttoning up a blue work shirt and smoothing down his hair.

'I thought someone might come around here,' he said, studying her. 'You're DI Longbright. I've heard all about you and your lot.'

'Sergeant Flowers, we have to clear this up,' she said. 'On

208

March the twelfth of this year a man being held under suspicion of arson committed suicide in the bathroom of Holborn Police Station while you were on night duty.'

'I've been over this with everyone concerned a dozen times already, and I've made an official statement to my own division which I'm sure you will have read.'

'I've no argument with what's in the statement. The problem is what you left out.' She paused to see if he would respond. 'Our pathologist's report on Mr Albu is going to be submitted today, and it will state that he was hanged with an elasticated belt, not with a strip of plastic torn from the mattress of his cell.'

Flowers' cheeks changed colour. 'You used your own pathologist. Why are you trying to stitch me up?'

'We just need to know exactly what happened. The bed cover had been cut with a penknife blade, and no knife was found on the deceased.'

He studied her in silence. She knew he would deny having anything to do with it. He was the type who would stay with his story no matter what happened. Huffing and eye-rolling failed to hide his panic.

'Before you speak, I want to check that you understand the implications of this. If you go on record insisting that you removed his belt, your testimony will change the verdict from suicide to murder by person or persons unknown. It seems obvious to me that you switched it because you forgot to take it from him when you booked him in. That's not a crime, George, it's an honest mistake.'

Flowers still said nothing but shifted awkwardly from one foot to the other.

'You've got one lad still at school and the other at uni, you have another twenty-three years on your mortgage and you're forty-six. I think I can save your job.'

'Negligence,' said Flowers finally, picking at his fingers.

'That's what they would say. That I caused his death by leaving him with the means to kill himself.'

'I don't think so,' replied Longbright. 'If Mr Albu had really wanted to kill himself he would have found a way to do it. We once had someone under arrest at Mornington Crescent who blocked a toilet bowl with paper and drowned himself. He couldn't do it in a cell because they're designed to prevent suicide, but the staff toilets aren't. Albu died in the toilet because Holborn has no provision for an in-cell facility. You didn't kill him, George.'

'I didn't do anything.' His gaze was steady and unflinching. 'That bloke was drunk and stank of petrol. I have no idea what his state of mind was like, and it's not my job to find out. All I know is that he wasn't wearing a belt. You can check the CCTV if you want. The cell has had a lot of occupants. Maybe one of them smuggled in a blade and started to cut the bed cover just to vandalize it. They do anything they can to show their disrespect. It's not a crime if none of us noticed.'

Longbright's conscience was clear; she had offered him a lifeline and Flowers had thrown it back at her.

She made her way across town to the ugly stone and glass box that housed the new Holborn Police Station. It was pelting with rain and her collapsible umbrella had done just that. The streets were suddenly deserted, improving the city no end.

As she reached the covered entrance, she tried to wipe the water from her face. Inside, she found herself alone. The duty desk was due to change at 8.00 p.m. It was now a quarter past and no one was around. She stopped a passing constable sporting the kind of weapons-grade acne that only afflicted the very young. He told her the incoming sergeant was running late because of flooding.

'Can you let me into the overnight cell?' she asked.

'Sorry, I can't do that without the duty officer's permission.' He looked apologetic.

'But he's not here.'

'You're PCU, aren't you?' He looked a little awed. 'I thought you'd been closed down.'

'We're on special assignment. I spoke to someone earlier.'

'They must have forgotten,' the constable replied. 'I was told not to let anyone down there by themselves.'

'Who said that?'

'Sergeant Flowers. He's off on sick leave at the moment. There's nothing I can do.'

'Fair enough.' Longbright ran a hand through her wet hair, making sure to get some water on the floor. 'Can I use the staff bathroom?'

He led her across the reception area and buzzed the door for her. 'Down the stairs, first door on the left.'

Inside the bathroom, she checked the sinks and taps. The place reeked of disinfectant. There were a few taped-up health and safety posters beside a mirror including 'Your Anonymous Tip-Off Helpline' and 'Call for a Free Chlamydia Kit'. Dispensers full of pink liquid soap were riveted to the wall. Nothing out of the ordinary. At the top of the rear wall was an opaque window covered in steel mesh. There was no handle and it looked as if it didn't open but she needed to be sure.

In the corridor outside she found a blue plastic chair and took it into the bathroom, placing it below the window. Hoping that the constable would remain upstairs to cover the empty desk, she climbed on the chair and pushed against the glass.

The window was sealed and unbreakable. Of course it would be. Overnight visitors were sometimes so drunk and full of anger that every edge and corner, every doorknob or imperfectly tightened screw became a possible cause of injury.

In the bathroom Albu had found a way to hang himself with a type of noose he could only have made if he'd had access to a knife.

Even setting aside the unlikeliness of the whole thing, it made no sense. If he was to be killed, why hadn't it happened in the alleyway near the bookshop? Or did it have to look as if he had taken his own life? No one would plan a murder in multiple stages: burn down a shop, blame an innocent, fake his suicide. It was just too complicated. Killers weren't usually very bright.

She returned the chair and headed upstairs.

'I thought you were going to dry your hair,' said the constable cheerfully.

'I think I'll stick with the wet look. What does Sergeant Flowers do when he's here all night?'

'He reads a lot of science fiction,' the constable told her. 'And he eats.'

'I'm going behind his desk – turn your back,' she warned. 'What does he eat?'

'Apples mostly. He's got this thing about getting the peel off in a single piece.'

In the bottom drawer she found a Swiss Army knife. It had so many blades and recesses that there was a good chance it had picked up plastic threads from the cell bed. She slipped it into her pocket.

'Who checks your CCTV?'

'Normally me but it's out of action at the moment. It's been out for a while. We're waiting for a service.'

'It's been out since Flowers went sick?'

'Yeah, about then.'

CCTV files were meant to be tamper-proof but she'd heard of staff getting into them. She was convinced now that Albu had been locked in the cell still wearing his belt. Proving it would be a problem if Flowers had cleaned up, but having made one mistake he had probably made others. Since it was impossible that Albu once dead had removed the belt from his own neck and substituted another material, the death would now appear on the books as unexplained, which the PCU classed as grounds for a murder investigation.

'Thanks anyway,' she told the constable, glancing out at the rain.

'Did you want the book?' the boy suddenly asked.

'What book?'

'The bloke who died. Albu.' He pointed vaguely in the direction of the cells. 'He had a little book in his jeans but it must have fallen out when he was lying down in his cell. I put it aside for you. Didn't George tell you?'

'Oh, yes,' she replied. 'Thanks for reminding me. I was supposed to pick it up.'

'Hang on.' He loped off and returned, handing her a tiny blue leather book, quite old, with onion-skin pages and gold edges. *The Poetry of Alfred Lord Tennyson.*

'You're a lifesaver.' She flashed him a smile and headed out to the staircase that led to the rainswept street.

25

OLD STUFF

Bryant's landlady was not a woman to be trifled with, even so soon after a stay in hospital. 'If you tell me you're going to be here for eight o'clock, that's when the dinner goes on the table,' Alma admonished, setting his reheated portion of stargazy pie before him.

'Madam, when I stare at a meal it's not supposed to stare back at me,' Bryant complained.

'The fish heads are meant to be above the crust like that. They're pilchards. It's a Cornish recipe.'

'You're from Antigua, not the West Country.'

'West Indies is still west.' She stuck her hands on her hips – never a good sign. 'You're having baked Alaska for dessert and I'm not from there either.'

'Then perhaps I should have a say in the weekly menu.'

'No thank you. I'm not having steak and kidney pudding every day, and crisps aren't a vegetable. Just try to get home on time.'

'I can't help the long hours. We've got a murderer on the loose.'

'You've *always* got a murderer on the loose. They're a bloody nuisance. Make them wait. Have you been to see John?'

'He's back at the unit.'

Alma looked horrified. 'He can't possibly be ready for work yet.'

'It's more harmful being stuck at home. Men are like parrots.'

'You mean they repeat everything you say.'

'No, they tear their feathers out if left unattended.' He propped a dust-encrusted copy of Gogol's *Diary of a Madman* against the cruet set and thrust a fork into his pie.

'Can you at least put that filthy thing down while you're eating? You'll give yourself indigestion.'

'This "filthy thing" is a masterpiece of Russian literature, madam, as you'd know if you'd ever opened a book.'

'Reading's never done you any good, has it? It's not stopped you from being rude to everyone. Instead of stuffing all those words into your head you could have given me a break and found yourself another wife. And Russians are nothing but trouble.'

Bryant tapped his book, releasing a shower of dirt from the pulverized binding, and spoke through a mouthful of pilchards. 'I was reading about the temple illusions of the ancient Greeks this morning and you didn't like me reading that either.'

'Only because it made you forget to lock the toilet door. You can't possibly be reading that rubbish for work.'

'I am, actually, and it's not rubbish. It will help me catch our man.'

'How do you know it's not a woman?'

'Because it hardly ever is. Over eighty per cent of all killers are male.'

'One day you'll make me change the percentage.' She closed

his book with great care and removed it from the dining table. 'What is this big case you're working on that's more important than your dinner?'

'I'm afraid that's classified information.'

'You think I'm going to tell the ladies at the church?'

A fair point, thought Bryant. Besides, he had always told her everything before. 'A woman named Chakira Rahman,' he began, 'she's—'

'Oh, I know all about that, it's been on the telly all afternoon.'

Bryant gratefully pushed away his pie and galloped into the living room, turning up the sound on the *BBC News*. A reporter was standing on the steps of St Martin-in-the-Fields interviewing the Reverend Stephen Mallory.

Bryant immediately rang his partner.

'Are you at home?' asked May, pre-empting him. 'I'm just around the corner from you.'

'You are? Then come by. There's a bucket of fish pie here that I'm desperate to get rid of.'

May arrived five minutes later to find another setting at the table. He folded his coat neatly on a chair and bent to kiss Alma's cheek. 'Alma, you're looking well. Are you feeling better?'

'Much better, thanks. You're the one we were all worried about. You've lost weight. Eat it all – he doesn't like it. Did they get the bullet out?'

'They gave it to me as a souvenir.' He took it from his pocket and passed it to her. She handled it as if it was the Koh-i-noor diamond.

Bryant sat well back as Alma ladled out hot pilchards. 'Who leaked the story?'

'I've a feeling Land might have put his foot in it,' said May. 'Unless someone was daft enough to talk to *Hard News*.'

'Ah – I think that was you. She told me you were after some

background information on your litigious millionaire businessman, Peter English. You shouldn't call people when you're on medication. I don't, any more.'

May was contrite. 'I wouldn't have told her anything about the case.'

'You wouldn't have to. She's incredibly suspicious. She'll have made the link at once, especially as you're rubbish at lying.'

May eyed his plate with suspicion. 'Have we heard how Michael Claremont is doing?'

'Janice called his private clinic earlier but wasn't allowed to speak to him.'

'What do you want to do?'

'Go after English, find out if he knew the victims.' There was nothing Bryant enjoyed more than interviewing someone who was dismissive of the police. 'Something else struck me as odd. Because of the locations of the deaths, neither of the victims could be left *in situ* for long.'

'Meaning what?' asked May.

'Meaning it wasn't possible to secure the site for forensics. Claremont lying in the road; Rahman dead on the steps. Dan had a moan about that. Ideally he likes people to be attacked in a more controlled environment.'

May tried to avoid catching the glassy eye of a pilchard. 'We have to spread the net wider and find more witnesses. There was supposed to be a facial recognition system working in the Strand but we've had nothing from it so far. The footage from the camera on Duncannon Street shows Chakira Rahman passing behind pillars just before the attack. The City of London Surveillance Centre are putting together a shot-reel for us.'

Alma opened the kitchen window. From downstairs came the shriek of their neighbour's TV. 'You can't rely on technology to find him,' said Bryant. 'Take a look at those.' He pointed to a wad of papers from the briefcase he had left on the sideboard. 'They're the witness reports from St Martin-in-the-Fields, a completely contradictory set of statements. The only thing they agree on is that there were others on the steps, and one person came close to the victim. We've got four sightings of a man, three of a woman.'

May read for a few minutes, then abandoned his meal and took the pages to the floor, where he began laying them out. 'There's a timeline here,' he said. 'We can work out when each of the witnesses arrived near the steps and departed. So these ones' – he waved a hand over the right side of the pages – 'are in the *before* group, heading towards Rahman, and these are predominantly *after* her encounter with the stranger who passed by. You see the problem.'

Bryant knew it was almost impossible to reconstruct an event exactly as it had happened. Even after decades of analysing the Zapruder footage of the Kennedy assassination, nothing definitive had ever been produced. Accurate recollection wasn't helped by the fact that witnesses did not like to give fragmentary accounts, and remade events into miniature stories.

May pressed his hand on the pages. 'Arthur, it takes a lot of nerve to attack someone in a public place. This is the action of someone operating with complete confidence. We need to look at his next target.'

'Very well. The third line of the song is: " 'When will you pay me?' say the bells of Old Bailey." '

'What do you know about that?'

'It's usually assumed that the bells refer to the twelfth-century church of St Sepulchre-without-Newgate.'

'The one near the Old Bailey.'

'That's right, by the Central Criminal Court. And the Fleet Prison nearby was mainly for debtors, so the "When will you pay me?" part makes sense. St Sepulchre is opposite, or *without* it. And it has an unusual bell, a handbell in a glass case fixed to one of the pillars inside the church in the south of the nave. It's known as the Execution Bell and was rung outside every condemned prisoner's cell at midnight before his execution. It's probably where we get "Here comes a candle to light you to bed" as well, seeing as the church clerk would have needed a lantern to find his way to the cell.'

'Which is all very fascinating but hardly helps us stop a killer,' said May.

'It's worse than that,' Bryant pointed out. 'The vicar won't let us put officers inside the church or in its grounds. He has the right to do so, but it means we'll have to get Met officers on the pavement near the junction with the Old Bailey, and that can't happen until tomorrow morning.'

'So in other words, anything could occur at any time to anyone and we have no way of stopping it,' said May.

'But we'll have done our job by reporting back on Michael Claremont's emotional state,' Bryant said. 'Everyone agrees he was mentally fine before the attack. They can write it off as an accident and say Chakira Rahman died in an unrelated case of mistaken identity or something, and everyone can go back to feeling safe and comfortable.'

'Until it happens again,' said May.

While she waited for her coffee in the Ladykillers Café, Janice Longbright took the blue leather volume of poetry from her pocket. Considering Cristian Albu had been found lying on his back in a puddle of linseed oil, the book had survived remarkably well. She flicked through it, stopping here and there to read a passage. As a teenager she had copied sections into her diary and memorized them.

'What are you reading?' asked Niven, handing over her flat white. She held up the cover. 'Oh, him. "Charge of the Light Brigade". "Theirs not to reason why, / Theirs but to do and die." What a load of old bollocks. I can't stand him and I have to face him every day.' Noting Longbright's quizzical look, he pointed over her shoulder to a pair of lines painted along the opposite wall of the café.

Kind hearts are more than coronets,
And simple faith than Norman blood.

'It's associated with the café,' Niven said. 'I don't get it myself.'

'There's nothing to get,' said Longbright, paying him. 'It means breeding isn't everything.'

She had never noticed the other painted slogans, posters and bits of memorabilia around the walls. They all related to the group of post-war films known as the Ealing comedies. The café was named after one of the most famous, which had been shot in King's Cross, just around the corner. She tried to recall the name of the poem that housed the quote on the wall and failed. She was about to look it up but saw she was running late and quickly rose.

'Oi, have you just left me cash?' called Niven. 'Haven't you got plastic? Nobody wants the old-fashioned stuff any more.'

'And yet you have a café dedicated to it,' she replied. 'Figure that one out.'

26

BECALMED

'I don't like him,' said Meera Mangeshkar as she changed at the staff lockers in the first-floor bathroom. 'My mother says you can't trust a man in tight trousers.'

'That's because she's obsessed with fertility,' said Colin Bimsley, swapping his blue PCU sweatshirt for what he referred to as his 'evening wear', a faded red T-shirt from the Repton Amateur Boxing Club.

'Plus, his beard is too neat, he smells too nice and I can't understand a bloody word he says.'

'That's because Mr Floris is public school. They didn't talk like that in your Southall comp, did they? He's probably a regular bloke once you get to know him.'

Meera shook her head. 'He still has to report everything back to his relatives at the Home Office. Faraday's done this to us before. What's that awful smell?'

Colin held up a bottle of aftershave. 'Mr Bryant gave it to me. Jaguar for Men. Price three shillings and sixpence. Also available as Soap on a Rope.'

'It smells like Toilet Duck.'

'Floris was pushed into this assignment by someone a lot more powerful than Faraday. But just to quell your suspicious little mind, let's find out from the man himself.'

'How do we do that?' asked Meera, pulling a black sweater over her head.

'Simple. We take him for a cleansing ale.'

'That's your answer to everything, isn't it?'

Colin threw his hands wide. 'Look around you. There's nothing going on. The investigation is stuck. The killer is dragging us around by the nose. All of our leads are dead ends. We're becalmed. We might as well take him to the pub and pump him for information.'

Meera sighed. 'Come on then.'

'I don't really drink,' said Floris when they offered to take him to the Racketeer for a beer.

Meera was incredulous. 'That's a challenge. You have to come for a quencher, it's traditional.'

'Yeah, I could smash a pint in the face,' said Colin. 'And I already chose the boozer for us. A little hipster hangout, top of the topknots, Banterbury Cathedral.'

Floris eyed them both suspiciously. 'Just one then.'

Taking a tray of glasses to the pub's candlelit basement, Colin settled on a sofa that looked as if it had lost a fight with a bear. A fake fire flickered in the grate, washing the floor with orange light.

Janice Longbright was in the corner of another sofa with Sidney, taking her through a folder of documents. In accordance with the rules of public house society the group had split in order to make rounds affordable, although they were all listening to each other's conversations.

Colin paid the barman to keep delivering beers until Floris started slurring. He had no meat on his bones so it didn't look as if it would take too long.

'I imagine it's a bit of a culture shock, coming to us after Whitehall.' Colin wiped a foam moustache from his upper lip.

'It's more chaotic than I'd expected,' said Floris. 'We only ever hear terrible things about Mr Bryant. I didn't know my boss had left you with no resources.'

Meera removed a slice of orange from her rum. 'You don't know the half of it, mate. Faraday's taken everything from us but old Bryant still has a few friends in government who can help out. Although I think we're running out of favours.'

Floris sipped his lager as if he'd never tried alcohol before. 'Perhaps you can explain something I don't understand.'

'Entropy. Relativity. Consciousness,' suggested Meera, sucking her fingers. Colin glared at her.

'I'm told the unit was founded by theorists and academics. Back-room boffins who were never meant to go out in the field.'

'The thinking was different in those days,' interjected Janice. 'It was believed that crime would one day be computed out of existence. We thought we'd understand human behaviour so completely that we'd be able to predict it and stop it from happening.'

'Your current investigation proves the theory wrong.' Floris set down his beer. 'You can't explain why people are being targeted. The unit appears dysfunctional. Your detectives' supposedly instinctive methodology doesn't seem to get results. You have no answers and the situation feels as if it's worsening, but you act as if it's just another working day.'

'Because that's what it is for us,' said Colin. 'We're not the Met. We don't run shifts. Even street cops go home eventually. They spend their days trying to stop kids from stabbing each other but don't go to the pub to discuss antisocial initiatives; they go to let off steam.'

'And Mr Bryant?' Floris checked to make sure he had not come in.

'He's different,' said Janice. 'He's looking for the impossible.

Real, definitive answers. He doesn't like Faraday hindering us with rules.'

'Mr Faraday has no control over me.' Floris loosened his tie. He was overheating. Some of his words were starting to elide. 'It was my idea to get the case to you, not his. You know the system from the ground up. This is my first job after university.'

Meera coughed rum over Floris's trousers. He turned down her offer to mop him dry.

'I've tried to tone down my accent. I think I'm starting to sound a bit more street.'

'Mate,' said Colin, 'trust me, you don't. First you've got to widen your mouth for vowels, lose most of your Ls and Ts, and watch Bob Hoskins in *The Long Good Friday*. He speaks proper Queen's English. An absolute ledge.'

'I take it you're both from London.'

'I'm Southall, then Elephant & Castle,' said Meera. 'He's East End. It's stamped through him like a stick of rock.'

The barman set down a cold collation. 'Ah, my master cheeseboardier,' said Colin, passing around plates.

'That's not a word.' Meera checked out the board. 'No pork scratchings.'

'I didn't mean to follow the rest of my family's big flat feet into policing,' Colin said. 'I wanted to be a boxer until I got whacked in the head and was left with spatial issues.'

'What sort of issues?'

'He walks into things,' said Meera, stealing a chunk of cheddar.

'It's a perceptual problem called Irlen Syndrome. The unit was prepared to take me.'

'I thought I'd find you all sitting behind desks in darkened rooms staring at screens,' said Floris.

'When the PCU started out it was all lab coats and slide rules until somebody realized you can't police people without talking to them. So a lot of it is still old school. Hands-on stuff, blagging your way into flats and going through bins.'

Meera could sense that Floris disagreed with the approach but was keeping his counsel. He'd never had to get his manicured hands dirty. He drained his glass and set it down. 'It seems to me that you do all the work and your detectives get all the acclaim.'

'The old man likes the limelight,' said Meera.

'That's not fair,' said Colin. 'He closes the cases.'

'So you don't mind Mr Bryant taking the credit?' Floris was intently gauging their reactions. 'We only ever hear about him and his partner in Whitehall, never anyone else.'

'We're not looking to be famous,' said Colin.

'Neither are they, I'm sure. But how will you ever advance through the unit if they remain at the top?'

'They'll see us right.' Colin looked to Meera for support but failed to catch her eye. The seed of doubt had been planted and the conversation quickly cooled.

Further along, Janice was struggling to understand Sidney, who sat poised and static, clutching a medicinal-looking pink cocktail.

'You need a few years' experience under your belt. Perhaps you should come back when you have more to offer.'

'It will be too late then. I'll be full of their rules. I can be useful now. You were young when you started.'

'Nineteen,' Janice admitted. 'But it was different in those days. None of us knew what we were getting into. I didn't go to university. I got the job because they saw something in me and took a leap of faith.'

Sidney stared down at her drink. 'They need to take a leap of faith with me.'

Longbright sat back in the sofa. 'And what are you going to teach us about policing this country?'

'I can see how our history drags us down. There's a new generation arriving that doesn't care about the past. You can't understand them and they won't understand you. I can bridge that.'

'I don't understand. How?'

'We never lived in any one country for long when I was growing up, so I never made friends. I lived online and studied. But I only studied the subjects that interested me.'

'Like this unit.'

'It became an obsession. So you see, I have a head start.'

'And that makes you think you can bring something fresh to this case.'

'To every case. I know them all, even the early investigations that Mr Bryant gave silly names to. The Leicester Square Vampire, the Dagenham Strangler, the Shepherd's Bush Blowtorch Murders. One hundred and twenty-eight major homicide cases on public record, plus all the others that were never listed.'

'OK, you've done your reading. But Mr Bryant doesn't think like anyone else. And no one thinks like him.'

Sidney held her gaze until she broke away.

'You can't possibly. The depth of his knowledge—'

'I don't have that yet but I know how his mind works because mine's the same.'

Janice tilted her head, trying to understand this delicate-featured girl in crazy trainers, one orange, one lemon. 'How is that possible?'

'I met him a long time ago,' said Sidney.

Floris knocked back the remains of his beer and accepted another. He was speaking rapidly and becoming inarticulate.

'Anything my father wanted he got, although I guess he didn't want the heart attack, and certainly not during an embassy ball. He told my mother he wanted her but dumped her, just as he'd done with his ex-wife. He certainly didn't want me. He once pulled a gun on a maid at a funeral. That's when they were still living in South Africa with my uncle, who became my aunt but no one ever mentioned it. We owned a cheetah that got loose at a party. Cheers, all.' Floris picked up his beer and drained it. 'Actually, I don't normally drink this much.'

'No shit,' said Meera, awed.

'Admit it, you fancy him,' said Colin after they had manoeuvred Floris on to his tube train. 'You were all over him like a rash. All it takes is a noncey haircut and a funny accent and you come over all *Pride and Prejudice*. I'm surprised you didn't get the vapours and pass out.'

'Well, what about you?' Meera shot back as they headed off along the wet pavement. 'All it takes to become your bezzie is a couple of hours in the nearest boozer.'

They argued all the way home until Meera realized that she was following Colin back to his flat, and he said well as you're nearly here you may as well stay over, and she said *may as well*, that's not very flattering is it, and he said I'm sorry your royal highness you know what I mean, and she said no, what, and he said I really, really want you to stay with me tonight, and she said that's better yeah I'll stay over then but don't think I'm going to stay every time you ask because I'm no booty call, and he said you got that right, and besides I can't get the duvet cover on by myself and the kitchen needs a tidy-up and she punched him hard in the stomach.

An hour after they left the pub an event occurred in another part of London that brought their respite to an end.

27

THE SHOUT

Script extract from Arthur Bryant's 'Peculiar London' walking tour guide. (Meet at St Paul's tube station. For details of upcoming tours consult my fully updated website. I'm joking.)

Straight ahead of you, ladies and gentleman, behold the Old Bailey, a bailey being another name for a city wall. The Central Criminal Court of England and Wales has been housed in several buildings near this one since the sixteenth century, but the current edifice was only built in 1902. Anyone can visit the public gallery and sit in on a case. It's good fun so long as you don't smuggle in a meat pie and open it in your lap before realizing it's really, really hot.

The twenty-two-ton golden statue on the top of its dome is Lady Justice. She holds the sword of retribution and the scales of justice, and contrary to popular belief she's not blindfolded, which explains a lot.

Inside, the courtrooms are all arranged the same way, with the accused standing in the dock facing the witness box and the judges. Before gas lighting the rooms were dark and shadowy, so mirrors were attached over the bar to reflect light on to the faces of the accused. The members of the court believed that studying their features would help them decide innocence or guilt.

In the nineteenth century, the courthouse was still part of Newgate Prison, and in 1868 anyone could catch the tube to see a good hanging, but Charles Dickens helped to get the practice stopped in public. Newgate was always an overpoweringly sinister place. It remained in use for over seven hundred years and didn't shut until the start of the twentieth century.

There's a secret tunnel running between the Old Bailey and the church of St Sepulchre-without-Newgate, so that the chaplain could nip over with his execution bell and administer last rites without having to plough through the waiting crowds. The ritual involved him ringing the handbell twelve times and reciting a bit of doggerel.

The next morning the prisoner would be given flowers and made to listen to another prayer before getting his neck stretched. He was led along Dead Man's Walk through a series of white-brick doorways that became incrementally smaller and smaller, a rare example of an architect practising psychological torture prior to the building of the Shard. At the end of this tunnel a huge crowd would gather to chuck rocks and rotten fruit at the condemned prisoner, and here he would eventually be buried. The church had a Watch House with windows facing into its graveyard so that the wardens could keep an eye out for Resurrectionists.

In 1670 a couple of Quakers (one of them the future founder of Pennsylvania) were arrested for preaching, and the Old Bailey's jury found them innocent. The judge refused to accept the verdict and locked the jurors away without food or water until they returned a guilty verdict. Instead of doing so they got a writ of habeas corpus issued, and established the right of juries to give verdicts according to their convictions. A big result for democracy. A few of our present-day leaders would do well remembering that.

Take a look around. The Old Bailey, the church and the Viaduct Tavern pub across the road look a bit stranded now. Few workers scurrying past this great court of justice appreciate its notoriety as a place of vengeful punishment.

The April wind had turned suddenly bitter. London was entering the season of unpredictable weather that usually lasted until Wimbledon. During this time it felt cold enough for a jacket and warm enough not to wear it.

PC Donnalee Martin stood on the corner of Green Arbour and Old Bailey, sweating slightly, looking over at the curved façade of the Viaduct Tavern. There were few cars and even fewer pedestrians. St Sepulchre was dark, its doors locked, hardly the welcoming community church its rector wished it to be. There were still some forty churches left in the Square Mile, but she imagined the area's residents would struggle to make up a single congregation.

It was just after midnight and PC Martin had only just come on shift. She hadn't expected to be stationed out here tonight, especially not until 7.00 a.m., but a directive had come through requesting officers for surveillance around St Sepulchre and the Old Bailey.

Usually some intel leaked through, but tonight they had

been told nothing. One of the superintendents had suggested it was linked to the death of a woman who had fallen down the stairs of a church, but how that connected to being sent here was a mystery. She was supposed to be paired with another officer, but the shift had started and he'd yet to appear.

The Square Mile was a lonely place to be posted late on a weeknight. It felt as if it had entered a state of suspended animation that only a workforce could bring back to life. There were probably more homes here now than there had been a hundred years ago, flashy penthouses tucked behind and above the endless offices, but where did anyone do their food shopping?

The sliding of the window alerted her, and a shout. She glanced around. There was nothing at ground level. Just past the curving cul-de-sac of Green Arbour she saw a man in the second-floor window of an office building.

As she watched, he took a little skip up on to the window ledge, then on to the stone sill. He turned his head and stared down at her. PC Martin was so surprised by his attention that she froze. Before she could call out he stepped off the sill, sending himself to the pavement.

He hit a rectangular brick flowerbed just in front of the building. One highly polished shoe flew off and bounced into the gutter. From where she was standing she could not see his fallen body. She looked back, wondering if there were any other witnesses, but the street was empty.

As she rounded the end of the concrete flowerbed his right leg appeared, bent forward at the knee. Under the yellow street lighting a spatter of blood showed up black on the paving stones.

She knelt down beside him, feeling for his pulse. His head looked like someone had taken a bite out of it. Unfortunately the corner of the flowerbed had caused a compound skull fracture. Blood still pumped from opened bone. An unmoving eye looked up at her. The small shiny object she picked up from the pavement turned out to be the crown on his front tooth. Unnerved, she could only reach for her phone.

By the time Janice Longbright arrived an EMT tent had been erected over the body. She had been the only member of staff still on duty at the PCU when the call came through. She took PC Martin to one side. 'Why were you out here by yourself?'

'There was supposed to be someone else on my shift but he didn't show up.'

'Always the night when something happens, eh?' She handed the officer her coffee. 'Go on, you need it more than me. You didn't go up there?'

'No, he was down here.'

'You say a shout attracted your attention. You mean from him?'

'I suppose so. I wasn't concentrating.' PC Martin looked embarrassed.

'But you heard the window open. Was that before or after the shout?'

'I think it was before. The shout came from inside the room.' There was a look of dread on PC Martin's face. 'I'm sorry, I should be better at this; I take enough statements.'

'It's always harder when it's you,' said Longbright patiently. 'How many voices?'

'Just one.'

'So he was, what, arguing with himself?'

'I guess so. He sounded surprised.'

Longbright looked at the still-open window. 'What is that building?'

PC Martin craned her neck back and looked up with half-closed eyes. 'I think there's some kind of financial company on the ground floor.'

'Do you wear glasses?'

'Disposable contacts. I usually – I thought I had some in my jacket.'

'Who's up there now?'

'A couple of my mob. I keep seeing him drop from that window like a dead weight. It was awful. His head hit the edge of the flowerbed with a terrible smack.'

'You saw him standing in the window. You heard him shout. Is there anything else you can remember?'

'There was something creepy about the way he stared at me.'

Longbright followed her eyeline. 'He just suddenly looked at you.'

'Yes, then at the church, and finally over at the Old Bailey.'

'Have you been over there?' Longbright ran across the road and checked the church's entrance and the wall of the Old Bailey, but found nothing.

'I thought of something else,' said PC Martin when she returned. 'The light.'

'What about it?'

'It was out. The room behind him was in darkness. He was only lit by the street lamps. And the way he moved was odd.'

'In what way?'

'Like he was dancing. He sort of swayed, then suddenly stepped up on to the window ledge. It was just an odd sort of movement.'

'Why do you think it was odd?'

'I'm not really sure. It didn't look natural. More like a skip. If I was going to climb out on to a ledge I'd grip the window frame on either side and pull myself up. His hands, that's it – they stayed by his sides. I'm sorry, it's not much.'

'You did good. I'm going inside,' said Longbright. 'Sit down and have a quiet think. See if there's anything you've missed.'

As she headed into the building Dan Banbury arrived and was annoyed to find the crime scene already tented. Across the road, behind the engulfing walls of St Sepulchre, the wall-mounted glass box that housed the executioner's bell was being smashed apart. The handbell was lifted out and stolen away, its task of ringing a pathway for the condemned not yet complete.

28

DEMOCRACY IN ACTION

By dawn's early light, the Peculiar Crimes Unit looked as if it had been bombed.

Nobody had been able to get the landlines working properly. Calls made everyone sound as if they were phoning from the bottom of the sea. One floorboard in the first-floor corridor was operating as a seesaw, and the flushing of the second-floor toilet periodically caused coffee cups in the kitchen to explode (it later transpired that the shaking pipes had the power to shift crockery along an unsecured shelf. 'Magnetic energy,' according to Maggie Armitage. 'Wrong-sized rawlplugs,' according to Dave One).

Speaking of whom, the two Daves had Frankenstein-stitched cabling across the building, turning it into an assault course and somehow electrifying everything made of metal in Raymond Land's office. By 8.00 a.m. the PCU staff were crowded into the operations room awaiting the arrival of their boss. May had made it back to the unit, and looked rejuvenated. Bryant was muttering to himself and filling his whiteboard from corner to corner with crabbed handwriting.

Land appeared to have slept in his car, even though he didn't own one. He stared at them with one jaundiced eye, then the other. *Perhaps he's turning into his pigeon*, Bryant thought.

'Do you want the good news or the bad news?' Land asked. 'Actually there is no good news, just bad and really bad, starting with the latest fatality, who turns out to have been a highly respected judge. I'll allow that to sink in for a moment, shall I? Who will tomorrow's victim be, I wonder? The Queen of Sweden or Elton John?'

'At the moment the death is being reported as a suicide,' said May.

Land glared at him. 'Judge Kenneth Tremain, working late and deciding on a whim to chuck himself from a second-floor window. He was due in the Old Bailey this morning to preside over a fraud case indirectly involving a certain Peter English, cited on this board as a Person of Interest, if I'm reading Mr Bryant's hieroglyphics accurately.'

'We haven't been able to get a foot in the door,' said May.

'You're officers of the law, not double-glazing salesmen.'

'Salespeople,' said Sidney without looking up from her notebook.

'What was he doing so close to the Old Bailey late at night anyway?' Land asked.

'The Central Criminal Court has a number of leased apartments nearby so that senior staff don't have to bother with hotels on late nights,' said Longbright. 'Tremain was in one of them doing some research. Dan, you went into the building.'

'There's a videophone in the flat, but its image quality is appalling,' said Banbury, rising to attach photographs of the building to the whiteboard. 'There's a camera over the main entrance. We've got footage of everyone who entered and left from the front. The problem is the back, which opens on to a walkway behind bushes.'

'Wait, he shouted, according to . . .' Bryant searched for his notes.

'PC Donnalee Martin,' said Longbright.

'So he was arguing with someone inside the flat.'

'Now hang on a minute . . .' Land began, raising an objecting hand.

'It's a couple of feet up to the window ledge.' Banbury added more shots. 'There's nothing below the sill. When he climbed out he didn't raise his hands to pull himself up. Instead she says he managed a sort of skip. He stared at her, then the church and the courthouse, moving his head to do so.'

Bryant's brow furrowed, although one more wrinkle made no difference.

'But that isn't how people look at things.' Dan drew the sightlines on the board. 'Our eyes use saccades, rapid eye movements between fixed points. When we see something that grabs our attention we move our eyes, not our heads, otherwise we'd look like robots. Then there's the odd climbing-out action with the hands kept straight down.'

'That fits.' Bryant looked from one puzzled face to the next. 'You must see how suggestive the eye and hand gestures are.'

'He killed himself,' cried Land. 'I don't know what you're on about.'

'Of course you don't, it would be like a cow trying to follow *Hamlet*, but I think this young lady might know.'

'He was already dead when he fell,' said Sidney, finally paying full attention.

'Precisely. Dan, please continue.'

The interruption threw Banbury, who had to refer to his notes. 'I went inside just after 4.00 a.m. I would have been there earlier but the traffic coming through Croydon was surprisingly—'

'Get on with it,' snapped Land. 'Why are middle-aged men always so interested in arterial roads?'

'I reached the room just after the local officers had finished trashing it.'

'So you didn't get anything?'

'I didn't say that. Even though the scene was contaminated I could see that someone else had been there. The floor rugs are new, so I got heel prints. Killer and victim.'

'Wait, back up,' said Land, raising his hands. 'At the moment this is still a suicide. The man stepped out of an upstairs window. You can't just make sweeping judgements. Were there two distinct sets of footprints?'

'No,' Banbury admitted. 'The rugs are woollen. But the patterns of movement suggest two.'

Bryant took the floor. 'Tremain hit the corner of the brick flowerbed in a way that smashed his frontal bone and opened up the coronal suture behind it. But according to Giles he also had a broken neck. The two traumas weren't dependent upon the same directional force. In other words, the injuries occurred separately.'

'And if that's the case I suppose you know how they were inflicted,' said Land.

Bryant rearranged the photographs. 'The judge's attacker broke his neck, set him down, opened the window and manoeuvred him outside.'

'Why on earth would he do that?' Land hated complications.

'His grievance may not be with these people but with what they stand for. He's taking them off their pedestals and showing that they have feet of clay, so they die by accidents or suicides, anything but murder. Confuse, distract, obfuscate: these are magicians' tricks.'

'So he wants it to look like Tremain killed himself,' added May.

'He could see that PC Martin was on duty. In her hi-vis jacket it was impossible to miss her. He showed Tremain climbing on to the window ledge by hiking him up and shoving out his right leg, but he couldn't make the movement look natural because the judge was heavy and his arms hung at his sides. Still, it was important to make PC Martin see everything. He wasn't to know that she had forgotten her contact lenses. He moved Tremain's head so that it looked like he was staring at the church – it was a bit blatant but he needed to connect the death to the others.'

'*Why?*' begged Land. 'Why does it have to look connected?'

'He doesn't think we're joining the dots. He wants recognition. He made sure Tremain went head-first, hoping injuries incurred in the fall would cover any marks he'd left, and we now have a matching MO.'

'How is that matching?' asked Land. 'It's nothing like the others.'

Bryant ticked off the points on tobacco-tarnished fingers. 'They're pre-planned, they're witnessed in public, they fit a song everyone knows. Claremont didn't suffer a mishap, Rahman didn't slip on the church steps and Tremain didn't suddenly decide to kill himself.'

'Then why make it look like they did?' Land persisted.

'Because—' Bryant began.

'Because it gives the killer a smokescreen,' said Sidney. Everyone waited for Bryant's reaction. Interrupters did not normally survive for long in the operations room.

Bryant nodded at the intern. 'Misinformation is his secret weapon. What he's doing and what he wants us to think he's doing are two different things.'

Raymond had the beginnings of a migraine. 'So what is he actually doing?'

'Perhaps he wants his targets to see that they've sinned in the eyes of God.'

'Fine, I'll subpoena an assortment of higher spiritual beings as witnesses. You're just making wild guesses now, aren't you? This is what it's come down to. The unit's celebrated left-field thinking is in fact a tombola of random thoughts.'

'You could put it like that.' Bryant considered the idea. 'Add this to our tombola – the handbell from St Sepulchre-without-Newgate was stolen last night. The church was locked but the staff are profligate with keys, so it was fairly easily accessed. The bell has a place in history but no monetary value. Its glass case was smashed. There was nothing left behind.' He shot Land a meaningful look. 'Why would somebody take it, if not to point public attention back towards the rhyme?'

Seen from a distance they appeared as a pair of sentinels, standing motionless at the railings of Waterloo Bridge, looking towards the Tower of London.

The sacrament took place during the course of every investigation. It was a rite of continuity and an homage to Bryant's lost love, who had died at the spot where they stood. Police officers are all a little superstitious: walls are touched, items stored in a certain order, working nights feel good or bad. Bryant and May stood on Waterloo Bridge, either at the end of the day or around this time, just before noon, in the calm lacuna before the lunchtime stampede.

The skyline resembled the contents of a knife drawer upended, but as rain silvered the surface of the Thames the buildings were reduced so that they appeared as they had in earlier centuries: low and dark. When the tide retreated this far the grey-green stones of the embankment were exposed and the shoreline looked ramparted.

The detectives were armed with umbrellas and coffees, and in Bryant's case a pipe, a walking stick and a croissant filled with apricot jam, although how he managed to eat and smoke at the same time had always been a mystery to May.

'After all this time I still see her,' said Bryant, chewing

ruminatively. 'I'll always associate Nathalie with the river. Hard not to, considering how I lost her.'

'You couldn't have done anything more than you did,' said May.

'Youthful high spirits. No reason to die.' Bryant had barely heard him. He stared down into the murky waters and into another time. 'The night of her eighteenth birthday,' he murmured. 'She'd climbed on to the balustrade and was walking along it. I should never have let her, but we'd been celebrating at the Anchor and were both a bit tipsy. I remember the bus honking, the driver thinking I was about to step back into the road, and how the noise made her start. When I turned around to grab her she'd gone. I jumped into the water but the current was too strong. I was instantly pulled under and had trouble saving myself. Nathalie couldn't swim. As I felt the stones beneath my feet I knew at that moment my world had ended. The search teams dragged the river for weeks, but never found her body. At this point there is nothing between where we stand and the infinity of the sea.'

May respectfully waited for his partner's memories to settle. Tilting back his umbrella, he tested the rain. 'I think we should talk about the case.'

Bryant came back. 'Of course.'

'I checked to see if our captain of industry, Peter English, left his residence last night. His assistant told me he was home, and his wife and children could vouch for him. I put in a formal request for an interview but it looks as though I'm unlikely to get it. English is setting up some kind of business initiative with the government so they're bound to protect their investment.'

'He's not above the law.' Bryant eyed his partner through raindrops and pipe smoke.

'Unless those in power are covering for him.'

'John, our country has a centuries-old tradition of being

fed up with its leaders. When democracy is working correctly *nobody* is satisfied. Even so, they don't usually offer sanctuary to murderers.' He finished his croissant and dusted flakes into the Thames. 'The fraud case will have to await a new judge. I can see why you want to go after English. He's a good fit with the victims, but don't go looking for conspiracies. We need to find a real connection between them. I'm consulting my experts about this.'

'Arthur, your experts are a bunch of mumbling dysfunctionals who hold their trousers up with string,' said May. 'I'm not dealing with psychics, necromancers or astrologers. I'd end up doing something they didn't see coming.'

'Very well. Janice can talk to the Conspirators' Club.'

'When you say conspirators . . .' May began.

'They're academic theorists, John. They feed me information I wouldn't otherwise hear about. Very little of it is of any use at all, but occasionally they point me in the right direction.'

May winced. Most officers of the law held their cards close to their chests. Bryant was fabulously indiscreet. 'If you're going off to talk to crazy people again, you can't let Floris find out what you're up to.'

'Don't worry, nothing will get back to him. The people I consult are cheerfully untroubled by social skills. The last time I went to a Conspirators' Club dinner they pelted me with boiled potatoes for suggesting that George Michael was dead.'

May raised his profile to the breeze, looking, Bryant noted, like one of Landseer's noble stone lions. 'I don't understand why some people insist on believing in alternatives to the truth.'

'Belief is the opposite of knowledge.' Bryant returned the lid to his coffee and placed it in his accommodating coat pocket. 'Even so, trusting facts is not enough; you need the

mind of an inventor. Churchill's boffins built the first lim-
pet mine with the aid of a porridge bowl and some aniseed
balls. Sometimes it's important to look at problems from
the side.'

'I know if I look sideways I'll miss something right in front
of me. I've always been rather straightforward, I'm afraid.'

'And it's one of your finest qualities, old chap. But lateral
thinking is a necessity nowadays.' Bryant leaned over the
parapet and knocked out the walnut bowl of his Spitfire.
'You always used to know where you stood, especially with
Londoners. Butcher, milkman, secretary, cleaning lady.
Nearly everyone did something tangible and practical for a
living. Set hours, nine to five, weekends in the garden with
the kids. You could arrest someone more easily if you knew
where they were. Not any more. Who knows what people do
now? Entrepreneur, influencer, money-mover, data-miner.
Do they have more satisfying lives than bakers? Twenty million ghost workers under minimum wage are doing all the
boring jobs we failed to automate. What if our criminal only
exists as an online cyber-thingy originating in the Philip-
pines? How do you find someone hidden in a digital labour
force? I wasn't trained to separate guilt from innocence on a
laptop.'

'Then concentrate on the parts you're good at and leave the
rest to me,' said May.

Bryant looked pointedly at his partner's damaged chest.
'Do you think you're up to it?'

'Arthur, if you can do it, I can too.'

He sipped his coffee, breathing steam from beneath his
umbrella. 'What is that supposed to mean? I'm in the pink.'

May gave him an old-fashioned look. 'I presume you remember thinking that the war was still on? We all assumed you had
Alzheimer's and it turned out you'd poisoned yourself.'

Bryant held up a forefinger. 'One time. I made one mistake.'

'You got strangled in the British Library and had the unit quarantined.'

'Pfft. Those are just facts.'

A truck thundered past, spraying rain-mist over them. May turned to face his partner. 'Suppose an Oranges & Lemons killer doesn't exist and Peter English is outsourcing hits on his enemies? He's halfway through, with three more to go, and then, "Here comes a chopper to chop off your head." But whose head?'

Bryant set down his pipe to reach into his coat pocket, which was playing a horrendously off-key theremin version of 'Bow, bow, ye lower middle classes' from *Iolanthe*. He read the text message. 'It appears your request to meet Peter English has been processed after all. He's expecting to meet you in an hour's time.'

29

RATTLING THE CAGE

The two Daves had managed to find the missing leg of the unit chief's desk and glue it back on, and even Stumpy the one-legged pigeon was back on Land's windowsill eyeing him malevolently. In order to feel as if everything had completely returned to normal Land needed something to go spectacularly wrong, and at two o'clock in the afternoon it did so.

He stared at his phone in horror.

'We're posting the piece on our site in one hour,' Paula Lambert told him. 'I wondered if you'd like to comment.'

'Where are you getting your information?'

'You know our sources are protected, Raymond. Your extremely minimal press release suggests that Justice Kenneth Tremain committed suicide, but we're hearing that he was murdered. Why are you hiding the truth?'

'How could you possibly have heard that? Let me put you on hold for a moment.' After trying Bryant's number and getting no answer, he called Longbright. 'Janice – where are you? It sounds like you're in a pub. Oh, you are. The press think we deliberately falsified the briefing on Tremain. We'll be accused of a cover-up prior to an Old Bailey trial. It'll look like we're working for Peter bloody English. Try and find out where they're getting their intelligence.' He switched calls to Paula. 'Obviously we can only give you the information we have at the time.'

'So you're changing your story now? It will throw suspicion on the participants in a major fraud case,' Lambert warned. 'We'll also be running a sidebar pointing out that the detectives in charge are searching through a compendium of nursery rhymes for a solution.'

Land was outraged. 'Who told you that?'

'It's true, isn't it?'

'A path of inquiry only, because of the locations, and one that was quickly dismissed.' The pigeon stared at him with one orange eye as if to say, *She'll never believe you.* 'We have other avenues of exploration. We'll be addressing your speculations very shortly.' *I wonder if it's too late to get back to the Isle of Wight before then*, he thought.

He could hear Paula tapping a pen against her teeth. 'Are you going to tell us he was murdered?'

'You'll have to wait to find out,' said Land. 'You only have to report the news, not manufacture it. I'm trying to keep this unit together, Paula, and you're not helping.'

'It's not our job to help.'

'It's not your job to hinder, either. Our past success rate speaks for itself.'

'The past is the beginning of this conversation, Raymond. That's how far back people's minds go. Nobody wants to hear about your greatest hits. They'll think a couple of old men in charge of a major case derailed a criminal trial.'

Land could feel his face heating with anger. 'If you print that we'll stop feeding you information.'

'Let me know how your avenues of exploration work out,' said Paula, ringing off.

Janice Longbright was in the Sutton Arms, a scuffed artisanal public house in Smithfield that had been redecorated via another selectively remembered past. The elegantly curved frontage gave way to an interior of early Victorian wall plates, plant pots and newly galvanized metal workshop stools. Sitting on one of the latter was Monica Greenwood, her red hair arranged in a chignon, her charcoal suit fresh from its dry-cleaning bag.

'We've met before, haven't we?' Monica held out her hand. 'You came to the Conspirators' Club one night.'

'That was a memorable evening,' said Janice, sitting beside her.

Monica ordered coffees for them. 'Our numbers have swelled since the whole fake-news thing. We have a lot of fun arguing about whether that Facebook fellow is a robot. The club is going through a bit of an existential crisis at the moment.'

'Why, what's happened?'

'Last week's lecture was about President Eisenhower destabilizing the Congo by ordering the CIA to murder its prime minister, but some of our members have started to adopt a rather alarming new stance.'

'What do you mean?'

'They're saying, who cares? It's a fact of life that America and Russia fix overseas elections. The hot new idea is "existential history" – that things are changing so rapidly the only way to deal with them is by confronting each issue afresh, carrying over no baggage from the past. It sort of makes sense. Most wars of attrition are based on historical antipathies. I think I preferred it when the talks were about the Loch Ness Monster.'

'We wondered if the group has started talking about the Oranges & Lemons deaths,' said Longbright.

'Not yet but I'm sure they'll come up at the next meeting, just as I'm sure that the speakers will suddenly start linking the deaths to Kurt Cobain, brainwashing and the moon landings. God, they love those moon landings.'

'You have a degree in understanding the neurological reasons for conspiracy theories – did I get that right?' asked Longbright. 'What do you make of it?'

'There's a unified-theory approach to conspiracies that says they're all interconnected, and in one sense it's true. All leaders desire power over others. First of all I'd decide if you're looking for a group or one person.'

'Which would you choose?'

'It's a loner's plan. Complicated and risky, but easy to adapt.'

'We have footage from several sites,' said Longbright. 'There's no single face common to all. You don't think they could be exactly what they look like: accidents and suicides?'

'I'm sure you already have forensic evidence proving they're not.' Monica sipped her coffee and smiled. 'But then I'm a paid-up member of a conspiracy society.'

John May had been summoned to Simpson's in the Strand, one of the most venerable restaurants in London. After nearly two centuries it was still serving marbled sirloins of beef and crimson saddles of mutton from silver-domed trolleys. The great wood-panelled room smelled of gravy, cabbage and something mustier, a hint of school dormitories remembered from forty years away.

The maître d' led May across the herringbone parquet floor to where Peter English was already seated, watching the ritual pouring of a pre-prandial gin. The businessman had perhaps not intentionally modelled himself on John Bull but the effect was the same. His red waistcoat, anachronistic enough to stick in the memory, was straining at its buttons even before his meal. Indeed, he appeared to have been stuffed into his clothes with great difficulty. The corporate stewards of Great Britain are not known for their fine grooming. Like old country houses far past their best they are usually in need of repointing and a damp course. English was no exception. He never reached the state of being hungover because he never entirely stopped drinking, and from bedroom to boardroom he did nothing for himself when there was someone else available to do it at a cheaper rate.

Accompanying English was a familiar face, Edgar Digby, a sunlight-deprived lawyer who had crossed swords with the unit several times in the past. English gave a desultory wave at the seat opposite.

'It's not been the same since they tarted up the menu,' he said to no one in particular, least of all the selectively deaf waiter who was pouring his cocktail. 'The Victorians used to play chess in this room. That's why the food comes around on trolleys, so the players wouldn't be interrupted. Now it's full of foreigners trying to work out which end of a fork to pick up. Do you want a drink? I suppose you're on duty.' He poured May a water. 'This is—'

'I know Mr Digby,' said May. 'You've come up in the world, Edgar. Not representing petty criminals any more?'

'No,' said Digby drily, 'I'm representing Mr English.'

'I'm seeing you because I gained the clear impression that you weren't going to go away,' said English.

'I'm afraid not,' said May. 'A brief chat may suffice to clear the matter up. I understand you and Michael Claremont were not the best of friends.'

'Oh, I don't think we're going to do this, are we?' English asked Digby. 'Interrogations at the luncheon table, really?' He turned his full gaze on May. 'Mr Claremont got a little too big for his Oxford toecaps. *Condemnant quod non intellegunt.* We clashed, ideologically speaking. If I found anyone in the House who fully agreed with me I wouldn't trust them.'

Arthur always tells me that only the unintelligent feel the need to quote Latin, May thought. 'Did you also know Chakira Rahman?'

'We crossed swords once or twice. I did the same with Kenneth Tremain.' He swirled his gin. 'Does that make me a suspect? My aides can fully account for my time. I have a penthouse at Potters Fields overlooking the Tower of London, and that's where I've been most nights with my staff. Of course I go out to eat – I own a restaurant on Piccadilly, although I had to fire the chef for being too damned French.'

'I can't imagine a person like yourself becoming physically involved in anything violent,' said May, 'but you must appreciate that many wealthy men and women have employed the services of someone else to handle unpleasant tasks.'

'Are you seriously suggesting that I hired a hit man? The Speaker of the House is still alive, isn't he? Have you tried talking to him?'

May felt as if he was being cornered by a predator. 'He can't be interviewed while his condition is being controlled by barbiturates.'

He glanced up and saw with horror that a tramp had wandered into the restaurant, and that the tramp was, on closer inspection, his partner. Bryant had his hands in the pockets of his immense brown overcoat and was openly inspecting everyone's meals as he passed between the tables. He was trailing toilet paper from his left heel. The maître d' led him over like a butler taking out a rat.

May could see with awful clarity what was about to occur. Bryant, his restless personality expanding in the confined, hushed space, would detonate the meeting. *Don't do it, Arthur,* he silently begged.

'Sorry I'm late,' said Bryant, patting English on the shoulder. 'I see you've brought along your familiar. I always wondered what it was like in here. How's the grub? The other tables all seem to be having school dinners. I suppose the sight of overcooked meat is enough to conjure happy memories of public-school spankings.'

'I don't entirely understand why you are here,' said English, furious but showing only polite contempt.

'You get both of us, Mr English. VIP treatment.' He dragged a chair over from another table and squeezed himself between them. 'I suppose my partner was explaining that you have something in common with the victims.' He pulled the toilet paper off his boot and daintily placed it on a side plate.

'You need to reconsider the tone you're taking with my client,' said Digby.

'Read the children's menu for a while, Edgar,' Bryant suggested. He waved at an ancient waiter. 'Can I get a decent cup of tea, sonny? A proper enamel stripper, no cat's piss.'

'I agreed to meet your partner in order to clear the air,' said English, lowering his voice. The Archbishop of Canterbury was seated two tables over. 'I was explaining that I've never had any direct contact with your victims.'

'But your paths crossed. You could have been summoned to court today if the judge hadn't left his frontal lobe in a flowerbed.'

'My corporate law team would have been there, not me.' English stabbed his finger on the tablecloth. 'There is no connection between us. Why would there be?'

May tried to think of something that would draw attention away from his partner, who was now scraping his boot with a fork.

'You're intending to enter politics, aren't you?' Bryant replied without looking up. 'I imagine the fraud case couldn't have come at a worse time.'

'It's a suit involving a distant subsidiary,' snapped English. 'I have bigger fish to fry.'

'Ah yes, your independent party.' Bryant turned over a silver mustard pot to examine its hallmark.

'I want to make this country feel respected again. As I walked here today I hardly heard a word spoken that I could understand.'

'Well, the English are notoriously bad at languages.' Bryant started to wipe up spilled mustard. 'You should have paid more attention at school.'

'You think this is funny, do you?' English was seething now. 'I'm a suspect because I disagreed with them? Why not add everyone I've ever argued with to that list? Some of them must be dead by now but I don't suppose that'll stop you. I know all about your unit, Mr Bryant. A bunch of woolly-minded liberals living in the London bubble, not giving a tinker's cuss for the working people of Britain. Some people have had enough of it. They want to go back to how things were.'

'How far back?' Bryant asked congenially. 'Tudor England? I suppose the downside to that would be a life expectancy of thirty-five years, so you'd have hit room temperature quite a while ago. Let's be honest, it's not the British people who want to go back, it's you. Back to a misremembered past cobbled together from old films and children's books where you once felt safe with Nanny. That's not why you're on our list. You're there because we have phone tapes of your clash with Mr Claremont and because Mr Tremain was about to question your business practices.'

'These killings of yours' – English aimed a forefinger at the pair as if personally holding them responsible – 'are the result of your unit's ineptitude. And when another death occurs you will once again have blood on your hands. You're the people that my party will go after first.' He pointed his stubby finger at Bryant. 'Especially you.'

'I thought that went rather well,' said Bryant when they reached street level a few minutes later. 'We rattled his cage a bit.'

'I didn't know we had phone recordings.' May opened his umbrella and looked for a taxi.

'We don't. Please admire my ability to spontaneously lie. There's nothing like a bit of brinkmanship to pep things up. Do you think he did it?'

'No,' said May reluctantly. 'There's too much at stake for him. He's rich and unpleasant but I'm sure he has subtler methods of revenge at his disposal, most involving phone calls to the press.'

'Unless that's what he wants us to think.' Bryant wiped a yellow streak from his coat pocket.

'Did you just steal the mustard pot?' asked May.

'Might have,' said Bryant. 'At least we've managed to upset him. The gloves are off now.'

30

MISINFORMATION

'Every step forward feels like two bloody great steps back,' fumed Raymond Land. Janice was the only member of staff within earshot, but she had stopped listening. 'It just gets messier and more confusing. I hope they take it all away from us, just take it – just – leave us in bloody peace and – and—'

'Raymond, breathe into a paper bag,' Longbright suggested, grabbing Sidney as she passed. 'Did you hear back from John?'

Sidney looked at her blankly. 'I already told you.'

'No you didn't.'

'Yes, I sent you an email.'

'I haven't had time to look at them. Just tell me.'

'You mean FaceTime you?'

'No, I mean actually physically tell me.'

'But you already have the email.' She turned to find the detectives returning. 'You don't have to read it now, they're here. Hey, I know what happened.'

'I'm Mr Bryant to you. Let me get my coat off.' Bryant set down his stick, his hat, his scarf, his overcoat and the silver mustard pot from Simpson's. 'Come into our office.'

He ushered her and Longbright in but held up his hand when Land tried to follow them. 'I'm sorry, you'd be exceeding the room's weight limit. You've got quite porky lately.'

'I should probably sit in on this,' called Tim Floris.

'All right, you can come in, you're thin,' Bryant agreed, waving him through. Land stepped forward but Bryant shut the door in his face.

Longbright was offered the only spare chair by Sidney, which made her feel old. Sidney turned to address the room. 'OK, so this girl I know is seeing a guy on and off who does podcasts from a studio on the same floor as Judge Tremain. He was working late last night and says he saw the killer going up to Tremain's door. He gave me a description.'

'What does he look like?' asked May.

'He has a woolly blue hat and a navy Puffa jacket and was hunched over, and there's something wrong with his leg.'

'What else?'

Sidney looked blank. 'That's it.'

'That's it? I'm guessing your friend didn't train with police observers. What time was this?'

'He doesn't know.'

'Did the judge come to the door? Were they friendly? Angry?'

'He doesn't know anything else, he just saw this lame guy.'

'When did the man leave?'

'He *doesn't know*, he was a bit off his face.' For the first time Sidney look rattled. 'He'd smoked a couple of joints. But he's sure about the limping man.'

'This – *this* – is what we're up against,' said Bryant. 'Hopeless witnesses. He confuses everything and slips away before anyone's sure of what's happened.'

'That's why I've been looking at the victims,' said Longbright. 'They have no work or social connections to one another, so do they have anything in common? Chakira

Rahman, hugely admired, a champion for diversity in media, leaves behind two young girls, the loves of her life. Kenneth Tremain, another dedicated family man, outspoken but with a reputation for fairness, his wife and son left devastated. We need to spend time with their families and friends.'

'Fine,' said May, 'but be aware – he knows what we're going to do because this is a race and he's still ahead of us.'

Strangeways squinted at the litter tray he'd inherited and deliberately micturated in the opposite corner before falling asleep on Meera's jacket, clawing at it in his dreams. He was disagreeable even when unconscious, snoring, shedding and producing prodigious amounts of mucus.

By late afternoon most of the staff had decamped to the operations room because it was the only place with fully functioning lighting. Bryant was wrapped inside a vast orange woollen scarf and fingerless mittens like a Dickensian book-keeper, and sat with his pug nose half an inch from his laptop screen. He had somehow managed to push its luminescence up so high that his screensaver – Géricault's *The Raft of the Medusa* – had turned his face green. May was still smarting from the meeting with Peter English, and was searching through press files looking for anything that might incriminate the entrepreneur.

It was the worst possible time for Maggie Armitage to turn up, bustling in and shaking water from a red lacquered Japanese parasol. 'Sorry, it's chucking it down out there,' she said, unfurling herself from a waterproof 'Monsieur Hulot' raincoat and a saggy-sleeved yellow cardigan. 'Your new pet just hissed at me. He looks like he's been flattened in a mangle. What is he?'

'A cat.'

'He might have been in a former life. I meant his breed.'

'I don't think he has one,' said May without looking up. 'He's called Strangeways, apparently.'

'Yes, I think I've just seen a couple of them.' She searched for somewhere to hang her dripping coat. 'Arthur, you're not answering your phone.'

'Ah, er, no, it got paint on it,' said Bryant, pushing aside his laptop with relief.

'Can't John fix it?'

'It's stuck to the window frame,' said May wearily. 'Don't go there.'

'I need you to come with me, Arthur.' Maggie tugged at his sleeve. 'We have to talk about the end of the world.'

'That's a good idea,' said May, typing his notes in. 'Go and discuss the coming apocalypse and leave the boring old investigating stuff to us.'

'Top plan,' Bryant agreed, grabbing his umbrella. 'I could do with some tea and a bun.'

'Incredible,' said May to himself, shaking his silver mane as he watched them go.

'There's a build-up occurring,' Maggie explained as she pushed open the door to the Ladykillers Café. 'The signs are everywhere.' She approached the counter. 'Do you have liquorice tea? Kombucha? Arrowroot? Thistle?'

Niven regarded her with a jaundiced eye. 'No.'

'Just builders' then, preferably Yorkshire Gold. And something sweet.'

'Anything in particular?' Niven asked, hand on hip. 'Spiced nettle and cranberry scorpion cake with walnut top-notes, or will you settle for a doughnut?'

'You're a caution, aren't you?' She turned to Bryant. 'I need to explain my thinking. I suppose it's because of the Dutch. Everyone knows three things about them. They're incredibly tall, have the worst cuisine in Europe and support voluntary euthanasia.'

'I was thinking windmills, tulips and saucy ladies, but go on,' Bryant replied.

'My friend Madame Tizia in Rotterdam is a Grand Order white witch like me. She researches social panics – everything from satanic abuse and false memory syndrome to anti-vaxxers. She calls to all the white witches on spring evenings.'

An image of bonfires being lit at dusk sprang into Bryant's mind. He hadn't considered that the witches might have something similar to the twilight bark. It seemed picturesque, if impractical.

'Does she do it telepathically?' he asked.

'No, through WitchNet. According to Tizia's data, human entropy has entered its terminal stage. The sixth extinction is now unstoppable, the global emergency is accelerating and technology is ending the information age. The predictions of H. G. Wells have come true. We still worship tribal deities and revert to superstition at the earliest opportunity.'

'Well, that's cheerful,' said Bryant, carrying his tea to a table. 'I hope your friend remembers to leave us a solution before she sticks her head in an oven.'

'These deaths you're looking into – I'm sorry, I read that horrible piece on the *Hard News* site about how useless you all are – they're worsening the situation for witches in the UK. Our members meet in the nation's church halls and conference centres, and they're already reporting a change in public attitudes.'

'Really? What kind of change?'

'My fellow witches feel they're being targeted for their beliefs.'

'I thought that was part of their job description. Sorry to be obtuse but what does that have to do with the victims in this case?'

Maggie leaned forward, keeping her voice low. 'There's a secret organization funded by billionaires that's socially engineering the country.'

Bryant leaned forward too. 'If it's secret how do you know about it?'

'They send us warnings. They're getting rid of everyone who's a threat.'

'Why are you whispering?' Bryant had a hard time imagining that a group of garlanded Wiccans singing folk songs and making seaweed tea could be a threat to anyone.

'We tried chanting but we're not strong enough to stop them. We need help to start a counter-revolution.'

'Maggie, you mustn't believe everything you read, otherwise you'll start thinking aliens are sending you messages through the fireplace.'

'I used to think that, but then I realized that the woman next door was a radio-cab controller.' She dug into a red plastic shopping bag. Bryant tried to read what was written on the side. 'It's recyclable,' she explained. 'Destroyed by sunlight in three days. I've had this one for over two years. Says a lot about the weather in London. Ah, here.' She whacked a sheaf of dog-eared papers on the table. 'I printed it all out so that nobody can steal the data.'

'You printed out a file your friend copied from a website,' said Bryant. 'Even I know that's daft.' Against his better judgement and only because she was avidly watching him, he flicked through the misspelled pages. 'I'll look into it,' he promised.

'I suppose King Lud was the country's first one,' she said, absently biting into a doughnut.

Bryant thought he must have zoned out of the conversation for a moment. 'The first what?'

'Social engineer,' she replied as if it was obvious. 'He named this the City of Lud over seventy years before the birth of Christ. He was an evil man in favour of culling the population and keeping strangers out.'

'That was because of the plague,' said Bryant with impatience. 'Not because he didn't like some people.'

'He wanted to remove everyone of "impure race". Maybe this new group is planning to replace those they assassinate with their own candidates. You know, replicants. From *you know where*.' She raised a glittery fingernail at the ceiling.

'The first floor?'

'No, Alpha Centauri.'

As much as he often admired her lateral thinking, Bryant feared that the white witch's somersault from King Lud to *Invasion of the Body Snatchers* would take them to UFOs, lately her pet subject.

'I've got enough on my plate without intergalactic conspiracies,' he warned her, handing back the pages. 'Maggie, I've always shown a lot of patience with you, but you've been duped by a fake-news site.'

The look of surprise on Maggie's face touched him. 'But how are people supposed to know that?' she asked, bewildered.

That, thought Bryant, *is what we're all wondering.*

Raymond Land highlighted a paragraph in his report and moved it to the top of the page but it promptly vanished, along with the rest of his document. Fifteen minutes later he was still trying to get it back when he became aware that Floris was prevaricating in his doorway. There was a look of indecisiveness on his face that probably captivated the emotionally susceptible but was utterly wasted on Land.

'Are you just going to hover about there or come in?'

'You've no door,' Floris said.

'Yes, I know. For a brief, blissful period there was one, but it was taken away again. What do you want?'

Floris cautiously approached and peered over the edge of Land's screen. 'Are you having trouble?'

'No, I often sit staring at a blank screen. Your colleague Mr Faraday wants a daily report. I've lost it.'

Floris reached over and tapped a couple of keys. The missing paragraph reappeared, which only annoyed Land more. 'Do you tell your bosses everything that goes on here?' he asked.

'Almost everything. They're not my bosses, Mr Land. As I explained, I report to the Home Secretary. You only see me in with Mr Faraday and his team because I'm seconded there until the investigation can be resolved.'

'Because I know how it looks to outsiders,' said Land. 'They stick their heads around where the door should be and think there's nothing going on and it's all a bit of a joke in here, but they're wrong. This is the nerve centre of a major homicide investigation. Only because the SCC initially turned it down, admittedly, but Faraday thinks we're incompetent. That lumbering diplodocus thinks *we're* incompetent. He's the one who was caught making racist jokes about Muslim women. Every time I enter his office I have to remind myself that it's not 1975. I even wrote him a document entitled "Understanding the modern PCU",' Land added with some pride. 'I included it in your introductory briefing.'

'Yes, I know, TLDR.* At the end of the week I have to submit an overview on the investigation. I can run it by you, although I won't be able to let you edit it.'

Land hated this young man's glib, patronizing tone. He hated his perfect beard, his shaved side-parting and his immaculately pressed white shirt. How could he have climbed the governmental food chain so quickly? There could only be one answer: family connections. Land had gone to a

---

* Too Long, Didn't Read

second-rate grammar school where he had been beaten up for his pocket money, and every hammering had stamped resentment into his heart.

'You don't have to run it by me,' he said. 'We have nothing to hide.' He suddenly wondered if Bryant had moved his marijuana plant back into his office.

'Fine,' said Floris with a disarming smile. 'If you have any further questions about our working relationship during this investigation please feel free to share them with me.'

I wouldn't share a Pret sandwich with you, matey, Land thought, *because Faraday will know I've opted for a crayfish and rocket before I've finished eating it.* 'Of course I'd be delighted to "share",' he said aloud, realizing he had put inverted commas around the verb.

'I've been informed that the HO's legal department has been fielding calls from Peter English's office this afternoon,' said Floris. 'Mr May's attempt to interview him in connection with the case did not go well, and Simpson's reported some kind of theft.'

'Were they just having a moan or are they planning to take action?' Land impatiently stabbed at his keyboard. 'I mean English's lot, not the restaurant.'

'They're demanding that both Mr Bryant and Mr May take the new PPCC test by the end of the week.'

Land blanched. He knew that the Met's new Police Psychometric Core Competency tests had to be conducted online without preparation, and checked for verbal reasoning skills, critical analysis and emotional awareness. John might be able to scrape through but Bryant wouldn't pass even if they wired his hearing aid to accept incoming advice from Stephen Fry.

'And if they don't take the test?'

'Mr English's lawyer, Edgar Digby, is going to file a harassment charge against them on behalf of his client.'

'All right. Fine, I'll arrange it,' snapped Land. He knew that Floris would have grown up with regular online evaluations and regarded them as entirely normal. 'They'll need to be printed out, though.'

A look of puzzlement crossed Floris's tender face.

'Mr Bryant prefers a fountain pen,' he ended, feeling as if he had just signed the unit's death warrant.

31

MAKING A MURDERER

So we come to the Event, and I'm sure you who understand the nature of men can already tell what came to pass. It is an old, old story, appropriately biblical.

After the handsome young sixth-former had ignored my mother in the street while he was out with his parents, he called on her to apologize. He admitted that he was embarrassed, and knew it was wrong.

She did not accept his apology. She was all too aware that her reception into his gilded circle only went as far as childhood games. She would never be allowed to cross the boundary of her street because although she was attractive she looked and sounded common. Perhaps that's too harsh. She was different. Wrong for him. She would be examined by his parents and instantly dismissed.

The boys were not bohemians, they did not set out to break down borders. Whatever their pretensions, they were really just suburban children anxious to fit in. And so they were duly slotted in, he to the middle class, she to a level below him marked 'Not good enough'.

Yet the boy was persistent. She turned sixteen and he continued to call, and one day she agreed to go out with him. She offered to come to his house, but he said his parents would not understand and he would rather collect her.

Her grandmother picked out a dress and paid for it, then sent her to a hairdresser.

He called for her on a warm July evening, and they set off along the street, and climbed through the old railings to St George's Church, just to stop there briefly for old times' sake.

The others were there waiting for her. One even complained that she was late. The girl who hid behind them all was there too, not willing to condone or condemn, and at some point she slipped away. My mother soon found out why.

'Remember how we used to play Oranges & Lemons?' he asked, handing her a bottle of rum. The others looked apprehensive. The evening took a sinister turn.

She remembered the boys' eyes, bright with excitement. They had started drinking as soon as the light faded. The songs and games were harder-edged than she remembered. Rougher. To each winner went the rum bottle, and then it went to each loser.

They played another game. He sang 'Oranges & Lemons' and she had to fill in the name of each church. If the questions had been about TV shows or pop songs she could have answered. She didn't know the names of churches. Each time she hesitated the rum bottle passed her way. She was laughing with the rest of them. They broke out joints, and soon no one could stop laughing.

It had been a little after 7.00 p.m. when she arrived in the ruins of the church. They let her leave at some time past nine, perhaps a quarter past. Her dress was not torn. Her face was not dirty. There were no marks or bruises on her skin. They had held her down gently and with great care, always checking to see that she was comfortable, but stifling her pleas to be released. It was a game that got out of hand, that's all.

Were they scared that she would tell someone? It seemed not to have crossed their minds. My mother was raised to be devoutly Church of England, so silent shame came more naturally than confession.

One of the questions that has stayed with me the longest is: Why did she not tell anyone?

Of course the silence couldn't last indefinitely. As summer turned to autumn she began to show with me. By then the boys had gone, moving smoothly from their schools to art colleges and universities, scattering across the country.

I assume her grandmother was shocked. My mother was uncomfortable with that part of her story. I imagine an alternative narrative where, after arguments and tears, she stayed at home and helped around the house, and in return her grandmother took care of her until I was born into a loving, understanding household.

That was not what happened.

Her grandmother called the police, who questioned my mother and eventually dragged a garbled story from her. They were at a loss to understand why she had said nothing at the time. They were especially interested in the part where she explained that she had been given copious amounts of alcohol and a joint. They made it quite clear that they suspected her complicity, but promised to investigate and arrest the young men who were responsible.

Of course, by this time the boys had long gone. The matter was further complicated by my mother's continued refusal to give up any names or descriptions. This is the part I have never been able to comprehend. I can only think that as a practising Christian she was not prepared to destroy their lives even though they had sinned against her. I am baffled, but can see no other explanation. Part of every heart is hidden.

According to my mother nothing came of the investigation, but shortly before she was due to give birth a complete stranger came running up to her in the street and punched her in the stomach. That's how I was born, delivered screaming on to a Greenwich backstreet, my soft-boned right thigh damaged in the attack. Whether or not it was connected to the boys no one ever found out. I think of her story as a book with some pages missing, and others containing only half-remembered truths.

I set out to write down her account, filling exercise pads with as many details as she would admit to me.

When my mother finally chose to tell me everything about how I was conceived, she believed her confession would begin a healing process and our lives would slowly improve.

Instead, things got much worse.

PART FOUR
The Bells of Shoreditch

How do you like London? How d'you like the town?
How d'you like the Strand now Temple Bar's pulled
  down?
How d'you like the La-Di-Da, the toothpick and the
  crutch?
How did you get those trousers on, and do they hurt
  you much?

Nelly Power, singer, 1880

32

CHASING GHOSTS

'They're looking at it the wrong way,' said Sidney, standing before the whiteboard with her arms folded.

'What do you mean?'

She waved her hand across the whiteboard. 'All this stuff about the nursery rhyme.'

It was 7.30 a.m. on Friday 12 April, and Tim Floris was the only other person in the unit. He had seen Sidney Hargreaves approaching the building; she was hard to miss in her red leather jacket and black leggings. Rain slashed the windows of the operations room, giving them a welcome spring-clean, but water was running from the sills across the floorboards, so the pair of them had to lay down towels and lift all the cables and connectors off the ground.

'It's taking them in the wrong direction. They should dump it and start at the other end.'

'What do you mean?'

She sat on the edge of a desk facing him. 'The victims are the cause. They've been targeted because of something they've done.'

'They're called victims because they're innocent,' Floris pointed out. He tried not to touch his beard but his fingers had a habit of straying to it.

'They were all born within two years of each other, Tim. Suppose they met somewhere before but not professionally? Maybe as students?'

'It doesn't seem likely, given that they're from different parts of the country.'

'They are now, but what if they weren't back then?'

'I'm an observer,' Floris reminded her, 'and you're an intern. We can't take the investigation in a different direction without their approval, and you won't get that without proof.'

'Then I'll find it,' she said. 'I may need your help. Do you have to put everything in your reports to Faraday?'

One look in his eyes told her he would do anything she suggested.

An hour later, Janice Longbright stood before the same whiteboard and studied Bryant's diagrams carefully, following lines, triangles, circles and three-dimensional boxes filled with tiny indecipherable scribble. She might as well have been staring at Egyptian hieroglyphics.

'Bloody hopeless,' she said aloud, wandering to the window.

The weather was like London itself, secretive in its intentions. Thunder trundled over the rooftops of the shops on Caledonian Road. In the street below, an elderly woman carrying a red and blue laundry bag was sprayed to her kneecaps with charcoal-coloured water displaced by a bus. A tramp had passed out beneath the window of the newsagent's, underneath a poster of the Seychelles that said, 'What are you waiting for?'

Janice needed a holiday, a proper one with beaches and outdoor restaurants overlooking the sea, but she was broke. She couldn't spend much more time peering out at one of the world's ugliest neighbourhoods without going mad. Sometimes when she got home, she moved through exotic cities on Google Street View, knowing that she would never go there. She had spent so much time doing this lately that it came as a surprise to go out on to a real street and see that the roads did not have white arrows on them.

What am I waiting for? she wondered, looking back at the poster, but Arthur had already answered her question, breezily telling her that she had a one in 45,057,474 chance of winning the National Lottery.

With an inward sigh she turned her attention back to the whiteboard. The nursery rhyme at its centre had three of its verses crossed through.

'*When I grow rich,*' *say the bells of Shoreditch.* The tabloid hacks had been starved of new details and had resorted to fantasy, but even their attention had suddenly evaporated this morning after receiving news that the police had foiled a major terrorism attempt. A van full of explosives had been discovered near Waterloo Station, timed to go off in the rush hour, but the timer had malfunctioned, with the result that the Oranges & Lemons Killer had been unceremoniously booted from the front pages.

She turned her attention back to Bryant's mad little drawings.

'Staring at them won't make them go away,' said John May, standing in the doorway.

'I wish it would,' said Longbright. 'Shoreditch is too big an area to cover. It's spread across two boroughs. There are hundreds of bars, restaurants and businesses. I can't find the staff to police it. Why is it we always get the personnel we need after an event, never before?'

'You can't investigate what hasn't happened yet. "When I grow rich,"' May repeated. 'Where do the rich hang out in Shoreditch?'

'There are half a dozen high-end hotels there now. God, to think that we used to patrol it in pairs for safety. Is that supposed to be the church in Shoreditch?' She pointed to Bryant's mysterious rendering.

May took a closer look. 'St Leonard's.'

'What does it say underneath? You'd think I'd be able to read his writing after all this time.'

'The trick is to imagine it the other way up. It says *twelve bells, Tudor actors buried here, parish stocks and whipping post still in porch.* That's all.'

'Nobody's been attacked inside a church.'

'Who have we got over there?'

'Colin and Meera, plus a couple of beat coppers keeping an eye out, and a patrol car passing every hour. The Met get more coverage for a robbery.'

'Then let's get a drone,' said May. 'Try Dan.'

Longbright called Banbury in. 'Can you put something in the air above St Leonard's Church?'

'You do know they're technically illegal.' Banbury came in eating a bowl of Shredded Wheat. The school run forced him to skip breakfast at home, but he got no sympathy because no one else in the unit could relate to the idea of having children. 'It's a pity because I've got a fantastic program for one, beta of course and full of bugs. It doesn't meet any of the regs but one day I hope we might—'

Janice cut in. 'Is the drone here?'

'I couldn't sanction that. It would be totally—'

'We just want to sneak it up there for a few minutes and have a look around,' said May. 'Is it in working order?'

'You have to understand that it's bespoke specialist equipment—'

'Meaning you cobbled it together from bits of old kit.'

'I'll have to make a lot of adjustments, then charge it.'

'How long will that take?'

'I can probably get it there by late afternoon.'

'That'll have to do. We're heading over there now,' said May. 'Bring it as soon as you can. I'll take full responsibility. Sidney needs to stay here. Where is Floris?'

'He went to Raymond's office.' Dan gave up on his breakfast. 'We really should keep him informed.'

'You're right, of course we should.'

They slipped past Land's room and made a run for it.

Script extract from Arthur Bryant's 'Peculiar London' walking tour guide. (Meet at Shoreditch Town Hall, stay close to me at all times and try not to look like tourists.)

This ancient, ill-used parish extends from Norton Folgate to Old Street, and from part of Finsbury to Bethnal Green. Originally it was a village on the old Roman northern road called Old Street by the Saxons.

There's a lovely romantic story about its name involving the mistress of Edward IV. It's not true. Shoreditch is appropriately named after a shithole, Soersditch, or Sewer Ditch. It wasn't even in London until the late nineteenth century. However, it was the home of London's first theatre, and the spot where *Romeo and Juliet* was first performed, although the audience must have had to narrow their eyes a bit to imagine themselves in fair Verona.

The area was dominated by St Leonard's, the Tudor actors' church of London. Its burial register lists Henry VIII's court jester and one Thomas Cam, who died aged 207. Actors always exaggerate. Having so many dodgy theatricals in one neighbourhood gave Shoreditch its first creative edge. People came here for saucy entertainment, and still do. It's had many famous residents: Richard

Burbage, Christopher Marlowe, Barbara Windsor and the singing bus driver Matt Monro.

Sadly Shoreditch declined from noble origins into poverty and prostitution. In the late twentieth century it aligned itself with neighbouring Hoxton to become 'vibrant', meaning it fills up with bare-ankled media plankton who can be tricked into purchasing Japanese bubble tea, bad graffiti art and hot dogs from vans that ironically reference Brazilian favelas. Shoreditch is now visited by tourists looking for the creative edge and finding only mouse mats and fridge magnets. There are still pockets of originality here, though. Last year I got a haircut on Brick Lane that was so original I had to wear a hat just to look out of a window.

In Shoreditch a day of surveillance crawled past without incident until late afternoon, when the streets suddenly filled with drinkers. They arrived in small groups that coalesced around hole-in-the-wall bars and cafés, and soon spilled beyond the kerbs. What were they celebrating? The end of the week, someone's promotion, a birthday, the awarding of a contract – who needed an excuse? The kerbs quickly filled up with empty bottles and street-food containers.

Dan Banbury had joined Colin armed with pieces of his drone. In an effort to fix its steering issues he wedged part of the guidance system into place using pieces from a Kinder Egg toy.

Colin Bimsley's walkie-talkie crackled. 'Colin, are you receiving me? Over.'

'Blimey, Meera, you don't have to shout, it's not *The Dam Busters*.'

'I do have to shout actually because this lot has already started and it's only six o'clock. At least you got a quiet corner. There are ten bars in a row here and the office workers are drinking for England.' She moved away from a couple locked in an agitated embrace. 'Jeez, get a room.'

'What's going on?'

'There's a couple next to me who are already rat-arsed. I don't think he's kissing her. It looks like he's trying to fish her tongue out of her mouth with his teeth. They haven't noticed it's raining.'

'Is it?' Colin was positioned in an alley beside Hackney Town Hall. He took a look across the main road. The far side was faintly eroded as if seen through kettle steam, the rain being damp enough to flatten your hair but not enough to make your shoulders wet. 'It sounds mad over there.'

'Is there football on or something?' Meera shouted. 'Can you hear them singing in the background? The gentleman on my other side just puked his Singapore noodles over a drain, which he managed to miss. Looks like he didn't chew the prawns.'

'Don't, Meera, I'm starving. Do you want to grab some noodles?'

'Not sure. He's got some hanging out of his nose that are putting me off. Hang on – that's it, mate, get it up while it's fresh on your stomach. All over his shoes. Nice, not even a thank-you.' There were cheers and hoots in the background. 'Have you seen anything over there yet?'

'I would have told you if I had.' Conscious that he was a plain-clothes officer speaking into his shoulder, Colin stepped back to allow three girls dressed as pink rabbits to pass. 'I've seen a lot of weird stuff in the past hour, but no one who looks like a murderer. Actually, I don't know who I'm looking for. How do you tell a killer from just another sketchy geezer? Dan's arrived with his Flymo – we're going to send it up for a test run in a minute.'

'I was planning to fit it with a facial recognition system,' said Dan, proudly eyeing the bulky black dragonfly in his arms, 'but you haven't got a face that needs recognizing.'

' 'Fraid not,' said Colin. 'We're chasing ghosts.'

'Are you still there?' asked Meera.

'There's nothing going on over this way,' Colin told her. 'We'll head in your direction. Can you ask that bloke where he got his noodles from?'

Dan sent the drone up but found it tricky negotiating the busy Shoreditch streets with the control box held before him. After stepping off the kerb and nearly vanishing under a lorry, he was grabbed by Colin's meaty fist and guided through the busy side streets. The drone tilted and flew on ahead, checking the pavements. The whine of its rotors was lost beneath the neighbourhood's high-decibel turmoil.

'If it spots a likely suspect, what are we going to do?' Colin asked.

'I'm hoping you'll figure that part out,' said Dan, studying the screen so intently that he fell over an outside table.

'I can't arrest someone on the grounds of looking dodgy.'

'We have to find him first,' Banbury reminded him, disentangling himself from a pair of metal chairs. The drinkers did not appear to mind that he had just prostrated himself in their midst, scattering plastic glasses. Indeed, they barely noticed. It was the ideal place to get away with murder.

33

BAD LUCK

Considering Shoreditch had been so heavily bombed during the war it seemed nothing short of miraculous that St Leonard's Church had survived at all. It had been built in an unfashionably delicate style once much disliked for its overt femininity. Set back from one of the busiest roads in East London, it was now ignored by virtually everyone who passed by.

The first thing that struck Janice about the building was its slender multi-tiered spire. Attached to one of the railings was a black-painted panel of wood that read, mysteriously, 'Oranges & Lemons letters'. The building was covered in scaffolding, but funding had been only partly raised for its never-ending refurbishment. There were clock faces everywhere, on the Tuscan portico and inside, gilded, beneath the organ.

'I had a chat with the vicar,' Janice told John May as they stood on the steps, the tentative rain sheening their coats. 'He's trying to find new ways of funding the repairs. The crypt contains some ornate tombs but it's falling apart.'

May walked back to the gates and looked out. 'Four major

roads, a railway bridge and hundreds of venues to cover. If he strikes, he'll make it look like an accident or a suicide again. How do we fight that?'

'This was always a trouble spot,' said Longbright. 'My mother used to patrol here. She said the locals were all on the cadge or on the grift.'

'No disrespect, Janice, but your mother had a low opinion of everyone. Where are the others?'

Longbright checked her phone. 'Colin's outside a motorcycle club called the Bike Shed by Hackney Town Hall. Meera's at the top of Shoreditch High Street. We can't cover all the routes. We should have had more officers here yesterday.'

The streets beyond were becoming busier. They could hear the hubbub rising from between the buildings, a great weight of humanity, no single voice discernible but part of a murmuring sound wall, underscored by the distant bass thump of outdoor speakers.

May wondered how someone could attack on these crowded pavements without being caught. Londoners had a long history of working together in times of danger. They would happily throw themselves at criminals and rugby-tackle them down so long as their best mate held their pint.

May and Longbright followed a path around the church, through unkempt, litter-strewn flowerbeds. 'We should have someone stationed at Silicon Roundabout,' he said. The sarcastic nickname had been assigned to a cluster of tech start-ups stacked around Old Street tube station.

'You can't see the church from there. It wouldn't have a link to the rhyme.'

'I was thinking about the "grow rich" part. Every one of these backstreets is packed out at night but there's nowhere that's especially wealthy.'

'The art galleries in Hoxton Square,' Janice suggested.

'They're not within sight of the church. We need more information, otherwise we're just wasting our time here.'

A cry came from across the road, from an antique shop that was possibly a bar, given the number of customers who were outside holding wine glasses. The screech resolved itself into laughter; in the shop window two girls were posing with an enormous gold-painted bison head.

'Perhaps Arthur will come up with something.'

'I doubt it this time. When I left him he was going to talk to someone about bookshops and poetry.'

'But it seems to help, doesn't it?' said Longbright. 'I mean, he goes off on these odd meetings and comes back with ideas. I know it's unscientific . . .'

'*Unscientific*? We're the homeopaths of law enforcement. It's why we're a laughing stock.'

'So you'd rather he stopped?'

'God no, of course not. He's brilliant at it. He gets results. But there must be a reason why he's the only person I've ever known to use such a system.'

Janice uprighted a fallen plant pot. 'John, he's the only one old enough to remember that such a system ever existed. When he goes, it's gone. It's unusable in anyone else's hands.'

'OK,' said May, 'what do you want to do?'

'One more circuit of the church and then we do the surrounding streets again.'

The gardens at the rear of St Leonard's must once have felt like countryside but were now overlooked by mean little houses. The former graveyard was deserted, its sheltering sycamores muffling the noise of people and traffic, leaving only sparrows and the faint susurration of rainfall. A few gravestones stood against a wall like the tabs on an old-fashioned cash register. The grass was studded with cigarette ends and empty fifths of Scotch.

'What is that?' May asked, stopping.

Janice sniffed the air. 'I don't know. Wood varnish? Something dusty.'

'Like old theatres.' He shrugged. 'A smell I remember as a kid.'

'You know we're near the site of the first London playhouse?' Janice said. 'That's why so many Elizabethan actors are buried here.'

'You've been listening to my partner again.'

'No, the vicar. I think he's a bit lonely.'

'You might get a date out of it.'

Janice's walkie-talkie blipped. 'We're across the road from you,' said Banbury. 'Look up.'

The drone had just arrived above them, a darting black spider unable to advance beyond the edge of the tree cover. Away from the street its buzz was annoyingly loud.

They carried on around the side of the building. The arched windows had long ago lost their stained glass and emerald moss extruded from the cracked brickwork. The building repairs appeared to have stalled. They stepped over a pair of graves garlanded with roots which burrowed beneath them, no doubt splitting the coffins below.

The bang made them start, a percussion of metal and glass cascading on stone. They headed towards the sound.

The church's pedimented portico was in such deep shadow that it was hard to see at first. A dark bird hopped across the steps as if scuttling away from trouble. Something lay on the flagstones. When Janice looked up she saw that where there had been a clock over the door there was now just a circular hole sifting dust.

'You've got to be kidding.' As she walked closer, drawing out her phone, she discerned the figure of a man lying face down with the clock mechanism smashed around him, the brass back of its white enamel face concealing his head. The gold minute-hand had been hurled to the stones nearby.

'We have the body of a fifty-something male, hit by falling debris at St Leonard's Church, Shoreditch,' she told the controller.

May lowered himself with difficulty to examine the shattered glass. ' "When",' he said. ' "*When* will you pay me?" '

Janice touched him on the shoulder. 'Who do you want me to call first?'

'Find Arthur,' he told her. 'And get hold of Giles.'

They both became aware of him at the same time: a slim dark man in his late twenties, Ethiopian in appearance, dressed in a dirty red tracksuit, standing in the open side door of the church. He suddenly snapped to attention and darted off into the bushes.

From his control box across the road, Dan picked up on the movement and directed the drone to follow. There was no gate at the rear of the churchyard. The suspect would have to pass by Longbright and May to get out. He was fast approaching the bushes before the rear wall and showed no sign of slowing down.

The runner smashed into the foliage without stopping, vaulting up at the wall and scrambling over the high railings as if he barely noticed them being there. The drone shot over the fence with him, blasting leaves from the ends of branches.

May could not move any faster. His limbs had grown suddenly heavy. He dropped his hands to his thighs, trying to catch his breath. A streak of fire shot through his chest and shoulder, a warning that he needed to remain where he was. Exhausted, he fell to the wet grass and sat back, waiting for his pulse to slow.

Janice had always been a powerful runner but the Ethiopian was moving like Mo Farah, bounding and striding, slipping along the crowded street like a fish in a stream. He turned into Columbia Road – *No flower market today, thank God*, she thought – then crossed into the park and notched up the speed.

There was no chance of catching him. As she ran, she called Meera Mangeshkar with their coordinates. 'Can you get to your bike?'

The connection crackled angrily. 'I'm right by it, just tell me where I'm going.'

The runner had already reached the far side of the park. Janice slowed up to concentrate on the call. 'He'll come out on to Ravenscroft Street and either turn on to Shipton Street or go for Hackney Road.' She gave Meera a description and rang off, heading back towards John May.

She found him lying on the grass and for a moment thought that he'd had a heart attack.

'I'm all right,' he told her as she gently raised him up. 'We need to stay with the body. Did he get away?'

'Meera's on it; she'll put out the word. Dan's got the drone above him and he'll be on my jacket-cam. I've seen another lad very similar to him, I'm sure of it.'

'Where?'

'In the CCTV footage from the steps of St Martin-in-the-Fields.'

May brushed wet grass from his waterproof jacket. 'Decoys. He employs them like a general sending in cannon fodder. It won't matter if we catch them or not.'

Meera slowed the bike on Hackney Road and checked the store fronts. *Artisanal cake shop. Vintage clothing. Tattoos. Plumbing supplies. Craft beer bar. Vietnamese supermarket.* Each ground-floor entrance led to a maze of small rooms, for these were terrace houses that had once been inhabited by large families. Nearly all had some kind of back entrance that led to

yards and storage units. A steady flow of customers streamed in
and out of them, making it the perfect place to disappear.

The ghostly rain had evaporated, and each pub and bar
now had a growing cluster of customers surrounding it. She
turned on to Shipton Street and cut up towards Columbia
Road, but knew she had lost him.

Driving around slowly, Meera watched the shops and pavements. People were buying supper, drinking with friends,
carrying shopping home. Ordinary life, something that
seemed almost alien to her now. She looked up as Dan's drone
tilted forward and buzzed past her, heading in the opposite
direction. It had spotted something.

She turned back towards Colin, passing a store with a red
neon sign that read 'Booze & Fags', very Shoreditch. She very
nearly missed him. White shoes, red tracksuit, soaked forehead, standing in the doorway of a bar called Sherpa Tenzing.
It had to be the runner. He had dark patches under his arms
and was fighting to catch his breath.

As he stepped outside he was engulfed by some kind of
event that required its participants to dress as Powerpuff
Girls and Power Rangers. There was an opening party taking
place. A girl in Turkish national dress was playing an accor-
dion. Beside her was a man selling large metallic animal
balloons.

Dan's drone was just above them. The drinkers looked up
at the whining spy and started jeering. Somebody threw a
plastic beer glass at it, which was enough to set the others off.
They grabbed a bunch of helium-filled unicorns from the
balloon-seller and floated them up around the flying
camera.

Banbury found his screen obscured by rainbow colours.
He tried to push the drone forward but the unicorns crowded
out his view.

'Bloody typical,' he complained into his headset. 'Londoners, a red rag to a bull, they just can't resist it, can they? Can you go and stop them?'

Meera cut across the street on her bike. She could see the runner fighting to get out of the jeering crowd as beer cascaded and unicorns bobbed about. When he tried to escape he found his exit blocked by Colin, who swiftly moved in, barrelling the drinkers out of his path. Tangled in red and silver ribbons, the drone hit the wall of the bar and fell on to the runner as a great roar went up. Moments later Colin had him locked down and handcuffed.

'I didn't do anything,' he called up at them. 'It's wet down here. There's beer everywhere. These are Nike Yeezys, man, first time I've worn them. Get me up.'

Colin pulled him up and checked out his trainers. 'Those aren't real Yeezys, they're Chinese knock-offs. You shouldn't have run.'

'I don't know nothing about it. Some bloke slipped me five hundred quid, it's in my right-hand pocket. Honest, take a look.' He wriggled about, trying to show them the money. Colin reached into his pocket and confirmed the fold of notes as Meera pushed the drinkers back.

He held out the billfold. 'What did he look like?'

'I don't know.'

'How could you *not know*?'

'I was in the churchyard. He come up behind me, told me not to turn around, asked me if I wanted to earn some fast money, nothing illegal.'

'What, and you said yes, just like that?'

The runner assessed him. 'Mate, are you joking me? Five hundred? To stand outside the church for five minutes? I'd do a lot more than that for a monkey.'

'What *do* you do?'

'I just sell a bit of weed but I used to be a professional runner.'

'Well, *mate*, you're involved in a professional murder now,' said Colin, hauling the prisoner to his feet. 'Let's go.'

Banbury came panting over and hunted for his downed drone. It lay on the pavement looking like a smashed crab. He was appalled. 'All that money spent on R&D, putting in dual optical, zoom and thermal cameras and it gets destroyed by a cheap balloon?'

'Oi, mate, it wasn't that cheap,' said one of the lads.

'You killed a unicorn,' said his friend. 'That's seven years' bad luck.'

34

BURNING PAGES

In the failing light Elise Albu was just able to recognize the shambling heap clattering his way past the bins outside her kitchen window. It could only be the poor old detective she had talked to about Cristian. Why was he here, and what on earth was he wearing? It crossed her mind that he might be senile.

She pulled open the front door before he had a chance to ring the bell with the end of his walking stick, which caused him to widen his eyes and startle her because they were a shocking shade of blue and he looked as if he might fall over backwards into the hydrangea bush.

'Hello, are you all right?' she asked, holding open the door.

'Of course I'm all right. I'm always all right. Can I come in?' Bryant lowered his stick and made a performance of stepping hugely across her threshold. 'Your husband. The bookshop. I've been thinking. My dear lady, I owe you an apology.'

'You'd better come and sit down.'

'I've been remiss. I promised to help you and then other matters stole away my attention. I was meant to tell you something, what was it? Well, several things, really. I wrestled your husband away from the City of London and had my top man take a look at his corp— corporeal form.'

Elise stared at him in astonishment.

'He committed suicide.'

'Oh. I'm not sure if—'

'—that's better or worse, I know. Well, here's where it gets a bit more . . .' He tried to remember the life lessons he had learned at the Golden Buddha temple but they had already faded, the curse of an ageing brain. Something about being more mindful of others. 'I'm sorry that your poor husband chose to, ah, divest himself of, ah, precious life with, um, so much to live for. We thought he'd been strangled.'

The strongest brandy available in the UK is the Polish Uderzyć vintage 1987, and comes in a bottle shaped like an angry bear. Elise Albu happened to have some in her kitchen cupboard, a gift from an alcoholic aunt. Guided to it under her instruction, Bryant poured her a large tot, taking a nip himself. Being nice to people clearly had its pitfalls.

'Don't you see,' he said, patting her hand in a consoling fashion, 'it changes everything.'

Much to his amazement, Elise burst into tears. She tried to speak but had to keep stopping. Bryant dragged a handkerchief from his pocket, looked inside it and hastily put it back.

'I think I've approached this the wrong way.' He pointed at the front door. 'I can go out and come in again if that would help.'

'No, I don't think it would,' said Elise. 'If you knew this why didn't you tell me earlier?'

'I wanted to talk to you first. Then I forgot. There's a lot going on at the office.' He took a deep, wheezy breath. 'Let me start over. Sergeant Flowers failed to remove your husband's belt when he took him down to the cell, and I'm afraid Mr Albu took his own life.' He explained how the belt had been replaced with a strip of material. 'Flowers complicated everything. We found traces of the mattress cover on a knife that belonged to the sergeant. Here's the tricky part. Although your husband, um, became deceased by his own hand, I think it was the direct result of meeting that man.'

Elise was momentarily lost. 'What man?'

'The one he went for a drink with. We spoke to the bar-maid at the Museum Tavern. She has a vague recollection of them sitting in a corner of the pub, but couldn't describe either of them. Do you know if any of the books Mr Albu had in stock were valuable?'

She tried to keep up. 'There was a glass case containing a few first editions, good ones, but we didn't have enough money to be serious dealers.' She wasn't sure whether to tell him about Cristian's cash-only trade in books of dubious provenance.

'So you were involved in the bookshop?'

'I helped out occasionally. I'm a medical practice manager – I don't have much free time. The bookshop wasn't really a going concern.'

'I wonder.' He scrabbled about in his overcoat pocket and produced the pocket edition of Alfred Lord Tennyson. 'Have you ever seen this before?'

Elise wiped her eyes and examined the leather cover. 'No, I don't think so.'

'There's a poem in it – hang on a mo.' He donned his spectacles and checked the index. ' "Lady Clara Vere de Vere" – ah, here it is. Tennyson was a baron who hung around with a lot of other aristos and wrote about one after he stayed at her country mansion.'

'I'm sorry,' Elise said, 'I don't know it. I don't understand what you're getting at.'

Bryant turned the open pages around to face her. 'There's a quote in the poem that was used for the title of a famous film. These words are heavily underlined, do you see? "Kind hearts are more than coronets". And as this book was found in your husband's cell after he died, I can't help thinking that it might be a clue.'

'A clue to what?'

'To his state of mind. You said you didn't know why he would go for a drink with his buyer. I think he had a very good reason for going. He had this little book on him when he went, and during the course of their time together he marked those words. He was found with a pen in his pocket. We'll need to match the ink.'

'But if he had something special to say why not write it out on one of the blank pages?'

'He couldn't; he was with the very person it concerns. He had to do something completely innocuous, so he thumbed through the book as he listened and drew a simple line under that phrase. Did he like films?'

'Very much, especially the old British ones.'

'And there we have it.' Bryant sat back, satisfied. 'Why would the buyer wish to destroy the books? I wondered from the start if there could be something in the shop that he wanted not to steal, but *to get rid of.*'

'I'm not sure I understand your thinking, Mr Bryant. I don't recall anything unusual on the shelves. Cristian didn't keep his records up to date but I'm familiar with his stock. At least I thought I was.'

Bryant had a gleam in his eye. 'Do you still have the keys to the shop?'

'Yes, but the fire brigade warned me—'

'Oh, they always do that. I take no notice. Can we go there?'

Elise worried at a nail, thinking. 'I don't know, I don't think I can – when?'

'There's no time like the present.'

*

Silver needles passed through the lamp lights as the pair made their way along Bury Place, Bloomsbury, to the boarded-over bookshop. The fire officers had sent in builders to seal the frontage and had inset a plywood door with a new Yale lock.

'Allow me,' said Bryant, hauling out a spectacular array of skeleton keys from his satchel.

'I thought those only worked in films,' said Elise, holding an umbrella over him.

'These just have the serrated edges removed. They're a bit fiddly but one of them usually does the trick.'

It took him moments to unlock the door. 'They'll have turned the electricity off,' he said, taking an ancient Fidelius battery-powered torch from his satchel. He shone its beam on the blackened floor, lighting Elise's way through the shop. Rainwater cascaded through a shattered light fitting. Many of the shelves had collapsed and the books upon them were carbonized, but near the floor a few had been shielded by an armchair. It felt as if they were in a cave.

Bryant shone his torch on a copy of *The Mystery of Edwin Drood*, its back half burned. 'I guess we'll never know how this one ends. Independent booksellers still write down the titles of the stock they sell, don't they?'

'Yes, Cristian was very thorough. If his ledgers survived they'll still be here. I wasn't allowed to take anything away with me.'

'Can you show me where?'

They stepped between oily pools, the floor crunching and crackling beneath their feet. The air was still acrid with charcoaled wood and burned paper. Bryant's torch beam picked out stalagmites of incinerated books.

Elise climbed behind the crusted remains of the counter. One side was untouched, the other virtually cremated. It reminded Bryant of a wartime photograph his mother had kept: a chemist's half blasted away, the other half still open for business.

'It breaks my heart to see a bookshop lost,' he said. 'I got very depressed when I realized that if I read one book every night between the ages of ten and eighty I could still only get through about 25,500 books.'

'I lost a husband,' said Elise.

'Fair point and sad obviously, but . . .' His eyes strayed to the burned books.

'I can't open this. Could you hold the light steady?' Elise pulled at the handle of a metal cabinet. Bryant went behind the counter, took a fair-sized hammer from his satchel and gave the drawer a thumping whack. It slid open with a metallic screech.

'What else have you got in there?' asked Elise.

'Madam, you don't want to know.'

Elise removed the accounts books. 'They're scorched but legible, just about.' She separated the top volume from the others. 'This is the most recent. What are we looking for?'

'Something valuable, listed and now gone. I'll take it with me if I may. What are these?' He pointed his beam at a sagging black shelf filled with swollen blank-spined paperbacks.

'Cristian had his own imprint. He privately published a few works,' she explained. 'He hardly ever sold a single copy but it made him feel that he was playing his part by helping aspiring authors.'

'Where were they printed?'

'At Tiptree in Essex, by a small private firm.'

'Did he clear the self-published editions for copyright or libel?'

'I don't imagine so. They weren't intended for widespread distribution.'

'Tell me about the books.'

'A few were based on unsolicited manuscripts he personally

liked, printed in small runs for private consumption. I think he hoped they might get noticed and picked up by a major publisher. And there was some vanity publishing – Cristian printed editions for would-be authors. It's a common practice that hurts no one. You know the sort of thing: *My Interesting Life as a Bus Driver*, twenty copies intended for the author's family.'

'I'm familiar with the practice,' said Bryant. 'Our fishmonger self-published a book about Rudolf Nureyev.'

Puzzled, she watched as he bundled armfuls of the books and dumped them on the remains of the counter, blackening himself in the process. 'What are you looking for?'

'Oh, it's just the way my mind works,' he said guiltily. 'In a case like this, one would instinctively search for an enemy bearing a grudge, someone personally known to you both, but my first thought was to check the stock and see if there was anything unusual about it. Where did your husband store the editions he printed?'

'Here,' said Elise. 'The print runs were tiny and he didn't want to pay for storage, so they all went into the first-floor stock room.'

'Which I'm now looking at because it fell through the floor.' Bryant began to check through the least damaged editions. 'I think I should take a few of these with me. And I might have to borrow that delightful copy of *Wood-Burning Stoves of the Soviet Union*.'

'I don't understand. You think someone would set fire to the entire stock in order to destroy one book?'

'Did Cristian ever get over-enthusiastic and publish something without telling the author?'

'He was passionate about his new discoveries.'

Bryant crouched with some difficulty and extracted an entirely unharmed volume from the lowest bookshelf. It had a strangely heavy grey cover. Leaning on his stick, he rose with it. 'This is a very rare edition, Mrs Albu. Ray Bradbury's *Fahrenheit 451*, bound in fireproof asbestos in 1953 and limited to two hundred copies. A book about book burning that couldn't be burned. It's worth a small fortune.'

'I didn't know.'

'You're not convincing me. Was your husband selling rare editions on the side? Don't say anything now. Perhaps it's best that you think about your answer for a while.'

Only the cover was flameproof, but it had perfectly protected the pages. Leafing through it, he came to a loose sheet of paper that was clearly not from the same volume.

'Mr Bryant, there's something you're not telling me either.'

Bryant removed a plastic bag from his coat pocket and slipped the page into it. 'I didn't want to raise any false hopes. If you've never seen the film *Kind Hearts and Coronets*, it's about an aggrieved gentleman who kills every member of the family who stands in his way. He tells the story by confessing all in his memoirs, but at the end he accidentally leaves the incriminating manuscript where someone will find it.'

'I'm not sure I understand what this has to do with—'

'Let's *hypothetically* imagine that your husband was illegally selling rare books. My first instinct is to assume that one of his buyers wanted something very badly that Mr Albu could not or would not sell, so he stole it and burned down the shop to shift attention from the theft. Book collectors are notoriously obsessive, and there are those who are prepared to do absolutely anything to get their hands on a rare edition.

'But now I wonder if I have that wrong. Suppose your husband went for a drink with one of the writers who had given him a manuscript and they demanded it back? Mr Albu pretended he didn't get around to reading it, but not only did he read it, he was so impressed that he printed up his own edition. But then he realized the dangerous situation he was in. The more his client demanded the return of the manuscript, the more your husband perversely wanted to keep hold of it. He had the Tennyson in his pocket and perhaps without even thinking, he underlined the title that pointed to the film.'

'But Cristian only published fiction, so how could such a thing be dangerous?' Elise asked.

'History shows us that books can be very dangerous. Perhaps it *was* just fiction. But suppose it explained crimes the writer was about to commit? Now it was incriminating. And what if your husband accidentally let it be known that there were printed copies? The writer would have to get them back at all costs and make sure they were destroyed.'

'Cristian could never bring himself to destroy books,' said Elise. 'He would have kept them in the shop.'

'The only sure way of removing the evidence was by setting fire to the bookshop.'

To Bryant the incident felt like a rehearsal for the Oranges & Lemons murders. Overwhelmed by financial problems, Albu would appear to have destroyed his own store. But his nemesis had reckoned without the incompetent Sergeant Flowers.

'There's hardly anything left,' said Elise, looking into the dripping darkness in despair. 'There can't be any copies left.'

'Maybe your husband sold some.' Bryant held up the scorched ledger. 'I'm hoping this will supply the answer.'

Back at the PCU, Raymond Land was feeling lost. Leslie Faraday had read his report and was far from happy. Phrases in Faraday's email jumped out and poked him in the eye. 'Unfortunately typical behaviour', 'offensive in the extreme', 'disappointed on every level' and the kicker, 'in reconsideration of your pension'.

Land knew he would have to cancel all leave and warn the staff that shifts would now run round the clock. He conveniently misremembered the past, telling himself that he hadn't wanted to come back to the unit in the first place, and that it didn't matter to him what the Home Office thought. Mortified, he consigned the email chain to the bin, then rang Paula Lambert at *Hard News*.

LAND: Yes, I know what time it is. We're making terrific progress with the case. I just wondered what the mood is like out there.

LAMBERT: When you say 'out there' do you mean our office, where everyone thinks you're doing a terrible job, or the general public, who all hate you?

LAND: Well, I was thinking of the general public really.

LAMBERT: They all hate you.

LAND: But apart from that—

LAMBERT: They're just hearing about another Oranges & Lemons death on the busy streets of their city right now, Raymond, how do you think they feel? If law-abiding citizens can't step out of their front doors—

LAND: Accidents, Paula, they've all been accidents.

LAMBERT: So the fact that the latest victim happened to be struck on the head by a falling clock on the very steps of the next church in your nursery rhyme is just a coincidence, is it?

LAND: It's not *my* nursery rhyme, it's hundreds of years—

LAMBERT: You're not getting behind this, are you? It's a dream case for us, the kind our readers live for. I'm amazed Netflix haven't sent a documentary team over yet. We're placing bets as to how long this can go on before one of you accidentally trips over the killer in the dark.

LAND: You're underestimating the amount of work involved—

LAMBERT: Just around the corner from where your clowns were this afternoon two seventeen-year-old kids were stabbed to death, and the Met arrested eight people less than an hour later. *Eight people.* On a day when they also managed to foil one of the country's biggest terror plots.

LAND: I say, that's a bit unfair—

LAMBERT: I'm just telling you what worries our subscribers, that's all. When they hear about kids being shot they think it's drug gangs and shrug. But when the targets are just like them they panic because it's relatable. We're going with the headline 'Oranges & Lemons Murders: Attacker Pips Police'.

LAND: You're running a punning headline and you're claiming the moral high ground?

LAMBERT: If you haven't had time to catch up with our coverage you can read all about it on our site. We're getting our information straight from source.

LAND: Wait, what do you mean? Has the killer been in contact with you?

LAMBERT: I've told you before, we're claiming press confidentiality on that.

LAND: If you've heard from him you have to turn over your evidence. You can't obstruct the investigation.

LAMBERT: What investigation? We don't see any progress being made at all. When you start getting somewhere, we'll consider sharing our information with you. Until then, I've got a team coming up with fruit-based jokes for future editions.

LAND: You're a very shallow human being, Paula.

LAMBERT: Darling, I'm a journalist.

LAND: You're way lower than that. You're a feature writer.

LAMBERT: See you tomorrow for the next headline event.

35

THE BOUNDARIES OF NORMALITY

It was past nine by the time the detectives met up with Giles Kershaw. There were no spring flowers crowding the tombstones outside the St Pancras morgue. Winter had crept back under cover of darkness. They approached the building beneath pattering umbrellas, Bryant stumbling over a gravestone in the gloom.

'We should leave this country and set up somewhere warm,' said May. 'It would do my rheumatism a world of good.'

'Except that most really sunny places are boring,' Bryant replied, enveloping them in pipe smoke. 'I took a holiday in Greece once. I ate a lot of olives and saw a goat. It's a trade-off; you have to choose between freezing and interesting or hot and dull. Although I wouldn't mind living in a country where it's practically a legal requirement to fall asleep after lunch. Janice says she sent you an ID on the victim who was clocked at St Leonard's.'

'His name is Jackson Crofting,' said John May. 'He lives in part of a warehouse off Columbia Road so St Leonard's Church was on the way home.'

'Bit of an odd place to head for after work, but go on.'

'He's twice divorced, a real loner – someone from his office came in to identify him. The director of a very successful video games company in Old Street. There were no messages on his phone but he has dozens of devices and accounts, so he could have been contacted and persuaded to go to the church in order to meet someone.'

'Any connection to the others?'

'Nothing yet.' May rang the doorbell and Kershaw admitted them.

The lanky pathologist looked absurdly fresh and healthy, as if he'd just come off a lawn tennis court.

'Hello, Giles, has Rosa gone home?' asked May. 'That spares her from being tormented by my comedy partner.'

'Go right through,' said Giles. 'Let's see if the latest victim puts a sense of urgency under you.'

The body in the white plastic bag was shorn of identity, the broad, fleshy face washed but bruised and peppered with small maroon cuts. Mr Crofting had been lifted out of a tangled, hurtling life and placed in this timeless room, calm and still and precise, where every action was considered and calibrated. Giles had set his computer to play Debussy nocturnes, from his playlists chosen for working with the dead.

'What did he do to incur this?' Bryant wondered. 'Do you have a cause of death?'

'See for yourself.' Kershaw carefully lifted Crofting's head and revealed a small but deep-looking incision above the left side of his collarbone. 'It looks like the same kind of blade that was used on Ms Rahman outside St Martin-in-the-Fields. Thin, strong, wielded by a right-hander. Obviously I haven't had time to run toxicology tests yet. I assume we're meant to think that the clock did the damage, but no forensic examiner would buy that.'

'He doesn't care about being believed,' Bryant replied. 'He wants to cause confusion.'

As Giles searched inside the incision May turned away from the body. The sight of death disturbed him more since his own brush with mortality. 'They *must* have all known each other,' he said. 'There would be no sense in planning something like this and then picking random victims.'

Arthur peered at the body with cheerful prurience. 'I suspect the answer lies in the book that Cristian Albu should never have had printed. The only trouble is, I can't find it.'

'Even for you two I have to say that this is extreme.' Kershaw removed his tweezers from Crofting's neck. 'Someone arranges to meet this chap in a church, stabs him and then drops a clock on him? In what world is that normal?'

'The boundaries of normality are shifting, Giles.' May kept his eyes averted. 'None of us ever imagined that the nature of criminality would change. Each time the world tilts a little more you have to readjust and work with it. When Russian spies start putting radioactive poison in teapots and perfume bottles, don't you think others might learn from them and follow suit? Crazy leaders teach us crazy habits. Do you have anything else?'

'Only that he was about to die anyway.'

'You haven't opened him up yet,' said Bryant, puzzled.

'I had a look at his NHS file,' Giles explained. 'Pancreatic cancer. He'd known about it for over a year.'

'I wonder if his killer knew,' said Bryant. 'You'd have to really hate someone to make sure you beat the reaper.'

'We have a suspect but we can't get to him,' May explained. 'He's surrounded by lawyers and comes up clean on every search. We've got some of his cached emails. Everything else has been declared off limits by the Commissioner.'

'Then may I make a suggestion?' Kershaw offered. 'If the

legal approach isn't working do something less legal. It wouldn't be the first time. Your evidence wouldn't be admissible in court but you might get a confirmation of guilt.'

'Perhaps we should burgle his offices,' Bryant pondered aloud.

'I merely posited a theory.' Kershaw looked blankly at May. 'Did you hear me say anything about a break-in?'

'You said "less legal".'

'Before we start arguing about semantics, here's what was in his pockets.' Kershaw handed over a clear plastic Ziploc bag, which Bryant promptly tore open and dumped out on to a non-sterile table. 'I give up,' said Giles, walking away.

Bryant thumbed through Crofting's wallet.

'I don't know what you expect to find in there,' said May dismissively. 'He ran a games company. He has a virtual wallet.'

'Virtual means nearly,' said Bryant. 'He can't nearly have a wallet but he does have this.' He held up a white plastic card. 'It's a swipey-thing.'

'It's not a *swipey-thing*,' said May, feeling suddenly tired. 'Any more than a phone app is a "buttony-thing" or a Kindle is a "plastic book". It must be exhausting to be in such a continual state of amazement at the modern world.'

'As soon as I get used to something it changes,' Bryant complained.

'That's because it takes decades for you to get used to anything. You're only just coming to terms with Wi-Fi.'

'I'm happier with cables. Anything solid. You used to know where you were with a piece of string.' Bryant flicked the card across to his partner. 'Look at the logo.'

The symbol above the name was a drawing of a green pea with a shoot rising from it. 'Pea?'

'P.E.A. Peter English Associates. It seems Mr Crofting had

his own pass for English's building. There's a barcodey-thing on the back.'

'You're just doing it to annoy me now. Why would he have this?'

'I assume English funds, part-owns or deals closely with Mr Crofting's company. We have a legitimate reason for going in. I'm sure I had another one but I've forgotten what it was.'

'Giles has a point,' Bryant said as they left the St Pancras morgue. 'Less legal might be better.'

May felt that the seed had now been planted in his partner's mind, but Bryant was way ahead of him, mentally filling a holdall with wire cutters, balaclavas, grappling hooks and coils of rope.

'We'll go in first thing tomorrow,' Bryant said. 'The weekend staff will be on.'

'Or we could keep it all above board and conduct an official inquiry,' said May.

'You know that will get us nowhere. You've already experienced how this fellow deals with the authorities. Deflect, lie, blame, confuse, avoid.'

'And what are we looking for?'

'A smoking gun,' Bryant replied. 'If you're all right with that image.'

May looked sceptical. 'I have a feeling it won't make any difference if we find one. You said it was all about planning. If that's the case, he'll have already thought of everything we might come up with.'

'Nevertheless, I think we should let him know we're on to him.'

May led the way through the tunnel that returned them to King's Cross. 'He'd never get his own hands dirty, but if he hired others to do it there'll be communications between them.'

'Unless they met in the park, like spies always do on TV.'
Bryant had to put on a burst of speed to avoid a pizza-delivery
bike. May noticed he didn't need his stick to do it, either. Had
he been faking the need for his brass-bevelled Malacca cane?

As they headed towards the unit, he wondered what else
the old devil was holding back from him.

36

COMPETENCY

Dan Banbury pushed back from his desk and pressed the heels of his hands over his eyes. He had been examining footage from all the locations for hours, and could no longer tell one blurred human shape from another. He was delaying the call he needed to make to his wife because he hadn't said goodnight to the kids and was going to be home late again.

He turned his attention back to the blue-grey pixels. The new security cameras were supposed to contain facial recognition software, but as always the biggest problem was a physical one: the lenses weren't rainproof. On dry days they accumulated a powdery fine-grain residue from vehicle tyres. The rain made it stick to the lenses and it had to be removed manually.

He had broken down the sequence from St Martin-in-the-Fields frame by frame, had watched the poor woman fall to her knees a hundred times, and still could not see the most vital moment. The killer had examined every camera angle before his victim's arrival. Rahman could have climbed at any number of different angles across the steps, which meant that her attacker had studied all of the sightlines and memorized their weak points.

Banbury had examined the remains of the clock from St Leonard's Church. It was almost two feet across but not as heavy as it looked, an almost empty cylinder that sat unsecured in a roundel carved in the stone. Not the original clock, the vicar had explained, but a battery-operated replacement made fifteen years ago, and slightly too small so that it was easily shifted. Access? Oh, that was easy, straight up the stairs to the side of the narthex and there it was, the back of the clock, but who would ever think of standing on a chair and pushing it out?

A *madman*, thought Banbury grimly, *but there's method in it*. He had stabbed Jackson Crofting first and positioned the body below the clock, running up the steps to send it down. Dan timed the run up the staircase and felt sure that the entire act could have been completed in less than a minute.

Colin Bimsley wandered past with a piece of toast wedged in his mouth. He extracted it and stared at the screen. 'Did you get anything from your drone?'

'Oh yes,' said Dan, 'I got some Power Rangers, a few unicorns and some sweaty little sod who'd been bunged a monkey to keep Her Majesty's law enforcement officers amused for the afternoon. Is there any more toast?'

'Last slice. You can have a bite of this one.'

'No thank you. You've got ketchup on – actually it's all over you. And lettuce and something else.'

'Liver sausage.' Colin flicked the debris away.

'I can't look at this any more. Either he's a master of disguise or I'm seeing a bunch of different people involved.'

'What, you mean like a group of subversives?'

'I don't know, Colin,' said Dan irritably. 'He's chucking money at a few chancers, getting them to stand around at his crime scenes and stir the mud a little. Like the van driver he

hired, Mohammed Alkesh. Make a delivery and get lost –
easy. I bet if you went out on to the Caledonian Road right
now and asked the first sketchy roadman you saw to go and
stand in the station, no questions asked, cash up front, he'd
volunteer and offer to bring a friend.'

'You could be right.' Colin dropped backwards on to the
swivel chair next to Banbury. 'If somebody wanted to desta-
bilize things, right, like the leader of a protest group, it would
be easy to make everyone paranoid about going out. I've
been looking into them. There's a bunch of incels demanding
justice for meat-eaters because they feel threatened by vege-
tarian options on menus – it was good for a laugh until they
started kicking in restaurant windows and poisoning food-
stuffs. It's like this bloke: the nursery rhyme stuff is great
publicity.'

'We should be holding a press conference to get all the
rumours dismissed,' said Dan. 'Raymond told me he wanted
to do it but Faraday never got back to him.'

'Why not?'

'They're playing silly buggers. How can you get anything
done when two people on the same side won't talk to each
other?' Banbury fast-forwarded to the end of his footage and
binned the file. 'What are you going to do after this is over?'

Colin stopped mid-chew. 'What do you mean? Career,
like? I kind of assumed everything was all right now, the way
it's always been in the past. Like when Meera says she never
wants to see me ever again and then asks me if I want to go
to the pub.'

'No, Colin, this was our last hurrah. Epic fail. We were
given it because everyone else knew it would be toxic. We'll
be punting around for new jobs within two to three days.'

'Unless Mr Bryant—' said Colin. He decided not to tempt
fate and swallowed his toast.

At the other end of the building, Meera yawned and

stretched her neck. 'I have to go home. I'm knackered. What a day. What time is it?'

'Half ten,' said Sidney, her face made paler by the light from her laptop. The pair were sharing an office full of plasterboard panels at the end of the first floor, but Meera had surrendered her territory without grace. Even so, it was hard to dislike the intern. She had a natural feel for the job, almost as if she had been briefed on what to expect. 'So,' Sidney said again, 'Mr Bryant. Tell me.'

'Why are you always asking about him?'

'He has to undergo a core competency test or he'll be thrown out.'

'How do you know that?'

'It was in Mr Land's emails.'

'You hacked into them?'

'He doesn't exactly make it difficult. I also tried to get into the Peter English Associates website but it's got dual-tier protection.'

'Should you have been doing that?'

'Someone's convinced your bosses that English is untouchable.' Sidney flicked through screens of data at a dizzying speed.

'Do you take all that in?' Meera rose and looked around for her PCU jacket. She wore it off duty as well because it stopped her thinking about what to wear.

'I know what I'm looking for. English looks invulnerable but he'll have a weak spot.'

Meera zipped up her jacket. 'Are you coming?'

'I'll stay here for a while.'

'You'll be able to get home OK?'

'You don't have to worry about me.'

As Meera left she looked back at Sidney, working in semi-darkness, hunched over a new window on her laptop screen. Something nagged at the back of her mind. The girl reminded her of someone or something else. She dismissed the thought and headed out, passing the detectives, who were coming up the stairs and looked as if they were just arriving for work, except that John May's face was grey with exhaustion. Bryant seemed to age backwards when he was on a case.

The detectives had returned in order to file their competency tests before their midnight deadline passed.

'It's ridiculous,' Bryant complained. 'It's late and we're both tired. I don't have time to waste on gibberish like this.'

He squinted at his laptop screen like a pawnbroker examining a disappointing engagement ring. Before him were thirty pages of multiple-choice questions.

'You have to do it if you want to stay on the case,' May said, pressing lightly at the sore muscles in his chest.

'My keyboard's sticking. I spilt some lamb pasanda on it but it's normally fine with Indian cuisine. I think clarified butter might work like WD40. It certainly does on me.'

'Here, have this one.' May handed over another keyboard and paired it for him. It was faster to supply Bryant with spare keyboards than try to clean food off them.

Armed with an extra cushion, Bryant settled to the task. 'Right. *Question one. A warehouse fire proves to be arson. A man was seen running away just after it started. He had been sacked from the company for stealing.*'

'Read it to yourself,' May suggested.

Bryant continued aloud. '*For each of the following statements, answer: A equals TRUE, B equals FALSE, C equals IMPOSSIBLE TO SAY.*

'*One. The man seen running away from the fire was the man who started it.* Well, that's ridiculous. Who wouldn't run from a fire? B, false.

'*Two. The incident is the second one to occur.* That obviously has nothing to do with it. How big is the factory? Is its

309

safety manager reliable? Are flammable items stored on the premises? B, false.

'*Three. The man who was sacked from the factory may have started the fire.* Well, that throws up more questions. Had the company unfairly docked his wages? Was he being exploited by the bosses? Was he framed after reporting health and safety infringements? This is exactly what's wrong with the police, narrow minds, limited imagination. How do they know it was a man and not a woman? What does the factory make? Has it been built in a storm corridor without lightning rods?'

'You're over-thinking it, Arthur.' May looked over his shoulder. 'And you've answered the questions in the wrong order.'

'I'm not a linear person. It's no good.' Bryant pushed the laptop away in exasperation. 'It's all a load of miscellaneous rubbish. I can't be expected to correct all of their mistaken suppositions.'

'Then just tick the boxes you think they'd like you to tick,' said May gently.

Bryant shook his head. 'My conscience would never allow me to do that.'

'If they take away the investigation you and your conscience won't get a look in.'

Bryant gave him a pleading look. 'Could you do mine?'

'Certainly not,' said May. 'There's other stuff that needs sorting out. We're short of information on Jackson Crofting's background. Sidney sent me an email. She's done some checking and found that all of the victims have disproportionate social reach.'

'I'm not sure I entirely grasp what that means,' said Bryant.

'It means they have influence, but successfully ring-fence their own private data. Outgoing but not incoming. They are followed but don't follow.'

'I don't follow you.'

May grabbed a sheet of paper from his partner's desk. 'Imagine a Venn diagram with each circle representing a victim's field of expertise. Politics, justice, technology: they cross into each other's lives, just not in the ways you're used to finding. They're not related, didn't go to university together, didn't have affairs with each other. But this' – he stabbed the diagram with his pen – 'shows they were connected in other ways. Dinners are work. Parties are work. It's peer group data-sharing.'

Bryant stuck a finger in his ear. 'No, you're not getting through. It's like distant waves crashing on the shore. Or it may be my tinnitus.'

'We're not finding a common causal link. Maybe they don't remember meeting, or were only distantly affected by something Peter English did. Or something they unwittingly did to him.'

Bryant had been barely listening. He had a habit of tuning out when May became enthusiastic about typing and time-tables. May did the same thing when his partner started going on about Greek mythology.

'Claremont,' Bryant said suddenly.

'What about him?'

'I can't get hold of him. This private clinic where his wife is keeping him: nobody answers the phone. I think we should send someone to check.'

'I'll add it to the list of things to do,' said May wearily.

'So we'll burgle English's place first thing in the morning, and that just leaves the competency test to sort out.' Bryant's blue eyes were saucer-like. 'Perhaps I could copy yours?'

May studied this strange childlike man who depended on him to navigate the treacherous shallows of modern life. He slid over his laptop with a sigh. 'Don't duplicate it exactly. At least make a couple of mistakes.'

'Don't worry, I'm fantastic at cheating,' said Bryant with a grin.

37

EQUAL TO THE LAW

They met at Holborn tube station at nine the following morning.

'What on earth are you wearing?' asked May as they headed towards Peter English's building in High Holborn. 'For God's sake, finish that before we go in.'

Bryant was eating a chocolate éclair. 'This is my casual attire,' he explained, running a hand down his clothes like a magician's assistant showing off a cabinet of swords. 'Appropriate clothes for an office worker relaxing at the weekend.'

'And that's what you think they wear, is it? A Christmas jumper and corduroy trousers.'

'I don't own any jeans and the top was knitted for me by Alma's church ladies.' He opened his coat to reveal the full horror of the jumper, which featured Santa Claus being blessed by Jesus.

'It looks like it was knitted by that woman who painted the Monkey Christ,' said May.

'This must be the place.' Bryant put the remains of the éclair in his pocket. The entrance before them was daunting:

a bronze and glass frontage with revolving doors and an acre of cream marble beyond. Within was a slab of sandstone that might have been stolen from Stonehenge, behind which sat a blank-faced young man in a blazer and tie, as smooth and unfeatured as a shop mannequin.

'Act casual,' said May. It would have been better not to say this, as Bryant's casual act involved a strange, arm-swinging gait that belonged in an old Norman Wisdom film.

'Hellooo.' Bryant cheerfully approached the receptionist. 'We're just doing some weekend work . . . at the weekend.'

'You still have to sign in.' The receptionist pointed to an open book on the counter.

Bryant scribbled a line, then printed a random set of consonants. If the receptionist asked he'd say his name was Hungarian. Taking May's arm, he aimed them at the brushed-steel barrier and waved his card at the panel.

Nothing happened. The receptionist started to take an interest.

'That's your Marks & Spencer card,' May whispered.

Bryant searched his wallet and switched it for the pass.

'Do you gentlemen know where you're going?' the receptionist asked.

'But of course,' said Bryant. 'We're doing a favour for Mr English, collecting . . . a thing.'

'He didn't leave anything for you down here. Maybe it's in their reception.'

'Of course. And where would that be?'

'On the sixth.'

'Oh, well, I'm sure that's where it is then. Waiting for us to collect it.' Bryant's voice had become inexplicably posh and vaguely Oliver Hardyish. He stepped through the barrier and slipped the card back to May. 'Thank you so much for your most caned concern.'

May was pulling a face at him. 'Accent. And stop explaining.'

They headed for the lifts, where the swipe card was needed again.

The sixth-floor reception area of Peter English Associates was a brash show of power: more marble, signature designer lights, glamorously uncomfortable furniture. A bank of monitors was running the kind of colour-saturated footage usually found in television showrooms: drone footage of South American waterfalls, Venice under clouds of pigeons, Machu Picchu with an orange sky.

Bryant peered down a corridor. 'Do you think anyone else is in? I should have asked the receptionist.'

'I'm glad you didn't while you were doing your Prince Charles impersonation,' said May. 'Come on, English is bound to have the largest corner office.'

They found it on their second try, but the door was closed with a traditional lock. This was where Bryant's skeleton Yale proved useful. Inside was a surprisingly modest room – no central desk, just an expensive Italian sofa and three fire-engine-red armchairs set around a marble mushroom.

'It's a pity there aren't laser beams criss-crossing the floor,' said Bryant. 'We could have rappelled through a heating duct.'

'Says the man who has trouble bending over to tie his laces.'

'Where do you think he keeps his stuff? Do people even have any stuff now or is it all online?'

'Well, it's not going to be in a grey filing cabinet full of manila envelopes, is it?' said May. 'This isn't the 1970s.'

'And yet it is.' Bryant pointed to a filing cabinet standing in the smaller adjoining office. 'Seventies wallpaper and an ironic filing cabinet. It'll probably be full of whiskies or something.'

His prediction proved correct. The drawers opened to reveal an extravagantly stocked bar.

'This place is geared for hospitality, not work,' said May, looking for charging points. 'There's no computer equipment. He must take his laptop with him.'

'There's a safe,' said Bryant, pointing to an unassuming black metal box set at the back of the bottom drawer.

'How did you spot that? You can't see buses.'

'I have my special trifocals today.' Bryant's moon-eyes swam up through thick lenses.

'Looks like it uses a Titan security key.' May peered at a tiny slot in the front. 'We won't get it open. Google use them in their buildings.'

'If he's that secretive, he has something to hide.'

May rose and looked about. 'I bet you that even in a company as security-conscious as this there's a closet Luddite working here. There's always one.'

They headed off along the corridor to look. In what appeared to be the HR department they found a single sheet of paper pinned to the back of someone's chair: 'English's schedule for the week'. May photographed the page. 'Nothing very revealing ... he's throwing a party at one of his properties on Sunday afternoon. Some kind of launch event.'

'Excuse me, who are you?'

They turned to find themselves confronted by a stern-faced young woman holding a cardboard coffee cup.

Bryant tried to recall the name he had written in the reception book. 'I'm Mr Harghzyszabó,' he said. 'I work here.'

'I don't think you do, Mr Harghzyszabó. You're far too old for a start, and this is my office.'

'You could have just said this is your office.'

Deciding that the best solution was partial honesty, May showed her his ID. 'We're working on an investigation into the death of one of Mr English's colleagues, Jackson Crofting. We'd heard that Mr English would be in this morning and were hoping to interview him.'

The young woman peered at them narrowly. 'He's never here at the weekend. You could have called me and saved yourself the trip. Is it something I can help you with at all?'

'We need to see certain documents pertaining to his deal with Mr Crofting,' said May.

'Unfortunately I'm afraid it's beyond my power to grant you access.' She had adopted a thermometer-lowering British tone that directly contradicted what she was saying.

'It's an official police investigation,' Bryant pointed out.

'Then I'm surprised you didn't arrange the interview in advance.' She checked her watch. 'It would be so much better if you weren't here.'

May squared up to her. 'Do you understand that we are senior law enforcement officers conducting a murder inquiry?'

She set her coffee down, ready for a fight. 'You may well be, but this is a public company sanctioned and represented internationally by the government that employs you, so I think you'll find you're beyond your jurisdiction.'

'Peter English does not make the law,' said Bryant.

'He doesn't need to. I'm afraid I must ask you to leave now.'

'So soon?' Bryant lifted up his boot. 'Can you direct me to the lavatory? I think I trod in something on the way in.' Much to her horror, he showed her. She pointed to a door in the corridor opposite, and Bryant limped theatrically over to it, followed by his partner.

'Who the hell does English think he is?' May fumed, closing the door behind him. 'God, you really did tread in something.'

'No, it's my chocolate éclair,' said Bryant. 'Give me a hand.' He leaned on May's shoulder and surprisingly nimbly climbed on to a counter holding three washbasins.

'She's probably calling English right this minute,' said May.

'Then let's give her something to call him about.'

Hauling a length of iron pipe from inside his coat, he

reached up and smashed the overhead sprinkler. A moment later water began spraying from points all over the ceiling and an electronic alarm sounded.

'You maniac!' May grabbed his partner and pulled him down. Outside, sprinklers had detonated in the corridor too, staining the walls and flooding across the polished wood floors.

'Wow,' said Bryant, 'I didn't expect that to work.'

'Be careful you don't slip.' May took hold of his partner's arm.

The assistant stood aghast, phone in hand, as sirens wailed above her and the detectives moved carefully on, leaving the building with as much dignity as they could muster.

The receptionist rose from his chair as they passed him, shaking themselves off like wet dogs, but decided he was not being paid enough to wrestle a pair of soaked seniors to the floor.

'I can't believe you brought an iron pipe with you,' said May as they hastened down the steps.

'It was part of that old rocket launcher. The one I used to fire chickens across the road with.'

'I can't even remember why you were doing that.'

'Neither can I.'

'What do we do now?' May asked.

'We wait,' said Bryant, wringing out his hat.

Meanwhile, Raymond Land had arrived at the unit and opened his emails to find something disturbing. He stared at his screen and wondered what on earth he'd done wrong. A note he had dashed off to Leslie Faraday in hasty anger had gone astray, and he couldn't tell where it had ended up. It was embarrassing having to call in Floris for help, so he tried turning his computer off and turning it on again. As his mailbox reopened he realized he had received a notification not intended for him because the sender had accidentally left him on a thread. It read:

Leslie –

Thanks for your note. On further investigation it appears to be distantly related to progeria. The disease in its purest form is incredibly rare and no one has survived it beyond the age of twenty-six, but there are more common versions with progeria-like side effects.

He was about to dismiss it as some bizarre form of spam but a name further down caught his eye. Before continuing he checked the word 'Progeria' and got 'an extremely rare autosomal dominant genetic disorder in which symptoms resemble the physiological ageing process'.

He read on:

One variant is not always fatal but indicates that the patient is subject to premature ageing. Unfortunately this isn't the only symptom as the disease also affects the brain, often causing hallucinations and reducing the patient's ability to tell dreams from reality, as well as adversely affecting their decision-making process.

I was not happy about releasing these details to you prior to my conversation with Mr Bryant, but I understand that, given the extreme seriousness of the unit's ongoing investigation, the circumstances in this case are exceptional. I suspect that Mr Bryant has long known about his illness and has never disclosed the facts about it. If for no reason other than withholding information, he should be removed from operations forthwith.

Arnold Gillespie

Land was astounded. The email was attached to some previous correspondence between Faraday and Dr Gillespie about staff medical insurance, and Gillespie had accidentally copied him in.

The more he thought about it, the more everything began to make sense. While the rest of the team, including his partner, had been immersing themselves in the nuts and bolts of the investigation, Bryant had been away with the fairies, chatting to his usual assortment of marginalized idiot-savants.

Something needed to be done. Bryant had to be taken off the case as quickly as possible.

38

INSOLUBLE

Hard News Video Report from Paula Lambert timed at 10.30 a.m. Saturday 13 April

A series of killings in broad daylight has placed Londoners on high alert this week. The latest victim has been confirmed as Jackson Crofting, CEO of the videogame company Geniusly. He was discovered outside St Leonard's Church, Shoreditch, apparently the victim of a bizarre accident, but there are suspicions that he was murdered by the Oranges & Lemons Killer. The police unit in charge of the investigation is refusing to comment on the risk to Londoners. In the meantime members of the public are warned to stay alert and avoid dimly lit areas.

'She's completely contradicting herself,' said Arthur Bryant indignantly, spanking his laptop screen. 'Why would you need to avoid dimly lit areas if the attacks occur in broad daylight? Why is daylight always broad? And why is the article headed with a photo of an unrelated woman?'

'Video games – that's Angelina Jolie,' May explained. 'She was in films based on a game. *Hard News* can link any story back to a celebrity.'

'Well, I hope nobody's stupid enough to fall for this rubbish.'

'People can only react to what they're told,' May replied reasonably. 'It's not their fault if they're fed lies.'

'It is if they believe them without evidence. Where's Paula getting her information from?'

'I think Raymond's been speaking to her. I just saw him in the corridor and he scuttled past me like a crab.'

'Do you think he's all right? Perhaps I should go and talk to him.'

'I wouldn't,' May said. 'It usually has a deleterious effect.'

'There is something very odd going on around here.' Bryant prowled to the window and wiped it with his sleeve. 'There are people outside just standing around and staring up at the building.'

'Have you looked at our website?'

'Don't be silly.'

'There's some pretty fierce feedback on it today about tax-payers' money being wasted. Apparently Faraday doesn't want us to hold a press conference because he thinks it'll turn into a PR disaster.'

'Of course, because he's not interested in whether the Oranges & Lemons Killer is ever found—'

'Please don't call him that, Arthur.'

'—but we have to let Faraday know that he doesn't control Raymond. *We* control Raymond.'

'All right, let's talk to him,' said May, grabbing his partner's hand and dragging him out into the half-repaired corridor.

Land was standing at the window too. His office looked barer and even less finished than before. Above his unstable desk the ceiling's innards were hanging out. 'What do those people want?' he asked as they entered. 'It's like . . . like . . .'

'*Night of the Living Dead*?' Bryant ventured. 'The Leeds Dripping Riot of 1865?'

'You had better have some very bloody good news for me,' Land warned, turning from the glass. 'This Jackson Crofting bloke copped it a week after winning the Business Personality of the Year Award. "Entrepreneurial excellence", apparently, not "Most likely to be brained with a clock".'

'He wasn't,' said Bryant. 'He was stabbed in the back of the neck.'

'Well, that makes it so much better, thank you. What was he doing at a church anyway? Nobody in London goes to church. Why can't anyone answer the simplest questions? Leslie Faraday seems to have stopped talking to me. He knows we're dead in the water. This is how dictators feel in their last days of power. Everyone walks away from them.' Bryant raised a puzzled eyebrow at his partner. 'And every time I open my computer it fills up with the most appalling lies about us from websites I've never heard of. Could you get Dan to come and clean it up for me?'

'Darling Raymond, as much as we'd love to discuss your janitorial issues, perhaps you could explain why we haven't held a press conference? I mean, apart from the fact that you always cock them up?'

'Faraday expressly forbade it—'

'—because he doesn't want it to come out that MI5 was investigating Claremont's mental health, I get that, but shouldn't you hold one anyway?'

'We need to get the public on our side,' May urged. 'We have no evidence and no suspects other than this fellow English and that poor dupe who was given five hundred pounds to stand in a churchyard. We're supposed to be putting all our energy into policing St Dunstan's now but we've barely started dealing with what happened yesterday. We're one step behind all the time.'

'St Dunstan's,' Land repeated. 'What's that?'

'It's a thousand-year-old Anglican church in Stepney,' said Bryant, 'the next connection to the rhyme. It's known as the Church of the High Seas because so many sailors are buried there. It has a delightfully arched nave, if memory serves.'

'I don't care if it has a jacuzzi and a disco ball, I don't want you going anywhere near it. The press will be there ahead of you.'

'There's another human life at stake,' May reminded him, 'or perhaps the victims have been forgotten in this travelling circus.'

Land stood firm. 'Your staff were on site at the time of the last attack and failed to catch even a glimpse of the killer, so why go there? It's physically impossible to run surveillance on the entire borough of Stepney.'

'We need to be near the church,' said Bryant.

'And do what?' Land almost screamed. 'You never put batteries in your hearing aid and he's starting to look like a man who's been recently shot.'

'We're perfectly capable of—' May began.

'I don't care what you're capable of, I care about what photographers see through their camera lenses, a sepia tint of two mature Victorian gentlemen who've just come from the park after feeding the pigeons, not the dynamic leaders of a major murder investigation. Don't you understand? This is out of your league now. People are saying that a cell of radicals is planning the country's downfall, warming up for bigger attacks.'

'We've heard that,' said Bryant defensively. 'Even if they exist they're hardly likely to hide clues in an old nursery rhyme.'

'Well, it's the word on the street,' said Land.

'The street?' Bryant was incredulous. 'You've never ever been to the street. You're like the captain of the *Pinafore*.'

'I thought he went to sea,' said May, confused.

'He never ever went to sea, that's the whole point,' Bryant explained. 'What have you heard about a radical cell?'

Land scrabbled about for his notes. 'Only that a bunch of disgruntled business leaders are forming a so-called populist political party to "take back control", as their slogan puts it. Let me tell you how this will play out. At some time in the near future a call will come through to arrest extremists. And *that* is what Faraday wants. That's what will clear the streets of dissidents in the eyes of the Home Office and win him a promotion.'

'I hardly think that's likely.'

'What, you think it couldn't happen here, given the way things are going?'

'No, Faraday being promoted. He has the mental agility of a beanbag.'

'I'm warning you to stay here.' Land was tempted to thump his desk but feared the leg might come off. 'Let Floris see that you're performing the duties expected of you. Don't disappear. You can send off Mangeshkar and Bimsley and anyone else with their body parts in full working order but I do not want to turn on my TV and see you threatening the Channel Four cameras with a walking stick, do you understand? I need a case built on solid evidence. You must have missed the last attack by seconds.'

'He was watching,' said Bryant. 'His clues aren't actually clues because they're not solvable, and he knows it. The "Oranges & Lemons" thing is a con.'

'I'm confused,' said Land, who was increasingly familiar with the sensation. 'Is he following the rhyme or not?'

'That's the problem,' said Bryant. 'It's not about the rhyme but it could be about the churches. Every ward in the city has at least one venerable place of worship. The general public barely notice any of them, whether they're Catholic, Anglican or pagan.'

'There aren't any pagan churches,' said Land irritably. 'Pagans are just nutters in headbands forming a conga line around old rocks four times a year.'

'You misunderstand, my dear old mumper. Historically, churches have a connection with paganism because many were built on top of temples, including our very own St Paul's Cathedral. The central image of Catholicism, Mary seated with her son, is drawn from the depiction of Isis with her child Horus. It's known as the *lactans* pose, and is—'

'Enough!' Abandoning caution, Land slammed his hand so hard on the desk that his tea mug slopped, surprising everyone, including himself. 'You've done this for the last time. I want you to catch a murderer, not give me a lecture in philately.'

'That's stamp collecting,' said Bryant calmly. 'Perhaps you mean theology – it's hard to tell when you get het up like this. Have one of your pills.'

'I don't need to take a Valium, I am quite—'

'Second drawer down.'

'—capable of—'

Bryant quietly slid his tea in front of him. 'Better take two.'

'Get him out of here,' Land pleaded to May, 'and don't let him leave the building. If anyone from the press calls you, you are *not* to speak to them.'

As soon as the detectives had gone, Land opened the drawer and reached for his tablets. After he reread Dr Gillespie's email about Bryant's health, he was left wondering what to truly believe.

39

DEVIL'S BREATH

The operations room looked like an abandoned cinema. The two Daves' plasterboard panels had been propped against the windows to block out light and increase the contrast of Banbury's images. Looped segments of camera footage stuttered across screens, flecking the walls with fragments of repeated action.

Janice Longbright looked around for her coffee cup and found it cold. She had catalogued the footage codes for Dan so that they could be edited into a single film clip that even Raymond Land, who had the attention span of a sugaraddicted toddler, could follow.

'The hardest part is working out where the killer is standing in all of these takes.' She pulled out chairs in front of the main monitor. Dan waited until the detectives had sat down and began spinning through the footage.

'In the Strand we have to assume he's inside the van with the driver. We can see through the window in some shots but the shadows are too deep to make out much. He either threatened Alkesh or paid him to turn a blind eye. No wonder the lad ran off afterwards. MI5 seems to think that Alkesh is no longer in the country. They're not keeping us informed about their findings.'

Banbury moved to the next sequence.

'The attack on Chakira Rahman. Two cameras picked her up on the steps of St Martin's. Watch this: there's an elderly Indian man, a middle-aged woman and ... I don't know what this guy is, he's dragging a piece of cardboard around, maybe begging. Here comes Rahman, cutting across the corner of the staircase, not really looking where she's going. Now, a little further on' – he checked the coding note and flicked forward – 'the cardboard guy passes closest.'

'How close?' asked John May.

'It's hard to tell exactly because the cardboard is under his left arm, which obstructs our view. Here's the crucial moment. We can see him start to raise his right hand. That's where the contact occurred.'

Banbury moved through the frames. Two grey figures were visible in a tangle of arms and coats. Nothing was clear, nothing definite.

'We can't see Rahman's face so we don't know what her reaction was. The cardboard guy moves on but doesn't speed up or change the way he's moving. His body language should give him away but it doesn't. Then nothing for three seconds, and finally we see Rahman go down the steps, here. We had Colin re-enact it and he nearly broke his nose. The cardboard sheet worked as a screen for the stabbing action.'

Dan froze the image. 'The toxin on the knife blade is interesting. There's a drug similar to scopolamine, the active ingredient in seasickness tablets, called burundanga. It's a ground-up extract from the seeds of the borrachero shrub and accounts for half of all ER admissions in Colombia. It's also known as the Devil's breath. It's commonly blown into the face, and is available here as a street drug. Lately it's

327

been used by Chinese nationals on women in West End night-clubs.'

'Two cheers for human ingenuity,' said Bryant. 'Let's move on before I get too depressed.'

'The next one won't make you feel any better,' Banbury warned, pulling forward another screen. 'The death of Judge Tremain presents us with a familiar problem. Evergreens. Why couldn't he have worked in an office behind a tree that sheds its leaves? The foliage obscures the window because the camera is only concerned with the doorway.

'Which brings me to the fourth, and here it gets messy. There were people and cameras everywhere in Shoreditch, but we've nothing from St Leonard's churchyard itself because it's on ecclesiastical land and they see no reason to spend money on cameras when the property is locked at night. I thought there must be a direct view of the portico from the other side of the road. There's a 360-degree camera installed on the first floor of that terrace, but guess what, it's been stolen. The property-owner looked shocked, couldn't remember the last time he checked it, et cetera. The failure would have been flagged up at the surveillance centre but no one seems to have noticed, which means we have no footage of the suspect's egress from the churchyard. We've plenty of video from the drone but it's of the runner who was hired to decoy us.'

'This is not working,' said Bryant, waving his hand at the screens. 'All this over-reliance on technological data. It's not your fault, Dan, it's what we all do now, sit around being fed electronic half-truths, using that' – here he stabbed a finger at Dan's monitor – 'when we should be using *this*.' He knuckled the side of his head. 'Whatever happened to hunches, feelings, taking a few chances?'

'Yeah, well, that's how Timothy Evans ended up being hanged by mistake,' said Meera.

'Who's been hanged?' asked Colin, who had momentarily zoned out.

'Evans was executed for murder in 1949 but his landlord was the serial killer Reginald Christie, who fed the police false information to cover up his own guilt,' Bryant explained.

'Why did the cops listen to him?'

'Because they liked him. They wanted to believe him.'

'Which was over seventy years ago and I know that seems like yesterday to you, Mr Bryant, but can we get back to the present?' Banbury asked. 'I can't fix the drone in time to use it for St Dunstan's.'

'Can't we borrow one?'

'I can try, but there's not a lot of goodwill out there at the moment,' said Dan. 'Do you know the area?'

'The streets are quiet. Anyone turning up at the church will be there for a reason. It isn't a place you just happen to be passing. It's flat and exposed. He won't be able to slip away into a crowd this time.'

Bryant had stopped listening. Tired and frustrated, he left the operations room and returned to his desk, settling himself with the items he had taken from Elise Albu: the sales ledger, four scorched self-published volumes and some correspondence that had survived the flames.

But he couldn't simply let go of the 'Oranges & Lemons' rhyme. There was something about its harshness that drew him back. He looked along his bookshelves and plucked down a title – *The Compendium of British Nursery Rhymes*, published the previous year by Eleanor Chester.

The chanted children's game of Oranges & Lemons began as a square dance with the same tune, which imitates the sound of church bells. It was first noted around the year of the Great Plague, 1665, and was sung on festival days. It is fanciful to think that the end of the song, 'Here comes a chopper to chop off your head', is the logical conclusion of the prisoner's journey to Tyburn Tree as debt was not a capital offence, although offenders could be hanged for 'fraudulent bankruptcy'. Charles Dickens's father was sent to the Marshalsea Prison in 1824 for a debt owed to a baker.

The rhyme is based on an older, considerably longer version called 'London Bells'. In it, ' "Bullseyes and targets," say the bells of St Margaret's' refers to nearby archery ranges and ' "Brickbats and tiles," say the bells of St Giles' is a reference to neighbouring builders' yards. ' "Pokers and tongs," say the bells of St John's' is more sinister. This church is situated on the second floor of the White Tower inside the Tower of London, where instruments of torture were stored.

Other verses refer to local tradespeople and businesses within the vicinity of each church. St Dunstan's has existed for well over a thousand years. It has been suggested that the reference ' "When will that be?" say the bells of Stepney' could refer to sailors' wives wondering when they would see their husbands again.

Eleanor Chester had an address in Bloomsbury, barely ten minutes' walk away. That was good enough for Bryant. He put in a call, then stuffed his battered hat on to his tonsured head and grabbed an umbrella.

'I'm coming with you.' Sidney was standing in the doorway.

'You don't even know where I'm going,' said Bryant in some irritation.

Sidney laughed. 'Do you know you talk to yourself? I literally just heard you say where you were going.'

'Are you sure you want to come with me?' Bryant eyed her red rain-hat, matching jacket and sparkly black leggings with suspicion. 'I thought perhaps you had a job interview at Cirque du Soleil.'

'Has anyone ever told you you're funny?'

'No, and—'

'—they never will,' they both said.

'Come on then.' He held out an arm to her. 'I could do with a walk.'

'Do you want me to book an Uber?'

'I do not wish to stare at a small drawing of a car turning back and forth while I shout, "You're going the wrong way" at it, thank you.'

'But I thought as you're old you would prefer—'

He patted her arm. 'Try not to speak.'

They argued all the way there.

40

THE IDEA OF LONDON

Raymond Land looked up as Sidney led a scrofulous pile of clothes past his door. 'He's not going out, is he?' he asked Tim Floris, who was seated beside him. 'Where's she taking him?'

'Who?' asked Floris, looking around.

'Him. That one-man slum. Bryant. I explicitly told him not to leave the building. You have to treat the staff here as if they're children. Sometimes they need to be smacked.'

He could feel Floris's disapproval. It never showed in his features, but it was there. Land didn't know how to deal with millennials. Floris's reaction to incoming news (usually bad) was odd in that he hardly reacted at all. He absorbed, processed and remained silent, never becoming involved or seeking to persuade. When Land made an effort to teach him a little about the workings of the unit, he'd said offhandedly, 'It's OK, I'm not going to be doing this for ever,' which left Land feeling crushed. Sidney was worse, an extrapolation of what had begun in Floris's generation.

He had expected Floris to ask him why he was not

stopping Bryant from leaving, but no such question was forthcoming. He told himself that the Home Office official was not on his side, or indeed the side of anyone at the PCU because he was duty-bound to report everything he saw and heard. Probably over dinner in Chelsea.

'Shall we try again with a new email?' Floris patiently suggested, moving his chair closer. Land was embarrassed at having his technological limitations exposed, but desperately needed help. Banbury had given up on him after realizing that his explanation of how attachments worked was being met with a look that suggested Land was engaged in a staring contest. The unit chief could no more grasp the concept of Cloud storage than he could imagine what the fourth dimension looked like.

As he laboriously opened a new window on his screen he asked, 'What's it like working for the Home Office?' This was perilously close to asking a personal question, so he expected a circumspect answer.

'Disappointing,' said Floris with a rare hint of forthrightness. 'They deal in statistics. They don't know any real people.'

'I always suspected that,' said Land. 'I applied for a position there once but Faraday turned me down.'

'Mr Faraday is . . .' Floris considered his choice of words. 'Challenging.'

'He's distancing himself from me, I can feel it. He stopped returning my emails but he's happy to contact you.'

'It's different for me. I'm staff. You're a rival.'

Land showed Floris what was on his screen. Out of the blue, Faraday had suddenly sent a furious demand to see him immediately.

'He says you're not answering your phone,' said Floris.

'There's still something wrong with the landlines. Although I have been reluctant to call him, I admit. One hates to be the bearer of endlessly bad news. He wants me to act without his sanction so that he has someone to blame when this is over. Could you possibly have a word with him?'

Floris looked uncomfortable at the turn in the conversation, but Land was always the last one to pick up on such things.

'You have the ear of the Home Secretary, you've been here all week making reports, couldn't you just – make up a little something extra?'

'I can't falsify information, Mr Land, if that's what you're implying.'

Land inwardly winced. 'Of course not, and I would be the last person to ever suggest such a thing.' He patted Floris on the arm. 'Let's forget we had this conversation.'

Arthur Bryant and Sidney Hargreaves sat in a small harshly lit room, the cheap furniture and bare walls suggestive of trimmed government funding. A pity, because Senate House was a grand edifice, as solid as a pyramid, the academic heart of the University of London. Its main hall had the solemnity and sweep of a Greek temple, as befitted the home of higher learning, but Eleanor Chester's room was hidden behind an upper deck of wood-panelled staircases, bridges and corridors, most of them now blocked off by incongruous steel swipe-card barriers.

'It was designed by the architect who created the art deco tube stations,' said Bryant, looking about.

'Not this room though.' Sidney looked as if she might pass out from boredom.

'You're being paid to observe.'

'I'm an intern, I'm not being paid anything.'

Eleanor Chester was younger than he had been expecting, but of course everyone was these days. *Forget the constables looking fresh-faced*, Bryant thought, *so are the judges*. 'I'm a musicologist,' she explained, setting down a tray of tea and biscuits. 'I see you brought the book with you.'

'I thought I might get a signature,' said Bryant, using up one of his big smiles.

'I wrote it because parents sing these songs to their children without knowing anything about them. Even the simplest songs tell a story. It's just that the meanings have been lost.'

'What about "Oranges & Lemons"?' Bryant suggested. 'I need anything that will spark my thinking in a new direction.'

'My first thought was George Orwell.'

'Oh, why?'

'*Nineteen Eighty-Four,*' said Sidney.

'That's right. The song is repeated throughout the book and feels more threatening as it becomes harder for Winston Smith to escape. It's used to show that his chances of survival are becoming impossible. After I spoke to you on the phone I had a quick rummage and found this.' Eleanor took a long roll of paper from her table. 'I've been following the investigation in the papers. They're saying some rather rude things about you.'

'Oh, I don't mind so long as the reports are wildly inaccurate.'

'Hold the corners, will you?' Together Sidney and Bryant rolled the paper out across the table, pinning the edges down with tea mugs and a sugar bowl.

'This is a pictorial nineteenth-century version of the original song "London Bells". There are fifteen bells referred to in the rhyme,' Eleanor explained. 'People struggle to make sense of the references. For example, there's an academic theory that this one, ' "Two sticks and an apple," say the bells of Whitechapel', refers to a famous crippled beggar who sold fruit outside the church. And a line about the Aldgate parish was supposedly cut because it was colloquially known as "the Prostitutes' Church". One of Jack the Ripper's victims, Catherine Eddowes, was seen outside it on the night she died.'

'So the nursery rhyme's tangled up with real-life murders,' said Sidney before Bryant silenced her with a look.

'Does it really matter what's true or false?' asked Eleanor. 'Over time all facts become legend. Our memories lie as we seek to humanize the past and rearrange it into something meaningful.'

'Very true,' said Bryant. 'I remember my mother as a joyful woman, but as I grew up I discovered she was deeply unhappy. I suppose false memories are more comforting.'

'Do the deaths correspond to the words of the rhyme?' Eleanor asked.

'At first they did explicitly, with the leaving of fruit and farthings at the crime scenes.' Bryant donned his trifocals to study the scroll. 'He's working from the song's shorter version so we've only the bells of Stepney and Bow left. All I know about the great bell of Bow is that Dick Whittington was called back by it.'

'Another piece of false witness.' Eleanor pointed to a drawing of Whittington resplendent in scarlet and green, peering over London with his boot on a milestone. 'The real Richard Whittington was on his way to Gloucester but turned back at Highgate Hill, so he'd obviously chosen the scenic route and got lost. His sense of direction might have been shot but there was nothing wrong with his hearing: he was over five miles away from St Mary-le-Bow when he heard its call. The great bell of Bow went on to represent London. The BBC always played the peal of Bow bells at the beginning of their broadcasts to occupied Europe during the war. Bow became a symbol of the city.'

'Which makes me a true cockney,' added Bryant. 'Born within the sound of Bow bells.'

'Yeah, and me,' said Sidney without looking up.

'But I think the symbolism of the bells goes deeper than that,' said Eleanor. 'You have to imagine what London was like when steeples still dominated the city skyline. No trucks or planes, no police sirens, no pneumatic drills. Religion was stitched through the city like threads in a tapestry. Each peal of bells delineated its neighbourhood. Away from London, chimes carried across counties. If you heard your church bell tolling you knew you were home. And you could sing along because the peals were so familiar and so full of major chords that words have always been affixed to them. The lyrics are largely single-syllable because the chimes are short and we hear one note at a time, hence "When – will – you – pay – me": simple and memorable.'

'So if Bow and the bells of London represent England, removing leading figures in our political, cultural and entre-preneurial life could be symbolic of its downfall.'

Eleanor laughed. 'That's a rather romantic idea. The Geor-gians and Victorians built fake follies to recreate ruined grandeur. The sciences roared towards the future while the arts took a great nostalgic step back. Greek and Roman legends were updated and relocated in mythic English landscapes. When the Victorians attained a great empire they tidied up their backstory. Their confidence became arrogance.'

'My point entirely,' said Bryant. 'To undermine a city you first destroy the self-assurance of its people. Churchill's propaganda machine convinced Londoners that they could never be beaten. It was a brilliant trick, but a trick all the same.'

'What you've described is the opposite, a nemesis seeking to destroy morale,' said Eleanor. 'But to what end? Public confidence is shaky but it isn't going to collapse because a few familiar faces disappear. The city has changed. In *Nineteen Eighty-Four* Winston Smith tries to recall the words to "Oranges & Lemons" because if he fails to do so the memory

337

will die, taking history with it. I hate to inform you, Mr Bryant, but that kind of history has gone.'

Told you, Sidney mouthed.

Eleanor rolled up the rhyme scroll. 'Only academics remember the bells or their meanings, or think they're of any importance at all. Now the city barely even takes a tangible form. It's a ghost version of itself that loosely inhabits the land plots of the past. Bomb it flat and it will still be there, an idea as much as a place.'

'Maybe he wants to become part of the legend,' said Sidney, and for once Bryant could not disagree with her.

41

MAKING A MURDERER

I remember my mother smiling but she was never happy. Why would she have been? Her grandmother opened the door for her and kicked her through it, although she slipped her some money to help her survive. I later discovered that something similar had happened to her when she was young.

We moved from one rented room to another, my mother and me, only stopping until the money ran out. Catford, Stonebridge Estate, New Cross, Dog Kennel Hill Estate, Tottenham – everywhere we lived had a bad reputation. ' "From Putney, Hackney Downs and Bow, with courage high and hearts aglow",' my mother said, because her name was Mattie, short for Matilda, and when she was little she read 'Matilda Who Told Lies, and Was Burned to Death'. It was the only poem she could recite, written for children. Pretty downbeat, but I guess it left an impression.

The flats got smaller, the houses shabbier, the neighbourhoods more dangerous. We always moved on before the back-rent got too high, and left a trail of debts and false promises. I was never christened. I didn't have an NHS number. It was as if I didn't exist. At first my mother was too ashamed to admit I was hers, although everyone knew. It's because she was raised religiously, with the burden of original sin. I was the memory of what had happened to her in a church.

We lived in streets that reeked of junk food, where sooner or later every dark trash-strewn corner filled with kids planning raids on each other. Any emotion other than hate was considered unmanly. I learned to keep out of everyone's way.

My mother was horrified by the idea of relying on anyone because she had been raised in gentility, and that meant being independent. Her relatives had all been connected with the church and in her hour of need none of them wanted anything to do with her – so much for the milk of human kindness. Soon we couldn't afford even the smallest rooms in the worst neighbourhoods, and began sharing illegal sublets.

By the time I was eight (and living, I recall, in a squat in Kensal Green) she and I had started to fight. Maybe it was because we spent all our time together but we seemed unable to sit down without an argument. I loathed the way we lived, always on the move, and locked myself away in libraries just to be alone. Learning became the only thing important to me. My mother worked here and there, finding jobs the old way by knocking on doors: cleaner, shelf-stacker, bed and breakfast staff, those were the jobs that paid, even though it was cash in hand so she could be dumped at a moment's notice. Sometimes I stole for her. It didn't bother me. There are ways to survive.

When you move around a lot, sharing accommodation and using public spaces like parks and libraries, you talk to a lot of strangers and you get good at it. You listen for clues, study body language, spot weaknesses, watch out for tells. I read about the great magicians and how their understanding of audiences was as important as the mechanics of a trick.

When I was eleven I had a friend, Atena. Her parents ran a Greek restaurant in Green Lanes and Atena waited on tables, which was unlawful because she was not quite ten. She was small, and most nights she slept behind the serving counter on a specially made shelf, which would have given all the nice liberal London diners heart attacks if they'd known they were eating their salt-baked sea bass three feet from illegal child labour.

Eventually the inspectors caught her parents out and they lost the restaurant, and I thought: What if that happens to me? What if they come to our place in the middle of the night and find me sharing an illegal room with my mother and two complete strangers and their drugs or whatever illegal stuff they had on them? Where will I be sent? And how could I be sent anywhere when I hadn't even been given a Christian name? When I was just a ghost kid?

To block out the sights and sounds of my life I read books on showmanship and magic; not the mundane manuals that showed you how to produce sponge balls or link metal rings, but ones that explained how deception worked on the mind. I was a fast learner. People are ready to believe anyone with more authority. They secretly want to have their choices praised. Deception works because people are lazy thinkers.

I returned to the library and started reading about the British police services so that I would be prepared for the day I would eventually have to meet them. Even then the idea had already formed in my mind. I just didn't know it was there yet.

PART FIVE
The Bells of Stepney

Be polite, be professional, but have a plan to kill everybody you meet.

James 'Mad Dog' Mattis

42

TRICKERY

*Script extract from Arthur Bryant's 'Peculiar London'
walking tour guide. (Meet at Stepney Green tube, keep
your hand on your tuppence and your wits about you.
Please note this tour is cheaper because it's not very
interesting.)*

When billionaires decide to buy their houses in London
because their kids liked the *Paddington* films, the same
shortlist of place names always appears: Belgravia,
Kensington, Holland Park, Notting Hill, Hampstead,
hollowed-out neighbourhoods that look so much like film
sets you wonder if a stroll behind them would reveal only
chipboard and scaffolding.

The names of places in London's East End resonate
for a different reason. Whitechapel, Limehouse, Shad-
well and Bow were marshy medieval villages built
around churches that became central to the lives of
immigrants. From the seventeenth century onwards the
French and the Irish and the Ashkenazi Jews arrived,

the Chinese and Italians and Germans, then in the 1960s the Bangladeshis.

In Stepney one house in three was destroyed during the war, and the effects can still be seen: small pockets of Georgian elegance left between the flat-packs of social housing. The area had a reputation for violence, overcrowding, poverty and political discord. Now it is quiet and residential, with a young middle class moving in. But those new residents would do well to look across at the Church of the High Seas, St Dunstan's, which dominated the area for so many centuries. They'll see what you see right now. A vast graveyard with hardly any headstones. That's because thousands of plague victims were hastily buried here. Did no new coffins enter the ground because the sexton dared not disturb the foul soil? After all, this was an area that believed the air was so pestilential it could only be halted from entering wealthy London by the erection of leafy barriers.

Over the church's main door are two carvings, one showing a ship, the other the Devil armed with a pair of red-hot tongs, because St Dunstan pinched Lucifer's nose to make him fly away.

As a child I played on the bomb-sites here, recreating Spitfire battles, forever being warned by my mother not to fall through the rusty corrugated roofs of Anderson shelters. The neighbourhood children limped home with cuts and grazes and unspent bullets that they hadn't been able to discharge despite pummelling them with bricks. Sometimes a child would bring an unexploded mortar bomb to school, which was usually good for half a day off. There was a breezy carelessness about the neighbourhood, held in shape by the rigid structure of family loyalty. I look at it now and feel the lack of atmosphere: no kids playing outside, no games, no songs, no Flash Harrys loitering on

346

street corners. Now the dangers come from frightened children after dark, dying to claim their turf.

There's a tip box on the way out, if you would be so kind. Don't talk to strangers outside the tube station.

Stepney on a wet spring evening.

An ancient avenue of tall claw-armed plane trees, their bark green from incessant rain, no passers-by, no one even walking their dogs.

The news teams that had threatened to stake out the terrain, lying in wait for the Oranges & Lemons Killer, had taken one look at the barren streets and hastened back to their newsrooms to report on the other main stories of the day. It was clear that nothing of interest would be happening around here.

Arthur Bryant felt the same way. St Dunstan's was much larger than he had remembered but the land around it was too featureless, too bare and open. You couldn't imagine Magwitch jumping out from behind a tombstone even if you could find one tall enough to hide him. The locals were locked indoors ordering pizzas and staring at their screens.

'Maybe we should head back to the unit,' said May, leading his partner across the over-clipped grassland. 'There's a forecast for more rain in half an hour.'

'He has struck at every church in the right order,' said Bryant steadfastly. He looked around and found nothing to hold the eye. 'He will be here. Where's Janice?'

'A couple of streets over. Turn your headset down, I don't want anyone knowing we're police.'

'Nobody ever mistakes us for police anyway,' Bryant complained. 'I haven't walked around here in decades but it looks even more depressing than I remember it.'

'It's changing. They have an organic farmers' market now,

and yoga in the park. There's no one here, Arthur. I don't think he's going to go through with any more. Four murder attempts in just under a week—'

'There were six fatal stabbings of teenagers in four days just last week,' Bryant pointed out. 'Their killers' motives were just as unfathomable.'

A crow left a tree, its branch springing up. Outside the churchyard railing, a boy was walking along the pavement with a plastic bag of shopping. White cords hung from his grey cotton hood. He bounced a little to his music.

'Have you got any of those weird sweets on you?' asked May.

'What weird sweets?'

'You know, those paper bags you have in your pockets full of sherbet saucers or shrimps or Spangles. You always have something they stopped making years ago. You're a mobile sweetshop.' He made a grab for Bryant's coat.

The shopping boy checked his phone, carried on walking, disappeared behind some bushes for a moment, reappeared on his way to the open park gates.

'All I've got is this.' Bryant pulled out a tin of treacle. 'It's quite difficult to eat on the move. Oh, hang on a minute.' He felt in the other pocket and produced some sachets of Marmite and a white chocolate Magnum in its sealed plastic wrapper.

'How long have you had an ice cream in there? It must be liquid by now.'

'Yes, but they're quite nice to drink. You have to be careful you don't swallow the stick.'

The boy was drawing level with them on the pavement beyond the railing, but was preparing to enter a gap in the churchyard railings and cut off the corner. Clearly most people did so; the grass was worn away in a diagonal path. He disappeared behind more bushes.

May looked disgusted. 'You're like a schoolboy who's been nicking stuff at the local tuck shop.'

'Things just accumulate,' Bryant admitted. 'Strangeways seems to like the Marmite sachets.'

'I can't go near him, he keeps trying to bite me.'

'Yes, he's not a people cat. He passes out if you make him jump.'

This time the hooded boy did not re-emerge. The change caught Bryant's attention. He looked around. 'Where's he gone?'

'Who?' asked May.

'There was a lad over there a second ago.' The street was empty.

They began moving towards the gate. As they reached the pavement they saw a trainer-clad foot twitching, its heel repeatedly hitting the pavement – *thump – thump – thump*. The plastic bag lay on its side, a split container of curry oozing out. The boy was grunting and clutching the top of his left arm. Crimson through grey cotton.

'He's been stabbed. There's no one around. How is that possible?' May dropped to his knees and tried to remove the crying boy's right hand from the wound so that he could assess the damage. 'It's a gash, about three inches long, not deep. Have you got any tissues?'

It did not surprise him when Bryant produced a full-sized tissue box from his coat. Ripping it apart, he wadded the tissues over the cut as the boy pointed towards the church.

'Where did he go?' asked Bryant, searching the street.

'He must be in the bushes,' said May. 'Call the unit.'

Bryant looked at his phone. 'I've got no signal.'

'Go closer to the church.'

Bryant hurried off to make his call. May pressed hard on the boy's shoulder. He checked the tissues and saw that the blood was still blooming. *This is the real face of violence in the East End*, he thought, *a teenaged kid lying on the pavement with a stab wound.*

'You're going to be OK, it's not deep,' he told the boy. 'We'll take care of you.'

He looked back towards St Dunstan's. He could not turn fully around without easing his pressure on the cut. Through the dark trees he saw the leaves of a bush rustle and part. He could sense the changing shadows, the displacement of branches as someone stepped out.

The boy coughed. Trying to keep his hand pressed on the bloodied tissues, May twisted. The figure was moving into the long narrow avenue of trees. They provided him with all the cover he needed. At their end was the edge of a housing estate where he could easily vanish within the corridors and staircases.

The tissues were soaked crimson but the boy's wound had started to clot. He was alert and trying to sit up. This time they would have a living witness. May showed his ID and conducted a search of the boy's pockets.

He found a phone, a sheathed knife and a small plastic Ziploc bag. Thinking it might be drugs, he unrolled it carefully. Inside were ten twenty-pound notes. He looked back and saw Bryant on his phone, leaning against a tree.

May wiped the wound again and saw now that it was only surface. He had seen plenty of self-inflicted cuts before. Releasing the boy, he started to rise. *No*, he thought, *no*. He began moving towards Bryant, who was now ambling into the church.

He broke into a run, but Bryant had vanished inside.

'Get out!' he shouted. 'Arthur, get out!'

He saw the flash before he heard the blast, a deep echoing note that funnelled through the nave and burst from the entrance in a haze of gravelly dust. He felt a hot wind in his face.

Pressing a tissue over his nose and mouth he headed inside

350

as the orange-grey cloud billowed over him. The stained-glass Christ in the apse had gone, and the unanchored front pews had been blasted backwards. The main stone structure and wooden fixtures of the church had not been damaged. The explosion had been highly localized.

He looked around for Bryant but found no sign of him. There was no fire. At the base of one of the stone columns he followed a thick smear of blood.

With a sinking heart he stepped back along the pew-strewn nave, searching for any sign of the body. *No*, he thought, *no, not after all we've been through, not like this.* How far could Bryant have been thrown?

On the floor lay a Bible, its pages blasted apart, as if there had been a visitation from an angry god. When he raised his eyes he realized he was looking at a ragged figure crumpled against the wall, beneath one of the low side arches. Behind him, something fell from the balcony and cracked on the tiled floor. Waving the dust from his face, he went to the body and eased himself down beside it.

He found himself looking at a short, barrel-stomached man in jeans and cowboy boots. Where his head should have been was a tattered grey stump. The rest of him had been dashed across the stones.

When May emerged he found his partner standing behind the church's thick protective wall. He appeared unharmed, although he was covered in more dust than usual.

'Were you there when I ran in?' May asked.

'I don't know. I couldn't see anything. I still can't.' He removed his glasses and gave them a rub.

'Your ears – one of them is bleeding.'

'Yes,' said Bryant vaguely. 'I've gone a bit deaf. My hearing aid fell out. It's OK, I have another one.' He concentrated on fishing it from his pocket while May tried to wipe his bloody ear.

'Will you get off me?' Bryant asked. 'It's only a scratch. You shouldn't be charging about. How's the poor devil in there?'

May looked surprised, which was a feat considering his hair was already standing up. 'How do you know?'

'Trickery,' he said, shaking out his hat. 'He has to stay one step ahead of us each time.'

'He paid the boy out there a couple of hundred quid to stick himself with his own knife,' said May. He ran outside, heading back to the spot where he had left him sitting on the pavement. There was no one there now.

May turned about, desperate to find anyone who could help. The houses opposite might have been shuttered against a storm. Had the noise of the blast not carried?

One man stood in the porch of his house, vaguely staring over in the direction of the church. 'Did you see a boy running?' May shouted. 'Black kid, tall, grey hooded top?'

The man stared back as if looking right through him.

His headset buzzed at his collarbone. He'd forgotten the sound was turned low. 'Next street, White Horse Road,' said Janice Longbright. 'I'm on the corner.'

They arrived to find Janice with the boy pinned against a garden wall, his wrists locked together with a plastic tie.

'How did you do that?' May asked, amazed.

'I could see you from the pavement. You ran off and this one upped sticks and came my way, so I thought I'd better bring him down.'

'Yes, but how?'

'I threw my brick at his shin.' Longbright always kept half a house brick in her bag, and had a deadly aim. 'He's going to be limping for a while.'

'Hey, sonny, who are you?' he asked the boy.

'His name's Jemaine Clarke,' she said, patting him on the head. 'Go easy on him. He didn't know he was being used as a decoy. He just wanted to make some quick money.'

'I knew it was too good to be true,' said Jemaine. His nose was running. Longbright wiped it.

'So next time follow your instincts,' Longbright suggested. 'Let's get your shoulder looked at, and don't worry, no one's going to tell your mates that you stabbed yourself.'

43

UPSIDE DOWN

'There's been a bomb at St Dunstan's, Stepney, one fatality,' Colin Bimsley called across the operations room. 'It's all a bit confused. Hang on.' He listened for a moment. 'I've got Janice on the line. The old boys are all right. She arrested a sixteen-year-old lad. The body of a man is being recovered from the church's interior.'

'Sixteen? He can't be the right one,' said Meera.

'You don't think sixteen-year-olds are capable of murder.' Sidney looked up, presenting a statement of fact.

'They were right by the church,' said Colin. 'The boy was paid to be a decoy, just like last time. They're taking the victim to St Pancras. There, now you know as much as me.'

'Which isn't much,' said Meera. 'All you've told me is that it's happened again and will keep happening because no one can stop it.'

'You're looking at me as if it's my fault.'

'It's not you, Colin, it's everything.' She turned about on herself in frustration. 'The system doesn't work any more, does it? Us, this place, this "radical alternative unit" no longer functions because someone has figured out a way around it.' Unable to sit still for a second longer, she angrily stormed out.

Sidney watched her go without a flicker of emotion.

Colin's phone rang again. 'Wait, slow down, repeat that.' He headed off to Raymond Land's office.

Tim Floris was in there with him, studying spreadsheets. The pair were becoming as thick as thieves. Knowing that Land was unable to keep his mouth shut, Colin wondered how much information he was passing through Floris to the ears of the Home Office. They looked up in unison when they saw him. Colin felt his face glowing with anger.

'John just called,' he said. 'It's happened again, inside St Dunstan's Church. Some kind of lightweight explosive device. Mr Bryant got blown up but he's all right.'

'Blown up?' Land stared at him in stupefaction. 'Again?'

'There's a man dead. We don't have an ID yet.'

'I tried to stop him from going,' said Land. 'You all heard me.'

As the calls poured in, the information they imparted grew stranger. While they were waiting for an ambulance, the boy Janice had arrested was attacked by another local teenager and was stabbed again. He had been taken to Mile End Hospital. John May was attempting to identify the victim and Bryant – well, as far as anyone could understand, it seemed he was heading for Warwick Avenue tube station. He called in to say that his ears were hurting but he was all right and had something very important to do.

'It's always like this around here these days,' said Land with a shrug, failing to notice the cynicism in Floris's eyes. 'I remember when work used to tail off around six o'clock and we all went to the pub.' He rolled his eyes in a what-can-you-do gesture, but found himself without an ally.

*

'I'm sorry I couldn't come to you this evening, I know how busy you are,' said Maggie Armitage, giving him a tight hug that left him covered with dog hairs and bits of something that looked like cake icing. She had toned down her usual funfair wardrobe to a graceful coordination of purple and black. 'I've just been at a Wiccan baking fundraiser at East Greenwich Library. Where were you?'

'I was blown up.'

'What, again?' She could smell smoke on him.

Bryant looked around. 'What are you doing here?'

She pointed to a nearby board announcing tonight's event: 'Hell's Spells, an evening of urban magic with Maggie Armitage, Grand Order Grade IV White Witch of the Coven of St James the Elder, Kentish Town'. 'I've got a few minutes before I'm on. Dame Maude Hackshaw gave a talk on owl-grooming last week and nobody showed up. Tip your head to the left. No, your other left.'

Bryant was puzzled but did as he was told. Some pieces of gravel fell out of his ear.

'Oh, that's much better.' He stuck in his little finger and wiggled it around. 'I think that was a bit of church.'

'You'd better have a glass of vermouth; I seem to have two.'

'It feels like I'm hallucinating. What is this place?' Bryant looked about the grand saloon at the ashlared stonework inset with chandeliers. Corinthian pilasters supported the encrusted gilt-beamed ceiling. There were too many cherubs. 'I think I need to sit down,' he said, and fell into the gold-legged red velvet chair behind him.

'It's a Lebanese restaurant. It used to be known as Crocker's Folly,' Maggie told him. 'A man called Frank Crocker built it to be ready for the Great Central Railway Terminus, but the officials moved the railway line to Marylebone, leaving him stranded. They say when he heard the news he threw himself out of a window and now his ghost haunts the place. Are you sure you're all right?'

'Not at all.' Bryant knocked back the vermouth in one gulp.

'What did you need to see me about?'

'Maggie, you're the only person who might understand. I'm having absolutely the worst week of my life. Death after death, and I can't stop them because I'm going the wrong way.'

Her kohl-rimmed eyes stared into his. 'Which way should you be going?'

'That's what I'm trying to understand. Could I have another vermouth? My ears hurt.'

Maggie passed him another immense drink from the hospitality tray.

'You know I went missing for a while? I was trying to understand something about myself.'

'Do you want me to read your mind?'

'No, it's simpler if I just tell you. The Grand Lama said I lack empathy but actually I don't care about people.'

'Well . . . that's what a lack of empathy is.' Maggie looked even more confused than usual.

He seemed pained for a moment, then removed a piece of rubble from inside his shirt. 'I rely on empirical truths because facts don't lie and human beings do.'

'A Wiccan would argue for the reverse,' said Maggie. 'Mr Crocker needed to believe in something untrue and built this place. That's what drew you to me today.'

'I can't change who I am, Maggie. I know I frighten people. I don't fit into the modern world. I don't want to share everything with everyone all the time.' He downed his drink.

'You're going to tell me something's changed.'

'I suppose I am. At the start of the investigation I talked to

Elise Albu, the wife of the man I believe to be the first victim. What she told me made me care about her, so I left all the Oranges & Lemons interviews to John and the others. I didn't want to feel any more of those painful emotions. Instead I concentrated on understanding the killer's methods, but I found nothing.'

'Arthur, your murderer is a chameleon, a liar, a shell. Damaged people are dangerous, you know that.'

'Is there any more vermouth?' Now that he had started to unburden himself, he felt like a deflating balloon. 'It's as if the world is half an inch from chaos and is about to collapse in on us, so why not just let it? Why keep trying to make sense of things? Why be the one who tries to hang on to the last little bit of irrefutable truth? Why should I be Winston Smith? Remembering the rest of "Oranges & Lemons" didn't do him any good, did it?'

'I have no idea what you're talking about, you dear old thing.' Maggie's smile held a strange sadness. 'It's in our nature to believe that truth will bring order to chaos. People always hope.'

'But why?'

'Because the last person left alive will still want to set a dinner table.'

'I'm not so sure about that.'

'I mean it. She runs a restaurant in Norway, a terribly nice lady. She hasn't been born yet, of course. She'll be the sole survivor of our planet's catastrophe. We had a lovely chat last week.' She batted away Bryant's look of incredulity. 'Oh, it was a space-time continuum thing. It was raining and there was nothing on the telly. I suppose you'd call it lucid dreaming.'

'I'd call it avoiding reality,' Bryant muttered.

'To answer the question you came here with: your disconnection from "normal people" as you call them is your blind spot. It prevents you from seeing the truth. What terrible thing could make you cease to value life?'

Bryant thought for a moment. 'Perhaps if I felt my own life had been damaged somehow—'

'Keep going.'

'Or even – taken away.'

'By whom?'

Bryant's eyes widened. 'Oh.'

'You see?' said Maggie. 'You put so much faith in facts that you've been blinded by them.'

He clutched at Maggie's arm. 'I need to think of it the other way up.'

'And if you do so, what does it tell you?'

'That the churches and rhymes are nothing, and the victims aren't as innocent as they appear. It's the villain who's had his life wiped away.'

'I'm just the facilitator,' Maggie reminded him. 'Whatever conclusion you reach is your own.'

'No, you're right. He's planned this carefully because it's the only thing that's important to him, so of course he's hard to find. He believes in his cause. And you have to keep believing in yours.'

She touched his arm. 'I must go on. By the way, Mr Crocker didn't jump out of a window. People just said he did. His memorial is all around you. Life is a trick played on the unsuspecting.'

He watched as she walked up to the microphone and tapped it, looking around the room. Only five of the chairs were filled, but she spoke as if there were a thousand.

44

PRESS PRIVILEGE

They had put the boy on the worst ward, with the disturbed yammerers and detoxing junkies. He was another stab victim, treated fairly and equally by amazing nurses working in a system that had stopped functioning efficiently years ago. Slipped into a pale-blue hospital gown and tucked up in bed without his hoodie and tracksuit bottoms, Clarke looked like a schoolboy again.

When Janice had finished the paperwork she came to find him. There were no parents beside Jemaine's bed, only an elderly Antiguan lady in a pleated floral dress.

'Alma?' she said. 'What are you doing here?'

Alma Sorrowbridge pointed to the church badge on her cardigan. 'We visit all the victims of knife crime, Janice. I was here seeing another boy. The nurse was just telling me that Jemaine lives with his granddad but he's in another hospital having a heart bypass. What happened?'

She hardly knew where to start. 'I arrested him. I had his hands behind his back to stop him from running. I was on the phone to the ambulance and a kid he knew came up. I told him to stay back but the EMT leader thought I was talking to her, and the next thing I knew the boys were shouting at each other and the other one stuck him.'

Jemaine had now been bandaged on the other arm. He lay staring at the ceiling, half-conscious and clearly hating his life.

Alma straightened the sheet under Jemaine's hand. 'What happened to the other boy?'

'He's in custody, something that seems to have come as a total surprise to him. He says he's going to sue me for wrongful arrest even though me and my little shoulder-cam saw the whole thing.'

'You can't help some of them. Look at the way they live.' Janice found it touching that the old lady was prepared to sit with an angry young stranger, expecting nothing. 'We find out what the boys need and try to stop them from stressing about the little things. Half a dozen this week and they can't be put on the same ward because sometimes they carry the fights into the hospital. The nurse said he was lucky, and I suppose she's right.'

'Has he spoken at all?'

'He was awake earlier but got a bit wound up, so the nurse gave him something to help him sleep. She's keeping him in overnight because of the medication.'

'He's had some pretty bad luck today.'

'That's what he told me, but it's hard to know if they're telling the truth or just giving their side of the story.'

'I wanted to ask him about the man who gave him this.' She showed Alma the money from Jemaine's pocket. 'He uses other people. He used this kid.' She handed Alma the money. 'Put it in his locker.'

Alma smiled up at her, calm and imperturbable. 'Healing needs privacy. I can't stay with him. There are others to see. When you've sorted all this out, come to dinner. I remember you like pork with sour cherries. Spend a little time with Arthur. He's been a bit lost lately.'

He's not the only one, Janice thought. Aloud she said, 'Dinner would be very nice.'

A man paid him to stand there, she remembered as she headed down the hospital steps. *He tricks them, he tricks us and we just don't see it.*

A dozen photographers were waiting outside the unit, ready to pounce on anyone who stepped outside. These were not the kind who made appointments, they were the ones who hung around the Ivy restaurant hoping to catch soap stars leaving in tears.

'I'm not sure you want to go out there,' said Meera, stopping in the shadow of the PCU's ground-floor entrance. 'Perhaps you should wait until they disperse. They're in every doorway. They won't just take photos of you, they'll try to wind you up.'

'And I want to get something to eat, so stand aside,' said Colin. 'Never get between a man and his food.'

'She's right,' said Tim Floris. 'We can keep you off the radar so long as you're in here, but not once you're outside.'

'Who's *we?*' Colin asked. 'You and your new best pal Raymond? Oh, wait a minute, you mean the Home Office is protecting us? That's a turnaround. Faraday has a history of trying to shag us over a hostess trolley. Don't make poor old Raymond think he's got an ally, because in a few days you'll be back in your uncle's office and we'll be stuck here with the mops and buckets. Open the door.'

Floris pushed it back and hastily stepped aside. Colin peered out. Where had the press been earlier, when Bryant was nearly killed in St Dunstan's?

The PCU building only had one exit, so the news teams and camera crews fought each other for space. They knew the names of every unit member, and the second Bimsley appeared they began shouting.

362

'Hey, Colin, how do you feel about letting another innocent victim die? What's your guilt on a scale of one to ten? Why are you all hiding away in there?'

'Oi, Colin, mate, over here! Who's dead this time? Anyone else been shot up there?'

'Shouldn't you be out on the streets looking for this nutter? Why aren't you telling us anything?'

One fat little photographer in a backward-facing Kangol cap kept shouting louder than the rest. 'Colin, where's your girlfriend? Can I get one of the two of you having a bit of facetime? My paper just needs one decent shot. You'd be helping me out of a hole.'

'I'll be helping you into one in a minute,' warned Colin.

He turned to see Meera storming out of the entrance with thunder in her eyes. 'Get away from the building or we'll arrest the lot of you,' she shouted.

The men all laughed. 'Like to see you try, love!'

'Press privilege! The public need to know, don't they?'

'Are you putting on weight?'

'Where's the young girl with the legs? Can we get the pretty one out here?'

'Oi, Colin, where's old Bryant?' called the annoying little one. 'Did we miss his funeral?'

Colin tore across the road. Picking up the photographer by his coat, he slammed him against the shop window at his back, cracking the glass from corner to corner. The gentlemen of the press yelled like geese and flapped about ineffectually.

Colin thought better of his action and set the snapper back on his feet, but the cameras had been ready and the shot of the day was captured. A few more were taken of the PCU members gathered in confusion and anger at the unit entrance, then the street cleared once more as word reached the photographers that a minor royal had been seen shopping in Oxford Street's Primark.

45

THE EPITOME OF LONDON

Eight o' clock on Sunday morning the press siege returned to the building on Caledonian Road, and John May arrived to find his partner already seated in their office. 'How did you get in?' he asked. 'I didn't see you outside.'

'I waited in the Ladykillers Café until everyone was distracted by the sound of a broken window.'

'That was a lucky chance.'

'That was Janice's brick.' Bryant popped two white pills from a blister pack and swallowed them with his tea.

'How do you feel after yesterday?'

'My ears are still ringing but I have tinnitus anyway.'

'You could have been killed,' said May with some vehemence.

'And I could have died years ago like a great many of my contemporaries,' Bryant replied. 'I have not done so. We need some way of getting officers stationed at St Mary-le-Bow. Who was the victim at St Dunstan's?'

May held up a page. 'Gavin Spencer, part-time shop fitter, fifty-six. He doesn't fit the profile at all. He's done time, six years for aggravated assault, by first accounts a nasty piece of work. The bomb was locked around his neck with a plastic cable tie. They're still looking for his ears. Dan says the device was small but concentrated, very simple, home-made. He says he sometimes knocks them up in his kitchen, which must thrill his wife.'

'Does Spencer have any connection to the others?'

'None that I can see. He grew up in South London, dropped out of university and fell into the usual tiresome pattern: DJ, club promoter, small-time drug-dealer. Soon got a couple of convictions under his belt. Met a girl at a party and knocked her about. Families complained about the lightness of his jail sentence, et cetera. I looked for connections to the others but only have the vaguest trace of one.'

'Even that will do,' said Bryant. 'The killer can't have hidden every single thing about his victims. He doesn't leave a hair behind. What does he do, carry a tiny vacuum cleaner around with him?'

'So there's this.' May handed him a photocopy of a note. 'Sidney spotted it in his Met file. Some bright spark thought to file it as proof of his home address.'

'What's it for?'

'Not itemized. Receipt for goods.'

'How did she even get to see it?'

'She seems to have electronic access to everything. When I asked her how, she looked at me as if I was mad.'

'She thinks we're not terribly *au fait* with technology here. She might have seen me trying to remove my SIM card with the end of a kebab stick. Go on.'

'Sidney checked for juvenile offences. When Gavin Spencer was seventeen he had his collar felt by some local cops. They came around his parents' house and asked him a few questions. There are no details of the suspected offence. The prison records base him at his mother's home in Essex but on this delivery receipt, which is older, they're in East Green-wich. The note has to be right because it bears a time stamp. We're aware that Michael Claremont was living somewhere nearby in Greenwich around that time, so there's a faint chance that they knew each other.'

'Not much to go on, is it?' Bryant threw his pencil stub across the room. 'We could come up with a hundred different theories for their crossed paths. Pass me that book behind you with the purple binding next to *Maltese Cross: Mediter-ranean Eye Injuries Volume Two.*'

May searched the shelf. 'What's Volume One called?'

'*Venetian Blind.*'

'I swear you have these specially printed. Is this it?' He blew the sawdust from a copy of *Mileposts of Old London*. 'What are you expecting to find?'

'Cockneys.' Bryant cracked the spine and ran his finger down the list of contents. 'Here we are. We know the killer's last site has to be St Mary-le-Bow in Cheapside. The great bell of Bow.'

'Ah, got you. Anyone born within its sound is a cockney.'

'Correct. Except it's gone.'

'What has?'

'The great bell of Bow was the tenor bell of the church's twelve bells. Hang on, let me find the page.'

'Why would it be in a book on mileposts?' May asked.

'You haven't done much research, have you?' He flattened out a double page and read. ' "The bell ... cast in 1762 ... weighed fifty-eight hundredweight" – yadda yadda yadda – "six tons of reinforced ironwork braces" – boring ... Ah, it was destroyed in an air raid in 1941:

'Of such importance is the church that on the road from London to the coast there are mileposts measuring out-wards from its doors. These are cut with cast-iron rebuses, pictographic puzzles. The Bow mileposts show four bells and an archer's bow. The bells ring out across the world and are regarded as the epitome of London. On top of the Bow steeple is a golden dragon with a St George's cross.'

'Which tells us plenty about the church but absolutely nothing about the killer,' said May.

'It's an appropriate ending for the task he's set himself, don't you think? An atrocity in the bedrock of England?'

'I don't know, Arthur. I don't know how he thinks. I don't know who he is.'

'But I do, sort of.' Bryant closed the book. May looked up. 'If Bow is to be his last attack, he'll make it especially tricky for us.'

'We need more staff on the ground, Arthur. The Met isn't going to help us out.'

'I realize that. But I need to talk to you about something else.' Bryant rose and closed the office door. 'The arson attack. Elise Albu and I went back to her husband's bookshop. I was looking for something that would link it with the later deaths.'

'Why?'

'I imagined a scenario in which one of Albu's customers gave him a manuscript to read, presenting it as a work of fiction. Albu over-enthusiastically printed a few copies. When the killer decided to turn his fantasy into deed he needed the manuscript back to protect himself from discovery. Perhaps he looked in on Cristian one day and asked for it casually, only to have the bookseller stall him, and that's when he realized he had opened himself up to blackmail. Worse, he discovered there was a printed edition!'

Bryant looked through the stack of books he had taken from the burned-out shop. 'Cristian was a connoisseur. I think he knew he wasn't just reading a novel but seeing a blueprint. In their pub meeting, he underlined "Kind Hearts are more than coronets" in his poetry volume, pointing out the marked similarity to a cheated murderer leaving behind his memoirs. The killer couldn't find all the copies so he torched everything.

'I found a number of intact books that Cristian had printed privately, but not the one we need. What I *did* find, however, was the one book in the shop that couldn't be burned.' He opened his desk drawer and drew it out. 'The rare asbestos-covered edition of Ray Bradbury's *Fahrenheit 451*, printed in 1953 and signed by the author, selling for twenty-eight thousand pounds, earmarked for his mystery buyer. There were some faint pencil marks on the title page so I had Dan take a look at it.'

He held it up so that John could read Peter English's name.

46

CROWN ESTATE

Sidney found her way to the map restoration department at the back of the British Library's first floor and was met by a bearded man-mountain in a checked flannel shirt, red braces and dungarees who looked as though he'd just been replacing a truck carburettor in Arkansas. Raymond Kirkpatrick, academic, antiquarian and heavy metal enthusiast, pulled his headphones from his ears and greeted her with a bone-crushing double-clasp handshake.

'Mr Bryant says you're the best,' said Sidney.

'I'm the best available on the PCU budget. And I come in on Sundays, just for the sheer bloody joy of working. I know all about you, Miss Hargreaves. Welcome, come on through.' He led the way through to the map room. 'I need a break. I've been hunched over a Stanford all week, recolouring a balloon-view of London. Janice warned me you'd be over. What have you got for me?'

Sidney opened her satchel and removed a clear plastic folder. 'I know you restore stuff. Can you get anything from this?'

Kirkpatrick carefully removed the blackened page from the

folder and placed it under an immense rectangular magnifying glass. 'Blimey, there's not much of it left, is there?'

'It got burned.'

He gave his beard a good scratch. 'May I ask where it came from?'

'Mr Bryant brought it back from a bookshop that suffered an arson attack. It's all there is left.'

'Why didn't he bring it to me himself?'

'He doesn't know I have it. It was stuck to the end of his scarf. I didn't want to waste his time.'

'So you thought you'd waste mine. What makes you think it contains anything?'

'I could read one word.' She pointed to the least burned corner.

' "Murderer". That'll do it. Well, I usually test paper for acidity, pH balance, thickness, age and weave but in this case it's best to start with these.' He tapped the side of his head. 'The peepers. We might be able to intuit something first.'

She watched as he bent over the sheet, working with a scraper and an eye-dropper containing a blue liquid. 'How's John doing? I heard he was out of hospital and back at work.'

'I've only just met him.'

'So how are you finding the PCU?'

'Nobody knows what they're doing. They muck around a lot.'

'There used to be lots of units like the PCU and they all had their own specific methodology. I can probably only recover part of this.'

'How?'

'Infrared.'

Sidney watched as the page was sprayed with a fine solution and flattened. Kirkpatrick subjected it to LEDs from a lamp shining at a forty-five-degree angle, which turned the blackened paper a sickly purple. He put his headphones back on while he worked, listening to a band called Satanic Disgust. The lead singer sounded as if he was being stabbed to death and his screams bled from the archivist's earpieces, making Sidney wonder what it must be doing to his brain.

Finally Kirkpatrick pulled off his phones and withdrew the burned sheet. 'There's some legible type in the centre.' He copied it out on to a separate sheet. 'There you go. At the top we've got what looks like a cap M, then lower-case a – k – i – n—'

'Making a Murderer,' said Sidney absently.

Kirkpatrick stepped back to show her the page.

'I think it's part of the manuscript Mr Bryant was looking for, but there's no author name. Have you ever heard of someone called Peter English?'

'Yeah. I met him at a drinks reception here last year. They hire out the atrium for sponsored events. He gave a speech.'

'What was he like?'

Kirkpatrick thought for a moment. 'I didn't spend much time with him, of course, but he struck me as a suppurating bunghole with all the allure of a hair on a toilet seat. His company never got around to paying their bill. Is he involved in this?'

'Everyone seems to think so. He may not have done it.'

'I hope you nail him, all the same. Preferably to something solid.' Kirkpatrick harrumphed. 'People like him have always done something.'

Meanwhile at the PCU, the detectives were getting ready for a party.

'I'm having doubts about Peter English,' said Bryant. 'It feels like we're clutching at straws.'

'The rich think they will never be caught,' May replied. 'We need to go to the launch event marked on English's office schedule. It starts at two.'

Bryant looked out of the window. Storm clouds were brewing above the Cally Road Pie Shop. 'I could have one glass of champagne, purely for medicinal purposes. There might be things on sticks.'

'Do you have a tie?' asked May

'No, I have a jumper,' Bryant suggested. 'I also have a comb and some aftershave.' He held up a lime-coloured glass bottle of Hai Karate.

'A budget cologne that was popular fifty years ago.' May took the bottle away from him and examined the label: 'Price five shillings and sixpence. How long have you had this?' he said. 'Let's go and surprise English.'

Three complementary London squares, Belgrave, Eaton and Chester, had housed everyone from Margaret Thatcher to Mick Jagger (it being the perennial fantasy of rebel rock stars to live like aged viscounts). Their houses now fetched thirty million pounds apiece. Today two hundred guests had gathered in Chester Square beneath an unseasonal yellow and white striped marquee that covered its unprepossessing flagstone cross. As English was head of the residents' committee there had been no complaints.

The occasion, the detectives gathered, was the launch of yet another Better British Business initiative, although the marquee roof was mercifully unadorned with its awkward Union Jack-styled logo, which was instead displayed on an easel by the entrance. Red, white and blue balloons clustered like polyps around the dark cave of the marquee. A pair of greeters, blank-eyed blondes freezing in evening dress, waited to take their names.

'You won't find us down there,' said Bryant, waving at the greeter's electronic pad. 'We're part of the security detail.' He showed his ID.

'I'll have to check,' said the blonde, a little thrown.

'Can we get some proper badges made, something with a shield and a bit of gold instead of a laminated card?' Bryant asked his partner. 'It looks like we're trying to sell photo-copying equipment. This photo doesn't do me justice.'

'We haven't got all day,' said May sternly as the girl let in a group of Chinese businessmen.

'Let me find someone,' she told him, half-heartedly look-ing around. While she did so Bryant pushed his partner forward and they suddenly found themselves inside.

A violin trio was playing a rendition of British maritime themes. As these had been composed mainly for brass instru-ments, they sounded like the *Last Night of the Proms* heard down the wrong end of an ear trumpet.

Bryant had a horror of corporate events. Worse, it looked as if speeches were about to begin. As they made their way to the raised platform he picked up a leaflet, read a few lines, scrunched it up and threw it over his shoulder, not noticing that it bounced off a woman's head.

'What's it about?' May asked.

'Oh, the usual rubbish about building bridges and making trade deals.'

'Are we actually going to lead him out of here past all his associates? We'll get hell for it.'

'We can threaten him with arrest if he refuses,' Bryant sug-gested, taking a lurid square of tuna ceviche from a passing tray. 'There he is.'

Peter English had the tanned complexion of someone who spent a lot of time on a yacht. It made him look wealthy and unsympathetic, as if at any moment the smile might be replaced by a call for guards. He was standing at the centre of a group that might have been meeting to plan a coup, and was eyeing the nearby lectern waiting for his cue.

'Arthur, are you sure?' May asked again, adjusting his col-lar. 'We're really going to do this?'

'Come on, it'll be fun. We haven't dragged anyone important off the street for ages.'

'Oh God. Let's get this over and done with.'

They walked to the platform just as the businessman was about to start speaking. It took a moment for English to register who they were. Without missing a beat he smoothly moved them to one side, turned to his audience and told them that his speech would start in a minute.

'What are you two clowns doing here?' His eyes were hard black marbles. 'How did you even get in?'

'It's not a social visit,' said Bryant, 'which is a shame as the vol-au-vents look enticing. We need to interview you in connection with the murders of, well, quite a few people actually.'

To their surprise, English started laughing. 'Most amusing. Did Faraday put you up to this?'

'Just gather anything you need to bring with you and we'll quietly take our leave,' Bryant suggested.

English looked from one to the other, incredulous. 'You can't be serious.'

The detectives did not move or speak.

'It's not going to happen, is it? I'm here with my wife, who is fragrant and high-born and has never had to come into contact with people like you.'

'I must remind you that it is illegal to resist or wilfully obstruct an officer of the law in the execution of their duty,' said May, 'and in this event you may be taken into custody under restraint.'

'Did you just come here to insult me?'

'No,' said Bryant, 'but the opportunity arose and we thought it was too good to miss.'

English's smile seemed to reveal rows and rows of sharp teeth. He appeared to grow before their eyes. 'Do you have the faintest idea how much trouble you're in? This is Crown Estate land. You have no jurisdiction here, no permission to set foot inside or even to speak to me. What I have, on the other hand, is a group of Westminster's most powerful MPs, including the Minister for International Trade, a battery of the country's finest lawyers and the God-given legal right to have you tossed out on your grubby little ears. Now, I'm about to take the stage and deliver a keynote address on the future of British exports to some of the most powerful investors in the country. You could humiliate yourselves by attempting to disrupt the event, or you can leave quietly and we'll pretend this embarrassing faux pas never happened and your careers didn't come to an abrupt, ugly end today.'

Bryant cleared his throat, never an attractive sound. 'In that case, I am arresting you. You do not have to say anything but it may harm your defence if you do not mention something which you later rely upon in court. Anything you do say may be given in evidence.' He turned to May. 'How was that? I thought I might have forgotten the words.'

May felt a dark presence at his side and turned. Two security men had slid into place beside them. Without taking his eye from English, May called in a support request. The amplified crackle of his shoulder-mic alerted the nearest guests that something was wrong.

It was an incredibly uncomfortable tableau, the detectives apprehensive and uncertain, the suspect seething. May switched to his mobile and waited while he was transferred between departments. By the sound of it, he didn't get much of a chance to speak.

'We have a Stand Down,' he finally told his partner, incredulous.

'Perhaps you now realize that there are places where you cannot go,' said English with soft menace. 'These enormous, volatile gentlemen will happily escort you off the premises. I want it to be known that I treated the pair of you with deference and respect – God knows why.'

47

MYTHICAL FRIENDS

The detectives stood in the doorway of Raymond Land's office looking so sheepish that they might have had tags in their ears.

'Perhaps I could prevail upon you to step inside instead of loitering in the corridor like a pair of superannuated Teddy Boys,' Land suggested. 'Say one word about me not having a door and I'll have you boiled.'

They stood awkwardly before him, knowing what lay ahead.

'Come further in,' said Land. 'I don't want Floris overhearing this.' He lowered his voice. 'Were either of you aware that Peter English is about to be made a knight of the realm? Perhaps if you had, you wouldn't have accused him of murder in front of the French ambassador. OK, nobody cares about the French but two members of the Awards Intelligence Service, who helped to get him there, were watching as you two attempted to entice him to the local cop shop with all the effectiveness of a pair of balloon animals.'

'Nobody can be allowed to walk away from a murder

inquiry,' said May. 'What does he have to do to get arrested – bash open someone's head in public? Oh I forgot, he's already done that.'

'Actually he hasn't,' said Bryant. 'He gets others to do the hands-on stuff for him, but we can't prove it. The Met could put a hundred officers out there tomorrow and all they'll do is make him change his plans.'

'I'm meant to be reprimanding you,' Land reminded them.

'Well, go on then,' said Bryant.

The unit chief ran his fingers across the spot where most of his hair used to be. 'You cannot wander in off the street and finger a suspect in the middle of a government-sponsored event.'

Bryant was indignant. 'We kick council-flat doors off their hinges. Why should he get special treatment? He's linked to a series of violent deaths. That should be enough to pull him in. The only people in the UK who can't be arrested are the Queen and children under ten – and him, apparently.'

'What do you even know about English?' Land demanded. 'You have nothing solid on him.'

'We have what we would normally need to bring a Person of Interest in for questioning,' said May.

'It's not enough. There's no forensic evidence linking English to any of the crime scenes. Once you've got that, I'll get the approval for his arrest.'

'For all we know he has a team of experts working day and night to cover his tracks,' said May, narrowing his eyes. 'Why are you so keen to take his side?'

'You're not the only one who's been doing a bit of research.' Land thrust out his chin. 'English is an easy target. People resent him for being a self-made man. Actually I used to know him. We were friends at school. He seemed a very nice chap.'

'Raymondo, you did not go to a posh school,' said Bryant. 'I'm amazed you went to school at all.'

'I meant at school at the same time. Schools.'

'So not the same school at all.'

'But I was always bumping into him. We were old friends and—'

'How many times?'

'What?'

'How many times did you bump into him?'

'Oh, often.'

'So you must have been really close. How often?'

'Ah – dozens – dozens of times probably.'

'Several times.'

'Oh yes, quite a few.'

'More than once? Because you went to a grammar school and he went private, and I seem to remember you lived in the wrong part of Greenwich and he probably lived in a nice bit and your paths would not naturally have crossed. I can't imagine he'd have wanted to be seen with you.'

May's ears pricked up. 'Michael Claremont lived in Greenwich for a couple of years. And the shop fitter, Gavin Spencer.'

'Raymondo, how old were you when this mythical friendship occurred?'

'I don't know exactly, about fourteen or fifteen,' said Land, 'but I don't see what that has to do with—'

They went to find Longbright in the operations room. 'Janice, did anyone else live near Michael Claremont or Gavin Spencer in South-East London when they were in their early to mid-teens?'

'We ran full checks on their background histories,' Janice told him. 'It was hard to find much on them at all. Only Claremont was required to provide a detailed history prior to his election as Speaker of the Commons, and Gavin Spencer had notes attached to his prison record. We didn't find anything to suggest they'd ever met. Besides, if something occurred way back then, why would anyone wait for so much time to pass before acting?'

'You didn't go and ask around the neighbourhood to see if anyone remembered their faces?' said Bryant.

'Of course not, it was too long ago. We don't have the time or resources to do that sort of thing any more,' said Janice. 'But we conducted thorough background checks online.'

'Online,' Bryant repeated.

'We have to be ready for any comeback from English,' said Land, who had followed them. 'You can bet his lawyers are drawing up a response right now.'

'He has to be kept under constant surveillance until this is over,' said May. 'I want you to get full approval for his arrest, Raymond. This is our last chance to catch him.'

48

MAKING A MURDERER

Atena waited on tables at her parents' restaurant in Green Lanes and slept under the counter between shifts. She grew up with the gift of confidence and easy conversation, and I heard she was planning to study law, something I longed to do if only I had the means. Instead I was forced to remain self-taught.

I heard she married well. My only friend. I never saw her again.

By this time I was suffering from bouts of depression, although I still took any work I could find and continued my studies in every spare moment. I watched and I waited. The powerless can only observe. That, I know now, is why social media remains so popular; it is the home of the powerless.

I remembered the only happy photograph I had seen of my mother, taken at a local funfair when she was young and pretty; I barely recognized the sickly thing that had taken her place. I never saw joy in her face, only the acceptance of defeat. I knew how others saw us, limping child and angry parent, searching charity shops, sitting in laundromats, watching the rain from cheap cafés, waiting for something better.

There's a stage of poverty you reach when you start to look different. It's very hard to get rid of that look. My mother died in a basement flat full of cockroaches with a needle hanging from her arm. She was not killed by drugs but sepsis. By this time she was overweight and severely diabetic. I knew the exact moment when her life had gone wrong. In my imagination I undertook a grand scheme that would rebalance my world and save me from her fate.

Right from the outset nothing went according to plan. Two of the six responsible were out of the country, one working in Madrid, the other in Singapore. But I was good at waiting. It gave me more time to plan.

They both returned within two months of each other, and then, infuriatingly, another one left for six months to work in Italy. I knew enough about them all to be sure that they weren't in contact with one another. Were they ever really friends, or merely drawn together out of devilry on dull summer nights when there was nothing to do but hang out and get into trouble? I wondered if they felt remorse, but a more terrible thought struck me. Did they remember what they had done? Did they even remember each other? What appeared momentous to me may have meant nothing to them.

I had left it too long to exact revenge. Modern policing involves DNA tests, face recognition software and electronic spoor. I knew a little about coding but not enough to erase whole histories, so I set myself incremental goals and practised until I could attain each one.

One of the first things I did was remove or alter the few

online residential addresses I could find for any of the six between the ages of seventeen and eighteen. I couldn't get to Claremont's details because they resided in a government file, and I found nothing on Gavin Spencer's background because he had an almost non-existent digital footprint.

Searching for them became more than just an exercise. It was a reason to stay alive.

The plan needed to be explored in almost infinite detail, so I went back to my memoir. Suddenly I found I was writing not just a fictional account of a murder spree but a memento mori. If I'm honest with myself, I think that by this time I had abandoned the idea of physically taking revenge. It was as if the act of writing it down was in itself a form of retribution.

I worried that the plan had flaws I could not see. They say authors grow so close to their fictions that they fail to realize what's wrong with them. I needed outside advice from someone, but who could I trust?

When I walked past the bookshop, I knew it was the kind of place that was run by an expert. The owner hardly ever had customers. I discovered that he read unsolicited manuscripts from new writers and offered them advice, so I submitted my creative exercise.

Cristian Albu read the book and wrote to tell me that it worked because I had made a clichéd plot believable. I had been in danger of losing my purpose but now I had found it once more, and decided to move forward at once with the plan. The time was right. All of my targets were in London at the same moment.

I knew I might never get another chance. When you approach a problem single-mindedly and concentrate on completing each section with the desired effect, you remove most of the chance elements and guarantee the outcome.

I promised they would die and I told myself I would deliver their deaths, even though I knew events might unfold differently to the way I had planned.

It transpired that I had made a single fundamental mistake.

There is no such thing as a perfect crime.

PART SIX
The Great Bell at Bow

Children of Cheape, hold you all still,
For you shall hear Bow bell rung at your will.

Clerk of the Bow Bell

49

QUESTION EVERYTHING

Script extract from Arthur Bryant's 'Peculiar London' walking tour guide. (Tour of the City's old market places. Bring more dosh than you think you'll need, you'll be buying a load of tat, trust me.)

Cheapside connects St Paul's Cathedral to the Bank of England. In medieval times 'cheap' meant 'market', and markets were everywhere in this ancient part of London's Square Mile.

The streets were named after the items sold: Bread Street, Poultry, Milk Street and Honey Lane were here in all their rambunctious glory, so it's no surprise that Chaucer was raised among the stalls. The highest members of royalty passed among the lowest tradespeople.

Cheapside was once described as 'the busiest thoroughfare in the world' and was long considered one of the most important streets in London, because you could buy cabbages and chickens here, but you could also buy gold. The street was devastated during the

Second World War and has now transformed itself into the pedestrianized shopping hell in which you find yourself today.

The cockney epicentre of London is St Mary-le-Bow, a church that has always had trouble with its bells. They were so often unringable that it became a matter of national concern, and even when they pealed there were problems. The bells shook the stonework from the spire and killed a merchant in Bow Lane. After the Blitz they were recast, each with an inscription from the Psalms on it. The first letter of each Psalm formed the acrostic 'D WHITTINGTON'. The British love word puzzles.

Cockneys are an endangered species now because the Bow bells can't be heard above the noise of traffic. They're dying out because hardly anyone lives in the area. The only hospital within earshot of Bow bells has no maternity ward.

I would like to read you a selection of bawdy speeches set in Cheapside from *Henry the Fourth Part One*. Anyone not wishing to be enlightened by the words of the immortal Bard may avail themselves of the myriad retail opportunities offered by Zara and H&M. If I'm left with fewer than three punters you will find me across the road in Williamson's Tavern.

They were stationed thirty yards from the church of St Mary-le-Bow, Cheapside, outside a tanning salon that was loudly advertising specials on leg waxing and muff management. A steady stream of half-asleep office workers passed them. Nobody looked up at the church. Hardly anyone looked up at all.

'I could kick the nuts off a chicken korma right now,' said

Colin, pinching his stomach through his PCU tunic. 'Look at me, I'm wasting away.'

'It's nine o'clock in the morning,' said Meera. 'Have a cereal bar like everyone else.'

'I'm not a budgie. You'll be suggesting a bell and a mirror next. Come on, there's a café over the road. It'll take five minutes.'

'And what if we miss him?'

'We can see just as much from there. Murderers don't get up this early. Look around. It's a lovely morning; we just need a bit of grub to make it perfect.'

Meera turned on him. 'How do you do it, Colin? How do you stay so bloody perky and cheerful no matter what happens? The seas are rising, the forests are vanishing, our leaders are imbeciles and murderers roam the streets, but when you look out there all you see is sunshine and food. It must be exhausting being you because it's exhausting even being near you.'

He looked at her as if she had spoken to him in Turkish. 'You can't do anything about the first three and the last one will be resolved by people with bigger brains than us, so why worry? We're foot soldiers, Meera. We're like thingy and whatsit, Rosencrantz and Guildenstern.'

Meera's eyes were like fireworks. 'At least they tried to get Hamlet murdered. I have ambitions too. You're just happy when it's not raining. I've set my bar a lot higher than that.'

'Than me, you mean.'

She softened and touched his arm. 'No, not you. It's just that there's more I can do. I've been meaning to tell you. I want to apply for specialist training.'

Colin's happy mood evaporated. He kicked at the wall behind him. 'But that would mean you leaving the PCU.'

'If that's what it takes. It doesn't affect us. This is probably our last day on the case anyway. We're no further on than we were when it started. Tomorrow it will go to the SCC, the Home Office will have proven their point and the unit will head into mothballs for the last time. That's why I need to think about moving on.'

'Why do you always say that?' Colin asked. '*I* this, *I* that, never we, never us.'

'I don't think of us as being together,' she replied carelessly. 'I've always been independent.'

'Too much independence cuts out everyone else. Don't become the person who does that.'

Meera was losing patience. 'I don't know what you're saying.'

Colin waited while someone shouting into his phone passed them. 'I'm saying you should learn to rely on me, Meera.'

'And how am I supposed to do that?'

'In my head it's really simple. We just get married.'

Meera could not have looked more amazed if she had gone to a football match and found herself attending a public hanging. She attempted to wipe the look of stupefaction from her face. 'Do you want to take a minute to think about what you just said?'

'I've already taken a lot longer than a minute to think about it,' said Colin, removing a ring box from his jacket pocket. 'I guess I loved you from the first moment I saw you.'

'You *guess*? It's not love at first sight if you're not sure.'

'I'm sure. I remember thinking, *I love her even if she is a bit short*. Meera, I need to know if you feel the same way about me.'

She stalled. 'It certainly wasn't reciprocated. You were eating. Anyone who can watch you fit a whole saveloy into your mouth in one go isn't going to fall in love with you at first sight. Or at second sight, when you've swallowed it and run your finger around your teeth to get the extra bits.'

Colin could feel the moment ebbing away. His hand with

the ring box was still outstretched. 'But do you think you
ever could—'

'Can you shut up for a minute?'

He closed his mouth. He wasn't sure about the way she was
watching him – like a child with a magnifying glass on a
sunny day waiting for an ant to stand still. He wanted to add
something profound and beautiful but decided against it
because he couldn't think of anything.

'If you want to win a maiden you must slay a dragon,' said
Meera.

'I don't know what that means.'

'You have to ask my mother first.'

'I don't want to marry your mother.'

'I mean you have to get permission from her.'

'Why?'

'Because if you do,' said Meera, 'she'll pay for the whole
thing.'

Colin looked as if his eyes were about to fall out. He
thought of all the happiest moments of his life, starting with
finding that he could now reach the shelf where his mother
kept the beer. This was better.

'What's that in your hand?'

He looked down, startled to find the box in his palm.
'There's nothing in it yet 'cause I'm a bit brassic at the moment,
but I'll fill it, I promise. I've got a can of Fanta in my bag; I
could give you the ring pull off that for now.'

'As irresistible as it sounds,' said Meera, 'I think I'll wait.'

'Oh my God.' He pinched his cheeks. 'I'm waiting for the
sky to fall.' He held her hand. 'My old man said I would never
amount to anything. He said I'd never make a copper because
no one would ever look up to me. I wish he was still alive. I
miss him.'

'You have a very good heart, Colin Bimsley,' said Meera.
'I'd be proud to marry you.'

He was about to kiss her when his phone rang. It was Janice. 'Stop whatever you're doing, Peter English has disappeared,' she said. 'We had two Met officers following him this morning from his flat to his office, but he managed to shake them off. We're sending you back-up. From this moment on you need to be really alert. Question everything you see and hear.'

50

THE GREAT BELL

'How did he slip away?' asked Bryant, stabbing at a hamburger carton with his walking stick and deftly flicking it into a bin. This afternoon he had chosen to bring along his ebony cane with the retractable spike.

'They saw him go into the building but couldn't follow him because they're not being allowed to enter without a warrant,' May explained. 'English's lawyer is trying to argue that there are no grounds for the granting of one. A few minutes later someone spotted English in the street behind.'

The pair headed over to a wooden bench in the little cobbled courtyard outside the church of St Mary-le-Bow and seated themselves. From here they could see anyone entering or leaving. There were supposed to be four Met constables stationed around the church. They couldn't be seen, but Bryant conceded that was the point.

'I should never have set off the fire alarm at Peter English's office,' he said out of the blue. 'It tipped him off because now he knows that I know.'

May struggled to see the point but gave up. 'What do you mean?'

His partner appeared not to have heard. 'I have been deceived and now we all have to face the consequences. Do you know about the bear?'

'I'm having enormous trouble following your thoughts,' May admitted.

'If you look at the art of deception from a neurological point of view it gets very interesting.' Bryant sorted through a paper bag of boiled sweets. 'I know my eyes don't work very well but I console myself with the knowledge that nobody's do. We need our brains, specifically shape-selective neurons, to make sense of what we see. Perspective and occlusion are tricks of depth perception that mess with our minds.'

He popped a barley sugar into his mouth, then remembered to offer May one. 'There are a number of famous experiments that show just how terrible our powers of observation are. One involves a student stopping to ask a porter for directions. Some workers pass between them carrying a large board, and a different person takes the place of the student without the porter even noticing his change of identity. Another experiment involves footage of a football match as a striker heads towards the goal. Nobody spots a big fellow in a bear suit dancing across the pitch because their brains have focused exclusively on the attempt to score. Deception is simply a system learned like any other.'

'Do you believe Peter English is guilty?' May asked.

'Oh, I know he is. That's not the problem.'

An elderly and somewhat infirm verger came out of the side entrance and undertook the adventure of crossing the cobbled courtyard. 'Ah, there you are,' he called. 'I'm afraid the vicar can't be here to greet you. He just wanted me to check that there wouldn't be too much disruption here today.'

'We're rather hoping for a miracle to occur,' Bryant replied.

'This is a church with modest expectations.' The verger exuded an air of natural melancholia, like rising damp. 'If you're having doubts perhaps our contemplative atmosphere can help. Just not today. The bells are being repaired again. It's a never-ending saga. Would it be sacrilege if we switched to recordings, I wonder? Would the congregation notice? I hope you get your miracle, although I imagine the chances are slim in this city of Mammon.'

May's shoulder transceiver buzzed. 'Peter English is approaching the church,' said Meera. 'He's walking down the middle of the pavement in plain sight. Should be coming into range – now.'

Dave One was a big man who would quite happily squirm his way through a tight doorway, but he was stuck. 'Pull on my boots,' he called back to Dave Two. 'If that doesn't work I'll have to take my trousers off.'

'I'd rather be spared the sight of your Noddy and Big Ears pants, thank you,' said Dave Two, tugging hard. How he knew about them was one of life's lesser mysteries.

His workmate re-emerged covered in plaster dust. 'There's something weird going on in there,' he said, pointing back through the doorway. 'We should have finished bricking it up or left it open, because that ain't right.'

The pair were in the unit's dank basement, where the low rumble of tube trains mixed with the gastric gurgle of the underground river. The small chamber beyond was all that was left of the old passageway connecting the basement to the below-street bar in the building next door.

'What do you mean, something weird?' asked Dave Two. 'There shouldn't be nothing in there because I relocated the junction box after all that trouble we had with that bleedin' corpse.'*

'Nothing in there, eh?' Dave One stepped aside to let his workmate see through the gap. 'What's all that then?'

A row of tiny red eyes winked back at them.

Sidney Hargreaves leapt along the corridor with her open laptop balanced in her right hand. She found Janice on the phone in the operations room.

'You have to see this.' She turned the screen towards Longbright and ran the clip.

Janice hung up the phone. 'Where did you get it?'

'It dropped on to Twitter for about thirty seconds before vanishing, but I was able to pull it in time. It was sent from a fake host.'

She ran it again. The video clip was taken from a phone on the steps of St Martin-in-the-Fields. It was only four seconds long. The audio was muddy and the visual was in deep focus but the foreground was diamond-sharp. Chakira Rahman was falling to her knees. The figure walking away from her only looked up at the camera for an instant, but was easy to identify. Peter English's dark eyes caught the camera lens for a split second, then continued onward.

'John's just spotted him arriving at St Mary-le-Bow,' said Janice, ringing him back. 'John, we have filmed evidence of Peter English a couple of seconds after the attack on Chakira Rahman,' she explained as he answered. 'Go ahead and make the arrest.'

The verger was confused. The detectives to whom he had been chatting had suddenly jumped to their feet and shot off like much younger men, following a smartly suited fellow

---

* See *Bryant & May: England's Finest*.

who was striding with speed and purpose towards the church entrance.

As Bryant set off after him May caught up.

'What's English doing? There's no one else here except him.' May thumbed back at the verger.

'The bells,' said Bryant. 'There's a man working on them.'

The church's blue and cream interior had been freshly painted. Instead of pews, plain chairs had been laid out in a semi-circle. The stained-glass windows on either side of the organ were blood red.

Bryant looked around and failed to find English, even though he had only just entered the church. Spying the door that led to the bell tower, he listened for the tap of shoes on stone, but his ears had yet to stop ringing after the bomb.

There was nowhere else he could have gone. Bryant knew that neither he nor May could get up there. He was about to call the others when Colin slid into the apse from the street and ran for the staircase, closely followed by Meera.

'Bring him down in one piece,' Bryant called after them. 'He's not going to hurt you.'

Colin entered the bell tower. Its interior was a maze of dusty wooden struts with ropes tethered to them like giant spiderwebs. Each arrangement of beams supported one of the great bells and its accompanying flywheel. At the centre of them stood the largest of all, a great bronze bowl deeper than a man, currently propped upside down so that it could be worked on.

On the staircase above him was English.

'Mate,' called Colin, holding his ID high, 'I don't know what you're doing but you need to come down from there.'

'This has nothing to do with you.' English stared into the upturned bell, then carried on climbing around it.

Colin waited a moment, then continued up. Above his head the octagonal walls narrowed. The steps turned to a slim wooden platform running around the edge of the steeple. There were no more handrails to rely upon. He was not the ideal person to send to the top of a spire, but none of the Met's back-up officers had appeared. He tried not to think about the drop beside him. He could sense Meera closing in behind.

There was a papery thrashing of wings as half a dozen pigeons were shaken from their roost, spraying feathers, dust and guano, batting their way up to the broken wood panels at the steeple's peak.

Edging past an immense brown curtain of dirt-encrusted cloth, Colin caught a glimpse of English as he reached the great bell at the top and leaned over the parapet towards it. What was he trying to do?

English was no more than ten feet away from him. Colin had gone as high as he could. The tower plunged away just beyond his right boot. The bolts holding the ramp in place squeaked and grated as he moved upwards.

English stretched out over the railing towards the bell, intent on his task.

Colin barrelled into him. The great bell of Bow shifted from its upturned position, but English threw himself after it as the flywheel rotated. The momentum was impossible to stop. He went over the edge as the bell swung down. His feet caught other bells, which began pealing cacophonously from the tower.

When the dust cleared Colin saw that English was hanging from the clapper of the great bell. His tie clip – who wore those any more? – pinged from his tie and bounced down through the bell chamber.

Colin ran back down to the point where the stairs became a ramp. He was underneath the great bell now. English was swinging helplessly back and forth above him, just out of reach. He looked less elegant with his stomach hanging out of his striped shirt. The echoing ring of metal shook down dust and pieces of mortar.

'Let go and I'll try to break your fall,' Colin shouted, unsure whether English could hear him over the din.

On the third swing English's grip slipped and he had no choice but to drop. Colin spread his arms wide and snagged his catch but the weight pulled them both over, crashing them on to the wooden platform as the bolts popped from the walls, firing across the interior of the spire like bullets.

Meera was less concerned about stopping English than making sure that her sudden offer of marriage didn't end before it had begun. Grabbing Colin and shoving him back from the edge, she dropped beside English and locked his arms behind his back just as a chunk of the platform pulled way from the wall.

They half dragged, half walked the bedraggled businessman back to safety, the clanging of the bells subsiding above them.

'You bloody idiots,' he warned them, 'you don't know what you're doing.'

When they reached the base of the spire Meera picked up the grimy paper packet that had fallen from its place on top of the upturned bell's clapper. She pushed it inside her jacket as Colin pulled English out of the church, the verger watching them in amazement.

'Get your hands off me, I'm not some grubby common little criminal.' English shook Colin's arm and tried to maintain his poise, but had been reduced. Out in the courtyard he quietly called his lawyer, then fell silent and allowed himself to be led away.

'We came in that patrol car,' said Bryant, watching them go. 'Why are we the ones who have to take the tube?'

'You know we can't travel with the prisoner,' said May. He turned to find an impossibly young Met officer running up to them.

'Sir, we just had a phone call about a stabbing on Bread Street. We heard some bloke got hit with a machete, really bad, like his head is hanging off.'

'Have you been there?' asked May, checking his badge: Adrian Tomkins.

'We had a quick shufti but couldn't see anything so I thought I should come and get you.'

'You should have conducted a thorough search first, Tomkins,' Bryant told him, but May was already heading over to the next street.

'You can see the church from there,' May called back. ' "Here comes a chopper to chop off your head." '

51

BAIT AND SWITCH

Ever temperamental, London had wiped away its azure sky to hurl rain at the windows of 231 Caledonian Road.

Raymond Land sat back in his chair and considered his choice of words. The email to Leslie Faraday sat unfinished on his computer screen.

He scanned the sentences once more and signed off the letter with a heavy heart. Having taken Faraday's periodic silences as a rebuke, he had written out a measured strategic retreat from the investigation. Although he was a good man at heart, Land gave up too easily. He had always been willing to snatch defeat from the jaws of victory. As he read back over his words, he realized he was looking at the unit's suicide note. It couldn't be helped. It was time to admit that they were beaten.

He hit *send*.

Sitting back in his chair, he waited for the whoosh that would signal the end. Any second now the dead weight of responsibility would begin to rise from his shoulders.

Nothing happened.

He checked that the sound was turned up. He tried to figure out whether the email had gone or not. It wasn't showing
in his sent folder. He was suddenly looking at a blank screen.
What had Tim repeatedly told him to do? Turn it off and turn
it on again.

That didn't work. There was something odd going on. He
wandered out into the corridor. Where was everyone?

Janice Longbright was not at her desk, and there was no
one in the operations room. Floris's office was empty. Land
picked up the framed photograph beside the civil servant's
laptop. It showed the Home Secretary and his police team
around a champagne-laden table at a black-tie bash. Nobody
at the PCU had been invited to a formal event since the jelly
fight at the Met Excellence Awards Dinner. From somewhere
upstairs came the sound of rainwater pinging into a bucket.

When he went back into his office something caught his
attention in the corner of the room. A tiny red eye was staring
at him. Had Dan installed some kind of new surveillance
equipment?

'Is there anyone around?' he called. Silence. Something
tapped at the window. He turned to find Stumpy the pigeon
on his sill, giving him a death stare.

As he headed back out and turned the corner he bumped
into Dave One and nearly went into cardiac arrest.

'Blimey, Mr L., don't creep about like that,' said Dave One.
'I wanted to see you. Have you got a sec?'

'I'm really busy,' Land lied, unnerved.

'It's just here, look.' He bent down and lifted the corner of
a corridor carpet tile. Beneath it was a fine black cable. 'It's
not one of ours. Someone's playing silly buggers. Has anyone
from outside got keys to the unit?'

'You know we're the only ones who can get in,' said Land.
'And sometimes even we can't. So what is it?'

'I don't know, but it goes all the way down to the basement

and it wasn't there a few days ago. Mr Faraday must have access to the site, mustn't he?'

'I suppose so,' said Land lamely.

'I've been thinking,' said Dave One, pulling at his moustache, 'the first victim, that Mr Claremont, he didn't die, did he? You lot have been trying to reach him without any luck, as far as I heard. That struck me as odd. 'Cause I read an Agatha Christie once where these people went to an island—'

'What, you want to be a detective as well now?' asked Land. 'We've already got a girl barely out of her teens running around giving us the benefit of her great experience. And what's wrong with the phones? Why can't you ever get them working properly?'

Dave One did not care to have his workmanship maligned. 'There's nothing wrong with them. Maybe the person you're calling sees your number come up and doesn't want to speak to you.'

Land had not thought of that.

As he went downstairs and hurried out of the building he realized he had set himself a daunting task: to find a working telephone box in King's Cross that didn't have someone breaking the law in it.

Trying to ignore the astonishing odour of McDonald's boxes marinated in urine, Land stepped into one and called Leslie Faraday's direct line, wiping the receiver before gingerly putting it to his ear.

Faraday's PA was screening his calls. After he laboriously explained why he was calling, she put him through just to get him off her phone.

'I've been trying to track you down for ages,' Faraday complained, which was clearly a lie. 'Where the hell have you been? Miss Hamadani rang you several times and kept getting put through to a Turkish gentleman who insisted he was an electrician. He tried to sell her a flat. Now Mr Floris informs me you've arrested Peter English without authorization.'

So much for promising to take our side, thought Land, misremembering their conversation. *I knew he was a creep from the moment I laid eyes on him*. He had already forgotten that Floris had just spent several days helping him out.

'We have new proof linking English to the investigation,' Land explained hurriedly. 'I tried to send you an email requesting a detention period of ninety-six hours. We have no holding cell at the moment but there's an arrangement in place with the hotel on the corner.'

'I don't even know where to begin with that last sentence,' said Faraday, suddenly sounding tired. 'Are you really committed to this?'

'It will end the investigation,' Land promised.

Faraday thought for a moment. 'You have to take full responsibility for him.'

'Fine,' said Land, accepting that whatever happened he would always get the blame. 'Any minute now we'll have the killer in custody.'

He rang off and ducked back through the rain, but when he reached the unit he found that the hall stairway lights were now out. The two Daves were supposed to have installed new LEDs in the ceiling, but he could see only bare wires hanging down. It looked as if someone had deliberately pulled the fittings out.

Thunder rumbled overhead, bouncing off the rooftops of Caledonian Road. As Land climbed the stairs, he wondered where Bimsley and Mangeshkar had got to. They should have arrived with English by now.

On the first floor he checked the operations room, then Longbright's office, but found no one around. The building was dark and wet and oddly deserted. There was usually someone left behind. He felt a prickle of cold air on the back of his neck, as if a window had suddenly opened.

Land turned sharply, but there was no one there.

With an involuntary shudder he returned to his office and tried the lights, but the switch did not work. His computer was still functioning so there had to be a problem with the fuses. The junction box was in the basement and he had no intention of going down there by himself.

What on earth was going on?

Bryant and May stood in the middle of Bread Street and looked along the glass palisade of offices that lined it. The pavements on both sides were empty but for a ragged lad with a sleeping bag at half mast, going through a bin.

'Who took the call about this chap with his head chopped off?' asked May.

PC Tomkins shifted uncomfortably. 'It came through on the emergency number. We thought what with the church being so near we'd better—'

'—walk over to us before checking whether it might possibly be a hoax,' said Bryant. 'You stupid boy.'

'I don't know what we're doing, sir. Everyone's telling us different things.'

Bryant angrily ground at the kerb with his stick. 'I sent a warning out to everyone: don't trust what you see, check it first. It was a hoax designed to get you all away from the church. It's a good job we got to him before he could cause any further harm.'

May gave up on his phone. 'I can't get through to anyone at the PCU. Tomkins, can you try?'

The officer called in, waited, rang again. 'No answer. It sounds like a line fault. I can have it checked.'

'No time – something's wrong.' Bryant headed to the junction, searching for a taxi. 'We need to get back right now.'

'Calm down,' said May, 'I'll find a cab. You know they don't like to stop for a scary old man waving a walking stick about.'

May hailed a black cab before it had a chance to turn into Bread Street and opened the door for his partner. 'English will set his lawyer on Colin and Meera. They won't get anywhere with him.'

Bryant climbed in and dug out his Spitfire.

'Oi, mate, you're not going to smoke that in here,' the driver warned.

'Police officers,' said Bryant. 'Open a window and get us to King's Cross within ten minutes or I'll find over thirty reasons to nick you.'

May fell back as the disgruntled driver tore away. Bryant filled the bowl of his pipe with Ancient Mariner Full Strength Naval Shag and lit it, sucking noisily.

'You know, late-sixteenth-century printers made up all kinds of wild stories to sell news pamphlets,' he said, as if continuing some academic banter that had begun earlier. 'They ran stories of seven-headed monsters and women who lived on nothing but air, men with goats' legs and battles that had been won instead of lost. The art of lying has been with us since the birth of civilization.'

'As usual I have no idea what you're on about, Arthur.'

'Why do we believe things we'd be better off not believing?' Bryant jabbed his point home with the end of his Spitfire, scattering sparks. 'Tricksters know how to override our natural instincts. By averting our gaze they turn us blind.' He threw his partner the grimy envelope English had collected from the great Bow bell. 'This is why he went to the church. Not to attack anyone but to get his hands on this. The one job he couldn't trust to anyone else. Take a look.'

May studied the bank statements in his hand. It didn't require a bookkeeper to see that the Better British Business deposit account held in the Cayman Islands contained an eye-watering amount of cash. 'Monthly transactions with no provenance,' May noted. 'Dan already checked that out but

found no red flags.' The second page showed the same transactions through a different bank. He gave a low whistle. 'No
wonder English was anxious to get this back. London, Al-
geria, Indonesia – it's a money-laundering route.'

Bryant tapped at the bottom line. 'The National Fraud
Intelligence Bureau will kill his party before it gets launched.'

'I don't understand,' said May. 'Why is someone black-
mailing English at the site where he's meant to commit his
final murder?'

'You have a knack for overcomplicating things,' said Bryant as they swung past St Paul's. 'I admit it takes some nerve
to use a man like English as a stooge, but it worked. We've
had the same bait-and-switch trick pulled on us again and
again, and we've fallen for it every time. They say the perfect
deception is the one that fools the victim twice.'

'But what's the point of sending English out to Bow and
phoning in a non-existent attack?' asked May. 'We have him
in custody. The end of the rhyme has been reached. All we
need to do now is wring a confession out of him.'

'Those pages are all you need,' said Bryant, puffing away
so furiously that the driver opened all of the windows despite
the rain and made retching noises. 'The fraud trial hasn't
received a revised date, so I guess this can be introduced as
new evidence.'

'What about his involvement in murder?'

'You asked me if he was guilty and I said yes – but not of
murder.'

May's eyes narrowed. 'You know what's going on.'

'And you know I'm superstitious. I can't explain until I'm
absolutely certain.' Bryant looked out of the window. They
were on Farringdon Road heading north, passing Exmouth
Market, climbing the incline to King's Cross. Thunder
boomed above them. Dumbfounded, John May watched as
the cab sped on through the evening rain towards the unit.

52

HERE COMES A CANDLE

Raymond Land pulled the plug out of his rebellious computer and followed its lead under his desk, lifting up carpet remnants to expose the trail. Crawling around on the floor covered him in cat hairs but finally proved pointless as the cable disappeared down a jagged hole in the floorboards. He was sure it had always been plugged into the skirting board by the window where Stumpy the pigeon sat watching him. Pressing his eye to the floor, he tried to see into the darkness below.

Something was faintly beeping.

There was a louder noise in the corridor, a roll and a thump. Were the two Daves still here? Now there was silence. He sat up and tilted his head, listening.

Clear and loud, chiming through the corridors, came the clamour of a bell being swung back and forth, back and forth. It sounded like a teacher in a school playground gathering her pupils.

Land couldn't work while the power was out but nor could he leave the building, not when their only suspect was about to be brought in and charged. There was more light in the operations room because it faced the dazzling bar of the youth hostel opposite and had taller windows, so he headed there.

The bell suddenly stopped ringing, as if a hand had clamped itself over the clapper.

The operations room was bathed in a cartoonish crimson chiaroscuro, much of it flooding in from a large bar sign in the street that was written in neon and read 'Soup of the day: Negroni'.

The grey pewter handbell had a pocked iron handle and was very old. It sat in the middle of the Formica-topped table at the front of the operations room. It looked suspiciously like the one that had been stolen from St Sepulchre-without-Newgate.

Land took another step forward and trod on the cat's tail. Strangeways screamed and sank its teeth into his trouser leg, mercifully missing flesh.

A candle flame popped alight on the other side of the table. Land could not see who was holding it. As unit chief this would have been a perfect time to assert his authority, but instead he said meekly, 'Look here, what's going on?'

The candle flickered and moved. The bell was raised – for a brief moment Land thought it was supernaturally lifting itself – and went along with it. The figure kept the light low. It seemed lopsided and somehow shortened, until Land realized that it was limping.

Downstairs, Sidney tried the newly installed electronic code and found that the main entrance's temporary door would not open. She had received an email from Janice asking if she would pick up a package at the railway station. Just as she was trying the door again, Longbright turned up.

'There was nothing there for me to collect,' Sidney said. 'Did I go to the wrong place?'

'I didn't ask you to collect anything.'

Sidney showed her the email she'd received. 'It was sent from your office laptop.'

Janice turned her attention to the door. 'Why do these codes never work?' She gave the door's base a hard back-kick with her boot. The lock popped and the chipboard panel swung open. 'Dave Two taught me that. Good job I wasn't wearing heels today.' She held the door wide.

'No one's answering,' Sidney told her, going ahead. 'The phones are down and it looks like all the lights are off.'

'That's nothing unusual,' said Janice. 'I've just arranged for the Happy Hotel & Bistro to take Peter English tonight. They have a secure room on the lower ground floor for "problem guests". It's like a drunk tank with a trouser press. It'll take us until tomorrow to get through the charge sheets.'

'We could put a cell in our basement,' Sidney suggested. 'It's big enough down there.'

The light from the street faded as they climbed. 'Have you been down there?'

'I've measured it,' said Sidney. 'They keep the plans online.'

Janice stopped her at the top of the stairs. 'You know we have to tell them the truth sooner or later, don't you?'

'I don't want to.'

'I'm surprised nobody's figured it out.'

Sidney stopped again. 'Are you sure you didn't send me an email?'

'Not me.'

Janice took out her brick. Together they went into the darkened corridor.

'What are you doing here?' Land nervously asked the pool of candlelight.

There was no answer. He was being led back to his office, the cat darting ahead of him. It was obviously unwise to keep following, but curiosity overcame his fear.

As he stepped into the room, the door swung shut behind him and a lock turned, which was surprising as he was pretty certain that the last time he looked his office had not only been missing a lock but was also minus a door.

The pewter handbell was rising again and began to toll with shocking loudness, its cavity swinging at him like the jaws of an animal.

Land tried to remember where his phone was. He felt his pockets. 'Put down the bell and we'll talk,' he said, trying to muster a commanding voice.

The candle grew brighter in the still air and Land saw who was holding it. The awful weight of the truth fell upon him. As did the bell, which caught him on the side of the head, knocking him off his feet.

The candle went out.

Peter English had forced Bimsley to stop the car at his lawyer's office in Duke Street, Mayfair. 'Because he has to be present at the meeting, you amoeba,' he said, stabbing at his phone.

'It's not a meeting, mate,' said Colin. 'There's nothing to negotiate. You're being charged with murder.'

'I am not your "mate". You are my public servant.' English turned his anger to the phone. 'I'm looking forward to seeing your face when you discover what a horrible mistake you've made. Digby, we're outside your office right now. Why the hell aren't you here?'

They waited as English's lawyer bobbed through the rain to the Vauxhall Astra. Edgar Digby burst into the vehicle, lowering a *Financial Times* from his head and spraying everyone with water. 'I was about to leave for the airport, Peter,' he said, budging into the back seat. 'A couple of days' golf in Geneva.'

'You wouldn't have got very far,' said Meera, pulling away. 'Your client's in for multiple counts of murder.'

'First of all, you're not allowed to share this information in the car,' warned Digby, who had been eating garlic. 'And second—'

Nobody found out what the second thing was, as a young woman on her phone ran across the road ahead and Meera was forced to brake sharply. The rain-slick road caused a Toyota Prius to drive into the back of them, spraining English's neck and giving him a bloody nose.

As the taxi drove away, Arthur Bryant stood at the edge of the pavement on Caledonian Road and looked up at the PCU's first floor. He saw a ghostly light drifting across the penumbral operations room.

'Why is it in darkness? And what's that?' asked May, pointing.

'He's striking at our heart. It's where he always intended to end this.'

May stared at his partner, appalled. 'Do you actually know what he's doing?'

'I have a pretty good idea. It makes sense. He'll have found ways to send everyone else away. He's terribly good at misdirection.'

Bryant set off for the front door.

There was no sign of the Incident Response Vehicle bringing in Peter English. May looked around. 'He should be here with Colin and Meera.'

'I'm sure he'll have found a way to stall them,' said Bryant. 'Everything he does now will just make him look more guilty. It's the superciliousness, coupled with the fact that he's not very bright. People fear his power but they don't like him. We decide within seconds whether we're drawn to someone or repelled by them. That's why the best actors are complete blanks offstage.'

'You didn't stop any of us suspecting English,' said May, even more confused.

'Perhaps not but I know you, John. You would have continued to be suspicious anyway. It was good fun annoying him, though.'

'Why on earth didn't you tell me earlier?'

'You'll see why in a moment.'

May grabbed Bryant's arm. 'Nobody died at Bow. We're still a victim short. Tell me who it is now.'

'Oh, John.' Bryant's eyes were filled with sorrow. 'If only it had been anyone other than Raymond.'

'Raymond? You mean *our* Raymond?'

'Oh yes. You see, that's why we're back here. All of this – it began with Raymond and it ends with him. We've come full circle, like the rondo bell-ringing in St Mary-le-Bow.'

May was dumbfounded. He reached the entrance and found the door hanging open. Pushing it back, he entered, hauling himself into the gloom.

Arthur overtook him. 'Let me go first; you've got your stitches to think about.'

'All right but be careful,' May warned.

Bryant reached the top of the stairs. 'At my age there's nothing more to be afraid of.'

At the end of the dark corridor they saw a distant flickering candle.

53

ERASING THE GHOST

Bryant reached Raymond Land's office and was surprised to find a door on it. He tried the handle and it swung open. There was no one at his desk.

He continued on to the operations room. He could see funfair lights ahead.

The PCU was most definitely not a church, yet here in the broad communal room that overlooked the street was a tableau as striking as any stained-glass window: a figure with its head bowed, kneeling on the floor, with an executioner standing tall beside him, the hilt of a sword resting in the executioner's fist, the tip of its blade touching the floorboards. The pair were motionless but alive with neon rivulets, yellow and purple flashing to scarlet.

Bryant kept back in the shadowed corridor, pushing May to the wall beside him. He held his finger to his lips. The detectives listened.

'I always knew you would have to be killed last,' said Tim Floris. 'The little coward who took the final turn. I can't think of it without becoming physically ill. I look at each of you as so-called respectable adults and find it impossible to imagine that you were there in the church at my conception.'

'Well, it's impossible for me to imagine it because I wasn't bloody there,' said Land, his indignation overriding his fear. 'I don't know what you're talking about.' He tried to push himself upright but was held firmly in place. 'I've got nothing whatsoever to do with this.'

'Of course you think you haven't. You've all been in denial for years. It's understandable, something to be so ashamed about. A very British trait, avoiding a subject until it goes away. You can say whatever you like but I will always know the truth.'

'Then you know bugger all,' said Land, chancing his arm. 'How do you know?'

'The truth came from the one person who would never lie to me.'

Land wanted to move his knees but was terrified of having his head cut off. 'I didn't know your mother. I never met her. How could I have done anything wrong?'

He thought back to the moment when he had finally studied the photograph on Floris's desk. The awards dinner, and the smiling line-up that included the sweating Faraday, the elegant Floris, the startled Fatima Hamadani and the clearly bored Home Secretary himself. He had glanced at it at least twenty times in the last week, but this time he truly saw.

MAKING A MURDERER

I suppose I should have taken it as a compliment, Cristian Albu editing and typesetting a copy of the manuscript I'd sent him to read, then having it printed and bound as a very attractive book. Twelve copies, he told me shyly, handing me the first. A deep-red cover, the title picked out in gold, my name underneath. He thought it could be a breakout success.

I was horrified.

If anyone read it my identity would be revealed, all the years of sacrifice and planning for nothing. He said the other copies were all in the shop but he wouldn't tell me exactly where they were. All obsessives have a greedy side, an attitude that makes them throw their arms around their valuables and draw them back like poker players gathering in winning chips. Sensing my panic, Albu had backed away and become possessive about his discovery. He promised me he would get rid of the copies but I knew he was lying. He had far too much love for his little sideline.

I'm good with chemicals. They're easy to learn about, easy to get hold of and carry around. I added a little benzodiazepine to his drink, a retro-amnesiac sedative about a dozen times more potent than Valium. The trick was getting him out of the pub before it kicked in so heavily that he became a dead weight. I sat him in the alley, took his keys and searched the shop.

Albu's filing system was non-existent. It was impossible to find anything. I only thought of torching it because he had cans of linseed oil left over from when he had varnished the wood floors. I poured it through the shop and lit it. I knew it would look like arson but it didn't matter. The important thing was to destroy every last one of the copies.

And then, the strangest thing happened.

A bowl of oranges burst into flame.

I had no idea that oranges could burn. It turns out that their oily skins contain a hydrocarbon called limonene that's highly flammable. All through the shop you could smell varnish and paper but, above all, oranges, sharp and overpowering.

I thought of my mother's story – she had just one, repeated

in endless variations until she could speak of nothing else. The church, the boys, the childish games that stopped being childish, a grotesque version of Oranges & Lemons, the pain of each of them on her in turn. The second half of her downfall, which could be elaborated infinitely over time – that being the one thing we always had – was my birth, her shame, the slow destruction of our lives.

She remembered their faces. She remembered all their names. Michael Claremont, who started it all. Chakira Rahman, who did nothing to stop it. Kenneth Tremain, Jackson Crofting, Gavin Spencer and Raymond Land. How could she have failed to remember every last detail about them?

When her grandmother reported it, she was far too frightened to tell the police much. She said she didn't know, couldn't remember, didn't want to know. Filled with guilt and shame, she cut herself off from everyone. She wanted to forget but the more she tried, the more she remembered. Whenever she felt the need to talk she sat at the end of my bed and told me. To begin with I didn't understand her because she left so much out. I was five years old the first time she spoke of it.

Gradually she described more and more. But even after she had explained everything I still didn't understand, because she hadn't told me how sex worked. I couldn't connect it all, the boys, the baby, it made no sense. So I started asking questions.

And then she never stopped explaining. The details never ceased. They grew ever more elaborate, ever more appalling. I was outwardly a normal child. I thought of myself as having a normal life, but it wasn't at all. She made me memorize their names. I went back to the church but it had become a pine merchant's, then the grounds were torn up and the site was filled with offices.

After she died I thought things would be better, but I woke every night to find her at the end of my bed reciting their names. There was only one way to rid myself of her ghost.

'She remembered wrongly,' said Land. He was not in a position to lie right now. 'I suppose I might have seen one or two of them in the street from time to time but I didn't know their names and I was never invited to their stupid bloody clubhouse. They wouldn't have had me, a kid whose parents lived above a newsagent's. Perhaps I saw them at the football fields on Blackheath or at the shops, how do I know? Boys often look nothing like the adults they become. I hated being a kid. My life was hell. I spent years trying to forget about it.'

'In these times of over-educated police chiefs you're a refreshing change,' said Floris. Land tried to remain motionless but Floris had brought down the edge of the sword blade until it touched the back of his neck.

There was a sharp sting as it cut the skin. Land cried out. He felt blood pooling inside his shirt collar. If anyone was coming to rescue him they were leaving it a bit bloody late.

'Your mother was wrong,' Land said again. 'I don't suppose she meant to lie to you but she made a mistake. She couldn't have remembered my name.'

The blade cut a touch deeper. 'Why not?' asked Floris.

Land forced himself to remain calm and coherent. It was crucial that he explained. 'Because after we moved away my mum remarried,' he said through gritted teeth. 'She married a man called Roger Land. When I was a teenager my name was Raymond Codd. I hated it because my classmates all made fish jokes, so I had it legally changed when I was in my early twenties. Your mother mixed me up with someone else. There was a posh kid about my age called Graham Land who used to hang out near the church. Sounds like she meant him.'

He felt the blade turning his neck to bloody ice.

'My mother would never have lied to me,' Floris replied, raising the sword high above Land's exposed neck.

Some years were bad, others bearable, but my mother always reappeared to me at twilight. She never left the end of my bed, and as long as she stayed there my luck followed hers downward.

I knew that in order to take a full and fair revenge I had much to learn.

While I was studying the structure of police divisions I came across the Peculiar Crimes Unit. I met an officer in the Met who told me that they only handled a very specific type of case, and noticed it was run by a man called Raymond Land.

I knew the police would soon be following my every move, so I used the 'Oranges & Lemons' rhyme to ensure that only the PCU could be appointed. I knew I would have to work from the inside, and that I needed them to trust me. I couldn't take the place of any unit member but I could be mistaken for someone from the outside.

The best solution was to pick a real person, someone close but slightly out of the frame, someone who would naturally stay away from the unit. Land visited the Home Office, so I chose someone in his liaison team. It was easy to find them online. I watched them all and listened to everything they said to each other in public. Lunchtimes were best; they always discussed the morning's work as they walked to their salad bar.

I set off the fire alarm at the Home Office so that we would meet outside the building in a street overcrowded with workers. Keeping a watchful eye out for the man I was planning to impersonate, I introduced myself to Land as Tim Floris. I wasn't sure if Land had met him, but if he had it would only have been once, and briefly. Floris and

I were both slim-built but I didn't look like him. The beard was a godsend, the sort of thing people focus on. They make many men look similar. It took a while to get right, but I learned to apply and remove it in less than a minute.

I needed to keep the real Floris away, so I cut all contact between Land and the Home Office and relayed Land's emails. Wherever I could, I added layers of confusion and mayhem. The devil was in the detail. I planted false memories, 'reminding' Land of when we had met at the Home Office, and he was happy to agree with me. I told lies, created suspicions, sowed doubts.

I mastered the art of misleading observers into making false assumptions. Even when they tried to get me drunk I managed to stay in character.

I made a few mistakes. I failed to ensure that Michael Claremont was dead, although I planned to finish him off after he left his clinic. I changed Land's email homepage but forgot to change the date, not that he noticed. When I found the photograph of the Home Office department at an awards dinner in a staff magazine I decided not to doctor it. I have never been able to look at my own face. Others say they find me attractive but I look in the glass and see a horrified Caliban reflected back.

I needed everyone to be more than just confused; I had to find someone innocent they could target. As soon as I realized that Peter English was being singled out, I shifted all the signs of blame to him.

I tried to fake camera footage of English on the steps of St Martin's but couldn't manage it. Finally I paid a girl who works in a comic shop to do it for me. I paid lots of people to get information, to perform little tasks, to obscure me, cover me, take the blame for me. I made everyone doubt what they had seen. My studies of magic paid off. But still the most satisfying part was the killing. I liked the killing best.

'She didn't lie to you. The mistake is with your memory,' said a figure in the doorway.

Arthur Bryant stepped into the room and turned electric yellow. He threw a book down on the floor between them. 'I checked. Raymond wasn't one of the boys who attacked your mother. His name was Graham Land. You probably misheard it the first time she told you.'

'If you come any closer I will kill him,' said Floris, aligning the blade.

'Then you will have failed.' Bryant stepped closer, never removing his gaze from Floris. 'Raymond isn't the one you want. He's nothing like the others. Think about it. The rest all had one thing in common: *presence*. Even Gavin Spencer was said to have charm. Girls were drawn to them. Raymond doesn't even have a clean tie. Look at him, he's a charisma-free zone.' He took off his hat and turned it in his hands.

May joined his partner. 'Let us have the sword,' he said, his tone calm and patient. 'You can't complete the rhyme. Your list has to remain incomplete. It's time to put your demons to rest.'

'You can do it,' said Bryant. 'We don't even know who you are.'

The hand with the sword remained perfectly steady. 'I was never really named, not officially. I wanted a magician's name. I thought I might call myself Nemo, and take my mother's surname, Nixon.'

'I wouldn't do that, there used to be a terrible magician called Nixon,' said Bryant, choosing the wrong time to start recalling old British television programmes.

The lights suddenly flared back on and everything happened at once.

Bryant's stick smacked at the sword blade, which very nearly removed Raymond's ear, while his partner stepped forward without a thought of the danger he was in. Floris – they never did bring themselves to use another name – stared at the detectives in astonishment. The idea that an elderly man might attack him with a walking stick while his friend simply waved his arms about had never crossed his mind.

When he made a grab for Bryant, he found himself gripping the old man's fishing hat. He cried out in pain, because even though he didn't fish Bryant kept a set of lethally sharp hooks sewn all around the brim.

'It was the bleeding junction box,' said Dave Two, wandering into the room with a screwdriver in one hand. 'Take a look at this. Chinese rubbish.'

Everyone froze in position and stared at Dave Two's junction box. He stared back. 'Blimey, don't all say thank you at once,' he complained.

Meera came in behind him, and while everyone was reassessing the situation Colin came charging into the operations room and planted a fistful of signet rings on Land's personal executioner. Everyone yelled, the cat shrieked so as not to be left out and Raymond Land fainted. By the time Peter English walked in with his lawyer, Bryant could see it would be a long night.

There was one thing at least that they could all agree on. Floris had been brought low not by the ruthless efficiency of the capital's law enforcement machine but by his own faulty memory.

54

MISSING A TRICK

The PCU staff should have celebrated, but it felt as if they were on shifting sands. The events of the last few days had shattered everyone.

Bryant had put his back out attempting to help disarm 'Floris' and May had strained a muscle in his chest.

Raymond Land got stitches in the back of his neck. Whenever he complained after this (and he complained a lot) the others would remind him that he might have had his head separated from his shoulders.

Everyone argued about who would call Leslie Faraday. Eventually names were put into Bryant's deactivated hat, and Sidney found herself granted the honour. She went into the detectives' office to do it, closing the door behind her. For some time after she refused to speak of what transpired between them.

Meanwhile, Dan Banbury removed the phantom router Floris had planted in the basement and dismantled it for spare parts. He kept the micro-cameras for himself. The sheer amount of disinformation involved in the case meant that the exact wording for the highly complex charge sheet was drafted more times than the Magna Carta.

Raymond Land was fully exonerated when a prisoner called Graham Land was discovered in Wormwood Scrubs. He had repeatedly confessed to assaulting a girl in his teens, but no one had listened to him.

Back in their office, the detectives found themselves staring at the framed photograph of the real Floris and his Home Office colleagues. 'I can't believe I didn't notice that,' said May, studying it, 'even after you told me about the experiment with the student. They do look a little alike, especially with the beards.'

'I think he kept it there out of hubris,' said Bryant. 'He wanted to see if we would notice. He had a lot of nerve. What do you suppose will happen to Michael Claremont now?'

'His past will surface and his reputation will be shredded,' said May, as sanguine as ever.

'The inquiry is going to be a nightmare,' Bryant complained. 'Poor old Raymondo can't handle the paperwork, he's far too shaken up.'

May shot his partner a look. 'Arthur, how did you *know* what was happening?'

'I wouldn't have known,' Bryant admitted, 'if it hadn't been for the smell of oranges. Citrus fruits contain a group of compounds called terpenes that give them a powerfully characteristic scent. I couldn't think of Claremont's accident without smelling them.'

'That couldn't have been the only thing.'

Bryant tipped back in his chair and unwrapped a chocolate, giving the matter some thought. 'The accidental triggering of the fire alarm when Raymond visited the Home Office struck me as overly convenient. I was thinking about it when I set English's sprinklers off at his office. I didn't see how it could be Floris and I had no idea that his victim might be Raymond. But the smell of oranges turned up again and again, and lingered everywhere, especially in here. It seemed to be leaving a trail.

'I thought that if we were being tricked by one thing – the supposed accident that Michael Claremont suffered – then what if we were being tricked by *everything*? But I also thought of Cristian Albu. Something was off right from the start. Why did he go for a drink with Floris? He could have just sold him the book and sent him on his way. Then I realized – he went because Floris turned on the charm. He *wanted* to go. Magicians are naturally charismatic. They practise being magisterial. Did you know there are virtually no female magicians? They only get to be the assistants to males.'

'Someone's missing a trick,' said May. 'I wonder how many times Floris came in here and searched through our notes. What was the book you threw down in front of him?'

'Oh, didn't I tell you?' Bryant's eyes twinkled annoyingly. He brought May over to his bookcase. 'Stand here and look straight ahead.'

When May checked the spot on the bookshelves being pointed out by his partner, he saw that between two of the volumes, *Enamelling For Beginners* and *Ring Any Bells? Memory & Cognizance in the Novels of Victor Hugo*, there was a third volume with a red leather spine.

Taking it down, he read the cover: *Making a Murderer*.

He glanced back up at the gap. How long had it been sitting there? 'I sit looking at that bloody bookcase all day. Where did you find it?'

'In a job lot I bought from the King's Cross book barge last month,' Bryant explained. 'I don't know how it got there from Bloomsbury but books do tend to migrate. I didn't get around to reading it, but I think it's going to prove very useful now.'

*

The following morning May's list of prisoner questions was rendered obsolete when the nameless man was found dead in Room 158 of the Happy Hotel, King's Cross. He had curled up in bed and with grim determination cut his throat, leaving behind the handwritten postscript to his memoir, which had been arranged at the bottom corner of the duvet, where he had always seen his mother telling her story.

Bryant was handed the memoir's addendum. To the printed volume he could now add the final chapter. He sent copies of both to Elise Albu.

55

MAKING A MURDERER

I'll never know the truth about what happened in the church that night.

Their crime was possible because they instinctively chose the right girl to attack. She did not tell a soul who they were, and they did not get caught. Their lives were, for the most part, a series of escalating successes, inversions of her downward path.

I was finally betrayed by my own memory. If I had not been driven to find Raymond Land I would not have diverted the investigation to the PCU, and would not now be in the basement of this poky little hotel in King's Cross.

Some people will point to a moment in their lives when everything began to go wrong. Mine occurred before I was born. I had no control over it, but I will have control over the end.

Tomorrow I am due to be charged with a long list of improbable-sounding crimes. Happily I will not be there for the farrago of lies they'll parade before me. I wish there was time to describe the incredible pleasure I felt when I claimed each life for her.

I have sharpened the plastic cutlery the waiter stupidly left with my evening meal by running it along the fashionably rough concrete bathroom wall. In the morning they will find me with an ugly but effectively cut throat. The rhyme will finally be complete, if in a different way from how I intended. It will have symbolic meaning.

I believe some people are cursed. Not just by poverty, although that will be the easy answer affixed to my story by the nation's hand-wringers. We are cursed by its by-product, a debilitating lack of confidence. It is why we stay silent, why we are controlled, why we apologize, why we are afraid. We are overruled by the ones who expect to be heard, and as they destroy our lives we thank them for it.

I see her here of course, my mother, still sitting at the end of the bed even in this overlit little room, but I know that by daylight she will be gone for ever. The only way to banish her is to take her with me. Finally we will no longer need to be afraid.

So, Mr Bryant and Mr May, as I'm sure you will both read this, let me leave you with a final thought.

There are no female magicians.

When they take out my cold body and ask themselves why I planned so long and hard for justice, they will discover my last secret.

I have always been my mother's daughter.

56

REMEMBRANCE

The following week involved grudging congratulations from an embarrassed Home Office, especially when Leslie Faraday discovered that the real Tim Floris had managed to misplace his swipe card for a couple of hours so that it could be duplicated by an energetic imposter. The public mood was briefly disturbed when it became known that the heroic victims the press had championed shared a sordid secret in their past. The topic trended on Twitter, then vanished.

It was not until the following Saturday that the PCU team got together to discuss what would happen next. In the evening Longbright hired a riverboat from the Thames Police at no cost (they owed her a favour for dealing with a long-immersed corpse; best not to go into the details). Longbright thought it would do them all good to get some moderately fresh air instead of sitting in the basement of a pub, even though their nostrils were filled with the reek of the river's dark recesses.

As Dan Banbury had his navigation licence and couldn't enjoy a drink because he was driving his wife back from her mindfulness workshop in Sevenoaks later that night, it seemed a good idea to let him pilot so that everyone else could get smashed.

'I say, Raymondo, do you have to keep that huge plaster on your neck?' Bryant asked, jouncing along in the stern. 'You look like you've just got a tattoo.'

'It's not a Gillette nick, I was attacked with a sword,' Land complained.

'It's a good job I saw the light moving in the window. I thought if there was a candle there could be a chopper. He managed to finish the rhyme.' Bryant knotted his scarf even higher around his throat and sat back, accepting a hefty gin and tonic in a plastic cup. London slid past, its illuminated bridges adding an oddly unreal sheen to the Thames, as if it had been photographically treated. The clouded sky reflected its gaudy new colours, yellow, purple and green.

'Hey, Sidney, I hope you've been keeping notes this week,' said Meera as they passed beneath Waterloo Bridge, now washed in bilious pink and orange. 'I've enjoyed watching you recoil every time Mr Bryant opens his mouth.'

'His language is offensive,' Sidney said breezily, 'but I can live with it.'

'Just as well because you're not going to change anyone.' Meera raised her beer cup in a toast.

'Just remember that before you were born he was fighting to ensure your rights,' said Longbright. 'If you're going into the force you'll need to be very patient and accepting.'

'And suspicious,' added Colin. They all raised their glasses to that.

'I know young people look at Mr Bryant and only see an old man but I know what he's done,' Sidney assured her.

'I am here, actually,' said Bryant. He had been staring at the racing black waters lost in thought. Something had changed in him these last few weeks. The truths upon which he had always relied had been turned on their heads. Nothing was as it seemed, and far from being perturbed by the thought of a world in flux he was exhilarated by the challenges this new life presented.

Banbury swerved to avoid something he hoped was a log and not a floating body. Freezing spray doused them, making everyone shout.

'How was your first case with the PCU?' May wanted to know.

Sidney studied him pointedly. 'First?'

'Of course, the decision's not up to me. The final decision is your mother's.' He looked at Longbright.

Everyone's eyes followed.

'You *are* Janice's daughter, are you not?'

'We were going to tell you,' Longbright began, warily awaiting Sidney's reaction.

'It was obvious from the outset,' said May. 'The name on her internship form is Hargreaves. I'm old enough to remember that you used to live with a detective inspector named Ian Hargreaves. His favourite actor was Sid James. Sidney looks exactly like a combination of you and him, although mercifully nothing like her namesake. Why didn't you say anything?'

'It was my fault,' Sidney said, stopping her mother from answering for her. 'I wanted to be judged on my own merits. I knew you'd be predisposed towards me if I told you who I was.'

'Well, you're not in yet,' said Bryant. 'Where have you been all this time?'

'I wasn't working at the unit when I had Sidney,' said Longbright. 'Ian was offered a management position in New Zealand that was too good to turn down. He wanted to take Sidney, and I let him. I came back to work at the PCU.' Longbright looked fondly at her daughter. 'When Ian announced he was moving to Madrid I talked to you both about leaving, but you convinced me to stay. Ian remarried. My daughter and I stayed in touch.'

'So that's why you have an unplaceable accent,' said Meera, turning to Sidney. 'I just assumed you were being annoying.'

'Anyone else got a surprise they'd like to share?' Land asked. 'Gender reassignment, spontaneous generation, evil twin?' He winced as he accepted a glass of wine. 'I've got one. I had an email from Dr Gillespie claiming that you' – and here he pointed at Bryant – 'have some kind of ageing disease that's making you prematurely decrepit, although I'd question *prematurely*.'

'Did you check to see if it was really from him?' asked Bryant, huddling himself around his gin.

'No! He is the company doctor; I shouldn't have to, should I? If you can't trust your own doctor . . .' He stopped himself. 'The real Tim Floris didn't consider that someone might have copied his swipe card. You can't check everything.'

'He guessed you wouldn't, my little *pierrot*,' said Bryant. 'That's what the disseminators of disinformation count on. Do you remember all that fuss back in the seventies about the Bermuda Triangle? How everyone thought planes and boats were vanishing from the map? Some time later the mystery was solved. It was all down to poor data research. Every so-called "missing" vessel in the North Atlantic could be accounted for. The full tracking information was eventually published but it was so densely detailed that nobody read it. The mystery is always more popular than the solution. Now when somebody leaks several thousand pages of incendiary material to a newspaper only a tiny handful of people ever read it all.'

'You didn't answer the question,' said Land.

'What, am I suffering from some kind of Methuselah syndrome? I can't believe that after all this you're still prepared to believe any old nonsense you're told. No I am not, thank you. I find the question most offensive. Although I may have lied about my age.'

'What, younger or older?' asked May, disconcerted.

'It happened in my teens,' Bryant explained. 'I wanted to get into a saucy Soho show but you had to be twenty-one, so I raised my age a little. Suddenly people treated me with more respect and I sort of forgot to go back. I'm actually the same age as John.'

May dropped his head in his hands. 'That was my one advantage over you. I demand to see your birth certificate.'

'Is there anyone on board who hasn't lied about something tonight?' called Land. 'Any more life-altering announcements?'

Colin caught Meera's eye but she gave her head a sharp little shake.

'I altered your multiple-choice competency tests,' said Sidney, turning to the detectives. She was seated at the bow and had droplets of river water in her hair. 'I was looking through your emails – sorry. The entries were full of mistakes so I corrected them.'

'How could you have done that?' asked Bryant. 'I sent them both off.'

'No, you didn't,' Sidney replied. 'They were still stuck in your outbox.'

'It was wrong of you to break the law,' said May.

'You set the example.'

'You do understand what you'll be taking on?' asked Bryant. 'We are the final repository of the city's knowledge. This lot, and a handful of other tiresome outsiders most people would cross the road to avoid, know and remember everything that has happened here. It is our joy and our curse.'

'What do you remember?' asked Sidney with a challenging gleam in her eye.

*

433

'It's patently absurd,' Simon Sartorius told him when they met in a tessellated time warp of a French restaurant in Knightsbridge. He set the manuscript aside, hopefully beyond the edge of his peripheral vision. 'I think we'd have to publish it under fiction.'

'You asked me for a big case,' said Bryant. 'It all happened, just quite not the way I've described it.'

'So you made parts up.'

'Certain scenes were edited to fit the format,' Bryant told him. 'Any changes will be made OMDB.'

'I don't think you're using these computer acronyms correctly,' said Simon. 'Perhaps you should stick to normal English.'

'Thank goodness for that. I'm saying that everything is true except for the parts that aren't,' Bryant mouthed at him. 'Our murderer really did turn out to be female. Her mother believed she would be safer if she dressed as a male. That's why she was never christened, why she went to nursery school under an assumed name and was immediately taken out of it. I assumed the killer was a man because it was more statistically likely, and to me the manuscript felt as if it had been written by a male. When I checked through it later, I saw that she had never lied. She must have been in terrible pain while she assumed the identity of Tim Floris. She could not be seen to limp because the real Floris walked normally, so she had to leave off her brace. She was very nearly the perfect trickster. We never did discover what happened to her mother, which only makes the truth more impossible to reach.'

'We'll have to edit the manuscript,' said Simon, his attention drifting to the ambitiously priced wine list. 'The second half is filled with the most shocking typing errors. How anyone could mistake the word "hostage" for "sausage" is beyond me.'

'I had to finish it myself at the office,' Bryant explained.

'My ghostwriter Cynthia made off with my laptop, our ice-cube trays, my Kings & Queens of England cigarette card collection and all our teaspoons. I've been unlucky with my biographers.'

The others had weaved their way home from the Bankside riverboat landing, leaving Bryant and May to head back from Blackfriars Station. 'What do I remember, she asked,' said Bryant, leaning against a dolphin lamp-post to look out across the tar-black Thames. 'The cheek of it. As if I could list all the things I remember. I've forgotten more than I can remember and I remember everything except the things I've forgotten.'

Just beyond them the tide furled and unfurled in brackish blooms. No other river possessed this strange atmosphere, of time and death and forgetfulness.

'Oh, I remember everything,' said Bryant softly. 'All the places, the people, the events and names from London's history. Everything that happens in this city has a phantom lurking behind it, and another phantom behind that, stretching back into the mist.'

He said no more, but as they walked in friendly silence he thought to himself, *I remember William the Conqueror building the Tower of London, Canaletto painting the Thames, Sargent, Whistler, Wilde and Radclyffe Hall all living in the same Chelsea street. I remember Samuel Johnson and William Blake, Derek Jarman and Hattie Jacques, the Hither Green disaster, the Judd Street bomb and the Cato Street conspiracy. So many protests! The suffragettes, the Battle of Cable Street, Ban the Bomb, Clause 28, the Notting Hill riots, the Poll Tax riots. All the royal fusses and political betrayals mean less to me than the things Londoners really care about: Windrush, Grenfell, the terrorist bombings. I close my eyes and my head is full of images: Violet Kray* blindly supporting her sons, Elisabeth Welch singing 'Stormy Weather', the Beatles crossing Abbey Road, the Pythons in the Caledonian Road pet shop. My head is filled with London faces: Charlie Chaplin, Joyce Grenfell, Alfred Hitchcock, Margaret Rutherford, Florence Nightingale, Karl Marx, Charles Darwin, Jimi Hendrix. In my mind Steptoe and Son are still in Oil Drum Lane, Shepherd's Bush, the Trotters are in Nelson Mandela House, Peckham, and Tony Hancock lives at 23 Railway Cuttings, East Cheam.

I remember the London pranks and anecdotes. Sir Thomas Beecham asking a lady in Fortnum's what her husband was doing nowadays, and her replying, 'He's still king.' The editor of the Sun firing his astrologer with a letter that began, 'As you already know . . .' Beachcomber leaving dozens of brown-ale bottles on stuck-up Virginia Woolf's doorstep, Sir John Gielgud accidentally insulting everyone. Most of this information is entirely useless but every now and again two names or events lock together to produce an unexpected third, and that is the moment I live for.

I have to remember it all because no one else will.

Now I must remember someone new. I will find a murderer's mother and put her child beside her. I'll give her the identity she was denied in life.

'You should have answered Sidney,' said May. 'Perhaps she's the right person to pass it all on to.'

'I'm not sure I want to do that,' said Bryant, taking his partner's arm. 'The past is a weight that can end up crushing your life.'

They stopped at the station entrance. 'Well, this is me,' said May. 'How are you getting home?'

Bryant smiled. 'I'm already home,' he said, adjusting his homburg and leaning on his snakehead walking stick. And looking at his unmistakeable outline against the shining Thames, it was very hard to disagree.

Bryant and May will return.

ACKNOWLEDGEMENTS

Considering this is the nineteenth Bryant & May book, I'm amazed how little the team has changed over the years. Editor Simon Taylor, who has forgiven me for actually writing him into the recent novels, and Kate Samano and Richenda Todd, who keep tabs on the most tangled of stories and gracefully steer me back on course, make my life so much easier that I can't imagine doing it without them. A warm welcome to Hayley Barnes on PR, and as ever a tip of the homburg to my agent James Wills, and Meg Davis, my film agent, who still believes that someone might be crazy enough to bring Bryant & May to TV.

Find me on Twitter @peculiar or on www.christopher-fowler.co.uk

Christopher Fowler is the author of more than forty novels (including the universally adored Bryant & May mysteries) and short-story collections. A winner of multiple awards, including the coveted CWA 'Dagger in the Library', Chris has also written screenplays, video games, graphic novels, audio plays and two acclaimed memoirs, *Paperboy* and *Film Freak*, and *The Book of Forgotten Authors*. He divides his time between London's King's Cross and Barcelona. You can find out more by visiting his website – www.christopherfowler.co.uk – and following him on Twitter @Peculiar.